:JERSEY
GIRL

RHONDA JAMES

Liz,

Thank you for
everything! Read
Superman "1" and his
and his brother
brother's come to
come to case :)

Rhonda James

Jersey Girl
(Sticks & Hearts Series Book 1)
Text Copyright © 2016 Rhonda James
All Rights Reserved
ISBN-13: 978-0692628126
ISBN-10: 0692628126
Published by Rhonda James, Author LLC
Cover Layout and Design: Taylor James
Editor: Julia Goda
Formatting: CP Smith Affordable Formatting

DEDICATION

This book is dedicated to three women who helped make this story what it is today.

Christine Tovey - I remember the day when I first ran this storyline and title by you. You were the first to champion it, and for that, I thank you.

Sarah Piechuta - Your love for B and Cassie is what kept me going, even on the days when it felt as if the words weren't there. Thank you for falling in love with B as hard as I did.

Melissa Mendoza - We did it! In this scary world of writing, I am nothing without you. I love that you see my inner 'Roni' and choose to love me anyway!

CASSIE

"*Welcome to Ann Arbor*," a soft-spoken female voice greets over the train's intercom.

It's two in the afternoon on a hot August day, and I'm dragging my oversized suitcase behind me, struggling to keep it upright due to the heavy contents I'd crammed inside. Standing on my tiptoes, I cup my hand over my eyes and scan the crowd for a recognizable face. After a few seconds, I spot him standing on the far side of the platform, hands shoved deep in his pockets, with a goofy grin plastered on his face. He takes five steps forward, and I abandon my suitcase to run toward him. When I get within three feet, I launch myself in the air, throwing my hands around his neck as he spins me around.

"Scotty!" I shriek loudly in his ear, then pull back to get a good look at him. He's changed a little since we've last seen each other. His hair is longer, and he's sporting a nice tan. "Nice color there, hot shot. Bet it feels good to play outside for a change." I ruffle my hand through his shaggy hair.

My brother is a hockey player. And a damn good one at that. Before finishing high school, he'd been recruited by Great Lakes

University and given a full scholarship to be their starting goalie. Ever since he was a kid he's spent the majority of his year either playing hockey, or training for the upcoming season. This is his last year of college, and he's already been drafted to play for a professional team in Detroit after graduation.

"Yeah, Ashley made me drive her to the lake nearly every day this week," he takes a step back to admire me. "Damn, Cass, you've gone and grown up on me. You look great, kid."

I punch him lightly in the arm, hating that he still thinks of me as a child. "I'm not a kid any longer. I'm nineteen, hardly the giggling teenager you left at home."

"You'll always be my baby sister, no matter how old you are. Get used to it." He gives me a playful wink and walks over to collect my suitcase. I follow him to his car, a black Dodge Charger our grandparents recently gave him as an early graduation present. He lifts my suitcase and tosses it in the backseat as if it weighs nothing, then motions with his hand for me to get in.

A low whistle blows through my teeth as I rub my hand over the leather seats. "Nice wheels. Bet this sucker is a chick magnet."

"I wouldn't know about that. Ashley's usually with me whenever I'm driving," he responds with a laugh. "But, yeah," he says, grinning like a little boy, "it is pretty sweet."

Scotty and Ashley began dating at the beginning of their sophomore year. I like her a lot, and she seems to be good for him, because after they started dating he took to calling mom and dad more often. Ashley is very close to her parents, so it was only natural for her to encourage him to work on his relationship with our parents. Not that there were ever any problems between them; he just pulled the 'I'm away at college and free from the shackles of my demanding parents' card and would go months without calling home. Mom used to fret over it, but dad would always assure her he would come around eventually. Usually when he needed money.

We ride in silence as I look out the window, taking in the architectural intricacy of the buildings near campus. I'm arriving a few days early, so the campus hasn't been flooded with students yet. The thought of spending three days at my brother's apartment, hanging out and seeing the way he's been living the past few years, makes me giddy. I've missed him.

"Thanks for letting me crash here," I call out to him, dropping my suitcase near the door as I make my way deep into the house he shares with three of his teammates. "Where should I put my stuff?" I poke around and see the telltale signs of four guys living together. Beer can towers. Towels left on the bathroom floor. Posters of half-naked women hanging on the wall. The one thing that surprises me is that the fridge is stocked with fresh fruits and vegetables.

"Cage is gone for a few days. You can crash in his room until the dorms open up." He comes around and leans over my shoulder to peer into the fridge. "You hungry? I could make something. Or I could order something from one of these places." He turns and opens a drawer crammed full of takeout menus.

"Geez, you guys must order out a lot." I pull out a few and ponder my choices. Thai food. Pizza. Gyros from a place just a block down the road. I only know this, because someone has taken the time to write it on the menu. The Chinese food menu

3

is tempting, but I steal a glance back over at the fridge and make a healthier choice. "I think I'll just have some of this fruit salad."

"It's nice to see someone eating it. Coach makes us meet with a nutritionist once a month, and she gave us a list. We're notorious for buying it and then letting a crap ton of it go to waste," he explains as I grab a fork and dig in.

"No one in their right mind would let food like this go to waste." I stuff a few bites of melon in my mouth. "This is how I eat when I'm at home."

"Come on. I'll show you Cage's room. He won't mind you're here. He's been up north, staying at Derek's family cottage and coaching a pee-wee hockey team for the last two weeks. Hell, I'll bet he's got some chick riding his—" His face turns a funny shade of crimson, and he cuts himself off mid-sentence.

"Is that your subtle way of saying your best friend is a player? Are you sure it's safe for me to sleep in his bed? I'm not going to catch anything, am I?" I counter sarcastically. I follow Scotty up the stairs, bowl in hand, and he opens the second door on the right.

He throws his head back and laughs, and I revel in the sound. I've missed this since he left for college. "No chance. I changed the sheets this morning. My room is just across the hall. If you need anything, just let me know. His room has an attached bathroom, and if you need towels, they're in the cupboard beneath the sink."

I take a look around the room, enjoying the masculine blue and grey color scheme. A large, king-sized bed takes up a huge chunk of the far corner. There's a desk in one corner, and a dresser on the other side of the room. I can't stop staring at his bed. It's freakishly huge. Who is this guy anyway?

"Is your best friend the Incredible Hulk?" I laugh and make eye contact with Scotty. The look on his face shows he doesn't get my humor. "That's probably the largest bed I've ever seen. You could sleep like six on that thing."

"I wouldn't be surprised if that theory hasn't already been tested," he looks over the room once more. "Listen, I have plans with Ash tonight. Do you think you'll be okay to hang here without me?"

"Oh, sure. I don't expect you to put your life on hold just because I'm here." I smile, doing my best to hide my disappointment. "Go. Have fun. I'll just curl up with a good book until I fall asleep. It's been a long day, so it probably won't take long." I offer up a wide smile to reassure him I won't fall apart in his absence.

"We'll hang out tomorrow. I promise."

"I'm going to hold you to that." I kiss him on the cheek and turn to pull a pair of yoga pants out of my suitcase. He lingers in the doorway for a moment before he smiles and turns to go.

I quickly change before heading back downstairs to have a look around. From what Scotty has told me, I know he lives with guys named Brantley, Jordan, and Derek, but I have yet to meet them. There's a flat screen television mounted on the living room wall, and the largest sectional sofa I've ever seen takes up the rest of the room. A small bookcase sits below the T.V., and I crouch down to check out their selection. *Fight Club, Fast and Furious, Die Hard.* All the typical choices a guy would make. Not to mention they have copies of every movie made in each series. I continue scanning and see a wide array of Adam Sandler movies, a few chick flicks, and a boatload of porn.

Rolling my eyes, I stand and come face-to-face with a shelf lined with picture frames, each one containing group shots of the four teammates. I notice how happy they look in each setting. In two of them they're wearing hockey gear and holding up a trophy from when they won the Frozen Four two years ago. Scotty has told me he believes they'll win it again this year, since most of the players are seniors who have kicked ass together over the last three years. One of the photos shows them in what looks to be a bar, standing side by side, arms draped over one another's shoulders, with a drink in one hand. The smiles on their faces tell me these guys are the best of friends. I pull that one down and run my finger around the rim of the frame, studying their faces. It dawns on me that I don't know anything about Scotty's life now. We'd always been close, but with him being two years older, and a guy, once he'd taken off for college, we practically lost touch. It's one of the reasons I chose to transfer to this college. I'm hoping we can reconnect before he leaves to play in the NHL and his life becomes filled with traveling and rubbing elbows with famous people. I have a feeling once he's gone, we'll lose touch completely. And this thought hurts me deeply.

I'm still holding the photo when my eyes land on one face in particular. I'm not sure which roommate this is, but he's standing next to Scotty. Where my brother and I have blond hair and blue eyes, this guy is the exact opposite. Dark, unruly hair falls down over his forehead, and the wide smile he's wearing makes the amber in his brown eyes sparkle. I trace a finger over his face, unable to turn away. Until the sound of a ringing phone pulls me out of my trance.

I place the frame back on the shelf and pull out my phone, swiping my thumb across to answer as I settle on the massive sofa.

"Hey, Justin," I answer wearily.

"Hey, babe. I miss you already. I was starting to worry. You never called to let me know you'd arrived safely."

"I know. I'm sorry, but Scotty brought me back to his house and I've just been getting settled. I was going to call." I rest my chin on a knee and aimlessly pick at my toenail polish. I'm not in the mood to have this conversation again.

"Don't worry about it. So, how is Scott? Tell him I said hi. You know what, just let me talk to him." Justin and my brother have known each other since we were little kids growing up in the same neighborhood.

"He's out with Ashley."

"Why would he invite you there if he wasn't going to be home? He shares that house with three other guys, right? Who else is there?"

"Calm down, Justin. I'm here alone. The dorms don't open for three days. Besides, I'm the one who told him to go out. I'm a big girl. I can take care of myself."

He makes it sound as if he's worried about me, but where had his worry been when I'd caught him cheating with my best friend? I broke up with him immediately, but he refuses to let go.

"Justin, you do know we broke up. Right?"

A heavy sigh fills the silence, and I know he's trying not to lose his shit. Justin has a really bad temper, which is great when he's on the ice. Unfortunately, I've been on the receiving end of his wrath, and it wasn't pretty.

"Justin, you *knew* this is what I wanted," I whisper.

"It's just hard, you know, hearing you say those things. Christ, for two years you've been my girl." There's pain laced in his words, and I get defensive, because he's the one responsible for this pain, and I'm tired of hurting.

"We stopped having sex when I broke up with you," I remind him.

"Doesn't matter. In my heart you'll always be mine. And I'm not ready to let you go."

"Listen, I'll always care for you. You were my first love, and you'll always hold a special place in my heart. But I *need* this. This isn't easy for me either, Jus—," my voice breaks. None of this has been easy. I care for him. I'm just not *in* love with him anymore.

"Could have fooled me. I'm sorry, Cassie, but I think you're giving up on us too soon."

"Maybe so, but I'm ready to move on," I answer defiantly.

"This isn't the end of us," he warns.

I let out a shaky breath and steel myself to deliver the final blow. "It's over, Justin. When are you going to accept that you need to let me go?"

"I'll never let you go. Never," he threatens, reminding me why I needed to get away from Minnesota. I hadn't planned on switching schools, but his actions left me no other choice. I needed a clean break. From Justin. From Charlotte. From everything that reminded me of what used to be. Now I just need to move forward.

I hang up, without saying goodbye, and make my way to the

bedroom where I'll be spending the next few nights. Letting go of someone you've spent a chunk of your life with isn't easy. Justin and I were friends for years before we started dating. I still remember the first orgasm he ever gave me. We were both virgins, or at least I was. At the time I thought he was as well. Looking back, it seems like so long ago. I have a lot of memories of our time together, and for a long time things were really good.

Until they went bad.

Coming here had been the right thing to do. Time to shake off the past and focus on moving forward. I wasted two years pretending to be someone I wasn't just to make Justin happy. It's time I learn what makes me happy.

BRANTLEY

It's two in the morning when I stumble into the house and make my way up to my room. I'm exhausted and looking forward to sleeping in my own bed. The house is dead silent, except for the snoring I hear coming from Davis' room. Doing my best to keep quiet, I duck into the bathroom to take a leak before stripping naked and crawling into bed.

I have a king-sized bed, and it's freaking huge. It takes up a good portion of my room, but at my height, I need room to spread out. Slipping between the sheets after being away for ten days feels better than anything I've ever felt. *Wait. Scratch that.* Feels *almost* better than anything I've ever felt. There's only one thing I can think of that could top this, and it's been a while since *that* has happened.

Just thinking about sex makes my dick hard, and I seriously consider rubbing one out, but I really need to get some sleep. I want to get some time in at the gym tomorrow morning, and then I need to meet with coach and talk to him about how things went at camp. I roll over, curling up on one side of the bed, and I'm out before I even have time to reconsider my decision.

It feels as if I've only been asleep a short time when I'm awakened by the sound of a garbage truck. Cracking one eye open, I see it's now light out, and I'm in my own bed. But I'm not alone. A warm, female body is tucked into mine, ass pressed tightly against my now *very* awake dick, and my left arm is draped loosely over her body, while one hand cups a perfectly shaped breast.

What the hell?

I squeeze my eyes closed and open them again, checking to see I am, in fact, awake. Still not believing what I'm seeing, because I'm fairly certain I was alone when I came in here last night, I press my fingers together and pinch a soft nipple.

"Ouch!" The strange blonde squeals, just before she elbows me in the gut.

"Hrrumph." The groan falls from my mouth before I can stop it. Using one hand to cover my junk, just in case her elbow starts flying again, I roll over onto my back. "Why the hell'd you do that?"

"Me?" she squeaks, frantically rubbing the sleep from her eyes. "I don't recall giving you permission to feel me up."

"Yeah, well, I wasn't expecting to find a hot girl in my bed this morning. Thought I was dreaming, wanted to see if you were real."

I've had my fair share of women in this bed. Women I've known. I don't recall meeting this one, but one glance tells me I'd like to rectify that.

The comforter's been pushed away, and she's wearing a pink lacy top over the skimpiest pair of shorts I've ever seen. She's really tiny, not only in body weight, but she must be a foot shorter than my six-three frame. Long, blond hair falls to the middle of her back, and this morning it's a hot mess of tangles, almost as if she went to bed with it wet. Before I know it, I'm picturing her naked in my shower, and suddenly my morning wood becomes a raging hard-on.

"You're not supposed to be home for two more days," she grumbles.

"Yeah, well, plans change, sweetheart. So, how'd you get in here, and why haven't we met before? You're really sexy. Are you aware of that?" My eyes skim over her once more before settling on the nipple I touched only moments ago. I find myself wondering how long she's been in my bed and which one of the guys I'll need to thank later.

"Ohmygod! Why are you naked? And why the hell are you aroused?" Her mouth gapes open in complete surprise. I glance to where the covers have been pushed down to my knees and can't help smiling when I see that not only am I hard, but my boy is so straight he's practically saluting us. I burst out laughing and link my hands behind my head, proudly leaving myself on display.

"Relax, sweetheart. I'm naked because this is *my* bed, and this is how I usually sleep. And, for the record, it's called morning wood, though the sight of you in that skimpy outfit doesn't hurt the situation." I smile smugly but she only glares in return before reaching down and grabbing the corner of the comforter to cover me. As her arm swings over me, her hair tickles my chest, sending another shock wave to my already aching lower half. I catch her by the wrist and can't mask my smirk when I ask her my next question. "So, any chance you wanna help me out?" My eyes dance between her and the obvious issue at hand.

She yanks her arm from my grasp and recoils as if I'm some sort of leper. This one is definitely not like the other women trying to make it into my bed. I normally have to fight them off. "No chance in hell."

"Okay, then. Guess I'll just have to take matters into my own hands." I reach beneath the comforter and give myself a stroke. Big mistake, seeing as how I never had any intention of going through with knocking one out while this chick sits only inches away. *Wait a minute. She hasn't taken her eyes off me. In fact, she's looking at the space between my legs as if she's hungry for it.* The tip of her pink tongue sneaks out to moisten her lips, and I picture what those lips could be doing. I give myself one more slow stroke. "You going to sit there with your mouth hanging open, or do you want to join in?"

She blinks a few times and shakes her head back and forth, not saying a word. "Is that a no?" I tease once more, but only because her eyes are still focused on the movement beneath the comforter.

"Are you really...? I mean... Would you actually do *that* while I'm sitting right here? You don't even know me." Her voice is soft and shaky as she offers me a shy, telling smile. One that reads both nervous, young woman and curious sex kitten. I for one would love to meet the latter of the two.

"Oh, yeah. I've got no problem beating off in front of you, if that's what you're into. However, there are other things we *could* be doing. One in particular comes to mind." I stroke myself slowly, and the way she's looking at my hand tells me I need to stop. If I'm not careful, I'll spew all over the sheets before she makes up her mind.

"Ew. Did you seriously just ask me to give you a blowjob? You don't even know me. That's just... gross." At this, she moves toward the edge of the bed, yet she still doesn't leave entirely, instead choosing to sit cross-legged and watch from further away. Unfortunately, her comment kills the moment. I've never had a woman look at me and utter the word *Ew*. Definitely an ego deflator.

Ego being my dick in this case.

"Annnnnddd, on that note..." I move to sit up but am immediately pushed back as she clambers up my body and plants a kiss on my lips. It's not the best kiss, but only because it's unexpected and clumsy. She smells sweet, kind of like strawberries or some shit like that. It's feminine, and I find I want to keep breathing her scent in. She pulls back, and we both stare at each other for a few seconds before either of us dares to make a move. I shift beneath her and study her expression. Her brows are drawn, as if she's trying to decide where to go from here, and her lips tremble slightly with each breath she draws in. I lift my hand to her cheek and trace my thumb over the swell of her bottom lip.

"Let's try that again." My words come out as a whisper between us as I cup my hand around the back of her neck and slant my mouth over hers. Her lips are soft, tentative at first, and I'm instantly caught up in the way she feels against me. It's like we meld together in perfect unison. We take our time, kissing, breathing heavily, learning each other's next move. And it's good. Really, *really* good. Her lips press firmly against mine, then part as my tongue glides along the seam. As our tongues brush together, she makes this soft keening sound I love hearing. My lips move of their own accord and I work my way over her delicate skin, feathering soft kisses along her jaw and down her neck. Chicks love it when you do that. Her pelvis rocks slowly, teasing me with a quiet promise of something more. The soft cotton of her shorts glides over my length, and it feels so incredibly good. It goes on for a few seconds until I grab her by the hips and still her before I lose it.

Since when did dry humping ever feel this damn good?

"Sweetheart," I murmur between wet kisses. "You never told me how you got in here." I kiss my way down her neck, intending to make my way down her gorgeous body.

"Scotty let me in last night," she answers breathlessly, arching her body until her breasts press firmly against my chest. "He didn't think you would mind."

"Trust me, honey, I don't mind. In fact, remind me to thank him later." I can see the outline of her nipples, and my mouth waters as I think about her squirming once I start licking and sucking them in the next twenty seconds. "How do you know Rivers?" I hum as my tongue prepares to get down to business.

She straddles my legs, grinding her pelvis over me, and it's driving me out of my everloving mind. Her hair falls softly around her sweet face, and while everything about her paints a perfect picture, the only thing I see are her breasts as they bounce less than three inches from my parted mouth. Then, without warning, she utters three words that would stop even the strongest of men in their tracks.

"He's my brother." My hands come up, shoving her off me as I scramble away. I can't get out of bed fast enough. I'm standing beside the bed, sporting a semi, while she's still kneeling, all sexed up and waiting to be taken. Only, I can't touch her.

Bro Code #1... NEVER EVER HAVE SEX WITH YOUR FRIEND'S SISTER

Bro Code #2... NEVER KISS YOUR FRIEND'S SISTER

Bro Code #3... DON'T EVEN CONSIDER CODE ONE OR TWO

I am so screwed...

"What's wrong?" She looks up with innocent, blue eyes, and all I want is to finish what we started. But there's no way I can. Rivers is my best friend. I would never do that to him. We both received a scholarship to play hockey and met on our first day of classes. Rivers is our goalie, and a damn good one too. Me, I'm a defenseman, one of the best around. He guards the net, and I guard the puck. We're protectors; it's what we do. Last month he asked all of us to watch over his little sister. Somehow, I don't think this is the type of protecting he'd intended.

Technically, I've already broken two codes, but in my defense, I had no idea who she was. *Note to self, always get a name before you shove your tongue down a girl's throat.* It's also obvious girls are completely ignorant to the whole friendship code guys have established. Maybe that's why guys with sisters are so quick to enforce it when they meet new friends. Me, I don't have any sisters, but if I did, I know I would lay that shit down within the first ten minutes of meeting a guy.

"What's wrong?" I choke out. "Rivers is my best friend. There are rules guys live by, and I just broke two of them in less than five minutes. And I would have broken another if I hadn't asked how you got in here." I drag my fingers through my hair and give it a yank as I pace the room. "Shit. He's going to kill me." Reaching for my pants, I pull them on and tuck myself inside, leaving the buttons undone.

Meanwhile, she remains in a kneeling position. Her hair is tousled a bit more from me burying my hands in those silky strands, and her nipples peek at me through the scrap of material covering them. I can feel her staring, and no matter how hard I fight it, I turn to face her. Her legs are slightly parted, and my eyes rake down her body, coming to rest on the juncture between her thighs. *Fuck, is that moisture on her shorts?* Suddenly, my hand is in my mouth, and I'm biting down hard on my fingers to keep from screaming.

"No, he won't. He doesn't have to know about this. It can be our little secret. Come back over here and join me." She grins devilishly, revealing two beautiful dimples, and it's all I can do to swallow the knot forming in my throat. Girls with dimples drive me absolutely wild, though this girl managed to do that all on her own. I can tell she's turned on by the breathless sounds that fall past her perfect lips and her pert breasts rise and fall with each labored breath. Like an idiot, I remain rooted, unable to turn away. I stand there, my erection thickening, and stare as she slowly draws her hand between her legs and begins touching herself.

I practically choke on my next words as I fight for control over my own body. "Can you *please* stop doing that?"

"Why? Doesn't this turn you on?" The devilish gleam in her eyes tells me she knows exactly how her little show is affecting me, both mentally *and* physically.

"Why?" My eyes squeeze shut and it's all I can do not to scream as I answer her insane question. "Because your brother is an early riser and these walls are paper thin." I stomp into the bathroom and close the door on the entire scene.

"That's ridiculous," she scoffs, and as if on cue I hear Rivers' voice outside the outer door. I button my jeans as my mind scrambles for a way to talk myself out of this.

"Cass? You up yet?" he calls out, before knocking once and throwing open the door. This is his trademark entry. However, I don't see what happens because I've made the decision to dive into the tub and feign sleep.

CASSIE

Even though my insides are shaking with laughter, I do my best to put on a calm front when I face Scotty. My girly bits are still tingly, but his friend's words ring loud and clear in my head when I see the look on my brother's face. It's quite clear he barged in expecting to find something going on between the sheets. I'm guessing he saw this guy's car outside and put two and two together. I'm thankful he didn't barge in five minutes ago when I was rubbing on his teammate like a stripper grinding up against a pole. It appears in my haste to get over Justin, I've bypassed kissing and jumped right into trying to have sex with a stranger. A stranger who just happens to be my brother's best friend.

"Hey, what were you doing in here? I thought I heard voices." His eyes scan the small space just as he turns to the closed bathroom door. My heart thumps wildly beneath my tank, and I pray to God he doesn't hear it.

"What are you talking about? I just woke up." I swing my legs over the side of the bed and stretch my arms up over my head. "Boy, I sure slept like a baby. This bed is so comfortable. I'm sure

after this, the dorm beds are going to be a huge disappointment."
I fake a yawn.

"Yeah," Scotty replies distractedly, then opens the bathroom
door. I cringe inwardly, prepared to lie if necessary. Without
warning, he starts laughing his ass off. "Cage, what the hell are
you doing sleeping in the bathtub?"

"What?" my handsome stranger asks, groggily. "Oh, hey, man.
Why am I sleeping in the tub? Maybe because you gave away my
bed."

"Sorry about that, buddy. You've gotta be stiff as hell. Here,
let me help you up." I hear movement, then the sounds of
someone stumbling, before they come out of the bathroom
together. "Cassie, I hope you're seeing this. My buddies love me
so much they'd choose a tub over climbing in bed with my little
sister." He slings an arm around his buddy's shoulder. "Sis, I'd
like you to meet my best friend, Brantley Cage."

"Hey, Cassie. Nice to meet you." Brantley raises his hand shyly
but refuses to make eye contact.

"Hi," I wiggle my fingers at him, trying my best not to let my
facial expression reveal what I'm thinking. "It's nice to meet you
as well."

Then our eyes connect, and it's as if little jolts of electricity
are firing inside me. His gaze lingers for a few seconds before
my brother rudely interrupts our connection.

"Cass, you have to see this guy on the ice. I swear watching
him skate is a thing of beauty. One of the best damn defensemen
to ever grace this campus." Scotty grins broadly while Brantley
remains silent. "Go on, tell her about your big play last season."

"Nah. She probably doesn't want to hear about that," he

replies all too quietly.

"Oh, I don't know about that. I think I'd enjoy hearing more about your moves." I give him a quick wink as I move to step in front of him. It may be just my imagination, but I swear I hear a noise when I get close. He swallows hard, and I watch as his Adam's apple bobs nervously up and down.

"Holy shit, Cass, what are you wearing? Put some clothes on and I'll take you out to breakfast." Scotty steps in front of me, trying to prevent Brantley from seeing me, and I almost laugh. I'm beginning to get a clearer picture of what it's going to be like having my big brother nearby.

"Get a grip, Scotty. I'm dressed perfectly fine." I flip my hair over my shoulder and give him a challenging stare.

"Please, your ass is practically hanging out of your shorts, and I can see right through your shirt. And if I can see it, I know Cage can see it too." At this, Brantley's eyes fall to my chest and he snickers. Scotty snaps his head around. "You got something to say, Cage?"

Brantley's lip curls between his teeth as his eyes dart between me and my angry brother. "Not at all. I'll just step out, so you can get dressed. It was a pleasure meeting you, Cassie." His tone is far too serious when he says this. A few minutes ago, we were flirting and about to have sex. Now, we've been reduced to casual formalities all because of some 'friend code.' Screw that. I like where we were headed better than where we've ended up.

"Trust me, the pleasure was all mine." I'm trying to sound flirty, but it comes out sounding breathy and full of sexual undertones. Brantley visibly slows, clutching the doorframe before he walks out without looking back.

"Stop that," Scotty growls. "I know what you're doing and it's not going to work."

"Yeah? And what is that?"

"You're flirting with him just to push my buttons. Well, knock it off. These guys aren't just my roommates. They're my teammates, and we don't need any shit between us. We need to be a unified team. I don't need to be worrying about one of them trying to screw my kid sister behind my back."

I grind the heels of my hands over my eyes as I shake my head at him. "Scotty, I'm not a little girl anymore. I'm a woman now. And I have needs, just like you do. I can't have you scaring off all of my prospects. It's not fair."

"Cass, as much as it pains me to say this, it's not the other guys I'm worried about. I just need you to stay away from my friends. Okay? They're not your prospects. You can hang around us and shit, but don't go acting all girly and dressing like this around them." He waves his hand in front of my shirt.

"They're called breasts, Scotty. I have them. Ashley has them. All women have them. I'm not going to hide them under a sack just to make you feel better. I can't help that I have them, nor can I help it that your friends can't stop looking at them. They're pretty spectacular." I glance down at my chest and rotate my shoulders back and forth.

"You did *not* just shake your tits at me. That was so uncalled for. I can never un-see that. That was so wrong." He throws up his hands, muttering as he walks out the door. "Be downstairs in twenty minutes and I'll take you to Angelo's."

After waiting in a very long line, we are finally seated at a small table in the center of the room. One by one, heaping plates of food are delivered to surrounding tables. The first thing I notice are the thick slices of homemade bread topped with powdered sugar and served with a side of warm maple syrup. My mouth practically salivates when a plate of it is placed on the table next to ours. I love French toast. Allow me to rephrase that. I am addicted to French toast. But this restaurant takes it to a whole new level by deep-frying it. By the time our waitress comes to take our order, I'm already speaking before she has a chance to ask what I want. When my breakfast is placed in front of me, and I take my first bite, it's clear it has been worth the wait.

Scotty watches with great interest as I enjoy my food. With each bite I savor, his smile grows deeper before turning into full-on laughter once I start moaning my appreciation.

"I've missed this," he says, moving his fork between us. "It's going to be great having you close by. We have a lot to catch up on."

"I'm looking forward to that. Things were never the same at the house after you left for school, then last year at Minnesota was a joke."

"Yeah? I was going to ask you about that. Did something happen between you and Justin? I mean, I know you followed him there," he asks, pausing to take another bite of his omelette. "Why the sudden need for change?"

"We grew apart," I answer, trying to avoid further explanation. I know those two remained close, despite the distance. Their love of the game keeps them in contact, especially during the off-season when they don't have to play against one another. "I just needed a change, and Great Lakes has an amazing music department." He gives me a look that says he knows there's more to it than I'm letting on. "Can't a girl miss her big brother?"

"Please tell me you didn't transfer here to be close to me." He pushes back his plate and lets out a frustrated groan. "Cass, I'm going to be really busy with hockey, and Ashley and I spend a lot of time together. She's pretty demanding."

I can't hide the disappointed look on my face. It's true; I did need to get away from Minnesota, but he was the real reason for my transfer. I know he doesn't intend to hurt my feelings, and it's probably wrong of me to expect him to change his life just because I showed up. But it would have made me feel better to hear him say he missed me too.

"That's fine. I don't expect you to drop everything for me. That's not what I'm implying. I just know your life is about to drastically change and this may be the last time we have to reconnect." I nervously chew the inside of my cheek as I push the last few bites of my breakfast around in a syrupy puddle.

"Hey," he leans forward and covers the back of my hand with his. "I don't care how far away my job takes me, or how busy I get, I'll always be your big brother and I'm always here for you. I just meant I might not be the same Scotty you remember from growing up. Things have changed. Time's changed me." He fidgets as he tries to explain himself. "I mean, my priorities are different than what they were when we were younger and you were trailing around after me."

"No they haven't. Your priorities are still the same. It's just now you have the freedom to pursue them without anyone hovering over you," I tease. "You think I didn't know what you were doing in your room when you were seventeen? I was fifteen. I may have been naïve, but I wasn't stupid." I laugh, watching as he turns three shades of red.

"And here I thought you were all sweet and innocent." His lip quirks as he eyes me warily. "So, you and Fairfax? I'm assuming you two..."

"Yes," I answer his unspoken question. "For nearly two years. See, I'm not sweet and innocent anymore."

"You'll always be my little sister, Cassie. I don't like thinking about some guy putting his hands on you."

"I know, Scotty, and I love you for that. But you have to know there are going to be other guys, regardless if you're ready to accept it or not."

"I suppose," he replies, giving me a half-hearted shrug.

"So tell me more about Brantley." His eyes narrow, and instantly I can tell he assumes I'm interested. Even though I *am* interested, I'm asking more out of curiosity. I want to know more about the sexy man who boldly stared into my eyes while touching himself. I have a feeling that image will remain frozen in my brain for months to come. "And before you ask, I'm not after him. I'm just curious to know more about the guy you call your best friend."

His shoulders visibly relax as he leans back, spreading his arms wide across the back of the booth. "For the most part, we're complete opposites. He's a planner, whereas I tend to jump right in without thinking. I'm a sucker for love, and he can't run away from it fast enough. But on the ice we're both driven and really fucking good at our job. He's just always been there for me. All of the guys are like that, but I know no matter what, Cage will have my back. He's the one friend I trust to be loyal until the end. There are not many people you come across who you can say that about, you know?"

As I listen, I find myself remembering the look on Brantley's face when he learned who I was, and now I understand. What scares me is the way his kisses left me longing for more. But what terrifies me even more is the fact that given all Scotty just told me, I'm fairly certain it won't stop me from wanting him. In fact, I think it makes me want him even more.

BRANTLEY

After Rivers leaves for breakfast, I pack a bag and head over to the frat house, where my buddy, John, has a futon I'll crash on for the next few days. There's no way in hell I'm putting myself back in *that* position. I mean, it's no surprise her brother will pummel my ass if he finds out what went down. But it's not just that. I hate to admit it, but I'm attracted to her. She's pretty, but at the same time, she's nothing like the girls I normally hook up with. Not that I hook up with a lot of girls. At least, I don't *think* I do.

So, for two days I divide my time between the frat house and the weight room, avoiding Scott like the plague. He texted yesterday, asking where the hell I'd gone. All I said was I didn't want to kick his kid sister to the couch. Little did I know he would see it as another noble gesture on my part. When he started praising me for being such a great friend, it was all I could do not to come clean. We've never kept secrets. We've never had to. Our whole group is like that. We're great as individuals, but even stronger as a team, which makes us a powerhouse on the ice.

"Cage, get in here and sit down," Coach calls out as I'm passing his office after a hard morning of practice. The first two weeks after summer are always an adjustment. Coach keeps us on a strict training schedule during the off-season. But coming back after being apart and trying to mesh with the new recruits always seems to take some getting used to. I mean, you've got the seasoned players who've already established their place on the team, then you bring in new guys who are itching to make their mark. Let's just say the trainers go through a lot of ice due to guys pushing too hard during those first few weeks.

I step into the room, and he motions for me to take a seat across from his desk. "How you doing, son? You looked good out there today."

"Thanks, Coach. It's good to be back."

Kevin Bishop's job involves much more than coaching this team of NHL hopefuls. For the past three years, I've been a part of this team, and he's taken on the role of surrogate father to a number of his players. Guys like me, whose own fathers are over a thousand miles away, often find themselves sitting in this very spot seeking advice or simply sharing minute details of our lives. I'll admit it's nice to know someone I respect so highly is always there for me if I ever need him.

"So, tell me about camp. See any future champions?" He smiles, and I spend the next twenty minutes telling him all about my week in Traverse City coaching a group of thirty hockey hopefuls, all under the age of eleven.

"Sounds like you had as much fun as the kids."

"Oh, yeah. I almost wish I could go back next summer. There

was one kid who was really fast, and he was wearing my jersey. I'm not going to lie, it was pretty cool," I grin happily as I think about my week with Tyler.

"I'm glad to hear it. I knew you'd be a great fit up there." He's still smiling, but concern washes over his face as he leans forward and studies me. "Is everything okay? You look tired. You getting enough sleep?"

"Hardly. Rivers' sister transferred here this year, and is staying with us until she can get into the dorms. She's in my bed, and I'm on John's futon at the frat."

He throws his head back, and the rich sound of laughter fills the room. "Cage, you're the only guy on this team who would hand over his bed to a woman and then move out. So, when do you get your bed back? The dorms opened this morning."

"Yeah. Rivers and Ashley are moving her in this afternoon. All should be back to normal when I get home tonight."

"Well, okay then. Everything else going okay? Course schedule, family, girlfriend?"

"I don't have a girlfriend, sir." I shift uncomfortably in my chair. "And my family is good. Spoke with my brother a few weeks ago; he said Mom and Dad are good. "

"Glad to hear it, kid. So, why no girl?" He leans forward until we're eye level and clasps his hands under his chin.

I shrug my shoulders and sit back, putting some distance between us, though I still feel as if I'm being scrutinized.

"What's the point? I don't want to be tied down. I'm headed to Detroit after graduation. I'm slammed with hockey and classes," I give him a list of excuses. Excuses I've firmly clung to since having my heart broken at the beginning of freshman year.

Coach remembers all the shit I went through with Vanessa. He knows how I feel about relationships, but I also know he worries about me being closed off to love. "It's just easier this way."

"You make it sound easy, but you can't hide from love forever. Sooner or later it's going to catch up with you. Then what are you going to do?"

"I don't know. Guess I'll just have to skate faster." I stand and make my way toward the door. "Thanks for everything. I better get going."

"Anytime, son. Hey, if you see Masterson out there, tell him to get his butt in here." I throw up a hand in acknowledgement and head to the locker room.

When I get back to my room, I find everything is just as I'd left it. There are even fresh sheets on the bed, and a note from Cassie.

Thanks for letting me stay here this week. I'm really sorry you had to leave for my sake, but I have to say I frigging LOVE your bed. And I'm sorry we didn't get to spend more time together, but it was fun while it lasted. Hope to see you again under different circumstances. ~Cassie

I laugh at her wit, imagining the gleam in her eye as she wrote it, then crumple the note up before throwing it in the trash. The house is quiet, which is rare once classes start, so I take advantage and turn on my music. My bed sits there, perfectly made, and it beckons me over. I stretch out my legs and remember the last time I lay in this exact spot. When my eyes close, it's her face I see, and her blond hair I feel where it fell forward and tickled my skin. Before long, I'm fast asleep, dreaming of when I was a young kid skating on Miller's Pond. Those were happy times, when all I cared about was what time the rink opened and when the lake would finally freeze over so we could put our skates on.

A ringing phone awakens me, and it takes a few seconds to find it in my sleep-induced state. It's dark, and I figure I must have slept a good five hours. My stomach rumbles loudly, and I realize I've slept right through dinner.

"Hello," I answer groggily.

"Sweetie?" Mom's voice breaks through the fog surrounding me. "Did I wake you?"

"Mom. Wow, it's good to hear your voice." I pause and shift my position so I can cradle the phone between my ear and the pillow. "Yeah, I was sleeping, but I never intended to sleep this long. I'm glad you called and woke me. How are you? How's Dad?"

"I'm fine." I sense the strain in her voice, and I am instantly wide awake.

"Mom, what is it? Something's wrong."

"Sweetie, I need to tell you something, and it's not going to be easy. I really wish I could be there with you when I tell you this."

The line goes silent for a few moments, and it gives my mind time to speculate what's going on. My grandmother had a heart attack. Or something has happened to my brother.

"Your father collapsed this afternoon. The doctor's believe he's had a heart attack," she says, catching me completely off guard. Her words strike me hard. It feels worse than the hit I took in the playoff game against Minnesota last season. That blow had been bad enough to take me out of the game. But this...

This one leaves me feeling as if I've been hit by the whole fucking Minnesota team all at once.

"Where was he? Was he at work, or with you?"

"We were in the kitchen, having an argument. He collapsed right before my eyes. I've never felt so helpless in all my life. They're running tests right now."

"Wait, what does this mean? There's something you're not telling me." By now my frustration has reached a dangerous level. I receive a phone call waking me out of a deep sleep, only to be told my father just had a heart attack and possibly almost died. Yet I sense there's something she's not telling me.

"Brantley, I need for you to try and calm down. None of this is easy for me. I hate having to tell you this over the phone."

"Mom, I'm sorry. It's just that I know there's something else. Just lay it on me," I plead with her. "Why were you and dad fighting? You never used to fight."

"People change, sweetheart. Your dad's business has been struggling for some time, and he hasn't really been himself. We were fighting because I found out a woman he works with has been texting him. They met for coffee a few times. I jumped to conclusions and confronted him."

"What?" I bellow, sitting up so fast it makes my head spin. "Why the hell would he be with another woman? He's a married man, or did he forget that?"

"Sweetheart, I know this is hard for you to hear. But right now I'm choosing to look past all of that because I want him to get through this. I can't afford to get held up on those details. He's my husband and he needs me. Now more than ever," she answers resolutely.

The rest of our conversation is a blur as I listen to the long list of tests scheduled. He'll be admitted to the hospital and will most likely be there for a couple of days. I suddenly feel guilty for being so far away, and I wonder if my brother is there with her.

"I'm sorry, but I don't understand. I just talked to him a few weeks ago and everything was fine. You both sounded so... so... normal. How can he go from normal to having a heart attack in just a few weeks? And how is it you sound so calm? Aren't you freaking out right now?"

"Sweetheart, I understand this comes as a shock. This isn't something any mother wants to tell her children. And it hasn't been easy for me. While I may appear calm on the outside, I can assure you on the inside I am barely holding it together. Your father and I have been together for twenty-seven years. It's hard as hell to see the man you love lying on a hospital bed with machines hooked up to him."

"I'm sorry, mom. Is Chris there with you? Do you want me to come home? I can probably get a flight out first thing tomorrow."

"No. You stay put. The doctors seem pretty confident he will be okay, and he's in good hands. Chris is on his way. We'll be okay without you here. I'll call you once I know more, or if anything changes." I know she's trying to ease my worry, but her words have the opposite effect. Knowing I could have gone to school in Colorado rather than take off across the country used to weigh heavily on me when I'd first come to Michigan. This situation just brings all of the guilt I thought I had buried straight back to the surface.

A strange tightness grips my chest, and I feel the sudden need to go out and get plastered. Maybe the alcohol will help me forget everything I just heard.

"Mom, I have to go." I can hear her talking as I hang up, but I don't care. Maybe tomorrow I'll wake up and discover it was all just a bad dream.

Even though in my heart I know it's not.

When I step out of my room, the first person I see is Davis. He's on the sofa, playing a video game and drinking a beer. I spin my keys on my finger and cock my head toward the door.

"Feel like getting wasted?" He's up and following me out the door faster than you can say *hell, yeah*.

CASSIE

I stand back and survey my side of the room, loving what I see. After Scotty and his roommates helped me get settled, Ashley and I spent the better part of the afternoon shopping for items to give my space a homey feel. Ashley is getting her degree in interior design, and she found the best selection of random stuff at rock bottom prices.

I find it laughable it took three grown men to help me move six boxes stuffed full of my most precious belongings. But they insisted on helping. Spending the past few days with them has been quite an experience. We laughed, played video games, watched multiple videos where men were blowing up stuff, and bonded over a few meals. My brother has really great friends. They are all sweet guys who support each other fully. The only absent member had been Brantley.

"Our space is totally bitchin'," exclaims my roommate, Veronica, as she comes up behind me and rests her chin on my shoulder. She has a dancer's body, long and lean, and at five-nine she stands a good five inches over me. "I have a feeling this is going to be a great year."

"Yeah, me too." I look around our small, overly decorated space and smile.

"I'm famished. You feel like grabbing a burger?" She reaches for her ID and a credit card. "I know this really great bar down by the train station, and there's a bus that will drop us off a few short blocks from there."

"Oh, yeah, Casey's Tavern. I saw it when Scotty picked me up the other day. Hell, yes I'm in." I stuff my pockets with the necessary items and close the door to our new home.

The place is wall-to-wall packed with GL students, and we wait forty-five minutes for a booth. The atmosphere is loud and full of energy. It's not a large space, but it's crammed full of local flavor. Images of Ann Arbor in ages past line the walls, along with chalkboards covered in decorative, handwritten menus. A fully stocked bar lines one entire wall, and the bar itself must be twenty feet long and is packed with customers standing shoulder-to-shoulder. I glance around and smile, getting the sense I'll be spending a lot of my time in this space over the next three years.

"This place is totally badass. I love it!"

Veronica beams with pride as her eyes scan over the small surroundings before hooking a thumb toward the bar. "Yeah, I've been coming here with my parents since I was little. I used to sit on one of those bar stools with my Dad and proudly declare one day I would work behind that bar."

"Well, at least I know where to find you after graduation," I laugh and take a sip of iced tea.

"My Dad used to look me in the eye and tell me "Roni, you can grow up and be anything you want to be. Why would you want to be a bartender?" to which I would happily reply, "So I can have as many cherry sodas as I want."

"That is so precious! I can totally picture you standing on one of those stools with your hands on your hips."

"I dare to venture the picture you're painting isn't too far from the truth." She shakes her head as she smiles.

I've only known her four hours, but I can already tell Veronica Parker and I are going to be the best of friends. You know how it is when you meet a kindred spirit. Within minutes, everything just clicks. I know I've gotten lucky. I've heard horror stories about people going off to college and having a roommate who makes their year a living hell. I have a feeling I've dodged a bullet, and I am very thankful.

We've already ordered our burgers, and after drinking two iced teas my bladder is screaming. Roni must read the desperate look in my eyes, because she turns and points to the corner furthest from where we're seated. After fighting my way through a throng of bar patrons, I wait in a short line to do my business. As I wash my hands I take a good look in the mirror. Rather than fight with my hair this morning, I'd pulled it into a quick braid that now hangs over one shoulder. My cheeks are flushed, but I figure it's due to the stuffiness of the room. I pull a lip balm from the pocket of my jean shorts and liberally apply it to my dry lips. Rubbing them together, I give my appearance a quick nod and turn to fight the crowd.

The number of bodies in the small space has increased. As I

walk back to where Roni is waiting, I'm jostled around. Just as I come to a clearing, I am knocked backwards and end up falling into an unsuspecting customer. My hands flail out and grasp the first thing they come in contact with, which happens to be a very lean body.

"I am so sorry." The words are out of my mouth before I even look up to see whom I've just manhandled. Amber eyes pierce straight through me as recognition sets in for both of us, and a smirk fills his handsome face.

"Whoa, Dimples. Better lay off the sauce." The playful catch in his voice catches me off guard, and it's the first time he's actually looked me in the eyes since Scotty interrupted what I affectionately refer to as *what could have been*. I want to be angry with him for ignoring me, but he had to go and give me a nickname. And not just any nickname. For some reason, this one feels personal. By looking at us you would never guess he's seen me before, but I know differently, and I curse my body for its traitorous response to his charming good looks. Using very capable hands, he rights me to standing and checks me over. "You okay? You didn't hurt yourself when you crashed into me, did you?" I can tell by the gleam in his eyes he's drunk, and for a few seconds we share an intense moment. One that tells me he's thinking the same thing I'm thinking. I blink up at him, unable to tear my eyes away.

I'm captivated by his presence. The last time I was in his arms I hadn't taken time to fully appreciate his beauty. That's most likely because I was distracted by his nakedness, but even still, how I didn't notice until now completely baffles me. The photos I studied fail to do him justice. His dark hair is longer on top and shorter on the sides. It looks as if he's used hair product to tame the longer pieces, but one rebellious strand has broken free and falls over his right eye. I want so badly to reach up and run my fingers through his hair under the guise of tucking it back in place, but I refrain. His full lips part, and he cracks a smile when he realizes I'm still staring.

"N-no, I'm fine." I smile through my nervousness and blow out the breath I've been holding. "How have you been? I'll bet you're glad to have your bed back. Though I have to admit I was sad to leave it." The minute the words are out, I wish I could take them back.

He's about to respond when a redhead approaches and wraps her hands possessively around his forearm. My eyes narrow in on her hand, and it's all I can do not to shout *Back off bitch. He's mine!* But sadly, that's not the case.

"Brantley, baby, who is this?" *Baby?* Is this the type of girl he goes for? With her super skinny jeans, heavy black eyeliner, and four-inch stiletto heels, she looks every bit the part of hooker-wanna-be. She stares coolly, sizing me up as if I may be looking to take away her man.

"Oh, this one here is Rivers' kid sister, Cassie." He reaches over and has the nerve to pat me on the top of my head like I'm a dog. If looks could kill, he would disintegrate right now. Much to my embarrassment, that's not how this cruel world operates. The redhead gives a smug smile of victory and titters with laughter.

"I wondered when they started allowing high school kids in here." And just like that, her attention is focused solely on the object of her desire. They both turn and walk away, dismissing me as if I were never there.

I'd be lying if I said I didn't watch him go, silently willing him to look my way one last time. But he never does.

BRANTLEY

It's only eleven in the morning, and it's already been a bitch of a day. Thanks to some of the guys partying too hard on Saturday, Coach put the entire team through the ringer at practice, and my whole body hurts. Hell, even my hair hurts.

I cut across campus in a daze, functioning on autopilot, when I hear someone calling my name.

"Brantley!" I turn and find a blonde frantically waving her arms to get my attention. We hooked up once after the team suffered a loss during our sophomore year, and she's been hounding me ever since. Don't get me wrong, she may be a nice girl, but once the alcohol wore off, I realized we had nothing in common. She's overly made up, fake in every sense of the word, and only wears designer fashions. I grew up in Colorado. If I'm not in uniform, you'll likely find me in a pair of Timberlands and jeans.

It takes everything I have not to pretend I don't hear her and keep walking. Instead, I stop and wait for her to catch up, because my mom raised a gentleman. "Hey, Summer. How've you been?"

"Boy, you sure know how to make a girl work for it." She gives my arm a playful smack. "So, are you going to Jake's party next month?"

"Uh, I wasn't planning on it. I guess it depends on my schedule. It's his birthday, right?" I ease my arm from her grasp and grip the back of my neck.

"Oh, yeah, and it's going to be out of control. You simply *have* to go. Parties just aren't the same when you're not there." She curls her overly glossed lips down in a pout while batting her lashes. While I'm sure this look leaves many guys falling at her feet, I couldn't be less interested if I tried.

"I'll consider it," I lie and turn to make my escape.

"Wait! I was wondering if you wanted to grab a cup of coffee. I have an hour to kill before my next class."

I've just opened my mouth to politely decline when my phone vibrates, saving me from hurting her feelings.

"Sorry, Summer. I have to answer this. Maybe some other time." I hurry away while opening the text.

Unknown: Hey there, B. Was hoping u might have time 2 discuss tutoring.

Me: Umm... Who's this, and how'd u get my #?

Unknown: Oh, this is Ca

Me: Don't know anyone by that name.

Unknown: Oops. This is Candy. I got your # off a study sheet.

Candy? Candy? I stop walking and rack my brain to remember if I know anyone by that name and decide it's a definite no. Then I begin drumming up an image of Candy. With a name like that, I can probably assume she's another member of the 'fake' club. And I'm fairly certain she probably has bubble gum pink hair.

Probably not a fair assumption, but I'm thinking it's a safe bet.

Me: Sorry, Candy. Don't think I can help.

Her: Why not?

Me: Busy playing hockey.

Her: But ur good at calculus?

For crying out loud. This chick obviously can't take a hint. I aced calculus last year. Just because I'm good at it doesn't mean I feel like helping someone who isn't.

Me: Well, yeah, but that's not the point.

Her: It is for me. There's a test next Friday I NEED 2 pass. After that, ur in the clear.

Me: That's where ur wrong. I'm already in the clear.

Her: So... No?

Me: Afraid so.

Her: Bummer. I was hoping 2 pass that test.

Me: Ask someone else.

Her: No can do, B-man. I heard ur the best, and that's what I want.

Me: What can I say? I am pretty good.

Her: See! This is why I need u. Come on, B. Just a few hours of your time. I promise 2 make it worth your while.

Me: Did u just proposition me?

Her: What? God no! I just meant I'd buy all the coffee u can drink.

Me: Too bad. I was almost ready 2 cave. Wish I could help...

Her: If u change your mind, I'll be the crying blonde hanging out at Comet.

Me: Ur funny. I like that. Nice chatting with u.

Her: U 2 B. Hope we can meet sometime and not talk math.

Me: Sure. Maybe. Well, bye.

I stare down at my phone and laugh. I'm beginning to think I may have judged Candy too hastily. She seemed... Well... She seemed sweet.

CASSIE

We're only three weeks into the first semester and I'm already struggling. In my haste to get enrolled, I'd piled on way too many tough credits. Music composition, calculus, American government. Ugh! Could my schedule get any worse? The only bright spot, other than comp class, is the psychology class I share with Brantley. We're surrounded by two hundred students, but there was no mistaking when he sauntered through the door on our first day of class. I don't believe he's even aware we're in the same class, but it doesn't surprise me. He's done everything he can to avoid running into me. On the few occasions I've stopped by Scott's to say hello, Brantley's either been out, or has chosen to remain hidden upstairs. So, each day I sit in the same seat, safely tucked between two football players, which is where I am today.

I'm not going to lie. Running into him at the bar had shaken me up. Just the feel of his body under my hands made me weak in the knees. Hell, just touching him would have been enough to make my head spin, but add that I've previously kissed him *and* seen him completely naked, and I turned into a complete mess. Then that redhead had to go and ruin everything. I don't know who she is, but the way he treated me after she joined us left me feeling humiliated.

When the psych lecture is over, I hold back and scowl as I look over my calculus notes. I'm really struggling in this class, and there's a test a week from Friday I *really* need to pass. I swear this professor is out to make my life a living hell. The class has only met six times, and we've already had two quizzes, both of which I nearly failed.

Then last week when I'd approached him about study groups, he'd merely pointed to a row of clipboards spread out along the wall. Seven clipboards contained spreadsheets listing students who were looking to join a study group. One clipboard in particular also listed contact information of students who offered tutoring. Since my situation required individual attention, I'd ignored the groups and gone straight for the tutoring, skimming the list until I came to a name I recognized.

B. Cage 719-688-5535

I texted him last Friday with the intention of telling him who I was, but I remembered how he acted at the bar and panicked. I figured he would totally blow me off. So I told him my name was Candy, and he blew me off anyway. I wasn't sure what hurt more, the fact I would probably fail again, or that he wouldn't have anything to do with me. All I want is five minutes of his time to tell him I'm sorry for the way I acted that morning. I'd humiliated myself and alienated him, all in the same moment.

I'm still holding my notes when I look up and see him walking up the aisle. He's talking with a fellow hockey player, but his gaze meets mine as he draws near. Rather than ignore me, he lifts his hand in a small wave as he passes, leaving me with a glimmer of hope he doesn't hate me as much as I fear.

Much to my relief, when I make it to calculus I find out Professor Briggs is ill and had to leave early. Class has been cancelled, but there's a note written on the whiteboard. STUDY FOR NEXT FRIDAY'S TEST.

When I open the door to my room I'm immediately deafened by a loud scream and a grunt as two bodies scramble for cover on Roni's side of the room.

"Sorry," I cover my eyes, "I'm leaving. Go back to whatever it is you were doing." My chest pounds as I slam the door and bolt down the hall with a hand covering my mouth. I shove open the exterior door and double over in laughter.

Ohmygod. I just caught my roommate riding some guy's di——

My thoughts are cut off when my phone vibrates with a text, and I do a happy dance when I see whom it's from. It's been three days since I first approached him, and to be honest, I've been on pins and needles, wondering if he would reach out to me.

Him: How's the studying?

My first inclination is to play it cool. I can't have him thinking I've been holding my breath, waiting for him to text me. Which I totally have. After our first conversation, I began second-guessing my decision to lie. I really hadn't thought it through very well. If he does agree to meet up, what will he say when Cassie Rivers shows up instead of Candy?

Me: I'm sorry. Who's this?

I'm still laughing when I press send. Within seconds, the three little dots appear and I wait for his response.

Him: Umm... It's B. U know, calculus god and all-around nice guy.

Me: Oh, yeah. I remember. Calculus god? Maybe. Nice guy? Jury's still out, B-Man.

Him: Now u doubt me? I have 2 say, I'm hurt.

Me: Not at all. I'm stating a fact. U haven't graced me with ur presence, ergo, I have nothing but a few texts 2 support your claim.

Him: Fair enough. U ready for this test?

Me: Not even close. But not for lack of trying. I shouldn't have signed up for this class.

Him: Ah, the curse 2 prove u can do it all. Been there.

Me: So u know my struggle?

Him: All 2 well.

Me: How'd u deal?

Him: Tequila. Lots of tequila.

Me: I'm afraid that's not a viable option.

Him: Don't drink?

Me: Underage. Lack of access 2 said tequila.

Him: Bummer.

Me: If I pass, u can treat me 2 a shot.

Him: U got it.

Me: I'm bored, B. Talk 2 me. Can't go 2 my room.

Him: Why not?

Me: Roommate's having sex.

Him: Yeah, been there 2.

Me: First 4 me.

Him: I'd say it gets easier, but that's a lie.

Me: Gee, thanks.

Him: Don't mention it.

Me: Can I ask u something, B?

Him: I'm all thumbs.

Me: Ha ha ur really funny. Do u have a girlfriend?

Him: Nope.

Me: That's a shame.

Him: Really? Why?

Me: Cause u seem like a sweet guy. I like u B-Man. Ur starting to grow on me.

Him: Thanks. I think ur growing on me 2.

Me: Does this mean u will tutor me?

Him: Maybe.

Me: Well, time's wasting. Will u tell me if that maybe turns into a yes?

Him: Maybe.

Me: I'm starting 2 not like u very much.

Five minutes pass before he responds and I'm grinning like an idiot when I read what it says.

Him: I'll risk it.

CASSIE

With today's classes behind me, I begin the long walk back to the dorms. This week has been rough. I'm not sleeping well, and my eating habits have gone to shit. My day ended after two torturous hours in music composition. Just before I left for Ann Arbor, I'd written a new song. I spent the better part of the morning sitting at a piano, working through a section that isn't coming together like I envisioned.

One thing I've learned since arriving is that it's nearly impossible to eat healthy. Okay, there's a salad bar in the cafeteria. And they have a wide assortment of pre-made salads and soups. But then I move to the other side of the room and see signs for pizza, hoagies, tacos, and Italian. Honestly, it's too much. If I'm not careful, I'll gain ten pounds in my first month on campus.

Climbing the steps to my room, I'm greeted by many of the acquaintances I've made since classes started. A group of us try to meet every Wednesday night just to hang out. We usually eat popcorn and watch a movie, though some nights all we do is sit around and gossip. For instance, just this week I learned a girl who lives down the hall from me is a dancer at a strip club. Some of the guys in our group went there last week and she performed for them. So, when I'm walking up the stairs and look up to see her coming my way, I'm naturally intrigued. I want to grab her by the arm and ask all about it. What's it like? How much money does she make? What prompted her to start stripping? The questions are endless. Not that I'm considering stripping for a living, or anything like that. I'm just naturally a curious person. I fight the urge, and we brush past each other without so much as a word or backward glance.

When I come to our door, I pause, knocking loudly four times before turning the handle.

"Geez, Louise. Come in, you dork." Veronica is stretched out on her bed, reading a book, when I poke my head in the room. "Will you knock it off already?"

"Hey, I've been traumatized. The last thing I want to see after a long day is your naked ass in the air." I drop my bag on the floor and collapse on the hard mattress.

"What's wrong with my ass?" she pouts, twisting her head around to check out her butt.

"Nothing at all. You have a perfectly fine ass. Nicely shaped. Pert in all the right places. I'm just not partial to staring at naked women."

"Would you be happier if I always have the guy's ass pointed toward the door?" She bites down on her lip to refrain from cracking up.

I ponder her offer for a moment and then shrug. "It depends. If he's standing, then it's a yes. But, if he's bent over and I see his balls, then definitely no."

"Ohmygod, you are so crazy!" She grabs a balled-up sock off the floor and throws it at me. Then she sits up and bounces on the edge of her bed. One thing I've learned about my new roommate, she's a very hyper person. "What are you doing tonight?"

"No plans. I'll probably study my calculus notes and start season 5 of SOA."

"Wrong. We're going to a party!"

"Yeah, I don't think so."

"Why not?" she pouts. "You never do anything, and Josh invited me, so now I'm inviting you."

"Who's Josh?" I narrow my eyes and wait while she squirms uncomfortably. "Veronica?"

"Okay, okay. He's the guy you caught me with."

"You mean the one you were riding like Seabiscuit? Yeah, no, thanks."

"Oh, come on. This will be good for you. You can get out and meet people. Besides, season 5 sucks. Something bad happens to Opie and Jax spends the rest of the season angry." She fans her hand in front of her as if my plans are insignificant. Not to mention, she just spoiled the entire season for me.

"Gee, thanks. I would have preferred finding out on my own. Now you've ruined it."

"Trust me, it was not pretty. I'm sparing you the gory discovery. Now, what do you say? Stay home and *not* be surprised, or go out with me and have fun?"

"You're not going to shut up until I say yes, are you?"

"Probably not."

I breathe out a long sigh and dangle my legs over the edge of the bed. "What time do we leave?"

I've been ready and waiting for fifteen minutes while Roni primps in the bathroom. While I hang out, I pass time scrolling through social media. I post a selfie on Instagram with the hashtag #partywithseabiscuit, then shoot off a quick text to my mom to say I'll call her on Sunday. I'm in the middle of typing out another to see how much longer Roni will be, when one comes through for me.

I know it's wrong, because he's my brother's friend who's made it clear he will never touch me again, but when I see his name, I get tingly all over.

Him: What's up?

Me: Not much. Heading 2 a party.

Him: The one at Sig Phi?

Me: Hmm, let me check.

"Hey, Veronica." I have to yell over the noise of her hairdryer. "This party we're going to, is it at Sig Phi?"

"Yeah. That's Josh's frat house." My eyes roll toward the ceiling. Great. I'm pretty sure she'll end up spending the night and I'll walk home alone. Lucky me.

Me: That's the one.

Him: Watch out for those Sig boys.

Me: Aww, ur worried about me.

Him: Well, u know, underage and all. I'd rather u share your first tequila shot with me.

Me: What makes u think I'm a tequila virgin?

Him: Call it a hunch. I've been thinking...

Me: Sounds dangerous.

Him: On occasion, yes.

Me: What's up?

Him: Remember that maybe?

Me: I do. I'm still angry with u.

Him: Well, I can't have that now, can I? Now it's a yes.

Me: Aww, B. I'm touched.

Him: Told u I'm a nice guy.

Me: U kinda dig me, don't u, B?

Him: Just meet me tomorrow at 5.

Me: I knew it!

Him: It's turning back into a maybe.

Me: Fine. Deny your true feelings. See u at 5.

What a goofball. I stare at the screen and feel a twinge of guilt for deceiving him. I know I run the risk of him showing up at the coffee house and storming back out when he realizes I'm Candy. I hate lying, yet I also hate he'd been so quick to push me away.

Wild doesn't begin to describe the scene greeting us when we walk through the door at Sigma Phi house. A half-naked girl comes screaming down the stairs and runs out the door we just entered, while a shirtless, tattooed guy darts between the gawkers to chase after her. My first inclination is to be concerned for her safety, then I hear her make a reference to their relationship being over, and I realize these two exhibitionists know one another.

After that, we all go back to what we were doing.

One glance around the room and I'm already preparing an early escape. To the left of the front door is a large room that must hold a hundred students, and most of them are crowded around a pool table or the bank of foosball tables lining the perimeter of the room. A secondary staircase sits on the far side of the room. Guys and girls wearing bathing suits are packed on the stairs like sardines as they wait their turn to dive into an awaiting blow-up pool filled with a red, gelatinous substance.

We weave our way through the room in search of the kitchen, somehow managing to avoid getting sprayed by red chunks flying through the air. Three large kegs greet us when we reach our destination and, not surprisingly, so does Josh.

"You made it!" he calls to Roni as she gets closer. Taking her by the hand, he pulls her in for an open-mouthed kiss, and it's hard not to recall the last time I saw him. Even if it was a brief glance, I've been scarred for life. I may never look at him the same way. He glances over, finally acknowledging my presence, and a scowl fills his face. "Who's your friend?"

"You remember my roommate, Cassie?" My eyes shoot daggers her way, but miraculously, she remains unaffected. The way she clings to Josh's chest only proves my earlier guesstimate I will be on my own heading home tonight.

"Oh, yeah. Hey, sorry about that little scare, but maybe you should try knocking next time." With that, he turns, leading Roni into the adjoining room, and I'm left standing with a look of pure hatred on my face. *What a jerk.*

Rolling my eyes, I fill a red plastic cup with beer and make my way through the crowded kitchen and into the next room. This house seems to be a never-ending maze of rooms, each one seemingly larger than the one you just left. While passing a group of nerdy looking guys standing in the corner, I learn this particular fraternity houses forty upperclassmen. I whistle under my breath, failing to understand the allure of living with that many people. I like solitude and value my privacy. Having a roommate sleeping less than five feet from my own bed took some getting used to, but the thought of that many people walking around, with the ability to get up in my personal space at any given moment, is enough to send shivers down my spine.

No matter how many times I've looked, I can't seem to find Roni anywhere. I take a sip of my beer and instantly want to spit it back out. Keg beer. *Yuck.* I'm most certainly not a fan. Finally, I give up my search and take up residence in one corner of the game room. The windowsill is lined with red solo cups, so I think nothing of adding one more to the mix. By now, the pool divers are completely covered in gelatinous goo, and I pity the poor sap charged with cleaning it up tomorrow. There's a spot on one of the sofas in the room, but I can only imagine what has taken place on those cushions, and that vision keeps me standing. All around me, couples are hooking up and seem completely oblivious to the fact a hundred other students surround them. I'm all for PDA, but what I'm witnessing goes way beyond that. The couple on the sofa looks like they're eating each other's faces off. Next to them, another girl is straddling some guy's lap while he plays with her breasts. Instantly, I feel my cheeks flush, so I turn my head and pretend I didn't see anything before I give up and move to the opposite side of the room.

At one point, I'm watching a heated game of foosball when I

get the feeling someone is checking me out. I look up, and when our eyes meet, he takes it as an invitation to join me, and I'm trapped while he talks about how wonderful life is at the frat house. From what I gather, since he's drunk and openly slurring, he's a junior who's solely responsible for planning the entire party. Somehow, I find that hard to believe, but I just smile and continue feigning interest.

The pleasantries come to an end when he starts getting touchy-feely. It starts with him running the knuckles of one hand over my cheek, while the other skims over my hip.

"What do you say we continue this conversation upstairs? I've got a room up there where it's quiet and we can get to know one another better." I raise my shoulder to my cheek in an attempt to remove his hand, while at the same time taking a small step to the side.

"Sorry. My roommate and I are meeting up in a few and heading out. Maybe some other time." I don't wait for him to respond, but the look on his face indicates he isn't drunk enough to miss I've just blown him off.

I duck away and head for the stairs. I still can't find Veronica, but I dash up the stairs for one last look around. I spot a couple on the landing, locked in what appears to be a tender embrace, but at second glance I realize I'm witnessing something much more intimate. She's wearing a short denim skirt, and his hand is between her parted legs. Her head is thrown back and her eyes are closed. His mouth covers hers, muffling her screams, but I'm unable to tear my eyes away as I watch the orgasm roll through her body and she collapses into him. Beads of sweat form at my temples, and suddenly I feel as if I have on way too many clothes.

Pleasure courses through my body, and I know if I reach between my own legs I'll find I'm soaking wet. It's been a long time since I've been on the receiving end of anything as stimulating as that.

I turn, embarrassed and feeling every bit the voyeur for watching their moment of intimacy. Although, in my defense, they were in the middle of a crowded frat house. I mean, who does that? People in love? Two people so sexually attracted to one another they can't keep their hands off each other? The last scenario strikes a nerve within me, and I'm back to longing for the touch of a stranger. Well, not just any stranger. One specific dark-haired hockey player comes to mind. I'm embarrassed to even think about him. I know he's off-limits. I've heard it from Scotty, and from Brantley himself, but it doesn't erase what transpired between us before he knew me as 'Scotty's kid sister.' God, sometimes I hate that label, and thinking about it upsets me further. I pass a bathroom that is miraculously available and duck inside to escape. Sagging against the door, I find myself wishing I were back home in Illinois.

If I'm completely honest, I hate it here. Outside of Veronica, I haven't made a lot of friends. I guess I could count Jordan and Davis, but I assume they're only being nice because of Scotty. And don't get me started on my brother. I came all this way, hoping we would be able to rekindle our bond. So far, the only quality time we've spent together was the morning I woke up in Brantley's bed and he took me out to breakfast. Since then, he's either had class, practice, or he's been hanging out with Ashley. My course schedule is too much, and I'm close to failing calculus. All of this has been piling up, and then add on the fact I'm at my first frat party at this school and the only person to pay me any interest was a drunken asshole who just wanted to show me his room.

When my eyes meet my reflection in the mirror I can't hold back any longer. Tears pool in the corners of my eyes, and before I can swipe them away, they fall down my face, soaking the front of my shirt. I'm bending down to splash cold water on my face when the door bursts open and someone steps through.

"Oh, wow, I'm sorry. I didn't know anyone was in here," says a familiar voice. I lift my gaze back to the mirror and stare at yet another person who wants nothing to do with me. I realize now I've never felt so lonely in my life. And just that quickly, the waterworks start up again. "Hey, don't cry. I'm sorry I surprised you like that."

He stands by the door, looking uncomfortable, with his hands tucked in the front pocket of his jeans. His eyes dart back and forth between my reflection and the closed door beside him. I can tell he's conflicted. On one hand, I'm Scott's little sister, and he may feel the need to protect me. On the other, that same loyalty to my brother calls him to uphold the bro' code he was spouting off about. In this moment, I couldn't care less about either. I'm upset and just want some damn privacy. To hell with all of these rules and obligations. Just once I'd like to come first in someone's life. When Justin and I were dating, he always talked about how I was number one in his life. But the irony was, his love for hockey and his family always kept me at a distant third.

Before I know it, strong arms envelop me, and I'm cocooned in the warmth of his body. "Shhh. It's okay, Cassie." His big hand smoothes over the back of my hair and down my back. "It's gonna be okay."

BRANTLEY

My arms are wrapped tightly around her tiny waist. She's taller than I first assumed, yet the top of her head barely reaches the top of my chest. I lower my head, breathing in the sweet fragrance of her strawberry-scented shampoo, and it's just as I remembered. I move to pull away, but she fists my shirt in her hands and cries even harder. My brows wrinkle in confusion, and I'm not sure what I should do.

"What happened? Did someone hurt you? Which one of these assholes do I have to kill?" I say it to try and make her laugh, but something inside me tells me if she says one of these dickheads laid a hand on her, I won't hesitate to follow through on that offer.

She doesn't answer right away, so I keep quiet and simply hold her. I've never had a sister, but I suppose this is what Rivers would do if he were here and she was crying uncontrollably. The only problem with that analogy is, being this close stirs up memories of her lying on top of me. Knowing how close I came to sleeping with her concerns me. There's a war going on inside my head right now. One voice is screaming, telling me to let go and walk away. While another is quietly pointing out how good she feels wrapped in my arms. It's only when she shifts beneath me that I take a much needed step back.

"No," she sniffs and wipes a hand over one side of her face. I reach around her to grab a few tissues then hold them out for her to take. "Thank you. I promise I'm fine. It's just a lot of shit kinda bubbled over and I needed a good cry. I think I'd just like to go back to the dorms." Her eyes shift between my face and the floor, and I can tell she's embarrassed about crying in front of me.

"Hey," I try keeping my voice soft, hoping it will help her calm down. My hand reaches out and lifts her chin, and I brush my thumb over her cheek. "Don't be embarrassed. We all need a good cry every now and again. Personally, I cried like a baby my first year."

"You?" A soft giggle escapes her throat as she shakes her head at my admission. "I don't believe that. You're too cool to lose it like this."

I use my finger to draw an imaginary X across my chest while nodding. "Cross my heart it's the honest truth. But do me a favor and don't tell the guys. I have a reputation to uphold." This gets me a deep laugh and I sense she's coming back around. "Listen, maybe it would be best if you headed home. This isn't the best scene to be around when you're feeling vulnerable. I would hate for something to happen." I'm thinking about some asshole trying to get in her pants, but I'm pretty sure she has no idea that's what I'm implying.

"I was trying to find my friend, but I think she's already in one of these rooms with her fuck buddy." She scrunches up her face when she says this.

"Not a fan of hooking up, I take it."

"It's not the hook-up that disgusts me. It's the guy she's with. He's a total D-bag. Like, seriously, straight up prick."

I nod, because I can only imagine which one of these losers her friend has set her sights on. Out of all the fraternities on campus, this one seems to have drawn the largest population of assholes.

"Would you like me to take you back to your dorm?" My feet shuffle over the tiled floor, and I realize I'm nervous. I want her to say yes, while at the same time I'm silently pleading with her to turn down my offer.

"Okay. That would be really nice. I was assuming I would have to walk back alone."

I blow out a nervous breath and take a step forward. My lips meet her forehead before I can second-guess my decision. Thankfully, I don't go lower, though I'd be lying if I said it wasn't where I'd originally intended to end up. There's just something about this girl that hits me like a stick to the gut. "Come on. Let's get you out of here."

It's a nice night, and for once I'm glad I chose to walk rather than drive the short distance. I hadn't even planned on stopping by. But one of the guys from the team said he wanted to check out the new freshmen babes. I'd followed along just to witness him make an ass of himself. He totally did, too. I swear, the guy's reputation precedes him because most of the new chicks flat out refused to speak to him. I couldn't help but laugh. Women talk, especially ones who have been burned before.

We see them all the time. Puck bunnies. They're chicks who hang around practice, go to every game, all in the hopes of hooking up with one of the players. The way they go about it is a joke. They walk around campus on game day, wearing the jersey of the player they hope to get busy with. Sometimes you'll see ten girls walking around with the same player's jersey, and you actually feel sorry for the poor sap for having to choose between them. I've been there, on more than one occasion, and I can honestly say it is quite the ego trip. The rules seem to be quite simple. The girl and the player know the score before they even do the deed. But, without fail, there's always one girl who becomes too attached, and when she discovers she was just another notch on his hockey stick, she gets angry and spreads all sorts of slanderous gossip.

For me, making the choice between girls was usually pretty easy. I prefer blondes, but I also like a girl I can have a stimulating conversation with. Even if we're just hooking up for sex. I don't want to listen to nonsense spewing forth from her mouth while we're making out. It's a complete turn off for me. But lately, I haven't been going home with any of them. After a while it became mundane, and I'm not looking for mundane. Quite frankly, I'm not looking for anything. I'd just prefer to meet someone I can make a connection with on a level that goes deeper than some girl looking to ride my stick. You know what I'm saying? That doesn't mean I want a relationship. *Screw that.* I would just like to have a chick for a friend. You know, maybe someone I can talk to about all of this shit going on inside my head related to my parents.

That's why I'm enjoying my chats with Candy. I'm actually looking forward to meeting her tomorrow. We've only been texting over a period of a week, but from the short replies she's been sending I get the impression we could hit it off.

On the opposite end of the spectrum, you have the girls we've affectionately dubbed as Jersey Girls. These are the girls you see in class, or on campus. The ones who make certain parts of your body stand up and take notice. And when you see them attending practice or a game you catch yourself skating faster, playing harder. They're the ones you want to find cheering for you. The girl you find yourself inviting to games, even going so far as to throw her a wave during warm ups. And, finally, she's the one you hope to see wearing your jersey while you're busting your ass out on the ice. If you're lucky, you'll get to see her wearing that same jersey, and nothing else, the morning after. Whether your team won or lost, it doesn't matter, cause when she's in your arms, you feel as if you've just won the Stanley Cup.

"How long have you been playing hockey?" Her words sound as if she's out of breath, and I notice she has to take three steps to match just one of mine. I chuckle and slow my pace.

"The earliest memory for me would have to be three years old, but mom swears my dad had me on the ice with him when I first started walking. My dad used to play when he was younger, and he had this pair of skates custom made for me. They were so small. They're displayed on a shelf in my old bedroom back in Colorado."

"Aw, that is really cute. I'd love to see a picture of those." She turns her head so our eyes meet, and in the evening light the blue of her eyes positively twinkles. *Holy shit.* I turn and look up at the sky to keep myself from staring at her.

"I'll see what I can do about that. Rivers told me you're a music major. What exactly do you do?"

"I write music, mainly. Music composition is my focus."

"That's really cool. So I guess that means you can play an instrument. Am I right?" I spin on my heel and walk backwards in order to see her face as she's talking. She gives me a look and bites nervously on her lip.

"Aren't you afraid of tripping or something?"

"Nah, I'm a highly skilled hockey player. I've spent most of my life balancing on a thin blade. I think I can manage walking backwards. Besides, it makes it easier to see you when you're talking."

"In that case, I'll leave you to it. I'm not coordinated enough to walk backwards and talk." She snorts out a laugh.

"Ah, a clumsy one. I take it your brother got all the coordination genes. That's cool. And thanks for the heads up. I'll be sure to watch out for cracks for you and stuff like that." I crack a smile at her expense, and she gives me an incredible gift: a smile that lights up her entire face. She has these perfectly straight teeth that can only have come from an excellent orthodontist, or lucky genes. But what really gets me is the pair of perfectly placed dimples located on either side of her mouth. When she gives me this full-on smile, I'm struck by how deep and adorable those simple little divots are. It's almost as if I've discovered a rare diamond on her face. Or some sappy crap like that. Honestly, I don't know what's going on with me right now.

I only know we're almost to her dormitory and I'm scrambling for a way to make this walk last longer.

"So, instrument?"

"Oh, yes. I almost forgot. Well, I play the piano and acoustic guitar." She does a little skip to avoid walking through a small puddle, and I find myself unable to stop staring at her mouth. "And, I also sing."

"No shit? I think I'd like to hear you sing for me sometime. Maybe you can come over and perform for me." I say this without thinking about how it might sound.

"Umm... I mean, sure. I can do that." She stops walking and I realize we've reached the entrance to her building. She hooks a thumb over her shoulder and turns back to me. "Well, this is me. Thanks for walking me home."

I stuff my hands in my pockets and rock back on my heels. "Cassie, I wanted-" I want to tell her that morning didn't mean anything, and I think we could be friends. But the words stay lodged in my throat. "I'm really glad I ran into you tonight."

"Yeah, me too." She tucks her hair behind her ear, and her gaze shifts nervously to the group of students approaching us. "Well, goodnight."

"Night," I mumble, but she's already gone inside.

CASSIE

I stand inside the door and watch him walk away, silently willing him to turn around one last time. But he doesn't. I roll my eyes, knowing this crush I have is completely ridiculous. But it doesn't take a genius to see he was totally flirting with me. It wasn't so much the words he said, but his body language spoke volumes. The way he held me in the bathroom. The tender kiss he placed on my forehead, for no apparent reason. Caring about me enough to walk me all the way home, when I know how far he lives from my dorm.

Nearly a month has passed since we first met, and the interest I have in him continues to grow. Maybe it's because I get to admire him from afar while in the lecture hall; and the secret texting we've been doing hasn't hurt. Every time I think about the way I've been deceiving him, I get this knife to the gut feeling, and I know I should put a stop to it. The first few days it had seemed harmless. Now, after the kindness he showed at the party, I know I can't continue with the lie. I figure it's best to end it now before anyone gets hurt. Besides, now that he's actually speaking to me, I don't need to keep up the charade.

I pull my phone out of my back pocket and see I've missed three texts from Roni.

Where'd u go?

OMG! UR not screwing that guy I saw u talking 2? R u?

Staying at Josh's.

Before I can talk myself out of it, I send him a text.

Me: Something came up. I can't meet. Sorry.

I change into something comfortable and head to the bathroom to brush my teeth. The bathroom is empty, and I figure most of my floor is still at the stupid party I just left. I see one of the girls from my Wednesday night crew and we chat for a few minutes before both heading back to our rooms to get on with our pathetic lives. When I get back, I check my phone and see I've missed Brantley's reply.

Him: What? I kinda had my heart set on our little study session.

Him: Now, whom do I have 2 pass all this knowledge on 2?

Me: Admit it. U kinda, sorta DO like me. Don't u?

Him: I guess we'll never know.

Me: I guess we won't.

Him: I'm not gonna lie. It makes me sad.

Him: I had this vision of u built up in my mind. I kinda wanted 2 see how close I was.

Me: Oh, now I'm curious. Do tell.

Him: Let's see... Hair: Red Eyes: Green Body: A perfect 10.

Me: Not even remotely close. But I seem 2 recall seeing that woman in the movie Who Framed Roger Rabbit.

Him: Ha ha. Duly noted. For the record, in my vision u were never a cartoon character. U were definitely real.

This is all too much for me to handle. He's super sweet and knowing nothing will ever happen between us makes my stomach hurt. I need to put an end to this whole lie right away.

Me: Sorry, I have 2 go. Thanks for the laughs. It's been fun.

Him:?

Him: Candy? Hello?

I decide not to respond, and turn off my phone before climbing into bed. Lying flat on my back, I stare at the ceiling, feeling like I've lost a good friend. I know it sounds crazy, but I've grown fond of our chats. Even though they were short and not very personal, I feel as if we've really connected. I'm going to miss this, but I know it's for the best.

I tell myself that thirty-seven more times before I finally drift off to sleep and dream of cartoon characters skating with sexy hockey players.

Veronica doesn't come back to the dorms by the time lunch rolls around, but she does send another text letting me know she's safe.

With nothing to keep me occupied, I head over to the music department to work on my song. It's Sunday, and the rehearsal rooms are empty, for the most part. I situate myself at one of the many available pianos and spread out my music. The song I've written is about a woman who's afraid to let herself love again. This isn't a personal story. I'm not afraid of love, or falling in love again. But I'm not exactly looking for it either. Truth be told, I didn't choose to write this song. This song chose me.

I love the entire process of composing. Writing the lyrics. Putting it to music. Laying down tracks. I've written two songs before this piece, all of which were done long before I moved to Ann Arbor. Not only will this song count towards my grade, but I also plan on utilizing the vast resources available through local recording studios. My goal is to take these songs and record them to be used as a demo. If I allowed myself to dream big, which I do, the icing on the cake would be for an artist to pick up one, or all, of my songs and record them as their own.

I play through a quick warm-up before moving on to the piece I wrote. The melody for this song always hits me hard. I was really struggling with it when I first started this class, but one of the instructors overheard me struggling and once we played through it a few times, he started playing this string of chords that brought it all together. As I play, I softly sing through the heart wrenching lyrics. Listening to this song, you'd think I've had my heart shattered into a million pieces, but that's not the case.

"I swear that sounds more beautiful every time I hear it." A quiet voice speaks behind me. I look over my shoulder and find one of my classmates standing in the doorway. I believe his name is Mitch, but we've never been formally introduced. "Sorry, I don't mean to interrupt, it's just a beautifully composed piece. May I?" He points to the other half of the piano bench. When I nod, he joins me and looks over my music. "It's Cassie, right? I'm Mitch."

"Yes, you're right." I offer a warm smile that he immediately returns. He has a nice face, and when he smiles, I can see that his bottom teeth are a little crooked. "It's nice to meet you, Mitch.

What year are you?"

"I'm a junior, but this is only my second year in this field. I spent my freshman year goofing off, so my parents told me I needed to buckle down and get my shit together or they wouldn't continue paying for college. So I moved out of the frat house and picked a major. Even after two years, I don't think I'm anywhere near your caliber. That song really is something special. It has this quality to it. It's almost..."

"Haunting?" I finish his thought, and he turns to me and nods.

"Exactly. I have to ask. Is this about you?" he asks, looking at my music sheets, reading through the lyrics. "It's so personal."

"No, it's not about me. But I get what you're saying. When I wrote it, I was actually sitting in the middle of the park, watching mothers push their children on the swings. I saw this one mom who couldn't have been more than her late twenties, and she looked so lost. The wheels in my mind started churning, and by the time I got up to leave, I'd manifested this whole scenario about her tragically losing her husband. The words practically wrote themselves." I stare straight ahead, picking at imaginary lint on my leggings.

"Well, it's really powerful. Your imagination has served you well." He moves to stand, while I remain on the bench, still fiddling with my pants. "I better get going. It's was nice to finally meet you, Cassie. Hope I see you around."

I offer up a small wave and then, as quietly as he arrived, he disappears down the hall.

I gather my belongings and stuff them in my backpack. I've been in this room for nearly three hours, but I'm still restless. I don't want to stay here, but I also don't feel like heading back to the dorms. I have my notes with me, so I decide to head over to the coffee house to study for my calculus test.

My phone vibrates as I'm walking out the door, and when I look down I see Justin's text.

I miss u, baby.

His words send chills up my spine. God, I hate his need to control everything. I quickly delete it, feeling a great sense of satisfaction as I watch it disappear, then text Roni to let her know I won't be joining her for dinner. I'm not sure where she is, but I don't want her to worry. Her response comes quickly.

Thnx. I'll grab dinner with Josh.

The coffee house is fairly quiet for a Sunday evening, so finding a cozy spot in the back is easy. Pulling my laptop, notes, and headphones out of my bag, I line everything up and press play on my favorite playlist. I'm so engrossed in my notes that I fail to see Brantley enter the room until it's too late. He spots me and offers up a half wave, which I return. When he makes a move to come my way I actually hold my breath. He reaches the booth and hesitates for a moment before sliding in across from me.

"Hey." It's not much, but it's all I can manage at the moment. It's a simple word, but it comes out sounding breathy, like I'm totally into him or something. Which I totally am, but I can't let him know that.

"Hey, yourself. Looks like you were really engrossed there. What are you studying?" He reaches for my notes, but I pull them protectively against my chest. If he sees what I'm studying, he may put two and two together. *After all, he is a calculus god.* A voice screams from deep inside my head. "Sorry, I didn't mean to offend you."

"No. I'm sorry. You didn't do anything wrong. It's just something personal. So, how have you been?"

"You mean since we talked last night?" He laughs, and it's this deep, sexy sound that goes straight to my lady bits. "I'm good, I guess. Just here, looking for someone. What about you?"

There's a part of me that wonders just who it is he's looking for, and I have to remind myself I have no right to be jealous. "Oh, I'm just passing time. I just left one of the rehearsal rooms and didn't feel like going back to an empty dorm."

"Is your roommate gone a lot?" As he asks this, he pulls out his phone and looks down. The frown on his face tells me he's not happy with what he sees. A pang of jealousy shoots straight through me as I picture him holding that redhead I saw at the bar. I wonder if she's been lucky enough to wake up in his arms. The way she looked at him that night tells me I already know the answer to that question. He's not even mine and I'm already feeling possessive. That can't be a good thing. Can it?

"Lately she is, but that's only because she's met her latest conquest," I laugh, and a snorting sound shoots out my nose, causing me to blush. "Sorry."

"Don't be sorry. It was..."

"Disgusting."

"Cute." We say simultaneously.

I quirk my brow at him, and he flashes me a quick wink. *I knew it!* I knew he'd been flirting with me last night.

We continue talking and enjoying one another's company. Although he frequently checks his phone, he seems to be engrossed in our conversation. At one point I see him typing and assume he's talking with another girl, or maybe Scotty. When my phone vibrates with a text, I casually glance to the right and see a text from him. Thankfully, he doesn't seem to notice, because he's too busy typing again. My phone vibrates again and I move my hand to slide it my way when another text comes through. This time, he's staring right at me, and when he glances down at my screen his eyes go wide with recognition.

BRANTLEY

When her phone vibrates, I think nothing of it. Girls text one another all the time. No big deal. And when she doesn't bother checking, I assume it's either her roommate or her brother. But when I fire off the next two texts, and her phone just happens to vibrate at the exact same time, I know it's more than a coincidence. The funny thing is, I should be really angry right now, and I am. But the feeling that takes me by surprise is I'm actually hurt she felt the need to lie to me. All these lies just to pass a stupid calculus test?

The silence between us is downright creepy. I'm quite certain the look on my face is one of confusion, but the look on hers pains me. It's one of complete mortification and despair. Now, I don't know her all that well, but I know the difference between someone pretending to be ashamed, and someone truly remorseful for what they've done. My first inclination is to get up and leave her to wallow in her shame, but when her eyes pool with tears I'm rooted in my chair. This is the second time I've seen her crying, and I don't like the way it makes me feel. I'm not sure how to describe it, other than as a tightness in my chest, but suffice it to say it's unsettling. I want to make sure she's okay, but I also need to hear why she felt the need to lie, and if there was ever a calculus test she needed help passing.

I push my chair back and stand, torn between staying and leaving. Her eyes are wide as saucers, revealing so much more than words could ever convey. There's an innocent quality to her I find refreshing in this sea of aggressive females. I know guys love the idea of having women who make themselves available whenever they call. But I'm willing to bet twice as many secretly desire having a woman look at them with eyes that tell a story like the one I'm reading right now. It's as if they're begging me to pull her close and hold her in my arms, not like we were before, but in a comforting 'I'm here for you' sort of way.

"Please, don't go. I can explain." Her voice is barely audible over the sound of machines whirring in the background, but her pleading tone is hard to miss. "Please," she begs.

My hesitation only increases her despair. She's staring at me, her eyes wide and teary, lips still parted by her last spoken word. It's all too much for me to handle.

"Save your tears for someone else, sweetheart. I'm sorry, but I can't deal with this right now. I thought... Hell, I don't know what I thought."

I storm out of the coffee shop without a backward glance. I know if I were to look back over my shoulder, I would probably find her crying, and I'm not ready to deal with that shit. I don't owe her anything. She lied. Pretended to be someone else. Who does that kind of shit? If she's trying to pay me back for the brush-off I gave her at the bar then I'd have to say job well done.

If she's trying to make me feel like a fool, she certainly achieved that. But when I think about it, none of those reasons make any sense.

I only make it three blocks before I turn around and haul ass back to the coffee shop. If I had an ounce of backbone, I'd listen to the voices in my head screaming this is a mistake. In my head, I know the smartest thing for me to do is keep walking and not look back. I try telling myself that in three or four days, this will all pass and she'll become a distant memory of another girl whose tears have been caused by something or other I've done. I know all of this, yet I still take a step forward and place my hand on the door.

The little bell over the door chimes loudly upon my entrance, and I turn my eyes in the direction of the booth. She's there, but her head is down, her forehead resting on the flat surface of the table. I approach the table slowly and rest my palms flat on its top as I lower my face down to hers.

"Answer one question. Why the elaborate lie?"

Startled, she lifts her head and blinks a few times. She doesn't answer at first, but I can see she's trying to get a read on my anger. I step back and draw a few cleansing breaths in an attempt to help me calm down. A few seconds pass, and the pounding in my heart slows to a steady staccato.

"It wasn't all a lie," she says quietly. I quirk my brow in question as our eyes lock together. "I mean, yeah, I lied about who I was, but I really do need help with my test."

"Why didn't you just come right out and tell me who you were the first time you texted?"

"I started to. But then I reflected back on the morning we

met, and I was afraid you wouldn't want anything to do with me."
As she speaks, her hands fidget nervously, and I wonder what it
is about me that makes her so uneasy. She acted the same way in
the bar the night we bumped into one another. "Look, I'm really
sorry about deceiving you this way. I was just hoping for a chance
to apologize for my behavior in your room. I was clearly out of
line and didn't respect your wishes."

"Your behavior wasn't that bad," I chuckle and lower myself
into the booth. Looking back on that morning, the look in her
eyes as she'd launched herself at me and the way her lips had felt
when pressed against mine, I couldn't help but smile. I'd spent
three whole days replaying that memory over and over in my
mind. She'd turned me on. There was no denying it then, and
there's no denying it today. If circumstances were different, and
she weren't my best friend's sister, I wouldn't be sitting across
from her and watching her struggle. She'd be in my lap and we'd
be locked in a kiss that would leave us both breathless and eager
to get the hell out of here. But the fact remains that however
desirable she may be, she's still off-limits.

So, I remind myself to proceed with caution.

"Come on, I acted like a complete idiot." She buries her face
in her hands and shakes her head. "First, I pretended to be
mortified by your arousal, then I threw myself at you and
proceeded to dry hump you for a good three minutes."

"Four minutes and twenty three seconds to be exact. But
who's counting?" At this, she lowers her hands and cracks a
welcome smile. "Listen, you don't have anything to be sorry or
embarrassed about that morning. It was what it was. And if
circumstances had been different, who knows what may have

happened. I'm just glad I had the chance to kiss you before finding out you were off-limits."

She rolls her eyes and begins playing with the end of her long braid. My eyes rake over her body, taking in her short-sleeved V-neck shirt, leggings, and red Chucks. She looks every bit the part of the college student she is. Yet she looks nothing like the hundreds of girls I see every day on campus. Something about her makes her different. Maybe it's the way she carries herself, or the fact that her lashes are thick and lustrous without the help of makeup. In fact, she doesn't seem to wear any makeup. She doesn't need to. Her skin isn't flawless, and her hair is a little wild when not tamed like it is today, but it works on her.

"Yet another reason why I was nervous about telling you who I was. You know, I get that you have a code to follow," she says, making air quotes when she says the word code. "I don't agree with it, but I respect it. I know I'm Scott's little sister. I don't need you reminding me every time you see me. For what it's worth, I'm not a child. You don't have to go out of your way to make me feel like one."

Her eyes drift toward the window and she goes quiet for a few minutes, watching as people pass by outside. I use that time to study her profile and note that even though I know they're related, the resemblance between them ends with their hair and eye color.

"Do you have any idea what it's like to constantly live in someone else's shadow? To never be recognized as your own person? Everywhere I go I'm always going to be Scott Rivers' sister. Just once, I'd like someone to look at me and only see Cassie."

I can't say I relate to what she's going through, but I've heard my younger brother utter those same words enough to know what she's saying is real. Growing up, Chris wasn't blessed with the same athletic prowess that came naturally to me. He could skate, but not nearly as fast or as gracefully. He was better with computers and video games. After a few years of being compared to me, he eventually gave up and stayed behind a desk. Although I'd never invited all the attention, I'm not sure I did much to deter it either. Chris tried his best to convince me it didn't affect him, but I knew different. Whenever I go home, I can't go anywhere in our town without being recognized or asked for an autograph. Ever since my high school years of playing hockey, I've been told I was going places. I guess the people in our town believed one day I would make it to the NHL. Listening to Cassie right now reminds me that Chris had been one of the first to congratulate me when I'd signed with the Detroit team.

"Hey," I reach out to cover her hand with my own and the jolt of electricity I feel is hard to ignore. By the look on her face I can tell she felt it too. "I can't say I know how you're feeling, but please trust me when I tell you that people *do* see you. And not everyone here knows you're related to Scott."

"Thanks. But how do you know they see me when you don't even seem to notice?"

"Because you're hard to miss." I lean forward to grab a napkin and use it to dab over the moisture she's missed. "I promise you I've noticed, and when I look at you, I see a hell of a lot more than Rivers' sister. I see a confident, sexy woman, who just needs to take a step to the right to get out of her brother's shadow. Hell, I barely know you, but I can already tell you have a lot more to offer than you give yourself credit for."

The words barely leave my mouth and her lips begin to tremble. I glance nervously at the customers around us, noticing the way they are watching us. They must figure we're a couple having trouble, or some sort of scene like that, because when my gaze meets theirs they give me a hard look before turning away. Her sobs are stifled, but still noticeable enough that people won't stop staring. I hate nosey-ass people, and people knowing my business. Even though this isn't my issue, I'm once again feeling the need to protect her.

"Listen, why don't we get out of here. You obviously have a lot on your mind. We can go somewhere else and talk privately." She sniffs twice before wiping her nose on a napkin. She peers up through tear-soaked lashes, and for a moment it's as if my heart has stopped beating. Her vulnerability in this moment is what gets me. It catches me off guard, and despite all of my previous reservations, I find myself wanting to spend more time with her.

"Are you hungry? Cause I'm starving." I rise and hold out my hand to help her up.

"Okay. Yes. I think I would like that." She bends to gather her books, takes my offered hand, and follows me out to my car.

Breakfast okay?" I ask, pulling up to an all-night diner that serves breakfast all day. We love coming here after a game, but tonight it's fairly quiet and thankfully none of the guys are here. It's not that I feel like I'm doing anything wrong by being with Cassie, but I wouldn't want anyone getting the wrong idea and running their mouth off to Rivers.

Once we're settled and have placed our order, I lean back against the booth and stretch my arms out wide behind me. She's no longer crying, but I can tell she's still fragile. I don't want to say the wrong thing by prying, but I'd be lying if I said I wasn't curious to know what had set her off. After a few seconds of staring, she saves me from having to ask.

"I'm sorry to be such a blubbering idiot around you. Normally, I'm not this sensitive. I've just had a lot come at me at once."

"You mentioned that before, in the bathroom at the party. So what is it that's weighing you down? Can you talk about it?"

"I'm lonely," she blurts out, and her thumb immediately goes in her mouth and she starts to chew nervously on the nail. "I know it sounds crazy. I'm surrounded by people, yet somehow it's not enough. It's just... coming here was a big change for me. I broke up with my boyfriend. And before you go thinking that's the cause for the tears, it's not. I'm the one who wanted to call it off, and I can assure you I'm over him. But it's still a big change. We'd been dating for a couple of years before I left."

"Wow, that's a long time. I've never had a relationship last that long. If you don't mind my asking, why did you end it?"

"It was time. He was moving back to Minnesota for school, and I wanted a fresh start. Catching him with his dick in someone else's mouth may have been another determining factor." I whistle under my breath and she tilts her head. "What was that for?"

"Nothing." She gives me a look that clearly says she isn't

buying it. "It's just that guys are assholes, Cassie. Most of the time, we're only looking for a hook-up, or we're wondering if we'll ever find someone. But then there are times we have everything we've ever wanted right in front of us and we don't even realize how great we've got it. Bottom line, the guy sounds like a giant douchebag. You don't spend that kind of time with a girl only to whip your cock out for the next one willing to suck it."

I glance up to find her looking at me funny, like she's trying to determine where that rant came from. Honestly, I'm asking myself the exact same thing.

"Sorry, I'm not entirely sure why I just said all that. My point is, I think you made the right decision," I let out a long breath and wait for her to say something. Anything.

"I think you're absolutely right. It was the right decision, and I feel good about it. But even if it felt right, it wasn't necessarily easy. I'd grown comfortable with what we had."

"How so?"

She shrugs her shoulder and picks nervously at her napkin. "I don't know. He wasn't the only boy I'd ever kissed, but I've certainly kissed him the most. And I've known him since we were in grade school. Scotty knows him also; they used to skate together. And then there's the whole 'I lost my virginity to him' argument. I mean, at the time I took that shit very seriously. We'd dated for almost a year before I gave myself to him, and when we finally slept together, I foolishly believed I was his first. I later learned that wasn't the case."

"That must have been hard to accept. How'd you find out?" I don't know why I'm asking, but here she is, pouring out her heart in the middle of a diner, and suddenly I find myself caught up in what she's saying. I think briefly about the girl I lost my virginity to. Where is she today? Is she happy? Does she ever wonder about me? Probably not, because honestly, this is the first time in six years she's crossed my mind. Then I find myself wondering what it would have been like to share my first time with a girl like Cassie, and I know right away it wouldn't take six years for me to wonder about her.

"He admitted it after I caught Charlotte sucking him like a lollipop. Oh god," she slaps both of her hands on the table and rolls her eyes skyward. "I don't even know why I'm telling you all of this. It's just that I don't really have any friends to speak of. I mean, I love my roommate, and we talk, but she doesn't want to listen to me whining about shit like this. Hell, I'm sure you don't want to listen to it either. I'm so sorry." A look of panic crosses over her face and I reach out to her again, feeling the same spark as before.

"No, don't be sorry." I shrug, showing her my best smile. "I honestly don't mind. I often find I need someone to talk to, other than the guys, you know. There're just some things they wouldn't understand."

She cocks her head again and offers me a small smile. "Like what?"

"I don't know. Personal things. Family things. Most of the time, all we talk about is hockey, video games, how much so and so drank, and who banged whom. You know, guy talk."

"Yeah. I know all about guy talk, being a girl and all." Her lip quirks up, teasing me with the faintest glimpse of her pink tongue. Our eyes meet, and for the briefest of moments, I see a flicker of sadness cross over her face. "You want to know something?"

Just as I'm about to answer, the waitress comes over and places our food before us. Two steaming plates, heaped with food, and smelling delicious. We sit back and pick up our silverware. I watch as she rearranges the food on her plate, moving the bacon to one side, and pushing the sausage patty to the far right corner. She ordered the French toast, and it has already been doused with powdered sugar, but she liberally applies a bunch more. When she catches me staring she only smiles and takes a huge bite.

"So, you started to tell me something earlier," I prompt, eager to hear what it is she was about to share. I've never had this kind of conversation with someone I barely know. I find talking with her to be easy, and effortless. I don't know why, but I like it and want to keep her talking.

She swirls a bite of bread around in the syrup before popping it in her dainty mouth. I watch, captivated as she wraps her lips around the tines and pulls the syrupy goodness inside. Her eyes close as she savors the moment, and the moan that follows doesn't go unnoticed. I swear to god, it's hot as hell.

"One of the reasons I moved here was to be closer to Scotty." She finishes chewing and pushes her plate away. I find myself hoping she isn't through eating. I'm enjoying watching her eat more than I'm enjoying my own food. "I thought by us being at the same school we would rekindle our relationship. Sadly, that hasn't happened. We used to be so close before he left for school. Now the only things he has time for are hockey, Ashley, and school. I've tried reaching out. I even drop by the house. But he usually isn't there, or says he doesn't have time to hang out."

I can see by the pain on her face this is probably the reason for her emotional breakdown. And I know what she's talking about, so I can sympathize with her. Rivers has Ashley crammed so far up his ass he hasn't had time for anything else. But I'm just his friend. I can handle it. Cassie is his sister, and she shouldn't have to try and win his affection. My anger toward him only increases when I see her eyes start to water again, and if he were here right now I'd probably punch him in the throat.

CASSIE

"You know what? I think right now we could both use a good friend. So, what do you say to you and me being that for each other?"

I'll be honest, his offer catches me off-guard. I mean, a few weeks ago he went from looking at me as if he wanted to devour me to looking at me as if I had suddenly sprouted two heads. Studying him now, the attention he's giving me registers somewhere between the two. He's smiling, so that leaves me feeling fairly hopeful this could go well. I'd like nothing more than to be his friend. He's easy to talk to. He has this way about him that leaves me feeling warm and peaceful. And it doesn't hurt he's easy on the eyes. I could stare at him all day and never grow tired of the view.

"You think you can handle being friends with Scott's little sister?" I tease him. "I wouldn't want you to jeopardize your vows of brotherhood or anything tragic like that."

"Ha ha, very funny." He reaches his fork over and steals the uneaten sausage patty off my plate. He takes a bite, chews for a few moments, then smacks his lips. "As long as you can keep your hands off me, I think I can handle it." He flashes me a flirty wink, and I stick out my tongue at him. "Now, now, none of that Miss Rivers. If we're going to be hanging out together, there will have to be some rules."

"Oh, do tell," I fold my arms across my chest.

"Okay, let's see. I think the most obvious rule is no sex."

"Well, duh. That's a no brainer. Next."

He chews on his lip for a moment, pretending to be deep in thought. While he thinks, I stare at his mouth and remember what it felt like to kiss him.

Stop it! I scold myself, very aware this may be harder than I'd originally bargained for. Clearly, I hadn't thought this out very well.

"Ummm, how about no naked study sessions?" He smiles proudly.

"Seriously? Are you pulling these rules out of your ass? I think I can refrain from getting naked in front of you."

"Oh, really? I seem to recall one morning when you were willing to get naked with me." A devilish chuckle falls from his gorgeous lips.

"Are you ever going to let that go? Yes, that first morning I'd have gladly sucked your dick and let you have your way with me. But that was all before you freaked out about your *precious* code." By now, he's practically on the floor from laughing so hard. The harder he laughs, the more frustrated I become. Leaning forward, I take both of his hands in mine and intertwine our fingers. It gets his attention and achieves shutting him up. He gives a pained look but doesn't pull away. "Can we please put that behind us and try to move forward? I really want to be your friend, B."

His hands press firmly against mine, his thumb brushing back and forth over my knuckle, and once again I'm lost to the sensation of being this close to him. "I'm sorry. I want that too. And I promise to stop teasing you about that shit. Though, I must admit, I'm not going to stop thinking about it. It was hot as hell, and you know it." He winks again then leans forward to kiss the back of my hand. "So, friend, when do you want to start studying?"

"Well, the test is this Friday, so the sooner the better. How about tomorrow night? You can come to my dorm and I'll even feed you." I smile and bat my lashes at him and I'm rewarded with another chuckle.

"Sweetheart, you don't have to bribe me, but I never turn down food. I have practice until five so it'll have to be after that. Will that work?" We stand and make our way out the door. A quick glance at the clock tells me we've been here more than two hours. That's funny; when I'm with him it feels as if time's standing still.

"I'll be ready and waiting." I laugh, climbing into the car. The ride back to the dorms doesn't take long, and when it's time to get out of the car, I find I don't want the night to end. "Well, I guess this is me," I announce, pointing to my building. "Just text me tomorrow when you're here. I'm in 322. I'll make sure my roommate is gone so we can concentrate."

"Uh huh, you sure you're not just trying to get me alone so you can finish what you started the first time you had me alone?" He laughs, bringing his arms in front of his face to block my hands from smacking him. "Last time I mention it, I swear." He's still laughing when I get out of the car and when I look over my shoulder as I enter the building I can see the whites of his teeth and know he's still cracking up at my expense.

"Idiot," I shake my head.

The following day seems to drag as I anxiously await our study session. I sail through music composition before spending a frustrating hour in calculus. Every day I have to sit through that class leaves me wanting to walk away and yell *I give up!* I'm fairly certain unless Brantley can pull off a miracle and teach me how to grasp the mathematical concepts of calculus in four days, there is no way in hell I'm going to pull off a passing grade in this class. Here's hoping he truly is the calculus god he claims to be.

It's a beautiful fall day, and as I make my way across campus, I marvel at the way the leaves on the trees are beginning to turn. The entire campus is dotted with a wide variety of trees. Oak, maple, sycamore, and linden provide a protective canopy over large sections of my walk back to the dorm. While I may hate my calculus class, I've fallen in love with this campus. One of my favorite buildings is Hill Auditorium, because of its subtle beauty. The outside is made up of concrete and brick with built-in columns at the entrance. But the inside will take your breath away. With its domed ceiling, oval stage, and seating for thirty-five hundred people, it's definitely a venue I covet to play my composed pieces.

I've barely stepped through the dorm's entrance when Dan

Harwood stops me on his way out. Dan sits next to me in Psych, but he doesn't live here so I assume he's visiting a friend. He's a junior who plays defensive tackle on the football team.

"Hey, Cassie. Do you live in South Quad?" He takes a step back to allow me through the door.

"Indeed I do. What are you doing over here?" I shuffle my backpack from one shoulder to the other and move aside as people pass by.

"One of our pledges lives here. I was just here to give him a hard time. You know how it is." His eye closes in a quick wink, as if I were somehow privy to one of his fraternity secrets. I haven't a clue what he's talking about, but rather than admit to it I just smile and offer a polite laugh. "You should come to one of our parties sometime. I'll let you know when the next one is coming up."

"Hey, congratulations on the win last Saturday. I heard you made a few great plays."

"Yeah," he shrugs, and I see the faintest hint of a blush spreading over his cheeks. "Don't you come to the games? I'd love to have you watch me play."

I shake my head while scrunching up my nose in distaste. "I'm not much of a football fan. I'm more of a hockey lover."

"I guess I can understand that, being Rivers' sister and all. I've been to a few of his games. He's an awesome player," he exclaims, and I beam with pride. I love watching my brother play hockey.

Growing up, it's how I spent most of my weekends during the winter. I remember how I used to complain that I was wasting my Saturday sitting in a freezing cold hockey arena, and then I discovered how cute hockey players were. Scotty used to hate it, because I would hang around after a game, hoping for a chance to talk to one of his teammates. He used to hassle me about it and was always quick to point out that his friends were way too old to be interested in a kid like me. I didn't allow his words to deter me. I was young and it was fun to dream. Then I started dating Justin, and rather than hanging around hoping for a chance to talk to a player, I spent every Saturday afternoon after practice kissing my favorite player.

But that's all in the past.

"Yep. He is pretty amazing," I glance longingly at the stairs and try to recall if I bothered making my bed before I left this morning. "Listen, I better be going. I have a killer calculus test coming up I have to study for. I'll see you in class tomorrow," I throw my hand up in a wave and leave before he has a chance to say anything else.

I finally enter my room and see that it's five o'clock. Roni is still here, but by the way she is gathering her belongings I can tell she is on her way out.

"Hey," I say as I drop my backpack on the bed. "Are you leaving?"

"Uh huh," she replies with her head down, digging under her bed to retrieve a wayward bra. She pulls it out and shoves it into her bag. "I might end up staying at Josh's tonight. You don't mind, do you?"

"What? No. Not at all," I furrow my brow in confusion. "Why do you think I would mind?"

"I don't know," she shrugs, "I mean, I know you don't like him that much."

I open my mouth to say something but close it before I get the words out. I don't want to hurt her feelings, but the truth is I'm not particularly fond of her choice in men. I don't say that because I saw him naked, though it did leave a lasting impression, and not a very good one, I might add. The real reason is, he isn't very nice. In fact, from what I've seen, he's even rude to her, though she seems completely oblivious to it.

"That's not true at all." I smile and hope she doesn't see right through me. "It probably only seems that way because we've never been properly introduced. I'm sure he'll grow on me with time."

"That's good, because he's definitely grown on me. I like being with him, for the most part, and the sex is really good." She waggles her brow as she says this, and I can't help but remember walking in on them. I hate to admit it, but it's happened more than once. Every time it happens, Josh never fails to remind me I should have knocked.

"Well, have fun and maybe I'll see you tonight." I turn and begin straightening up my half of the room before Brantley gets here.

"Do you have plans?" she asks hopefully.

I sit down, allowing my legs to dangle over the side of the bed. Brantley will be the first guest I've invited to our room, and I wonder what it will be like having him all to myself in this crowded space. It dawns on me that I really don't know much about him, other than the fact he plays hockey and has been Scotty's best friend since freshman year. I wonder if he liked living in the dorms, or what he thinks about spending his evening hanging out with me when he could be with that red-headed bitch who had her hands all over him at the bar.

"I have someone coming over to study. We'll probably just hang out afterwards."

"So, who is this mystery tutor? Is it the hottie you've been texting for the past week? Maybe you'll get some tonight." Her eyebrows dance wildly up and down as she claps her hands together.

"As a matter of fact, it is, but nothing is happening. Sex will not be taking place here tonight."

"Suit yourself. But if things change I'll expect a full report in the morning." She wiggles her fingers on her way out the door, and I stare after her, wishing for everything I could be that carefree.

BRANTLEY

The shrill sound of Coach Bishop's whistle echoes throughout the arena, as does the collective swearing from everyone on the ice. We've been practicing for two hours, and coach has been running the same play for the last forty-five minutes. Four weeks into our practice season and we still aren't gelling. I'm usually on a line with Kevrick and Masterson, but two days ago Coach decided to move Masterson to a new line and have him work with one of the freshmen. I'm not sure what's going on with Davis, but I'm certain he's going to have a raw ass by the time Coach gets finished chewing it off.

"Davis! What the hell is wrong with you? If you've got a problem you need to talk about, come see me; otherwise, get your head out of your ass and show me some hustle." The whistle sounds once more, and we take our positions. "Again!"

As the puck drops Kevrick owns it, moving across the ice with lightning speed. I skate to his right, reaching the blue line as he passes off to Davis, who finally seems to be paying attention. Davis moves fluidly toward the net, circling around Masterson and behind the net to hand the puck off to me at the last minute, where I launch it high and to the right of Rivers. He never had a chance at stopping it. We make eye contact and I toss him a playful wink, adding insult to injury. I've spent enough years playing with him to know that nothing pisses him off more than me sneaking one past him during practice.

"Fuck you, Cage," he growls from behind his mask, but I see the glimmer of a smile forming at the corners of his mouth. He may get ornery, but he still loves to see me shine. Our jealousy only stems from sheer competitiveness, but we always give each other our full support. When he was drafted before me, I was the first to shake his hand and congratulate him. If circumstances had been different, and I hadn't been drafted the following week, I still would have been happy for him.

Our celebration is short lived as Coach's whistle gives off two quick chirps, indicating it's time for drills. Sticks, gloves, and helmets are tossed on the bench before we line up at one end of the rink. Twenty sprints later, we head to the locker room, a sweaty, exhausted mess.

I toss my helmet and gloves in the top cubby of my locker. My practice jersey comes off next, before I drop to the bench and bend to take off my skates. Davis stomps in and his helmet whizzes past my head. It bounces off the lockers and skips over the floor before finally coming to rest just outside the entrance to the showers.

"I take it you got reamed out again. What's going on?" I don't bother looking up, by now he's seated beside me and grumbling under his breath.

"Nothing. Just got some shit on my mind. You got plans later?

You want to head over to Skeeps with me?" he asks, referring to a local bar that's actually called Scorekeepers. A group of us usually head over there on nights we don't have practice.

"Sorry, buddy, I'm heading over to South Quad after I shower." I peel off my compression shorts and drop them in my hockey bag. Leaning forward, I'm hit with the stench that can only come from the inside of a hockey player's duffle. It's a strange combination of sweat, shit, and vomit, all neatly rolled into one package and trapped inside the walls of a four-foot poly bag.

"The Quad, what's over there? You got a hot little underclassmen you're keeping tucked away?" he laughs, chucking a skate over his shoulder.

"Actually, I'm meeting up with Cassie for a tutoring session," I reply then make my way to the showers. He's hot on my heels as I reach forward and turn on the water.

"Holy shit!' He leans forward and lowers his voice. "Does Rivers know about this? He's gonna flip his shit when he hears you're spending quality time in his kid sister's room."

"Why the hell does everyone think I'm out to screw her just because I'm hanging out with her? It's calculus, nothing more. Besides, we're friends, and I wouldn't want to do anything to screw that up," I insist.

"Since when are you and Cassie friends? Matter of fact, since when are you friends with *any* girl? Most of them only want one thing from you, my friend." He makes a clucking noise with his mouth before turning away and I flip the double bird at his back.

"Since I ran into her at a party one night and walked her home. She's a really nice girl who's looking for a friend."

"And you're that friend? Interesting," his voice trails off as he turns off the water and heads back to the locker room.

I grab a towel and knot it around my waist before trailing after him. "What the hell is that supposed to mean?"

"Oh, come on, Cage. Spending time with a woman isn't usually your thing, unless it's between the sheets. And that's all fine and good," he looks around to be sure no one else is within earshot before continuing, "but we're talking about Scott's sister. What about the code?"

"Trust me, the code will remain safely adhered to. She's just a friend, and if he has a problem with that then maybe he should consider making more time for her instead of cramming his head so far up Ashley's ass." I yank on a pair of jeans and grab my bag. "Catch you later."

When I open the door to South Quad, I'm instantly taken back to my first year on campus. The building has been renovated since I lived here, but the memory of dormitory living will never be erased from my memory. Confined spaces. An abundance of study partners to choose from. Late night sneak attacks on the girls who lived across the hall. Meals with hundreds as opposed to the family of four you'd grown accustomed to. I love the privacy of having my own place, but I wouldn't trade that time for anything. I'd learned a lot and had more than my fair share of good times while calling this place home.

Cutting through corridors, I make my way up to room 322, only to stand in front of her door for a full three minutes before

I finally raise my hand and knock. I hear music coming from her room but she turns it down just before pulling the door open and flashing me a warm smile. All my doubts about coming up here vanish when I take one look at her standing there in white cuffed shorts topped with a lightweight black and white stripped sweater that hangs slightly off her narrow shoulders. Her feet are bare, and the blue polish on her toes matches the blue in her eyes. Her head tilts to the side, and the sun shining through her window dances off the stone piercing on the right side of her delicate nose.

"Welcome to my humble abode." She bends at the waist and makes a show of inviting me in with a wave of her arm. "Thanks for slumming on a Monday night." Her eyes meet mine and she shoots me a quick wink before closing the door.

"This is hardly slumming and a hell of a lot nicer than where I live," I laugh, looking around the small but tidy space. "It wasn't nearly this nice when I lived here."

"You lived in South Quad?" She sits down on her bed, scooting back until she's leaning against the wall, and pats the space next to her. "Sorry, I don't have more places to sit. But my roommate will be gone for the rest of the night."

I glance nervously between her and the door while squeezing the back of my neck with one hand. "Um, I thought I was coming over to study calculus." Her eyes go wide just before she cracks up, and now I'm really confused. "What's so funny?"

"Sorry." She's still laughing as she wipes at her tears. "That wasn't an invitation for something to take place. I only meant you could sit on her bed if you'd be more comfortable over there."

My body visibly relaxes, and I drop my backpack at the end of her bed, feeling the need to prove I'm capable of being close to her. "No, here will be fine. You just caught me off guard." Taking a seat next to her, I stretch out my legs and wait for her to show me her notes. She doesn't say anything for a few minutes, so I turn my head to find her staring. "What?"

"I wasn't coming on to you, if that's what you're thinking. Our relationship is purely platonic, so there's no need for you to be nervous around me. I promise I won't jump on you and kiss you again," she laughs, tucking her hair behind her ear, and I notice a strip of five pink studs lining the shell of her ear.

That's too bad, cause I'd really like to kiss you again.

Where the hell did that thought come from?

Somewhat shaken, I try and play it off like it's no big deal. "No, it's cool. I'm good with where things stand. I mean, I didn't really think you were coming on to me, but you have to admit it sounded a little like a proposition."

"Yeah, I'm sure you've heard enough of those to know the difference," she laughs then twists her body to face me, crisscrossing her legs beneath her like a pretzel.

"Maybe a few," I chuckle at my own expense. "So, where's this calculus you need help with?"

She orders a pizza that we share while spending the next three hours going over equations and a few tips and tricks I've learned along the way. By the time we're finished, it's clear that while she may not have mastered the concept, I don't think she'll have a problem passing the test. Not everyone has the headspace to grasp mathematical equations, but I do believe they are capable of memorizing a few formulas to help them get through a class.

"I think you'll be fine," I assure her as she places her notes back in the front section of her backpack. "But if you still feel like you need another dry run, you can stop by the house tomorrow night. I have an early practice and my last class lets out at six."

"That would be great. I think I have a handle on parts of it, but there a a few problems I want to run through while you watch. Maybe then you can see where I am stumbling." Leaning forward, I snag the last slice of pizza and pick off a piece of cold pepperoni and offer it to her. She takes it without missing a beat. "I really appreciate you doing this for me. I'm a creative person, my brain doesn't *do* logic as easily as yours."

"Yeah, well, I can't play a guitar and you can. So now we're even." I lean back, rubbing a hand over my face to mask a yawn. It's been a long day.

"Hey, maybe I can teach you," she moves forward, placing the palms of her hands flat on the bed as her torso stretches toward me. Face full of enthusiasm, she beats out a rhythm on the mattress, the wheels in her head clearly putting together a plan. "You help me pass this test, and then I'll show you a few chords; and after a few lessons, I'll have you playing a song."

I draw my eyebrows together in confusion. "Like, which song?"

"I don't know, what would you like to learn?"

I think about it for a moment, not really caring what I choose because I don't foresee myself sitting long enough to learn the guitar. "How about Stairway to Heaven?"

"Hmmm, probably too much for your first song." She sticks her thumbnail between her teeth and nibbles on the tip as she ponders my options. "Let me think about it and I'll pick one out for you."

I laugh at her willingness to pursue this harebrained idea. But I have to give her credit; she seems truly interested in returning the favor. Though it's not at all necessary. "You really think you can teach me to play the guitar? You don't even know me that well. What if I'm all thumbs?"

"You'll just have to trust me. I can teach anybody to play an instrument. Besides, you've had your capable hands on me once before, so I definitely know you're not all thumbs."

The smile she gives me nearly knocks me back a foot, and I catch myself before drawing a sharp breath. This girl could offer to teach me anything and I'd willingly agree to it. I know right away I'm in trouble and should probably get out while I can, but I'll be damned if I'm not ready to jump off this crazy train just yet.

CASSIE

I woke this morning with a smile on my face. Come to think of it, I'd gone to bed with one plastered there as well.

Those few hours Brantley spent in my room last night had done wonders for my outlook on Friday's test. Even so, I'd told him I needed another study session to go over a few problems. I have no illusions that I'll master the concepts of calculus after only days of studying his tips, but if I can pass with a C+, I'll be satisfied.

I go through the motions of the day, somehow managing to remain awake while listening to the most boring government lecture ever given. Roni texts me as I'm leaving class, asking if I want to meet up after lunch. Of course, I say yes. She got in late last night, so we haven't had a chance to catch up. As I make my way across campus, I hear a familiar voice calling after me. I stop and turn in time to see Davis coming up behind me.

In his red Henley and baseball cap turned backwards, he looks every bit the mixture of hot athlete and shy college boy. I offer a warm smile, which he immediately returns. Davis is cute. Really cute. He's shorter than Brantley, but the rippling muscles beneath his shirt tell me that on the ice he's a force to be reckoned with. Brown eyes dance behind his smile, and I like the way his sandy-blond hair curls around the edges of his hat. I take it all in, but while my eyes appreciate his boy-next-door good looks, he doesn't make my heart flutter the way Brantley does.

"Hey, Cassie, how've you been? I haven't seen you around." We resume walking, shoulder-to-shoulder, and appear to be headed in the same direction.

"I'm good, busy, but still good," I laugh and hook my thumb toward the dining hall. "Are you heading there?"

"Yeah," he smiles again. "I have practice in two hours. Gotta beat the rush. How are classes?"

"Fine, for the most part. I have Briggs for calculus and he's kicking my ass," I frown, reaching for the door handle. Davis shuffles around me and reaches it first, then proceeds to hold it open for me. I pause and step aside as he holds it for a few more students, who don't bother to acknowledge his act of courtesy. "Thanks, Davis. Some people are so rude," I bite out, hoping they hear me.

"No problem," he chuckles. "I see you take after your brother." I blush, embarrassed my comment may have come out nastier than I'd intended. "Hey, I like that in a woman. It tells me she won't take any shit from me or any other man she's with."

Still blushing, I glance sideways and nudge him with my shoulder. "Thanks."

"Don't mention it." He nudges back. "Hey, I heard Cage was tutoring you. You're in good hands; he's a math whiz. Yeah, you wouldn't know it by looking at him, but the guy's a closet nerd.

He's got an entire collection of DC comics stashed away in his closet. He's helped me through my share of tests. Personally, I think the guy has a superhero complex."

"Why do you say that?" I wrinkle my nose.

"Guess it's because he likes helping people," he shrugs his shoulder, "I don't know."

"Yeah, we met last night, and he was really cool about it. I'm heading over to your place after practice. My test is tomorrow afternoon and I'm nervous."

"I'm sure you'll do fine. But if you fail, I'll help you kick his ass." He gives me a flirty wink.

By now we've reached the line, so we both grab a tray and load up. I reach for soup and a salad, while Davis seems to take a little of everything until there isn't any room left on his tray.

"What?" he asks innocently upon meeting my arched brow. "I'm a growing boy. Besides, I'll burn twice as many calories during practice. Coach is kicking our asses after losing to Penn." He places a foil wrapped burger on my nearly empty tray.

We pay and make our way to the edge of the dining hall. The place is pretty crowded, even at this early hour, and I'm surprised when instead of heading over to a table where his teammates are sitting, he chooses to follow me. I notice the way Brantley's eyes connect with mine, and the question behind his gaze leaves me unsettled. We locate an empty table, and I work to regain my composure as I sit across from him. As we eat, he tells me about their upcoming game against Mercyhurst. Davis seems to think they'll come out the victor, and judging by the way they've been playing, I would have to agree. We're halfway through our lunches when Brantley decides to join us. Frankly, after the look he'd given me, I wondered why it had taken him this long. He lowers himself into a chair beside Davis and burns me with his gaze. While the questions may go unspoken, I can still read his mind.

What's up with you two?

Are you interested in Davis?

And my personal favorite, but only because it tells me he's jealous.

Are you gonna to start dry humping him now?

Rather than answer him with a look of my own, I shift my gaze back to Davis and attempt a genuine smile.

"How's it hanging, Cage?" Davis addresses him as they fist bump one another in greeting.

"A little low on the left, same as always. What are you lovebirds up to?" he asks, quirking his lip wickedly as I turn fifteen shades of red.

"What?" Davis casts a nervous glance my way and throws up his hands. "It's not like that. We're just having lunch and talking. Sorry about this idiot." He rolls his eyes to the right toward Brantley, whose smug smile has disappeared.

"It's okay." I laser my stare at Brantley and flash him a million dollar smile. "He's only jealous because he's afraid I'll ask you to tutor me next. But don't worry, B, I can only handle one hot tutor at a time." I stand and gather my tray. "Thanks for hanging with me. Let's do this again sometime. Brantley, I'll see you tonight?"

"Yeah, sure," he replies, clearly flustered by my casual attitude.

"Later, boys," I sing-song and sashay my way across the crowded dining hall, fully aware their eyes are glued to my ass the entire time.

Roni's already seated at the counter by the time I stroll through the door. Comet Coffee is nestled just off a brick paved alley lined with quirky little shops, and in my opinion, it's the heart and soul of the Nickel's Arcade shopping district. The place is packed with students, as it always is this time of day, and I shove my way through the crowd to fill the empty seat next to her.

"I took the liberty of ordering you a macchiato." She slides a cup across the small space. "I'm glad I got here early and beat the crowd. This is crazy," she blinks, looking at the long line of bodies waiting for their caffeine fix. There are plenty of coffee shops on campus, but there's something about this place that seems to draw a crowd. For me, I prefer the cozy atmosphere, but it's also about the experience of arriving here. The entire alley is covered by a glass ceiling that hovers four stories above the hustle and bustle of foot traffic below. Small café tables line the alley outside some of the shops, and I often spy students sitting with their computers and studying, or at least that's what I envision they are doing.

I take a sip of coffee and smile, appreciating the rich notes of caramel and cream, then turn to find her staring at me. "What? Why are you looking at me like that?"

"I'm not looking at you in any specific way. I'm just waiting for you to fill me in on how your evening went. You were still sound asleep when I got in this morning."

"Well, I tried waiting up, but gave up when one o'clock rolled around and you still hadn't shown your face." I give her a knowing wink and take another sip. "I take it you had a good time."

"You know, just because I'm with Josh doesn't mean we're having sex. We hung out with his frat buddies, played a few games of pool, and ordered pizza." She picks up her mug and smiles as she brings it to her perfectly painted lips. "After *that* we had sex. Amazing sex."

"Naturally, because sex with Josh is always amazing," I tease.

"Well, not always, but most of the time it's pretty spectacular." She actually blushes as she admits this. "But enough about me. How was your hottie?"

"He has a name, you know."

"No, I don't know, because you haven't bothered telling it to me." She pokes me playfully in the ribs, and I squirm away, fearful of being tickled. After years of being held down and tortured by Scott, I have quick reflexes.

"It's Brantley Cage," I tell her, the words coming out on a whisper, as if the mention of his name will send those around me running back and reporting gossip to my brother.

Her chin drops, leaving her mouth open for a few moments. "Whoa, that's one serious hottie. Jesus, Cassie, I had no idea *that's* who you were spending the evening with." She goes quiet and takes a sip before continuing. "What about your brother's ridiculous rules? Won't this be breaking them somehow?" She knows all about my introduction to Brantley and had been quick to point out that most of the students on campus have harbored a crush on him at some point in time. And that isn't limited only to the female population.

"Please, don't get me started on that," I wave her off and lean back in my chair. "Besides, it's not like that. I told you, we have an understanding."

"What sort of understanding is this?" She arches her brow and rests her chin on her hand.

"Well, we established a few rules before he would agree to tutoring me. For instance, there'll be no naked study sessions and absolutely no sex," I clear my throat, suddenly feeling silly after repeating them out loud.

"Seriously? That's what you guys came up with?" she lets out a snort of derision.

"What? Oh, come on. I know they sound ridiculous, but establishing these parameters seemed to make him feel better."

"Cassie, the fact he felt the need to establish them at all tells me he's into you. I think you two are a ticking time bomb waiting to explode, and when it finally does, it's going to be hot and sexy and very sticky." She bursts into a fit of laughter, drawing the attention of the crowd behind us.

"Stop it!" I glance over my shoulder and offer a weak smile at the group of guys behind us. I think one of them is in my calculus class. "I'm not having sex with him. He's helping me pass a class, end of story."

"Oh, please. You can't tell me you're not the least bit into this guy. He's hot as fuck." She leans over to whisper in my ear. "And from what I've been told, he's great in the sack."

"Gee, thanks. Now that's the only thing I'm going to think of every time I see him. It's bad enough I know what his dick looks like, now I have to know he's skilled in using it too."

"Sweetie, from what I've been told most hockey players know how to handle their stick, both on *and* off the ice." She winks once again and finishes her coffee. "I'm just saying you may want to re-think those parameters."

"Okay, on that note, I think I'll be going." I stand, feeling my face turn multiple shades of red as the image of Brantley's *stick* flashes through my mind. She grabs her purse and follows me out, never once taking her eyes off my scarlet cheeks.

"Admit it, you're thinking about sex with him right now, aren't you?" she asks as a satisfied smirk fills her perky face.

"Fine." I stop short and turn to face her. "Yes, right now, I'm thinking about how great it would feel to have him take me from behind. I'm envisioning his lips kissing my spine as one hand keeps a tight hold on my throat as he pounds into me. Does that make you happy?"

"It'd make me happy if I could do that to you. Name the time and place, sweetheart," comes a strange, male voice.

Roni and I both turn and find the guys from the coffee shop standing behind us in the alley, and all three of them wear a huge grin.

"That's a really nice offer, honey, but not now," Roni dismisses them and links her arm through mine to drag me down the brick walkway.

"Maybe some other time then. I'm not picky. You're both hot as hell," calculus guy calls after us as we both release a flurry of giggles.

"That was fun," she laughs, rubbing tears from the corners of her eyes.

"For you, maybe, but that guy's in my math class. Now he's going to think I like rough sex."

"Hey, don't knock it."

"Only you would say that to me at a time like this." I give her a shove and adjust the strap of my backpack. "Listen, thanks for hanging out. I've missed this. I have to get going. I need to run and practice my song before meeting Brantley."

"Oooh, another study session. Remember what I said about those rules." She waggles her eyebrows a few times before tossing a wave over her shoulder and heading in the opposite direction. "Have fun, sweetie. I want to hear *all* about it later tonight."

Rather than answer, I simply shake my head, knowing I'll probably be asleep before she rolls in.

CASSIE

A blast of cold air hits me in the face as I step through the doors of the arena. I got my calculus test back today, and I'm here to share the good news. Ever since that day at the diner, we've been hanging out. On the days he's too tired from practice, we usually text or he'll video chat with me before falling asleep. We make each other laugh, and he's easy to talk to. In a short span of time we've gone from acquaintances to something along the lines of best friends. My friendship with B seems to have been formed of its own mold. It's organic in the sense that we came together to satisfy a base need of having someone to talk with, who would accept us for who we are without expectations. Even though I know the chance for a relationship is off the table, I'd be lying if I said I'm not attracted to him. It's hard not to be captivated by him. His sex appeal makes every hair on my body stand up and take notice whenever he's near. It also doesn't help that he's a very *hands on* kind of friend. We'll be walking around campus and he thinks nothing of slinging his arm around my shoulder. Or, when we cross the street, he takes the time to hold my hand and drag me across. He claims it's because I'm so short it takes me twice as long and he's worried oncoming traffic will plaster me. Normally, I would accept that response, but that doesn't explain why he continues holding on long after we've reached the other side.

Practice started an hour ago, and there's a crowd of girls huddled near the boards. Of the ten or so girls gathered, at least half of them are wearing jerseys. I slip past, and they don't acknowledge my existence. This isn't my first time attending practice, and the same girls are always present. I know most of them, though only by name. For example, Mandy Cunningham is a junior lusting over Danny Simpson. I know this because she not only wears his jersey, but she also squeals every time he steps out on the ice. Then there's Stacy Preston, and she currently has the hots for Gavin Turner. Rumor has it she's slept with most of the team, but that doesn't stop her from wearing a Great Lakes jersey with the number seventeen plastered over the back. I can't be certain, but either these girls have a never-ending supply of cash to spend on trivial items such as jerseys, or there's a community closet where they can reach in a pull out their favorite flavor of the week.

I take a seat five rows up and rest my elbows on my knees. Threading my fingers together, I lean forward and survey the lineup currently on the ice. At the moment, they're gathered around Coach Bishop. I give a small finger wave to Scotty and he gives me a nod of acknowledgement before waving to Ashley and taking his place between the pipes. For as long as I can remember, my brother has wanted to be a goalie. Every year when winter would come around he would wait for the pond at the end of our street to freeze and he would beg my dad to help him drag the net out and set it in place. Then, he would take up his position while my dad would fire shots at him one by one. I loved going with them, but I hated getting all bundled up to go, so I would never be dressed properly and would end up heading home before everyone else in order to prevent getting frost bite. Watching him this year is bittersweet because I know these times are coming to an end.

The puck drops, and I watch as they practice a few plays. Brantley's skates glide gracefully over the ice, and watching him makes me feel as if I'm already watching a professional athlete. Based on what Scott's told me, I know he and Brantley are headed to Detroit at the end of the year, and I realize I'm going to miss them both.

Suddenly, Kevrick sends the puck sailing across the ice and Brantley takes off after it with Danny Simpson close behind. Brantley's stick makes contact, but Simpson slams him into the boards and they both fight to gain possession. I stand, eager to see if Brantley comes out the victor, and realize my mistake too late as Brantley makes eye contact with me and loses control of the puck. I make a face and mouth *sorry,* but he simply gives me a wink and a gloved wave.

I sit back down, still smiling from the simple interaction, and am quickly surrounded by a cackling brood of puck bunnies. No one speaks for a few minutes, and we sit in awkward silence as they take turns sizing me up. I stare at each of them, wondering if any of them have been in B's bed, and bite back the snarky comment that hangs on my tongue.

"Hi, I'm Stacy, and this is Mandy, Tiffany, Lana, Lisa, and

Tina." She continues speaking and pointing to each girl, but honestly, all I hear is *blah, blah, blah*. I have zero interest in meeting these girls, let alone wasting any time speaking with them. They're catty, shallow, and viciously cruel in the way they try to tear apart relationships of players with legitimate girlfriends. I know this because Ashley has mentioned on more than one occasion that Tiffany's tried her best to get her claws into Scott.

Before I can answer, she voices the very words they're all wondering. "Are you dating Brantley?"

To the average, unsuspecting female her question would appear harmless. But I'm neither of those things, therefore I know this question stems not from simple curiosity but from pure jealousy. From the corner of my eye, I see Brantley watching the interaction. I avoid looking in his direction, but only to prevent adding fuel to their fire. What we share is none of their damn business, and I'm about to tell them that very fact when I'm interrupted by the sound of Ashley's voice.

"Hey, Cassie, what's going on here?" Ashley steps between them as if they're in her way, and they immediately part to make room for her. Ashley is a longstanding Jersey Girl, and it's clear she's not intimidated by their presence. They may travel in a pack, but it's obvious who their leader is, and she's busy eyeing the two of us as if trying to figure out what we have that she doesn't.

"Hi, Ashley, we were just introducing ourselves to Brantley's little girlfriend." Ashley's eyes narrow, but I can tell she's trying not to react. "Yeah, she's been here a few times over the last week, and just a short time ago he saw her and waved. We all know what *that* means," Stacy stands and begins to walk away.

The rest of her brood follows close behind. "However, I feel I should warn you he's aggressive in the sack. I only say this because you're so tiny and I'd hate for you to go in without that knowledge. I simply couldn't live with myself if you were split in half by his giant co—"

"Cassie, you okay?" Brantley's deep voice cuts her off before she can finish her sentence, though I know for a fact the only thing she was trying to tell me was that she's been on the receiving end of something I've only dreamed about. But I did have to agree with one thing; it *had* been pretty damn big. His eyes question mine; the worry on his face is evident. To. Everyone. Present.

Stacy's eyes dart from Brantley's to mine as a snarl fills her face. "Guess we have our answer, girls. Cassie, don't say I didn't warn you. Brantley, be careful out there sweetie." With that said, they march down the aisle and straight out of the arena.

"I'm okay."

"Care to tell me what all of that was about? I mean, I know it's not any of my business, but you know how your brother is about these guys," she gestures toward the ice.

"It's not what you think, okay. He's helping me with calculus and we hang out." She gives me a confused look. "Look, neither of us is looking for a relationship. We get along, like the same movies, and before you say anything I'm not in denial." I hold a hand in front of me as if this is helping me get my point across. "He's a really nice guy who's my friend. Nothing more."

"Okay. As long as you know what you're doing." From her smile I can't tell if she believes me or if she's just agreeing with me to appease me.

"Please, Ash, if Scotty asks, you need to let him know nothing is going on. Brantley was very clear establishing the rules. Scotty can trust him."

"Hey, don't worry, I'll be sure to defend you both. Actually, you spending time with Brantley is going to benefit me, because now he may stop nagging the shit out of Scott to stop spending all of his time with me. Honestly, I was beginning to wonder if he didn't have a thing for Scott." She lets out a soft giggle and straightens out her sweater.

"Yeah, I don't think you need to worry about B crushing on your man. He's all about the ladies. I mean, you heard Stacy."

"Oh, please. You can't believe a word that girl says. I'm not so sure she's slept with Brantley, though he does make the rounds." Her last words are almost a whisper as she looks at everything but me.

"Ash, he can sleep with whomever he wants. I told you, nothing's going on." An hour later a whistle sounds, announcing the end of practice, and we make our way toward the locker room.

Twenty minutes later, Scotty walks out and Ashley pounces on him, wrapping her long legs around his waist as he slants his mouth over hers and walks toward the exit with her in his arms. I watch with mild envy, wondering if I'll ever have that again. I remember being that way with Justin. I would hang around after practice, waiting for him to shower me with kisses. We'd grab a bite to eat, because he was usually famished after practice, then head back to his place and spend the evening between the sheets. Witnessing their brief interaction makes me realize I miss connecting with someone on that level. My body craves human contact. I find myself wondering what B would do if I were to throw myself at him when he walks through the door.

The hall starts to clear, and I begin thinking he's either snuck out a back door or he's meeting with Coach Bishop. Finally, the doors open and he walks out, smiling when he sees me leaning against the wall. His smile beckons me over, and without a second thought, I catch him by surprise and launch myself in his arms. He stumbles but circles his arms around me as I wrap my legs around his waist. His brows draw together in confusion when I lean forward and plant a kiss on his cheek.

"What was that for?" Our foreheads meet, and we quietly stare into one another's eyes. A moment passes between us, and I wonder if he has any idea what being this close does to me. There are times we're together when the he way he looks at me pierces my soul. Swallowing my emotions, I release my hold and lower my legs to the floor.

"I got my test back today." I reach down and retrieve a piece of paper from my backpack. I hand it over and watch as a smile fills his gorgeous face when he sees my grade. Without warning, he picks me back up and spins me around. I squeal with delight when he spins me three more times before setting me down once more. His hands rest on my elbows until I'm steady on my feet, and I'm still giggling when he lowers his head and kisses the corner of my mouth.

"You got a B+! I'm so proud of you. We have to celebrate. You don't have any plans tonight, do you?" I grab my backpack and we head outside.

"No, why, what do you have in mind?" My legs work double time to keep up.

"Tequila shots. You and me. My place. Let's go." He reaches out and laces his fingers through mine. As if the near kiss hadn't been enough to get me going, his warm skin against mine makes the area between my legs tingle with desire. Desire that won't be satisfied until later tonight when I'm home alone.

BRANTLEY

I line up four shot glasses on my dresser then look to my right and find her staring up at me with wide eyes. Normally, I would be downstairs drinking shots with the guys, but tonight is all about Cassie. Passing that test the way she did is definitely worthy of a celebratory shot, or three. It's not my intention to get her drunk; she's far too tiny to put down a lot of liquor. I have to be very careful, because she's my best friend's little sister, *and* she's underage. Besides, I don't want to get drunk. Not because I don't enjoy alcohol, but because I don't want to lose control and do anything stupid. Coach has a rule about us drinking during season, but that doesn't stop us from partaking in a few beers every now and again.

"Okay, so you said you've never drunk tequila, right?" I ask as I finish setting up our drinking station. She quickly nods, leaning closer to observe as I demonstrate the proper technique. Holding my thumb and forefinger apart, I point to the soft webbing between the two digits. "See this area here? Give it a lick, then sprinkle on some salt," I show her what I mean. "Take the lime

in the same hand and your shot in the other. Lick. Drink. Suck."
I raise my glass and give a quick toast. "Here's to kicking calculus'
ass!" I follow each step before slamming the glass back down.

"That looks easy enough." Her lips part, and the tip of her
tongue darts out to moisten her skin before tipping the shaker
like I showed her. She brings the glass to her wet lips and
shudders as the liquor burns its way down.

"How was it?" I laugh as she wipes her mouth with the back
of her hand.

"Not as bad as I expected, but I don't like licking the salt off
my hand. That just feels gross." She scrunches up her tiny nose
in disgust as I pour two more.

"Tell you what, you can lick my hand this time." I swipe my
tongue over the salty skin before coating it with more salt and
holding it out in front of her. She leans forward, taking my hand
between both of hers, then slowly licks away every grain of salt
before knocking back the shot and reaching for the lime. My dick
hardens as the memory of her tongue on my skin leaves me ready
to lose control. It's all I can do to swallow as my throat threatens
to constrict.

Wtf was that?

"Let's watch a movie," she announces in a voice that's slightly
elevated. The flush on her cheeks tells me the alcohol is working,
though I'm not shocked, because she doesn't weigh more than a
hundred pounds. She drops to her knees and scrambles over to
my rack of DVDs to select one. I toss back one more shot then
turn on the T.V. and settle in on the bed to wait. After a minute
she pops back up with her selection and places it in the player.

"Sweet Home Alabama?" I cock my head in question when

the title appears on the screen. "I don't own this movie."

"I know. I snuck it in earlier this week. I love this movie, and it's much more fun to watch with a guy than it is to sit home alone and watch it like a lovesick sap." She crawls in next to me with her head at the foot of the bed. Her feet rest beside my ribs, and every once in a while she crosses her feet in the air. She's wearing the same blue polish as before, and a thin, silver band adorns one of her toes.

The movie goes on, and I have to admit it's not as bad as I'd originally suspected. It's a sappy love story, but with a comedic twist. Halfway through the movie, I find myself rooting for the guy to just take her in his arms and lay one on her. By now, Cassie's toes have found a home between my fingers as I use my thumbs to massage the balls of her feet. Neither of us speak as we pretend to be engrossed in the movie, but her soft moans tell me she enjoys what I'm doing a hell of a lot more than watching former lovers try to connect. And I have to admit, I'm enjoying the hell out of making her moan.

I don't recall falling asleep, but I wake to find Cassie wrapped in my arms. The end of the movie is a blur, though I seem to recall them kissing on the beach. Her back is flush with my chest, and soft hair tickles my cheek as I work to shake off the fog of sleep. I shift my position and she presses further into me, and of course my dick chooses that moment to react. We're both fully dressed, but there's no denying my hard-on.

"Brantley," her soft voice breaks through the quiet. "Please tell me you're wearing pants this time." The giggle is out before she even finishes her sentence, and soon we're both laughing quietly, remembering the first time we'd woken up in my bed.

The funny thing is, even though we're both awake, neither of us has made an attempt at breaking away. Instead, I pull her close and drop a kiss on her jaw.

"Good morning, sweetheart. I love waking up to find you in my bed." She huffs and swings a pillow at my head before getting up and shuffling to the bathroom. I get up, run a hand through my hair, and quickly straighten the bed just in case anyone chooses this moment to walk in. The house is silent, so maybe they are still sleeping. I pick up the glasses and saltshaker and take them back to the kitchen. When I make it back to the bedroom, I find her sitting on the edge of the bed with her hands in her lap. "You okay? You don't have a headache or anything, do you?"

"No, I'm good. Listen, about last night... I didn't do anything stupid, like throw myself at you again, did I?"

My hand immediately goes to my chest in a show of mock disappointment. "Gosh, Dimples, it was so beautiful. We kissed, we did things to each other's bodies. We made sweet, passionate love, and you told me that no other man will ever satisfy you the way I do. Frankly, I'm hurt that you don't remember." It's hard keeping a straight face when I see the look of panic on hers. When she sees I'm only kidding, she quickly stands and marches over.

"Ugh! You big jerk. For a second I believed you!" She punches me in the arm before shoving me out of the way. "Goodbye, Brantley."

"I'll call you later, okay, baby?" I call after her retreating form.

"Yeah, yeah, whatever." She throws up her hand and takes off. I wait for the sound of the closing door before doubling over in laughter.

Cage, wait up!" I pause and turn to find Rivers making his way out of the locker room. When he finally catches up, he falls in step with me as we exit the arena and make our way to the adjacent parking lot. Thanks to the 3-1 win in last week's opening game, tonight's practice had been cut short by thirty minutes. I'm grateful, because we have late practice on Mondays, and this way I have more free time to get a jump-start on some of my assignments. I've always found it easier to be ahead of things, because once the season gets rolling, we'll be spending more and more time on the ice, and I really hate trying to do homework while riding on a bus. Our first away game is this weekend, two games at Kohl Center in Wisconsin. Even though it's early in the season, we're pretty confident in bringing home another victory.

"You looked sharp out there tonight. I think Kazmerski's going to shit his pants when he sees you coming after him this year," he says, referring to Wisconsin's top senior defenseman.

I huff out a laugh in agreement. "That's what I'm counting on, my friend. That, and the hope he hasn't grown another two inches. You heading out with Ash tonight?"

"Nah, she's got some chick thing going on over at her apartment, bunch of girls getting together to drink wine and watch Magic Mike XXL."

"Definitely sounds like something to steer clear of," I say, tossing my gear into the backseat. "She didn't happen to invite Cassie, did she?"

He frowns before responding. "I'm pretty sure she didn't. Why, are you suddenly concerned about whom my girlfriend spends her time with?"

"I'm not. I just thought since Cassie was relatively new to the area, and on occasion I've seen them talking during practice. I don't know, I guess I thought maybe they got along."

"I think they get along just fine, but Ash has this circle of friends, and they only get together once a month. Honestly, I don't give a shit. It gives me a night off. Speaking of which, you want to head over to Skeeps? First two rounds are on me." He spins his keys on his finger while waiting for my answer.

I answer, yes, of course. Scott is my best friend, and I couldn't tell you the last time just the two of us went out for a drink at the bar. Hell, this used to be our regular thing, but something had happened between he and Ashley over the summer that turned him into a whipped puppy dog.

We drop our cars at the apartment and make the short walk to the bar. After securing two seats, Scott wastes no time ordering up a couple of beers and two shots a piece. We spend a few minutes greeting a few of our teammates and other faces that recognize us, then he leans back on his stool and studies me with great intensity.

"What is it?" I finally ask after his staring starts to make me nervous.

"How are things going with Cassie? Is she making it hard on you? Math has never been her best subject." He takes a swig of beer.

Memories of her making me hard flash through my head, and the alcohol nearly chokes me on its way down. But I don't dare joke about that, not where Cassie is concerned. I almost feel bad thinking those thoughts about her. *Almost*.

"Actually, it's quite the opposite. She works hard and pulled a B+ on her test." I give my shoulder a casual shrug.

"So that's it? A few nights of tutoring and you go your separate ways?" He throws this out there as if he could care less what my answer will be, but I know better.

"I'm not really sure," I answer honestly. "I enjoy spending time with her. She's really easy to talk to and we get along pretty well. She did mention needing more help preparing for her midterm, so I'll probably hang around for that."

His lips practically disappear as he processes my confession, but he surprises me by encouraging me to keep hanging out with her.

"Listen, Cage, I really appreciate you looking out for her this way. I know the transition hasn't been easy for her. She left a pretty serious relationship to come here. I think she's still dealing with the breakup. Just do me a favor and keep your hands to yourself," he says it in a joking manner, but his threat comes through loud and clear.

"I've already told you, she's just a friend." *A friend with the sweetest lips I've ever tasted*. It's in this moment I'm thankful I have a really good poker face, 'cause I have a feeling if he knew of the dreams I've had, we'd be having an entirely different conversation.

He claps me on the shoulder then grabs his beer before standing. "I'm just giving you a hard time, buddy. You know I trust you implicitly. Now, I'm gonna kick your ass in a game of darts."

"Oh, yeah? You really think you can beat me?" I tease. "Have you forgotten about the last time we played in this very bar? I seem to recall being the one to serve up the ass whipping." He laughs, and it's a rich sound I've grown fond of hearing over the years. I get up and follow, knowing I should feel relieved he's okay that I'm spending so much time with Cassie, but I can't shake the nagging feeling I'm already treading on thin ice, only I just don't know it yet.

CASSIE

I rap my knuckles loudly against the cool metal one final time and adjust the strap of the guitar case hanging on my shoulder. When he doesn't answer, I assume he's not home, or with one of those annoying puck bunnies always hanging around. I never bothered to tell him I might be stopping by. Seeing as how I know his schedule by heart, I assumed he would be home. We've spent the better part of three weeks together under the guise of tutoring, but mostly we hang out and watch Sons of Anarchy. Sometimes we talk about things that are bothering us. Half the time I'm complaining about my brother, while his only gripe seems to be centered around the lack of unity on the team. He's not the only one feeling it. I've also heard Scotty mention it, and Davis was going on and on about it over lunch yesterday.

As far as I'm concerned, my brother couldn't have chosen three nicer guys to live with. They always welcome me with a warm greeting, and they're quick to include me when I'm caught sitting alone in the dining hall. In fact, Davis and I have taken to eating lunch together every Wednesday since we first ran into one another on our way to the dining hall.

Three minutes have lapsed since I last knocked and I finally accept the fact he's not home. Just as I'm stepping off the porch, I hear a thumping noise behind me as the door swings open to reveal Brantley. Allow me to rephrase that. A very wet Brantley, with a towel tied low on his hips, tattoos on full display.

Sweet Mother Mary. My B is freaking gorgeous.

"Hey, Cass," he smiles, bringing up a hand to drag it through his unruly hair. For half a second, I'm rendered speechless. It's only been six weeks since I last saw this much of his skin, but staring at him now my eyes zero in on his chest and the happy trail leading to a part of him I'm dying to know more intimately, and I'd swear to you it's been years.

"Hi." My voice comes out raspy, and I have to clear it before continuing. "Thought if you had time, I'd give you your first lesson." I pat the side of my guitar case and offer him a sheepish smile. It's probably dirty of me to drop an impromptu lesson on him this way, but I figured if I asked when a good time would be, he would've tried to blow me off. I get the impression he's afraid of failing in front of me. I also get the impression Brantley Cage rarely fails at anything. If ever. That's what gives me confidence to keep applying pressure. I have no doubt I can teach him; in fact, I'm looking forward to it.

"Gee, Cass, I don't know." He rubs a hand over his freshly shaven jaw, and I have this sudden urge to bury my nose in there and inhale deeply. I love the smell of a man after he shaves.

"Oh, come on, give me an hour. If you hate it that much, we never have to try it again." I flash him my best, dimpled smile and can tell instantly I've won him over.

"How can I say no to this face?" He gives my cheek a slight tug and steps back to let me pass. "Get in here." I step over the threshold and sneak a sniff as I pass. For an instant, my breath hitches in my throat and I have to remind myself to keep walking. "Let's go to my room. That way if one of the guys comes in, they won't see me making an ass of myself." He chuckles and steps in front of me to take the stairs two at a time.

I watch his every move with great interest, wondering how his towel manages to remain in place, and secretly will it to fall gracefully to the floor. He has a great ass. I only know this from staring at it so often. But it's one part of his body I haven't had the pleasure of viewing without clothes on. Until now. When he reaches his room, he drops the towel and steps into the first pair of jeans he finds lying on the floor. My jaw drops, and I'm unable to tear my eyes away. Even though we've established rules, he has no qualms about baring himself to me. In a way it's totally unfair, and I find myself wondering how he'd react if the tables were turned. He casts a glance over his shoulder and grins when he finds me staring.

"Where do you want me?" Oh god, now my mind is in the gutter. That's not the question he should be asking after I've just seen him from behind. Damn, he has a fine ass. Of course he does. He's probably the closest thing to perfection I'm ever going to encounter, and the fact he doesn't act like he knows it makes him even better.

"Umm, how about we both sit on the floor, that way I can help you position your fingers." I clear my throat once more and pull Willow from her case.

I have three guitars, each given to me by a different family member. My father gave Willow to me when I was fifteen. It was quite an expensive gift for someone so young, but when he handed it to me that Christmas morning, he told me he had no doubt we'd make beautiful music together. We wrote my first song together, and ever since, I've called her my good luck charm. She's made out of cocobolo wood, and has an intricate design to her that still takes my breath away. Besides being beautiful to look at, she has a sound quality none of the other guitars in my collection possess.

We sit cross-legged, facing one another. "B, meet Willow. She's my favorite guitar. Go on and take her, she won't bite." He looks slightly apprehensive as he reaches out to take her in his capable hands. I'm so close to this piece of wood, I almost swear I can hear her moan with pleasure as his fingers wrap around her neck.

"She's beautiful," he says quietly, never taking his eyes off mine. For a moment, I'm not sure if he's talking about Willow or me. "What's the proper way to hold her?" Rising up to my knees, I wiggle my way behind him and reach my arms around his middle.

"First of all, you have to make sure your posture is good. Sit straight up and place this hand here." I guide his left hand up the neck of the guitar. "Keep your thumb behind the neck, bend your first three fingers and gently rest them over the chords. Your thumb is going to remain loose while your fingers will move back and forth between the chords you're playing."

"Here," he lifts the guitar and places it in my hands. "Show me first by doing it yourself. I want to watch the pro in action."

"I'm not sure about the pro reference, but I'll show you the way I do it. Pay close attention." I take her in my hands and the act is so natural I don't even have to think about what I'm doing.

"Play something for me." He leans back on his hands and watches me in expectation.

"Hmmm, any requests?" I ask playfully, as my fingers move over the chords to warm up. "Never mind, I know what I'm playing." I begin strumming the opening chords to one of my favorite songs by the band, Paradox. They're a rock band out of L.A. I've been following since their first release. This song was written for the lead singer's wife. She sang it with him at an awards show a year ago and I fell in love with it. It has more of a country feel, which might be why it spoke to me, but it probably had a lot more to do with the lyrics than anything else.

"Don't just play it, you also have to sing it for me."

When I strum the first C chord, my mouth opens and the words come out without giving it another thought. Before I know it, I'm lost in the music.

There's a picture of you, still hanging on the wall
I sit home every evening, just hoping you might call.
My world came closing in on me, the day you said goodbye
I thought I would get over you, but all I do is cry.
Come back to me I'm begging you darlin'
Come back to me so I can hold you one more time.
Don't leave me hanging, I can't face the world without you
Come back to me, I'll love you right this time.
Ev'ry day you're not here, reminds me of all I've lost
Do whatever it takes to win you back, not caring 'bout the cost.
Give anything to have you here, and hold you all night long

Fight like hell to stop the tears, but I'm just not that strong.
Come back to me, I'm begging you darlin'
Come back to me, I'll believe in you this time.
The bed's too big without you, don't leave me alone tonight
Come back to me, I'll make everything alright
Come back to me, I'll make everything alright.

I finish the song and open my eyes to find him staring at me with his mouth hanging open in wonder. I'm used to this sort of reaction. Most people look at me and have no idea I pack such a powerful voice in my tiny body. Dad always told me I'd knock 'em dead one day. Looks like I came close just now.

"I'm... I have no words." His head shakes back and forth as he claps for me. I blush out of embarrassment, but only because it's him. Normally, I'm not this shy when receiving compliments. Somehow the compliment seems bigger when coming from him. "That was amazing. I know this is probably going to sound cheap and cliché, but you have the voice of an angel." He scoots closer, and I know it's only to make it easier for me to teach him, but a small shiver courses through me when his shoulder brushes against mine. "You don't expect me to learn that one, do you?"

"No." I smile a crooked smile and tuck my hair behind my ear. His eyes track the movement, and when our eyes meet, I know something has shifted between us. "Let me show you a few chords."

He holds the guitar like I showed him and fumbles with the whole combination of strumming while moving his fingers. After a few tries, he seems to catch on. And when he strums a C chord and D major successfully, I give a small round of applause.

He carefully moves the guitar aside and leans toward me, resting his weight on his right forearm. "What was that song? I've never heard it before."

"It's called "Come Back to Me" by Paradox, who happen to be my favorite band on the planet. I've actually met the lead singer, Sebastian Miles, one time at the airport in Chicago. He was super sweet, signing everything the crowd threw his way, and outside of the fact of him being drop dead gorgeous you would have never known he wasn't like the rest of the world. He seemed so down to earth."

"That's cool," he moves his fingers over the carpet, inching closer to mine with every pass. "So, this guy, what's he look like? What is it about him that gets you hot?" he asks in a teasing voice. When I don't respond immediately, he jumps on my silence. "Oh, come on, Cassie. I know he does it for you. I can tell by the way your eyes glaze over. And there's so much energy coursing through you right now you're practically humming beside me. What is it about this particular guy that gets to you?"

"Why are you asking me this?" I whisper.

"I don't know," he shrugs, and for a moment I think he's going to let it go. "Maybe it's because right now, you look the same way I remember that first morning I found you in my bed. Right after we kissed."

"Oh," I let out a shaky breath as I ponder my answer. "He has dark hair and tattoos, with eyes that pull you in." I lick my lips nervously, aware of the similarities between the man I'm describing and the one sitting less than six inches from me. "Then he wears these sexy as hell lip rings, and his voice melts me into a puddle of goo. I don't know, guess I'm just a sucker for dark-haired men."

Our eyes meet once more, and this time I know I'm not imagining things. He leans closer and slowly moistens his upper lip with his tongue.

Wait, is he going to kiss me?

I don't breathe, terrified any movement may scare him off. I want so badly for him to kiss me. I've dreamed of his lips on mine since first tasting them. I'm not sure what this will mean for our friendship, or the rules we've set in place. All I think about are Roni's words.

The fact he felt the need to establish them at all tells me he's into you.

Maybe she'd been right after all.

He's so close. I can feel his breath on my cheek as he leans in at a painstakingly slow pace. I'm shaking inside. The throbbing between my legs tells me I'm so turned on by the thought of his tongue mingling with mine, I could probably have an orgasm without him touching me.

"Cass," he murmurs softly, inching closer.

Please kiss me.

"B," I whisper, parting my lips in invitation.

"Cage!" Davis bellows before barging through the closed door as we scramble apart. "I just walked in on Masterson getting a blow—" He stops abruptly when he sees me sitting on the floor. "Hey, Cassie." He rubs the back of his neck uncomfortably and looks between us. "What's going on in here?" He waggles his brow suggestively and I wonder what we'd have done if he'd walked in just a few seconds later.

"Nothing," Brantley snaps.

It hadn't felt like *nothing* to me.

"I was just giving Brantley a guitar lesson." I stand and lift Willow off the floor. "I better be going. Your hour's up anyway." I quickly collect my things and head for the door. Davis is still in the room, so I can't say what's on my mind. I can't tell him I wanted him to kiss me more than anything in the world. Or that I've fantasized about him every day since we met. Instead, I look back and offer a parting wave he doesn't bother returning. I'm not sure if he regrets what almost happened, or if he's actually pissed it didn't. Either way, he doesn't take his eyes off Davis long enough to acknowledge my exit.

BRANTLEY

I toss my hockey duffle in the back of the truck before climbing inside and plugging in my phone. Things were much more productive at practice tonight, so much so that Coach let us out a few minutes early. Whatever was bothering Davis seems to have been forgotten, because he was on top of his game tonight. The rookies finally seem to be meshing with the rest of the guys, and I couldn't be happier. The timing couldn't be better, because we play our first game against Ohio State this weekend. After claiming the win in our first two games, then tanking out big time during the last two, our season hasn't gotten off to a great start. We have to be on top of our game this weekend if we want any hope of sending Ohio home with their tail between their legs. Ohio has a rock solid team. Their defenders are fast, and their offensive line is impressive. They have one of the best goalies in the NCAA league. Notice how I said 'one of the best'. Rivers holds the number one slot, and I'm banking money he'll end the year with that title. The guy is just that talented, which explains why the Detroit team had drafted him so quickly. He was always good, but last season the guy hit his stride and doesn't appear to be slowing down.

My phone beeps as I turn over the ignition and I look down to see a text from Cassie.

Her: Thinking of u. Wanted 2 say hi. Is it wrong that I miss u? Lol

I smile to myself, imagining her skinny butt sitting in that tiny dorm room. It's only been a few days since my first guitar lesson, but a part of me gets what she's talking about. I still can't believe I almost let myself kiss her. Fuck. I wanted to more than anything. Listening to her sing that song. Watching the way her fingers moved effortlessly over the part she calls the fretboard. She's a natural, and I can see myself getting lost in her voice. If Davis hadn't barged in the way he did, who knows how far things would have gone. I'm ready to take things to the the next level, but I'm not ready to ruin what we've built just because I can't keep my dick in my pants. After our talk at the diner, we've somehow found ourselves inseparable. We rarely go a day without some form of communication. I find myself checking my phone for texts, or scrolling through her Snapchat to see what she's been up to when I'm not around. Every Wednesday she posts a photo of her eating lunch with Davis, and I won't lie, it rubs me the wrong way. I know they're just friends, but isn't that what we are? If I'm thinking about something more with her, could Davis be thinking the same thing? Something about her makes me smile. And I have to admit it's nice spending time with a girl I can be myself around. Cassie doesn't expect anything from me, yet somehow I find myself going out of my way with her.

I open Spotify and soon James Bay's voice fills the cab of my truck. I'm about to shoot off a reply when my phone rings in my hand and I answer without checking to see who it is.

"I was just thinking about you." My face nearly splits in two from the smile stretching across it. It's been a long ass day and I know she can make me laugh.

"Well, isn't that what every mother wants to hear from her handsome son. How are you darling? You sound tired."

Would someone please explain to me how a mom can pick up on that shit?

"Mom, hey. How are you? How's dad doing? Last I talked to him he sounded well." I throw my truck in gear and pull out into traffic. It's after seven on a Thursday, but for some reason the traffic on State Street is still bumper-to-bumper.

"Your dad is doing really well. The doctors are impressed with how well his recovery is going. But you know how he hates being idle. Missing work has really put him in a foul mood, which is the reason for my call."

"Here I thought you just wanted to hear your baby boy's voice," I say in a teasing voice, making her laugh.

"Oh, darling, you know how true that is, but I must admit I'm calling for purely selfish reasons. What are the odds you can find somewhere to go during Thanksgiving break? I only ask because I've gone behind your father's back and booked us a getaway. I know the timing is poor, but given recent circumstances, I think it will do us some good. Maybe it will remind us of how things used to be." I can hear the desperate plea in her voice, and even though I don't have a freaking clue where I'll end up spending the day, I don't have the heart to crush her spirits.

"I'm fairly certain I know of a family or two who'd be willing to feed another mouth. I'm glad to hear you and dad are getting away. I can't remember the last time you did something like that for yourselves. But aren't you worried about dad not getting his fill of sweet potato casserole?"

"I've already got it covered. The hotel we're staying in is preparing a complete Thanksgiving feast for their guests, and it's a buffet. Your father will be in sweet potato heaven, though I may have to remind him to control himself, seeing as how he did just have open heart surgery," she laughs, and I welcome the sound. The last few times we've spoken, I could hear the strain the in her voice, though I know she worked hard to hide it. "Thank you for understanding. I hated the thought of calling, but the timing worked out perfectly. His office is closed that week anyway, so he won't feel guilty about not being there. I want you to promise you'll be home for Christmas. This may be the last year we get to see you once you become famous."

"Come on, mom. I'll never be too famous for my family," I answer honestly. "Besides, I'd be a fool to pass up your Christmas morning hugs. Hey, where's dad? Can I talk to him?"

"He fell asleep on the sofa just before I called, and I don't want to wake him just yet. Why don't you try calling back in the morning? Listen, I better go, sweetie. We love you."

"Yeah, love you guys too. I'll try calling tomorrow, but I can't make any promises. I have an early practice." I end the call on a sigh, not in the mood to think about Thanksgiving when October has barely begun. Pulling into the driveway, I cut the engine and pull open my messages.

Me: It's not wrong. I miss u 2.

I dance through the shower, then lie on my bed to read a few chapters in my econ book. Two pages later and my mind drifts from what I'm reading. Hearing mom's voice brought everything I'd been trying to suppress back to the surface. Even though mom seems perfectly content on acting as if nothing happened, I can't seem to shake the heavy weight crushing against me. Dad and another woman? Trying to picture my dad with anyone besides mom just feels weird. Would he really cheat on her? And if so, why? I want to ask these questions, but I never seem to get him on the phone for longer than five minutes. Maybe mom's been running interference so I'm not able to corner him. But the thought of asking him over the phone doesn't sit well either. No, these are questions that should be asked and answered face-to-face. That way, I can look him in the eye when he responds. Now that I won't be going home for Thanksgiving, it will have to wait another month, and by then it may start to feel like old news to them. They'll have moved on while I'm still holding onto misplaced hatred. No, hatred isn't quite the word I would use. Too harsh. But I do have resentment because, no matter how you look at it, if he stepped out of line in any way, I'm afraid it may rock the pedestal I've kept him on all these years.

I'm afraid maybe it already has.

I don't know how long I've been asleep before the phone starts ringing. "Hello?" My voice is thick with sleep, and I cover the phone with my hand to clear my throat.

"I'm so sorry I woke you. Just call me tomorrow," she blurts and I have to work fast to catch her before she ends the call.

"Wait, I want to talk. How are you? I've missed you." It feels weird saying the actual words out loud, but they're true. And now that they're out there, I can't take them back, not that I want to.

We haven't seen each other much this week, and right now, I could really use a friend.

"B? Are you okay? Your voice sounds funny."

"I'm okay. Wait... I mean, not really." I try to compose myself. I felt fine until I heard the concern in her voice. Knowing she's out there worried about me does weird things to my head. "It's my dad. He had a heart attack after I got back from Traverse City."

"And you're just now telling me? Is he okay?"

"Honestly? I'm not sure. And that's not even the worst of it. Mom suspected he'd been having an affair and—" That's as far as I get before she cuts me off.

"Stay right where you are. I'll be right there." The call ends abruptly, and I'm left holding the phone to my ear as if waiting for her to pick it back up and tell me she was only kidding. Fifteen minutes later, there's a soft knock on my door, and when I open it, she falls into my tired arms.

"Oh, honey. I'm so sorry." Her blue eyes peer up at me, and for the first time since we've met, I'm not looking at her with lust or longing. All I see is someone who dropped everything to be with me because she sensed I needed a friend. Holding her in my arms feels so nice it makes me wonder why I haven't opened up sooner. "Do you wanna talk about it?"

I don't respond with words. I simply nod my head, and she guides me over to the bed and crawls in beside me. With her back against the headboard, she pulls me in so my head is on her shoulder. She strokes my hair and speaks in a low, soothing voice.

"What happened?" I open my mouth, and before I know it, I've told her everything I know, which isn't a whole lot. "But his surgery went well and he's recovering? How's your mom holding up? This must be difficult for her. I can't imagine watching someone I love go through something like that."

My arms circle her waist to pull her close. There's barely an inch between us, but I can't seem to get close enough. She seems to know exactly what I need before I have to ask.

"When we talk, she sounds normal, but I'm sure it's been hard as hell. My dad doesn't handle sitting still very well. I'm sure he's driving her crazy, but you wouldn't know it from talking with her. I don't get it, you know? If she suspected anything of an affair, how can she go from confronting him to taking care of him as if nothing happened? In my eyes, there's no excuse for any of it, and the excuses mom made for him sound like pure bullshit to me. He says he loves her, but, there was a brief period where he was questioning everything in his life. Screw that. In my opinion, if you're in love, then you're all in, there is no in-between."

She goes quiet for a few minutes, and when she finally speaks, I cling to her words as if they're a lifeline. "I suppose when you've been with someone a long time, it would be hard to walk away. Think about it, they promised to love each other through good times and bad. I'm sure after what, twenty-plus years, they've weathered a hell of a lot of storms together. No. When times get hard, you don't run away and seek shelter; you get right in there and sling a little mud if that's what it takes. I know I would fight for the man I loved, no matter how messy things got. She probably forgave him, because that's what love does to you. You love not only when there's laughter, but also when there's pain. I'm certain she feels after this long she's earned the right to stay by his side, and I hope he realizes how fortunate he is to have a woman like that."

"So you're saying I should forgive him even if he made a mistake? That I love him no matter what?"

"Yeah, B, that's exactly what I'm saying." Her finger slips below my chin, lifting my face to hers. "I'm not saying it will be easy, but he's your father, and whatever it is he's going through, it sounds to me like he needs his family now more than ever."

I bury my face in her shirt, silently crying as I try and absorb the words she's just spoken. She's quiet now, waiting for me to say something, but allowing me to do it on my own terms. There's safety in the friendship we've formed. A sense of freedom I've never experienced with another human being outside of my parents. I'm not sure how it happened; all I know is I like it, and I find myself wanting to cling to it for as long as she'll let me.

"Stay with me. I don't want to be alone tonight." She smiles and without a word gets up and uses the bathroom to change into one of my T-shirts. I like seeing her in my clothes. I'm not sure why. I just do. On her way back to bed she makes sure to lock the door before shutting off the light and snuggling in beside me. With my face pressed up against her back, I breathe in the sweet fragrance of her shampoo and listen to the soft sounds of her even breathing. It's only after she goes quiet that I give in to the pull of sleep and enter a peaceful slumber while holding onto my best friend.

The next three weeks morph into much of the same.

Practice. Class. Time with Cassie.

Class. Practice. Time with Cassie.

It doesn't matter how the day starts, all that matters is they end the same. Spending time with Cassie has become my new normal. Whether together or simply talking on the phone, I always feel good when she's around.

"You want to catch a movie, or hang out in my room and practice some more?" I ask as we make our way toward the exit of the lecture hall. Two nights a week she's been meeting with me to have me play for her. I'm only a third of the way through the song, but last week she left Willow so I can practice on the nights she isn't giving me a lesson. She's a great teacher. Patient. Demanding without being harsh. And very thorough. She'll make me play the same chords over and over until she feels my movements are natural rather than forced. She says I'm a good student too, but that's probably due to the years of disciplined training I've had to endure for hockey season.

"I can't get together tonight. I already made plans with Roni. She complained you're monopolizing my time, so I gave in and agreed to go to a party with her." She links her arm with mine and gives me a sideways glance as we continue walking.

"Party? Which one? I haven't heard about any parties." I play along, knowing full well what 'party' she'll be attending. Her birthday is this weekend, but a bunch of us decided to surprise her by all meeting up at Rick's. Last week, Roni texted to fill me in on her plan, and before we knew it, Scott and Davis were in on the surprise. Roni has this grand plan to distract her before arriving at the bar much later tonight.

"Umm..." she stalls, and I can tell she's embarrassed to admit where she's going. "It's not that kind of party. She's taking me to a sex toy party," she mumbles the last part into her hand so I can't make out what she's just said. But I already know, so it's kinda funny.

"I'm sorry, I didn't hear that. What kind of party?" I turn my head so she doesn't see me smirk, and I have to make sure it's not present when I turn back around.

"A sex toy party," she shouts at the top of her lungs, and this draws the attention of several students. "What?" She throws her hand up in question, but they all turn away and keep walking. She turns to me and rolls her eyes, annoyed I made her admit it out loud. "Are you happy now?"

"Hmmm, let me see... Ask me later when I see what toys you've bought." I give her a teasing wink.

"Oh, you wish. I'm not planning on buying anything. I'm not even taking my wallet. I'll just be observing."

"I'll spot you twenty bucks if you're worried about wasting your own money," I offer happily.

"Brantley," she warns, and I concede by shutting my mouth and slipping a twenty in her front pocket. It really is fun to watch her blush.

Rick's is another venue where students congregate throughout the school year. For the most part, it's usually crowded on the weekends, but tonight is Wednesday so we have no problem finding a few available tables. Pulling them together to accommodate ten bodies, we situate the chairs and order a round of drinks. Davis is on my right, which also happens to be the direction the door is in, so while he goes on about some girl in his econ class, I listen and watch the door simultaneously.

Thirty minutes after we arrive, they walk through the door. I'm two beers in and finally starting to relax when she approaches the table and pulls back the seat I've been saving for her. The one right next to mine. The same one I've kept a watchful eye over since everybody and their neighbor kept trying to snag it. Now that she's here, I can let down my guard and kick back.

She takes a look around the tables, spying her closest friends, and immediately senses something is up.

"What's going on? Why are you all here on a Wednesday?" she asks skeptically.

"Surprise!" We all scream in unison. "Happy Birthday!"

"No way." She drops her face into her hands and shakes her head.

"Yes, way." I pull her hand away and give her a barely noticeable wink. Rivers is sitting two seats down and across from us, and I can feel him watching my every move. I lower my hand and raise my beer in a toast just as Ashley brings out a cake with twenty glowing candles. "Happy early Birthday, Dimples. I hope all your wishes come true." She smiles a smile that I'm sure is meant solely for me before blowing out all her candles in one breath.

"Me too," she whispers and throws a wink back at me.

"Woo hoo! Cut the cake!" Masterson calls out. "Happy Birthday, Cassie."

One by one, they all come around to our side of the table, while she stands to give each one a hug. I watch with a smile, thinking back to that night at the frat house when I'd walked in on her crying. Back then she'd been lonely, longing for the very thing now surrounding her. Everyone here loves her in their own way.

"Happy Birthday, sis." Rivers makes like he's going to muss her hair, and she reflexively dodges his hand. But instead of giving her a hard time, he pulls her close and gives her a hug and a kiss. "Love you." Ashley follows after him, and then I hear him tell her they're taking off. She stares after them as they leave, and I can sense her disappointment.

"Hey." I tug on her sleeve, and she lowers her head to look at me. Now that the watchdog is gone, I pull her back on my lap and whisper in her ear. "Did you put my money to good use?"

"Wouldn't you like to know," she answers seductively, and all I can do is laugh as I lean in and plant a kiss on her cheek.

I'm fairly certain if I were to reach my hand in her pocket, I wouldn't find that money. No. Something tells me she spent it at that party, and I'm dying to know what she bought. A small part of me hopes I'll get to find out.

By the time I drop her off at the dorm, I'm horny as hell. It's been weeks since I've gotten laid, and I'm worried if I don't remedy that soon, I may end up doing something to jeopardize our friendship, not to mention give her brother reason to kick my horny ass.

CASSIE

How are things? It's been a while
I miss your laugh. I miss your smile
The late night talks, we used to share
Your hand in mine, because you cared
All of these things, remind me of
Those days when I still had your love

"Dammit." My hands slam against the piano keys, creating a haunting sound that echoes off the walls. I've been in this room for nearly an hour, but the music isn't working and it's really pissing me off. It's not as if the song is a requirement for my class; it was just something that came to me while I was in the shower. Lately, that appears to be one of the many inconvenient places that sparks my creative juices. Driving a car, the middle of night, or during sex also make that list.

"I need Willow," I announce to the empty room. Working quickly, I shove the music sheets in my bag and hustle out the door.

I'm halfway back to the dorms when I remember Willow isn't in my room. She's nestled safely inside Brantley's room, where we've been meeting for his lessons. Surprisingly, he's put a lot of effort into learning, and when I offered to leave the guitar with him to practice, he'd been all for it. I send him a quick text to let him know I'm stopping by, and keep walking toward the bus stop.

I suppose I could have borrowed a guitar from the music department, but Willow's been present for every song I've composed. I'll feel better having her with me for this one, even if I'm just messing around.

It's a quick ride to his apartment, and the bus lets me off at the stop just three doors down. When I knock on the door it swings open before I have a chance to lower my hand. Scotty stands on the other side and looks surprised to see me.

"Cass? What's up?" he asks when I breeze past him.

"I'm just here to pick up Willow. I left her here so B would have more time to practice."

"B. So what, you two have nicknames for each other now? Anything else I should know about?" His eyebrows shoot up an inch on his forehead.

I roll my eyes and shove my way past him. "I believe we've already covered this topic. Is he home or not?"

"Can't say for sure," he shrugs his shoulders and closes the door. "I just got home myself. But his truck's out front."

"Okay, thanks. I'll just run up and grab her." I don't wait for his response. It's not as if I need his permission to enter Brantley's room. I've hung out with him enough to feel comfortable in this house.

His door is slightly ajar when I approach, so I rap my knuckles once before pushing it open only to receive the surprise of my life.

He's shirtless and lying on his bed with a half-naked redhead straddling his jean-clad legs. And she's not just any redhead. She's the same girl who'd called him baby that night at Casey's.

They're oblivious to my presence. I could turn and walk out and he'd never know I was here. But to my horror, my legs are frozen in place. I watch helplessly as she gyrates over him, feeling their connection, and the look in his eyes makes my mouth go dry. When their lips meet in a kiss the pang of jealousy that hits is so sharp I let out a garbled cry. The girl glances lazily in my direction without missing a beat. I stumble backwards, embarrassed I've been caught. Brantley's eyes find mine and there's panic behind them.

"Shit!" I exclaim, grasping the doorframe for stability before bolting down the stairs. Tears sting my eyes as I speed past Scott without an explanation. The last thing I see is the puzzled look in his eyes as he gapes after me. I run down the street as fast as my legs will carry me, catching the bus just before it pulls away from the curb. Sinking into the first empty seat, I steal a backward glance in time to catch Brantley sprinting across the lawn in my direction, stopping only after the bus turns the corner.

I cower in the corner and work to catch my breath. Humiliated doesn't even begin to describe how I'm feeling right now. Just days ago I'd been happy because I thought he was going to kiss me. That same night I even dreamed he harbored a secret crush on me. Truth is, even if he *had* kissed me that night,

I would just be one more girl added to his lineup. Hell, it's no secret he's slept with more than his share of girls on campus. Just last week I heard about this list; apparently it's legendary and has been a long-standing tradition among the sororities on campus. It's called the Campus Conquest and, according to several girls in South Quad, Brantley is #2 on the list.

I'm pretty sure I never stood a chance at being more than his friend, but that doesn't stop me from wanting more.

Lucky for me, the bus is almost empty, because I can't stop the tears from trickling down my cheeks.

BRANTLEY

"Shit," I murmur, shoving Natasha aside to go after Cassie.

What the fuck had she been doing?

And how long had she been standing there?

Taking the steps two at a time, I sprint past Scott and frantically scan the street for any sign of her. Forgetting my pants are unbuttoned, I haul ass across the lawn, screaming her name. From the corner of my eye, I catch a glimpse of blond curls entering a bus just as the door closes and it pulls away.

"What the fuck just happened?" One minute, I'm messing around with Natasha, and the next, I'm running down the street after some chick.

No, you asshole. Not some chick.

It was Cassie. And you've just hurt her.

A sinking feeling settles in the pit of my stomach, yet I don't fully understand what I'm sick over. Cassie and I hang out. Nothing more. Ground rules were set, and we've stuck to them.

Sort of...

But what about the little touches?

The hand holding that lasts longer than necessary?

And what about the times we've almost kissed?

Shit. I'd made it perfectly clear nothing could ever happen between us. It wouldn't work. Scott is my best friend, and I don't want to betray his trust.

I *won't* betray his trust.

However...

I won't deny I feel something for her. Hell, I dreamed of her only two nights ago. Dreamed of her smooth skin. Her perfect tits that were made to fit my hand. Her soft lips parting just before they surround my...

Oh, for Chrissake. That's not helping.

When I walk back into the house, Scott's standing in the living room with his arms crossed and his eyes narrowed in my direction.

"You mind telling me what the fuck that was about?"

I run my fingers through my hair and shake my head. "I don't know, man. She just came into my room. I had no idea she was coming over," I shake my head, trying to figure out how I'll ever be able to look her in the eyes again. But why am I letting this bother me? I don't owe her an explanation for my actions. I'm a single guy with needs.

Needs she shouldn't fill.

"Um, hell-o? Did you forget something?" I look up and see Natasha standing with her hands on her hips, scantily dressed and clearly annoyed. I blink several times until it registers I must have forgotten she was upstairs. I have zero desire of picking up where we left off. And honestly, despite how sexy she looks in her black, lacy bra, I don't even think I could achieve a hard-on right now. Nor do I want to.

I saunter over and give her a quick kiss before asking her to leave. "Natasha, baby. I'll call you later." Thankfully, she gets it. There are no ulterior motives when it comes to Natasha. She uses me for sex. But that's okay, because until now, I've been doing the same thing. She quietly gathers her belongings, what little she brought with her, and walks out the door.

"Nice," he comments while watching her go. Then turns and glances down at the open waistband of my jeans. "I take it Cassie saw more than she bargained for when she went up there. I think you should know, she was pretty upset."

"Yeah, I know," I stammer, unsure how to begin explaining what's going through my head right now. And the hardest part is, I can't tell him even if I wanted to. Which I truly do because he's my best friend.

When I finally make it back to my room, I reach for my phone and see that Cassie sent me a text nearly an hour ago.

Her: Fighting with a new song. Coming over 2 get Willow. C u soon!

A knot forms in my chest when I picture the look on her face. Without a doubt she'd been shocked, but I'm certain I saw something else. Something I never meant to cause.

Pain...

Practice is scheduled to start in thirty minutes, and Coach will ream my ass if I'm late. I snag a clean shirt and throw my hockey duffle over my shoulder. On the way out, I spot her guitar in the corner where I last left it. Lifting it carefully, I decide to drop by her dorm after practice. I have no idea if she'll speak to me, but I sure as hell have to give it a try.

CASSIE

Veronica and I are on our beds studying when I hear a knock at the door. My stomach lurches in fear it may be Brantley; after all, he had been chasing me down only two hours ago. I came back and poured my heart out to Roni, hiding my face the whole time. She'd been quick to remind me that B is a player, and I get that. It's not as if I walk around oblivious to the rumors, but I never expected to have reality slap me in the face. And I hadn't been prepared for how it would leave me feeling. Honestly, I'm confused about what's happening between us. We seem to go out of our way to push the boundaries of every parameter we've established. At some point, one of us is bound to cross an imaginary line and what happens then? Would our friendship be over? I truly hope not, because I'm not sure I'd want to remain here if B wasn't in my life. Being with him warms my heart in the same way I feel whenever I perform a new piece of music for the first time.

It's a feeling that says *I'm complete*.

Honestly, it's scares the crap out of me. Because anything that leaves you feeling *that* good is also something you can lose in the blink of an eye.

The knock comes again, followed by Brantley's deep voice, "Cassie, we need to talk."

"What are you gonna do?" she whispers when I fail to get up.

"I'm not ready to face him. Just tell him I'm not here," I whisper back and cower near the end of the bed so he won't see me.

"Hey, Brantley," she greets him, cracking the door open only a few inches. "Cassie's not here."

"Hi Veronica. Do you know where she is? I really need to talk to her." There's desperation in his voice.

"No, I'm sorry, I don't. Is everything okay? You seem stressed," she asks sweetly.

"Umm, I'd rather talk to Cassie about it. Something happened earlier today and... I can't stop thinking about her. I need to know she's okay and I haven't fucked things up between us," he says sadly. I can feel his pain from where I'm hiding. I feel it because my pain goes just as deep.

"I know about what happened. She came back and told me all about the little performance you gave."

"She did? I swear I had no idea she was even there. Be honest, is she avoiding me? She's in there hiding right now, isn't she?"

"No. I told you. She's not here. But I'll tell her you stopped by," Roni replies calmly. I swear the girl could win an Oscar for her performance.

"Okay," he concedes. "I brought Willow. She was looking for it earlier, and I figured she would like it back."

"Sure thing. I'm sure she'll appreciate the gesture."

"Listen, can you do me another favor? Tell her I'm really sorry. I feel like a complete asshole, and would give anything for one of her hugs right now. Just tell her that for me and let her know I'll be waiting for her whenever she's ready to talk."

"I'll do that. See you later," she says, closing the door in his face. Then, she whips around and crosses the room in two steps. "You *have* to go after him."

"What? Why? I told you. I'm not ready to face him."

"Cassie, you should have seen his face. He looked so sad. I don't care what you say. That man is crazy about you. I can see it in his eyes when he talks about you. Damn, what I wouldn't give to have him going all teary eyed over me."

"Wait, he almost cried?" I nearly chew my bottom lip off as I debate my next move.

"Yeah, I swear if he'd kept going, they would have spilled down his cheeks. Guys don't cry over you unless they have feelings for you. You're a fool if you don't at least listen to what he has to say." I don't wait to hear the rest of her speech. I'm out the door and chasing after him in a flash.

"Brantley," I call after his retreating form. He's less than a hundred feet away, but apparently he doesn't hear me. My heart beats rapidly as I sprint after him and scream his name. "B!" He turns just as I launch myself at him, and when we collide my face smashes against his solid chest.

"Come here. I can't see your face," he grumbles, picking me up so I'm wrapped around him like a pretzel. A tear rolls down my cheek, but he quickly brushes it away. "Much better," he smiles, and I trace the curve of his lip with my thumb. When our eyes meet and his lips part, I lean forward. And just like the day we met, I go for it.

His lips taste heavenly, and if the kiss ended here, I'd be completely satisfied, but it doesn't end, it only intensifies. Our tongues brush together, and as the kiss deepens, he tangles his fingers in my hair and holds my head in place. The kisses skim down my neck and stop when they reach my bare shoulder. Soft nips and licks sear my skin until a moan passes my lips and the spell we're caught up in is broken. Our eyes open and we hastily pull apart.

"Cassie, I'm so sorry—" he starts, but I press my fingers over his lips.

"Don't you dare, B. Don't apologize for kissing me. We were caught up in the moment. Nothing more."

He gives me a funny look before shaking his head. "No. I wasn't going to apologize for that. It was hot as hell." His lips curve into a wicked smile. "You can greet me like that every day if you want." I give him a poke in the ribs, and he makes a grunting noise. "I'm kidding, okay. Listen, I'm sorry about this afternoon. I never meant to hurt you."

"I wasn't hurt." The lie falls from my lips with ease. "It just shocked me, that's all. From now on, I'll remember to knock."

"There won't be a next time, Cassie," he says with sincerity.

"Brantley, I don't expect you to stop having sex just because we're hanging out. You have needs, so go ahead and fulfill them. I honestly don't care whom you stick your di—" he cuts me off with another mind-blowing kiss, and when we break apart, I wrinkle my nose in confusion. "What was that for?"

"Will you please stop? Yes, I have needs. And, yeah, I've been with my share of bunnies. But I'm tired of that shit. I like hanging out with you. I like spending time with you, because you're with me for who I am as a person and not as a status symbol. I consider you my best girl friend, Dimples. I'm through spending time with skanks. At the end of the day I just feel empty after being with them. But when I'm with you, it's different." He swallows hard, leveling his gaze with mine, and it's hard to hide my disappointment at being called his girl friend. With emphasis on the separation of the two words.

"Why were you with her?" I know it's a stupid question, but I need to hear his answer.

"Honestly? Because of you."

"Me?" I ask incredulously. "How exactly did I drive you into the arms of a skank?" I wiggle against him, and he releases his hold.

"Well, not *you*, exactly." I roll my eyes and he continues. "Remember your birthday? After everyone left and you were sitting on my lap?" I nod and curl my finger around one of his. His eyes cast down to our joined hands and a smile forms at the corners of his mouth. "We were joking about that sex toy party, and you wouldn't tell me if you'd spent my money. I went home that night and couldn't stop thinking about it."

"Thinking about what?" I tip my head back and look up at him. His eyes dart nervously from side to side before settling on my lips. For a moment I think he may kiss me again.

"You," he folds his hands, locking them behind his head. "I couldn't stop thinking about *you*. I swear, my dick was so hard I had to jack off twice before falling asleep."

"I'm sorry," I smirk, "I'm sure that must have been hard for you."

He frowns at my choice of words. "Trust me, you have no idea. But it's still wrong of me to think of you that way. You're my friend, not to mention my best friend's sister." I roll my eyes again, and he grabs hold of my wrists. "I know you hate being reminded of that, but it's true. Anyway, I figured the best way to get those thoughts out of my system was by fucking someone else."

I pull one of my hands away and run it through my hair. "And how'd that work out for you?"

"I didn't sleep with her. I wanted to, or at least I thought I did, until I saw your eyes. After that, I couldn't go through with it."

"Well, that's just crazy. You can't give up sex because you're worried my feelings may get hurt. I don't expect that of you." I weave my fingers through his belt loops and draw him to me. "I promise I won't think less of you if you need to hook up with someone. But as your *friend,* I do have one request."

"Oh yeah? What's that?" The calloused pad of his thumbs caress my hips and, because it feels *really* good, I have a hard time thinking straight.

"No matter how desperate you become, promise me you won't sleep with Stacy Preston." His brow arches, and he gives me a smile.

"Pfft, that's easy." He lowers his forehead to mine to look me square in the eye. "I promise I will *never* sleep with Stacy Preston again."

"Thank you," I mouth the words.

"For the record, it only happened one time." He slings an arm around my shoulder and we turn toward the dorms. "Worst lay

162

I've ever had." I throw him a dubious look and he makes an X over his chest. "Swear to god. She's a selfish fuck. Ask any guy on the team."

"No, thanks." I swat at him. He motions toward his back and I hop on for a piggy-back ride to my room. And just like that we're back to being *us*.

CASSIE

Saturday morning I'm at my desk working on my song when I hear a knock at the door. I check the time and know it's not Brantley; he's down at the gym with Davis working on his already perfect abs. As I open the door, I'm startled to find Scotty standing there.

"Scotty!" I throw my arms around his neck, and he pulls me in for a really tight, brotherly hug. In the middle of it, I'm struck with the reality of how much I've needed this from him. Words can't begin to explain how much I've missed spending time with him. I've expressed this to B, and he keeps telling me to talk to Scott, but something keeps holding me back. I guess a part of me is afraid if I push to hard he'll pull away completely. Scott is sometimes like a timid dog; he can only handle so much before he retreats into a corner and it takes a while for him to rebuild his trust. I don't get it, but I know enough to stand back and let him come to me. That's why this gesture means so much.

"What's up? Is everything okay?" I motion for him to step inside. We haven't seen each other since the afternoon at his apartment, though he had called me that night to check on me.

"Nothing's wrong. Geez, does a guy need a reason to visit his baby sister?" he closes the door behind him and looks around our small space. "Holy shit, these rooms are so small. I still can't believe I lived here for a year." He pushes his beanie back on his head and drops into Roni's desk chair.

"Yeah, I guess I've gotten used to it by now. Anyhow, we try not to spend too much time here." I tuck my legs under me and sit back down on the edge of the bed. "It's good to see you. I've missed your face."

"Yeah, I've missed you too. Listen, I just wanted to check in and see if you're okay. I know we talked the other night, but the look on your face when I last saw you had me worried. You want to talk about it?" He's clearly in big brother mode, which makes me smile, because this is the Scotty I've been missing.

"Thanks for coming over, and for worrying about me, but I'm okay now. Brantley came by that night and apologized."

"He did?" His brow furrows but it's quickly replaced with a smile. "So, you two good now? Back to being buddies?"

"Yeah, we're good," I answer, returning his smile.

"Good to hear. I know you two have gotten close." He rubs his hand over the back of his neck as he says this. "You know, I was thinking maybe you'd like to hang out tonight? I could take you to that Cuban place I was telling you about, Frita Batidos, over on Washington." His eyes light up with excitement, and it reminds me of when we were kids and he would try and talk me into doing something that may get us into trouble.

"Oh, yeah. That's the place where they make those sour lime shakes you were telling me about." I'm practically bouncing on the edge of the bed just thinking about them. I love anything sour, and my brother knows this. "What time do you want to go?"

"I'll pick you up at six. We can eat, then maybe catch a movie or something. That sound good?" He stands, and I jump up to give him another hug. His arms are so long they swallow me whole when he wraps them around me. I'm so moved by this show of affection that I'm unable to prevent a few tears from escaping down my cheeks. It's only when I sniff and refuse to let go that he realizes I'm crying. He takes a step back and lifts my chin. "Hey, I didn't come over here to make you cry. It's just dinner and a movie, Cassie. It's not like a date or something. Geez," he winks and ruffles a hand through my hair. "See you in a few hours."

I mumble a response and watch as he lets himself out. It's only then I realize Veronica must have slipped out sometime during our little bonding moment. It's just as well. I'm suddenly in the mood to be alone and cry. Before I do that, I decide to text Brantley letting him know what just happened. His response comes quick and brings a smile to my teary face.

Him: It's about time his dumb ass woke up and saw how lucky he is. Have a great time. Text me later.

I set my phone on the nightstand and smile all the way to the shower.

My smile fades when I step outside and see Ashley sitting in the passenger seat of the Charger. Without uttering a word, I give him a look that says *I thought we were hanging out alone.* He flashes me one that says *I'm sorry, she just showed up and I couldn't say no.*

I climb in the backseat, knowing my brother is too nice a guy to blow off his girlfriend for me. It's only a short distance, but Ashley talks nonstop the entire way. What shocks me even more than seeing her in the front seat is what she's talking about. Apparently, they are leaving tomorrow after the game and going to Ohio to see her family. This weekend is my recital, and he's supposed to be there for me. I guess this explains why he suddenly had an interest in spending time with me. Guilt. I remain quiet in the backseat, but I'm boiling inside. He tries to make eye contact but I simply smile and avoid his gaze, refusing to let him see my pain. It's only when we stop in front of the restaurant that I finally let out my frustration.

"Um, why are we stopping here? Scott knows I don't like this place. Scott?" She turns and bats an eye at him and he immediately caves. Gah! Why are men so weak when it comes to women?

"Cass, would you mind eating across the street at Zola? We can do Frita's another night." He looks at me hopefully. On any other occasion I may concede to his request, but not tonight. I've been looking forward to our time together, and I was really hoping to see his face after my performance tomorrow night. I've worked really hard on this piece. He hasn't even asked to hear it. I've played it a few times for Brantley and he clapped and cheered for damn near ten minutes. Why is it Brantley gets it, but my brother seems completely clueless?

"You know what, no. I've been looking forward to eating here, and that's where I'm eating. Feel free to eat across the street. We can meet up afterwards and go to the movies. Enjoy your scallops." I flash a fake smile and go inside the restaurant. I'm instantly hit with the delicious aroma of garlic and cilantro. I look down and see a group of students munching on a large bowl of garlic-cilantro French fries, and my mouth begins to water in response.

The line is really long, and the place is packed. I take my place in line and settle in for the long wait. From the smells wafting past as the kitchen door opens I can tell the wait will be worth it when they set that heavenly platter of food before me. I glance around and note the seating is simply rows of white picnic tables strung together and everyone eats sitting next to other patrons. At least I won't be alone while I'm eating. I'm lost in thought when my phone buzzes in my pocket.

Him: I envision u with a plate of garlic fries. Are they as good as u expected?

Me: Not that lucky yet. Still standing in line. Place is packed.

Him: Oh, the torture. At least Scott is entertaining company.

Me: He would be if he were with me.

Him: Don't tell me he's running behind.

Me: Nope. He's across the street with Ashley. She didn't want 2 eat here.

Him: You're fucking kidding. Right?

Me: Sure. Haha. I'm so hungry I'm ordering one of everything.

When he doesn't respond, I assume he's gone back to whatever it was he was doing before he texted. The guys in front of me are having a conversation about last week's hockey game, and I find myself eavesdropping.

"Did you catch that save Rivers made? Man, I don't know if

that guy is lucky or just that talented. He's on fire this season," dark-haired guy says.

"Yeah, and he's headed to the pros after graduation," cute blond responds. "He and Cage both signed on as free agents over the summer."

"Shit, just what Cage needs, another reason for women to drop their panties for him. I swear that guy is bathing in bunnies," dark-haired guy gives a sarcastic laugh, and I can't help smiling because it's painfully obvious he's jealous.

My back is turned to the door when I hear one of the guys smack the other and tell him to look over his shoulder. Out of curiosity, I automatically turn in time to see Brantley walking over to where I'm standing.

"Holy shit, it's Brantley Cage! Hey man, how the hell are you?" Blond guy sticks out his hand, and Brantley politely shakes it, but his eyes are focused solely on me.

"Hey, doll." He cups my cheek in his large hand, and I lean into him, seeking comfort in any form it's being offered. "You okay?" I step forward and fall into his arms. Suddenly, everything seems better. His hands move up and down my back as he whispers softly in my ear. "I'm so sorry, baby. It'll be okay. I'm here now."

"What are you doing here?" I murmur against his warm chest. I don't want to move, he smells so good, and it feels like heaven to be wrapped in the safety of his arms.

"What do you mean? My girl needed me, so I came running." He gives his shoulder a shrug as if it's no big deal. He truly has no idea how big a deal it is to me.

"You came running just so I wouldn't have to eat alone?" I

shake my head at his reasoning.

"Of course. I'll always come running for you." He nudges me with his elbow before running a hand through his hair. I look up, meeting his eyes, and see the sincerity within them. This right here. This is what a true friend looks like. I stretch out my hand and stroke the smooth skin of his cheek, not giving a thought to how it may appear to those around us.

"My very own Superman," I whisper, and he smiles at the superhero reference. "Thank you. This means so much to me."

"No problem, Dimples." The tip of his finger brushes down my nose and continues until it reaches the divot in my cheek. I love his affectionate nickname, and he usually saves it for special moments. Moments like this. His slings an arm around my shoulders and leads me to the counter to place our order. A lot of words are spoken before he hands the guy his credit card.

"Did you seriously order one of everything?" I ask as we take a seat at the nearest available table.

"Not everything, but I think it's safe to say we're going to need a lot of space for our food. You said you were hungry."

We make small talk for a short time while they prepare our food. In the meantime, I keep sipping on my lime Batido. It's amazing and creamy, and I'd seriously live on these if it weren't for the fact I'd be gaining twenty pounds. When they bring our food, it takes three people to carry it out. I burst out laughing after they walk away.

"Ask and you shall receive, my queen." He gives a mock bow and reaches for a plantain. When the flavors of garlic and cilantro meet my tongue I moan my appreciation. "Be careful over there. A guy can only take so many of those moans before his mind gets away from him."

"Ohmygod, you really need to stop talking about sex." I squirm uncomfortably in my seat, and it doesn't help his body is pressed so close to mine I can feel the heat from his skin burning straight through my jeans. "I swear, for someone who's vowed to keep our relationship platonic, you sure like pushing the boundaries of our little agreement." I smile coyly at him. "Did you know there's a link between the reaction a woman has to sex and good food?"

"Is that so? Do tell." His eyebrows dance with interest as he leans even closer.

"Um hmm. In fact, some people believe food is the ultimate aphrodisiac." When I'm finished talking I take a plantain between my fingers and slide it back and forth between my lips before biting into the creamy center. Now, he's the one squirming in his seat. In fact, he adjusts himself a couple of times after I repeat the move with a few of his fries.

"Shit, Cassie. You need to stop, or I'm gonna say fuck the rules and take you back to my bed," his deep voice growls in my ear, and when he speaks, his lips tickle my flesh. "I don't want to mess up our friendship with sex, so just eat without making it sound like a porno and everything will be okay. Sound good?" I think I would have been fine if he had stopped there, then his lips press against my neck, and he leaves a trail of hot kisses down my shoulder before shoving a fistful of fries in his mouth as if nothing ever happened.

"You're going to pay for that one day." I ruffle my hand through his hair and steal a fry from between his fingers.

"I don't mind being indebted to you," he mumbles under his

breath.

BRANTLEY

Her body stills next to mine, visibly affected by what I've just admitted. If someone were to ask why I made that statement, I'm not sure how I would answer. I like Cassie. I mean, she's great fun and the only thing she's ever asked for were a few hours spent teaching her something that comes naturally to me. She never expected my friendship, at least not the one developing between us. To be honest, I think what's happening has taken us both by surprise. When her text first came through tonight, I'd been heading out the door to join the guys over at Skeeps. My decision to ditch those plans and come here hadn't required any thought. I knew she was hurting, and the thought of her sitting here alone didn't sit well with me. Before I knew what I was doing, I found myself opening the door to the restaurant. I spotted her right away, her blond hair spilling down her back in loose curls. The look on her face when she saw me confirmed I'd made the right decision. She tried playing it off as if Scott's actions hadn't hurt her, but we've spent enough time talking for me to read between the lines. He'd hurt her, again. I can't bring myself to believe he's deliberately trying to crush her spirit, but I see it taking place. Many times I've wanted to tell him how badly he's hurting her, but I know Cassie wouldn't want that. She wants him to realize it on his own, and I'm trying to respect her wishes, but that doesn't mean I have to be happy with them.

"Did you get enough to eat?"

"Yeah." She sucks down the rest of her shake and belches. For such a tiny thing she achieves substantial volume. Out of habit, I bring up my hand and she meets me in a fist bump, then we both cut loose with laughter. Just like that, the sexual tension dissipates and we're back to being us, which is fine with me. I'm not sure I can handle any more temptation before I finally cave. The kiss we shared the other day is still imprinted on my lips, and I have a feeling the desire to kiss her again isn't going away any time soon.

Looking over the uneaten food, she pushes away the basket of plantains and rubs her flat belly. "I don't think I'll need to eat for a week."

We're clearing the table when Scott and Ashley appear outside the restaurant. Walking outside, I'm quick to pick up on Scott's surprise at finding me here, though he recovers before Cassie catches on. I throw up my hand in a wave and brace myself for an interrogation.

"Hey, man, what are you doing here? I figured by now you and Masterson would be surrounded by bunnies and throwing back shots." He takes a half step and we meet for that one-armed hug that men do. "Cass, you still up for that movie?"

"No. I think maybe... Wait, yes. Yes, I'm up for it." She shifts her gaze between us before finally landing on me. "What do you say,

B? Care to join me for two hours of guaranteed action-packed entertainment?"

Right now, the battle between my head and my dick is pretty fierce. The thought of sitting beside her in a darkened theater for that amount of time gives me all kinds of ideas. On one hand, it means more time with her, but our little incident at the table gives me pause, and I know more time is probably the last thing we need right now. I'm about to give a lame excuse as to why I should head back to my apartment, alone, when she tilts her head and flashes me her dimples. Just like that, I'm a goner.

"Please?"

Aw, hell. How can I say no to that? So I let out a hasty breath and utter the very words I've been trying to bite back.

"I'd love to."

The theater is packed when we enter, and a quick surveillance of the room tells me we'll never find four seats together. Cassie grabs hold of my forearm and balances on the balls of her feet to try and get a better look around. Her lips tip up in a brief smirk before changing into a frown and turning back to Scott.

"Bummer. Looks like we'll be better off splitting up." She hooks a thumb over her shoulder and gives my arm a tug. "We're heading this way." Scott simply shrugs as Ashley pulls him in the opposite direction to find the only seats left at the front of the theater. She watches them go before turning back to me. "God, I thought they'd never leave."

I chuckle, despite the knot forming in my stomach. Two

hours.

How the hell am I going to make it through two more hours without this girl getting to me?

The only empty seats are in the back row, and just my luck it's a row that contains only two seats. We settle in, and my leg begins to bounce nervously. I can't get the taste of her out of my mouth. A few kisses on her neck and I'm salivating like a fucking dog. I sneak a sideways glance, and she seems completely relaxed, as if she doesn't have a care in the world. Shit, maybe I've lost my touch. This is the same girl who rubbed herself all over me without knowing who I was. The same one who begged me to fuck her and I'd turned her down. Maybe my rules have finally killed any desire she once had. But if that were the case, why'd she allow me to tongue fuck her the other day? I'm sweating bullets, and she's cool as a cucumber. If I don't pull it together, I'm going to blow a nut in my seat.

Rules... Yeah, I just have to reacquaint myself with them.

No naked study sessions. Okay, that one doesn't help. It doesn't even apply here.

No sex. Right. Got it. I repeat those two words a few times in my head, trying to make them stick. Great, now all I can think about is sex. And not just any sex. Sex with her. Sex with the most amazing girl I've ever met.

God, I'm such an asshole.

"Do you want some popcorn or something?" All of a sudden my throat feels dry. "I need something to drink." I stand abruptly and wait for her response.

"No thanks, I'm good." She peers up at me with big doe eyes, and my traitorous dick immediately reacts. I nod in response,

176

because it's all I can fucking manage at this point, and then bolt for the door.

Once I'm in the lobby, I sink against the wall and look up at the ceiling. *Shit, what the fuck is wrong with me?* My best friend is less than a hundred feet away and all I can think about is banging his kid sister. If he had any idea what's going through my mind he'd have my balls in a vice.

I grab a soda and a bag of popcorn. I'm not hungry, but when the kid behind the counter offers it, I say yes without thinking. I carry my stash back to our seats and settle back in. The movie's already started, so her eyes are fixed on the scene. I stash my drink in the cup holder and instinctively hold the popcorn out for her. She palms a handful, never taking her eyes off the action taking place on the big screen.

We're forty-five minutes into the movie and James Bond has already slept with four women. So much for not thinking about sex. During these scenes, Cassie leans closer and rests her head on my shoulder. Every few minutes, a whimper slips through her parted lips, and I have to adjust my junk. The scene really appears to affect her, and when she reaches over and links her fingers with mine, I relax for the first time since arriving.

When the credits start rolling, she stretches her tiny body over the armrest and brings her soft lips to my cheek. "Thank you for staying with me tonight. You turned what would have been a shitty evening into one of the best nights I've had in a very long time."

I swallow hard, knowing if I were to move my head two inches our lips would meet again. Is it worth the risk? And what would it even mean? I'm not looking for another relationship.

But isn't that what a girl like Cassie deserves? She'd never agree to anything less. And why should she? Do I even deserve to have her lips on mine? Plenty of guys on campus would kill for the opportunity to hold her in their arms. To wake up next to her every morning. Or lose themselves inside her every fucking night. Why is she even wasting her time on a guy like me? If I cross that line I'll only end up breaking the very spirit I've been fighting so hard to protect.

"You're a really great friend, B," she whispers softly. I respond by lifting our joined hands and tenderly kissing the back of hers.

"You're a pretty great friend yourself," I tell her, and the word *friend* nearly chokes me on its way out.

This is good. This is what I wanted. In my room later that evening I try saying it out loud to see if it makes me feel any better.

Cassie Rivers is my friend. Nothing more.

I throw in that last bit for good measure. I find saying them out loud doesn't make me feel better. In fact, saying them out loud makes me doubt their truth even more.

The next morning I'm in the kitchen, leaning back in my chair with my fingers laced behind my head, attempting to listen as Rivers rambles on about his current dilemma. It's not that I don't care about his situation. Well, maybe I don't, but the point is I have other shit on my mind and his incessant droning makes it impossible for me to focus. I can't stop thinking about this shit with Cassie. Our relationship is confusing as hell. One minute, we'll be talking about last week's game, and then we're talking about sex toys and I'm kissing her neck. The fact we can shift from one subject to almost making out scares the hell out of me. If we keep this up, I'm not sure how much longer I'll be able to hold it together. A man can only take so much before he finally cracks.

"Shit, man, my mom's going to chew me a new asshole over this. Cassie's first performance is tomorrow afternoon, and I promised to be there. Now she knows I'm going to miss it because of this family event with Ashley. And let me tell you, she made it perfectly clear at the movies last night that she's pissed." He pulls at his hair while pacing anxiously back and forth. "What am I supposed to do? I mean, it's kind of a no-brainer, right? If I tell my mom I'm not going, she'll be pissed at me for a few days, tops. If I tell Ash I can't go to Ohio for her parents' anniversary party, she'll cut out sex for a week, maybe even longer. Fuck that, I'm not about to go down that road."

"Yeah, wouldn't want to risk going a whole week without getting your ego stroked," I reply, sarcasm dripping from every word. I've heard him complain about being cut off one too many times. Those stupid-ass games are just one of the reasons I've fought to avoid the pitfalls of a relationship. You make your heart vulnerable and someone's bound to get hurt.

"What would you know about going without? Your dick's seen more pussy than most guys' on campus," he angrily retorts.

I roll my eyes at the exaggeration and lean forward in my chair. I've spent four years on this campus, and one exaggerated rumor spread like wildfire. Now I'm known as a pussy magnet. He knows me better than anyone, yet somehow he still holds onto that gossip like it's the gospel truth. "Don't believe everything you hear."

"Dude, it's kind of hard when I can hear them screaming their appreciation in the middle of the night. Hello," he points to the hallway, "our rooms are less than twenty feet apart."

"Last year maybe," I reply hoarsely. "Face it, buddy, it's been months since you've had to endure that kind of torture." He narrows his eyes and ponders my words, only offering a shrug of his shoulder to indicate his acceptance of my statement. Given the fact that I've been spending so much time with his sister, and how I really don't want him bringing *that* up, I quickly change the subject. "So, what's it going to be?"

"I guess I don't have a choice. I'll have to call up Ash." He rises from his chair and starts down the hall, probably going to hide and grovel. All of a sudden, he stops, turns around, and gives me the widest grin I've ever seen on a human face. "YOU!" He points a finger at me as he slowly approaches. "I don't know why I didn't think of it before. It's perfect." He smacks his palm across his forehead and continues grinning.

"What's perfect? And wipe that grin off your face. You're starting to freak me out."

"Cassie adores you." He throws an arm around my shoulders and pulls me close. "Who better than my best buddy to come to my rescue? This is genius." He drops his arm and struts around, proud of himself for coming up with a solution to his self-made crisis.

"No way, not happening," I cross my arms over my chest and feign annoyance. Truth is, I'd be honored to go and support her. She never asked if I wanted to attend; she probably assumed I wouldn't be interested. Nothing could be further from the truth. I love listening to her play, but I've never seen her perform in front of an audience. All the times she's played for me have been when we were alone.

"Why not?" He crosses his arms.

Why not? I want to scream at him. How about because she's *your* sister, and she came to this school to be closer to you. Yet all you do is find ways to avoid spending time with her. Don't you realize how lucky you are to have her in your life? I want to scream all of this at him, but I know it won't make a difference.

"Because I have plans." It's a lie, but he doesn't need to know that.

"Come on, Cage. You know if the tables were turned, I'd be there for you."

I decide if I'm going to do this, I may as well benefit from it. "If I'm giving up a date with a hot chick, then what do I get in return?"

"My undying appreciation." He looks over and sees the firm set of my jaw then quickly adds, "And I'll get Ash to hook you up with one of her roommates."

I mull it over, my brain scanning over the list of Ashley's friends. Honestly, there's not a single one I'd agree to date, but I don't tell him that. "Deal, just make sure it's not that chick Marshall tapped last month. She gave him a nasty case of crabs." I laugh and remember how Marshal had looked ripping off his cup and digging at his junk.

"Cage, I think it goes without saying that my sister isn't one of your conquests. Got it? I don't want you touching her, or trying to kiss her, and I most certainly do *not* want you fucking her. Am I making myself clear?"

"What the hell? You make it sound as if I treat women like a piece of meat." A playful smile tugs at the corners of my mouth when I think about Cassie. It's a good thing he hadn't been there to see the look on my face when she licked salt off my body, or if he knew whose face I picture every morning when I rub one out. If he had a clue about any of those things, he wouldn't be asking for my help.

"Cage," he threatens in a low growl.

I throw my hands up and feign defeat. "I hear you. I promise to be a perfect gentleman. I'll attend her performance and even buy her flowers if that makes you feel better."

"That's all I'm asking, man. Thanks."

CASSIE

Today is Saturday, November 14. I know this not because I've bothered to look at a calendar in the last few days, though it does come up every time I open my phone. I know this because today is my recital. The day I've been preparing for, staying up late for, playing my heart out over for the last six months. Ever since the day I sat in that park and penned this very song I'm about to showcase. Is it my best work? Probably not. Would I choose to play it if I had something else in my bag of tricks? That's a difficult question. Am I proud of the way the arrangement turned out? You bet your ass I am. I have no doubt it's a great piece. I only wish I'd written it after meeting Brantley.

Six months ago I was in a different place. Mentally and physically. While I had been dating Justin back then, he'd never been able to stir up the kind of emotions I feel every time I'm around Brantley. I've grown to depend on him. It's hard not to when he loves coming to my rescue. A few nights ago, I playfully called him my Superman, but a part of me had been serious. There's something about knowing he's out there, watching out for me, and ready to stop locomotives at a moment's notice. Well, that kind of attention does something to your heart. Softens it just a little. Molds it into something better. Something stronger.

In twelve short weeks he's managed to turn my heart into a puddle of goo. I often wonder if we would've reached this level if I hadn't told him who I was that first morning? Probably not. Most likely I would have become just another girl he hooked up with and never contacted again. Twelve weeks ago I could have killed Scotty for ruining that opportunity. Today I realize it had worked in my favor after all. What we have feels special, and I want to tell him so, so badly. But I'm terrified of scaring him off. I know he cares for me. And I'm certain he's attracted to me. He's been pretty obvious in the way he touches me or holds my hand. A shiver courses through my body when I think of his lips on my mine.

I never asked him to come for me today. I didn't want him to feel obligated. I'd rather he be here because he wants to, not because he feels he has to. Sitting backstage by myself leaves me wishing I'd taken the chance and invited him. It would be nice to know *someone* I loved was out there cheering for me.

There's a party later tonight at one of the frat houses. I'd heard about it last week and invited B to join me but he'd declined. I don't think it was because he didn't want to be with me. I think it had more to do with the fact he isn't crazy about the fraternity hosting the party. Then, the other day after class Dan Harwood caught me off guard by inviting me to attend the party as his date. I like Dan, he's nice enough, but to call what we're doing tonight a date would be quite a stretch. I agreed to go with him only on the condition he keep his hands to himself.

I agreed to go, but now I don't want to be there without B.

"I think I'm going to be sick," I jump up and quickly make my way down the hall to the restroom, nearly knocking over a young girl in my haste. I've seen her before in the music department. Dana, I think that's her name. Thankfully, the room is empty when I push open the door. I pause to lock it just before leaning over the porcelain bowl. The room feels like it's spinning, and the yogurt and granola I had this morning threaten to come back up.

I remain in one position, afraid to move for fear I'll vomit or pass out. Sweat pools under my arms, and I begin doubting the claims made by my deodorant manufacturer. When the sweat trickles down my back, I look at the sparkling tile floor and seriously consider lying flat on my back. It looks cool and inviting.

I spent most of the day yesterday locked in a practice room at the music school working on my arrangement. During that time, I can't recall breaking for water or food. I know I drank water at some point, but outside of the yogurt this morning I haven't eaten a meal since Thursday evening with Brantley.

I'm still flattered he dropped everything he was doing so I wouldn't be alone. He knew I'd been looking forward to my evening with Scott, and when he'd heard I'd been let down he just showed up and made everything right again. I know it's probably unfair to always expect him to be in superhero mode, but I must admit he'd look pretty hot in a pair of Superman's tights.

The wave of nausea passes so I close the lid on the toilet and take a seat. This isn't the first time I've played in front of an audience, but tonight I'm nervous as hell. I keep going over the opening chords in my head. I've played them so many times I know them backwards and forwards. There's no reason for me to be bent over this toilet, but for some reason my hands won't stop shaking.

I replay the arrangement over in my head, moving my fingers as if a grand piano were here in this tiny stall. Everything feels right. Everything is in sequence. I've got this. I know I do.

I can do this.

Then I think about Brantley, and I want to see him and tell him how I feel about him, then my insides tumble once again. Suddenly, I feel claustrophobic and my fingers become useless appendages as they struggle to open the sliding lock trapping me the stall. Then I begin to panic. If I can't make my fingers work to open a friggin' door, how on earth will I play a four-minute arrangement? It takes a few moments to finally pry it open, and by the time I'm finally out in the hall, I'm bent in half and fighting for a full breath of air. Eventually, my breathing evens out and when I stand, I walk straight into the arms of my hero.

BRANTLEY

I take a seat in a row toward the middle of the auditorium. Shifting the bouquet of roses to the crook of my arm. I peruse the program handed to me upon entering. I note that Cassie's piece isn't until the middle of the recital so I get an idea to go backstage and wish her luck. Somehow I managed to avoid telling her I'd be here tonight. The time we spent together Thursday night had been amazing, in so many ways. I love spending time with her and being her friend. But there's a part of me deep down that wonders what more with her would look like. I'm fairly certain it would supersede all my expectations, but having something that good would only mean I have something wonderful to lose. I know I don't want to go through that kind of pain again. It's not worth it. Besides, I would be too afraid of messing up what we have. What we're doing now seems to work. We hang out, we flirt, we support one another. It's as if I have everything I've ever wanted with a woman; the only thing missing is sex. And dammit, I *want* to have sex with her. I think about it all the time, but I have to be strong for both of us. I can see in her eyes that she wants me too, though I don't think she'll ever admit it.

The door to the performance area is locked, but I luck out when one of the girls working backstage recognizes me and lets me through. I search the rooms for any sign of Cassie, but I come up empty. The same girl who let me in finds me wandering aimlessly and offers to help.

"Are you looking for someone?" she asks, eyeing the large bouquet of pink roses.

"Um, yeah." I clear my throat and smile an awkward smile. "Cassie Rivers."

"I think I just saw her down by the women's bathroom. She looked pretty nervous. I'm sure those roses will cheer her up."

"Thanks, uh, Dana?" I take a stab at her name and hope I get it right.

"Yeah, that's right. You're welcome, Brantley." She giggles softly before turning on her heel and continuing down the darkened hall.

I find her bent over outside the women's bathroom and make my way down the hall as fast as I can. She stands, and without looking, walks straight into my arms. When she takes a step back, her face is pale, and I notice her hands are shaking.

"B? What on earth are you doing here?" She checks over her shoulder as if expecting to find someone else I would be looking for.

"I came for you, baby. You know, for a smart girl you sure are dense sometimes." I bend to place a kiss on her forehead and find it's damp. "Hey, are you alright? You're not going to pass out or anything like that?" I take her hand and pull her back inside the bathroom. "Sit." I order, motioning to the covered garbage can. I wet a few paper towels and press them to her forehead.

"What are you doing?" she calmly questions.

"You're clammy, and you looked like you were going to faint. Have you had any water today?"

"Umm, I honestly don't remember." Her blue eyes go round with panic. "Holy shit, B. I don't know if I can do this. I'm shaking like a leaf."

"We need to get you a bottle of water. You're probably dehydrated. You've got a crowd to wow, and I'm not about to let you fall apart on my watch." With that said I bend and scoop her up in my arms. She's light as a feather, and her thin arms lock around my neck as I carry her down the hall, following her directions to a room where she'll be more comfortable. As we step through the door I look around and see a group of anxious faces. These must be the other musicians performing tonight. Two guys stand and make room for me to place her on the sofa. I ask one of them to run and grab me a bottle of water and within a minute he returns with not one but two. I thank him and turn back to her. I crouch beside her and lift the bottle to her lips.

"I can drink a bottle of water. I don't need you to do it for me." She gently chastises, taking the bottle from my grasp. After downing half of it, she comes up for air. "The flowers are gorgeous, thank you. So, tell me, why are you really here? Did Scotty ask you to come? And please don't lie to me."

I sigh, knowing she'll see right through me if I try to tell anything but the honest truth. "Yes, he asked me yesterday, but I would've come anyway."

"Why?" she whispers.

"I told you, Cassie. I'll always be there for you. Besides, I love hearing you play. Now, finish your water and go out there and knock these people on their uptight asses."

"I'll do my best." She cracks a smile, and I thread our fingers together. They fit perfectly. She stares at our joined hands, while I stare at her. She's breathtakingly beautiful. "You better get going and find a seat, the recital's about to start." I only make it five feet before her voice pulls me back. "Hey, Superman, thanks for saving me again."

I lean down and kiss the tip of her pert nose. "It's my pleasure, Dimples."

The smile she offers is one I'll store in my memory for years to come, maybe forever, because as soon as it leaves her lips it comes straight for me and pierces my tattered heart. At this moment I have no doubt I'm falling for this girl, and that knowledge paralyzes me with fear.

I bypass the seats and take up residence near one of the exits. I watch in awe as she walks out and takes her place at the piano. The way her fingers move over the keys and knowing how committed she is to this song, tt hits me. Hard. If it weren't for the wall holding me up, I'd surely have fallen to my knees, just as I feel myself falling for her.

When her piece is over and the crowd comes alive with applause, I take that opportunity to sneak out and head home. I was going to surprise her by taking her out to dinner, but I don't think I'm able to face her right now. Everything feels like it's coming at me so fast, and I spend most of the night locked in my room, going over every day we've spent together. Every word we've ever spoken. I analyze it all. I come to the realization I've felt this way about her from the start. She'd wanted me then, and I'd been the one to throw those stupid rules in her face.

Now, I'm the one about to break them all.

I considered not coming to this party. They all end the same, and I usually end up back at my apartment drunk and asking myself why the hell I'd gone in the first place. Cassie asked me last week if I was planning on going, and I'd told her no, but I changed my mind after hearing she agreed to go as Dan Harwood's date. Dan Fucking Harwood. For the life of me I can't understand why she even bothered saying yes. Lately, he's been showing up wherever she is, and it's pissing me off. He tries talking to her before class, then waits by her chair afterwards to walk her out. She's always polite, but in the end she walks out with me, and I always make a point of throwing my arm around her shoulder as I walk her to her dorm. I've begun to wonder if maybe she does like him and I've just been too blind to notice.

When I enter the frat house the first person who latches onto me is Natasha. There was a time when I would have welcomed her attention. But after that night outside the dorms, Cassie's the only girl I've had on my mind.

I have every intention of going further inside the house with hopes of finding her, but I don't make it far before someone stops me to talk about last week's game-winning play. Before I know it, fifteen more minutes have passed, and I excuse myself from that conversation only to find myself locked in another not more than a minute later. This is precisely why I avoid these parties. I love that people enjoy watching me play, but secretly despise all the attention once I'm off the ice. Right now, I'd like nothing more than to be home, watching SOA with Cassie. If we were there, we'd be lying on my bed. She'd be on her stomach with her head at the foot of the bed, while I would lean against the headboard and give her a foot massage. She would be eating popcorn, going on and on about the guy who plays Jax. While I'd fantasize about riding a Harley down the California coastline with the wind at my back and her arms wrapped around my waist.

I find myself thinking about the way she smells. I think about how hot it would be to see her hand holding my cock. Or how good it would feel to bury myself inside her. I know it's wrong, and against everything I swore to uphold, but I think about her all the fucking time, and it's confusing the hell out of me.

We move deeper into the house, and I finally manage to lose Natasha to a group gathered around the keg. Music thumps loudly from the next room, and I hear guys chanting *more* and *take it off*. Naturally, I'm intrigued, so I push my way through the crowd, blocking the doorway to the conference room. A group of guys have gathered around a large table that's been turned into a makeshift bar for the party. Beyoncé blasts through the speakers and three girls are using the table for their own version of Coyote Ugly. They're dancing seductively, every move cheered on by their personal cheering section. I push my way through to get a better view, and what I see stops me dead in my tracks.

Cassie is up there, swaying her hips and touching herself in a seductive manner. She looks sexy as hell, and perhaps a bit drunk. Her arms rest behind her head, holding her hair away from her neck, and as she dances, her eyes are closed. It's clear half the room is lusting over her. Raw sensuality and confidence oozes from every pore with each sway of her hips. She rocks forward, spinning on her heel, then stumbles when one of the guys grabs her by the ankle. I turn and find Dan standing next to me. His eyes are glued to Cassie's chest and his mouth hangs open, making him look like a perv.

My anger quickly builds, and I tear into his ass. "Dude, what the fuck are you doing? She shouldn't be up there. These guys will be all over her in a second. I'm putting an end to it."

"Why the hell would you do that? I'm horny as fuck and she's just the girl to take care of me." His words come out slurred, and any idiot can see the guy is clearly wasted, but that's no excuse for what he said. There's no way in hell this guy, or anyone else for that matter, will get the chance to be with her. My fist connects with his nose, and he hits the ground like a sack of potatoes.

Stepping over him, I plow forward, shoving back a few bodies as I go. A few guys start to mouth off, but when they see who I am, they back the fuck up. No one bothers paying attention to their buddy on the floor. The guys on the football team are pretty big, but everyone knows a hockey player will never back down from a fight, even if he is outnumbered. Several guys take a step back and let me through. Without a word, I reach up, scoop her off the table, and cradle her my arms.

"Hey, B. You came to my rescue," she snuggles against the crook of my neck as I carry her up the stairs to John's room. Thankfully, the room is empty. I reach one arm behind me and lock the door so no one will barge in on us. "I love being in your arms. I feel safe when I'm with you," she whispers in my ear.

"You are safe. I won't let anyone hurt you. Ever," I reply immediately. Without a doubt, I know I would do anything to protect her.

"See," she places her lips on my neck and the heat from her kiss sears my skin. "I knew you liked me." She pinches her thumb and forefinger together before releasing them to allow a fraction of space between the parted digits. "Maybe just a teeny tiny bit."

I shake my head but don't verbally deny it. "Just how much have you had to drink tonight?" I lean back and get a good look at her eyes. Now that I'm up close I can see her eyes are crystal clear, not glassy at all.

It's only when I'm sure she's okay that I release her legs and set her back down. Looking her over, I take in the vision before me. She's wearing a pair of skinny jeans with a black camisole and cropped jean jacket. I look at her feet and find her signature Chucks, only tonight they're deep purple. The left side of her mouth quirks into a smile, showing off the dimple in her left cheek.

"One beer and a shot. I'm not drunk, B. We've both been dancing around this subject for weeks. I'm just finally brave enough to tell you how I feel." Her tongue peeks out and glides slowly over her bottom lip. My eyes track the movement hungrily as her fingers reach forward and delicately trace the hard planes of my chest. "Thank you for rescuing me from those guys down there."

"Yeah, well, someone had to. Besides, your brother would have killed me if I hadn't stepped in. There's no telling what those assholes might have done if you'd stayed up there much longer."

She takes another step, and I put my hands behind my back to keep myself from pulling her against me. But I want to.

"Uh huh," she speaks softly, licking her lips once more as she moves closer, until there's no more space between us. Her hand slides up my body until her fingers thread through my hair. "I'm not buying it. You didn't pull me off that table for Scotty's sake. You did it for your own benefit, and you know it."

My breathing comes to a halt, and I know I should tell her to stop, but it feels too damn good. I've missed having a woman touch me this way. The way she looks at me with those big, blue eyes that scream *take me*. And believe me, I want to so fucking badly.

"Cassie," I hiss as she caresses me with the palm of her hand. I'm already hard. Christ, I've been hard since I saw her on that table.

She covers my mouth with her fingers and stands on her tiptoes. "Shhhh. Don't talk. Just shut up and kiss me."

My hands settle on the curve of her hips, and my thumbs toy with the hem of her shirt. The pad of my thumb makes contact with her skin, and a low hum falls from her lips. I carry her over to the futon in the corner of the room. Her hands lock around my neck as our mouths come together, and when they meet, it's as if we've never been apart. She's so familiar. The slant of her mouth. The curve of her tongue.

I don't want to rush this. It may be a one-time opportunity, but I'm taking it. I've suppressed my feelings far too long and it's killing me inside. For three solid months my dick has been painfully hard for this girl. All I've thought about was what it would feel like to call her mine, and just for tonight I'm going with it. Consequences be damned. She feels too good to let go of.

Her soft moans tell me she wants more and she slides lower on the futon, allowing me to fill the space between her parted legs. Even though we're separated by denim, I can feel the heat between her legs as she grinds herself over my erection. I'm lost to the sensation, having denied myself pleasure for far too long. I know if she keeps this up, I won't last long.

Her arms press into my shoulders, drawing me closer, as her lips graze the space below my ear. I feel soft, sensual kisses on my neck, and my fingers slide under her shirt to brush over her breasts. Using the tip of my thumb, I trace over her pebbled nipple as she whispers in my ear.

"I want you, Brantley. I want your hands on me. Your mouth kissing me. Everywhere. I want you whispering dirty things in my ear. But mostly, I need to feel you inside me. I've wanted that for so long. Don't make me beg, 'cause you know I will."

I don't hesitate in voicing my reply. "You won't have to. I want you too, but not here. Not like this."

Her eyes close as she let's out a pained sigh. "Okay. You're right. Maybe we should wait."

"What? Hell no. I mean let's get out of here. We can go back to my place. Your brother's still out of town, and we can have the whole night to ourselves."

"The whole night, huh?" She smiles sheepishly, and my dick presses painfully against my button-fly jeans. "That sounds promising."

"Uh huh, and I plan on taking advantage of every last minute." My lips leave a trail of kisses, starting at her shoulder and moving slowly until finally coming to rest on her waiting mouth. "I just need to say one thing," I murmur between kisses. "After this weekend, we go back to the way we were. I can't pull off anything more with your brother around. I don't know if I'm strong enough to deal with that. Can you handle those terms?"

She places a gentle kiss on my lips. "I don't care about your terms, B. I'll take you any way I can get you."

I take control of the kiss, driving my tongue in deep, punishing strokes that leave her with a small taste of what's to come. "If I were you, I wouldn't plan on getting any sleep tonight."

CASSIE

The raspy sound of his voice, combined with what he's saying, leaves me breathless. Our friendship has meant so much these past few months, but I've dreamed of having him inside me since that first morning. Spending time together has only added fuel to the ever-present spark that's been smoldering between us. When he asks if I can handle being nothing more than a hookup, I immediately say yes. I don't allow myself time to second-guess my decision. I only want to feel his body on mine. Deep down I know the aftermath might destroy me, but right now I'll follow him anywhere. Consequences be damned.

His hand finds mine and he leads me down the stairs, somehow managing to avoid being stopped by the crowd as we make our way out the door and down the walk to where his truck is parked. I hear the click of the lock, and then he's behind me, one hand on the door handle, the other on my hip. My breath hitches when he leans forward to whisper in my ear.

"Are you sure about this?" I feel his lips tickle over my skin and shiver in anticipation. He smells heavenly, a heady mixture of mint and the cologne he always wears. His body presses tight against mine, and I feel the hard lines of his chiseled physique. Years of training, skating nearly every day of his life, have left him lean and firm in all the right places. I arch my body until my ass brushes over his arousal, and he draws in a sharp breath. Overcome with lust, I'm able to nod, but just barely, before reaching behind me to run a hand over the front of his jeans.

With great effort, we break apart and I climb into the cab of his truck. We say nothing on the way over to his apartment, but we aren't able to keep our hands to ourselves. The slow stroke of his finger up my thigh feels so good. It speaks of slow seduction, infinite possibilities, and the promise of more. And I want a whole lot more. More kissing. More touching. More of everything. My heart thuds wildly in my chest, the dampness between my legs increasing as his finger reaches the apex of my thighs.

"Is it just me, or does this drive seem to be taking way too long?" My voice shakes as I lay my head back in the seat, while he makes slow circles over the seam of my jeans. I tilt my hips to meet his hand, and he lets out a low laugh.

"Patience, sweetheart, we're nearly there." His demeanor is far too calm compared to mine. I feel like I'm on edge and he's acting like we're going out for ice cream. I want to be angry with his easy-going attitude, but at the moment, I'm too preoccupied by what his hand is busy doing between my legs.

We finally pull in the drive, and when he reaches for the door, I grab his arm. "Wait! Are you one hundred percent certain no one else is home?"

He lowers his head and squints through the windshield to

look up at the house. "Hmmm, I'm ninety-six percent sure." I narrow my eyes in frustration. "Tell you what, you stay here for a minute while I go check. If we're not alone, I can take you back to the dorm and we can finish this another time." He may appear calm on the outside, but the strain in his voice tells me that postponing this for another time is not the way he wants this night to end. That knowledge makes me feel better, and I nod for him to go inside. "I'll be right back. I promise." He leaves me with a light kiss before dashing inside.

No more than a minute passes before he comes out smiling like he's just won the lottery. Seeing his excitement makes my stomach flip-flop, and I have to remind myself this is just sex, nothing more. He's not my boyfriend, nor will he ever be. We're simply two people, who've agreed to give in to the lust we've been denying for so long. Lust that's been burning deep within the two of us for twelve long weeks.

I follow him inside, eyes nervously scanning the room despite the fact he told me we have the house to ourselves. Taking me by the hand, he leads me through the house and pauses in front of the kitchen.

With his free hand he grips the back of his neck and glances down at me. "Can I get you anything? Something to drink, or maybe you're hungry?"

I draw my bottom lip between my teeth and rock forward on my tiptoes. "The only thing I'm hungry for is you."

"Fuck, that sounded hot," he growls, lowering his head to kiss me. With one hand on my waist he pulls me flush with his body and runs his fingers slowly up my back. I can feel his arousal pressing against my belly, and I shiver, knowing exactly what's waiting for me behind those jeans.

Although I love what he's doing, I'm fearful of getting caught. "Maybe we should move this to the bedroom. I'd hate for someone to walk in on us."

"I like the way you think." He smiles seductively as he leans in to capture my mouth once more. The slant of his lips and the way his hands settle on my ass leave me moaning with pleasure. Mouths still locked, he lifts me in his arms and my legs wrap around his waist. We walk backwards until we reach the stairs, our tongues swaying in time with each step before we break apart breathlessly. "I can't wait to have you in my bed again."

My lips curl into a smile before coming to rest on his throat. Tracing with my tongue in slow strokes, I follow the bob of his Adam's apple as he swallows. "Then stop waiting and take me there before I beg you to have your way with me right here."

Within seconds, we're in his room behind a locked door. My heart is pounding, and I know his is too, because I place my hand on his chest and feel the strong beat beneath my palm.

"You feel that? That's all you, sweetheart. Being this close to you drives me crazy." His lips crash against mine as we fall onto the massive bed. This isn't my first time here, but it is the first time I've laid in this same spot with the intention of taking our relationship to the next level. I let my head fall back on the pillow, lost in the sensation as his tongue mingles with mine. Moments ago we were anxious to get here, but lying beneath him I feel no sense of urgency in his movements.

"You're wearing too many clothes," I tug at the hem of his shirt. He rewards me by pulling it over his head and tossing it carelessly on the floor. I drink in the sight of him, shirtless and aroused because of me. Holding his breath, his muscles contract as my seeking fingertips tickle over the taut muscles that define his stomach.

I am lying on my back beside him when he braces one arm on the bed and hovers above me, kissing my jaw as he makes his way down my neck. Taking his time as if savoring every kiss and nibble of my flesh. He straddles my waist while his hands slip under my tank to slide it up and over my shoulders. His eyes rake over me, taking in my black bra with tiny pink bows. It's sexy with just a touch of sweetness. Kind of like me.

"I like this," he says huskily, fingering one of the satin bows. The tip of one finger circles my nipple through the soft material as his thumb finds its way inside. I arch my back, craving more of his touch. I've longed for this. Dreamed of it night after night. But dreams couldn't prepare me for the way it feels to be at the mercy of his gentle hand.

His mouth covers my breast, soaking the lace with his tongue, while his hand slides down my body and slips beneath my jeans. His fingers make a sweeping pass, teasing as they go, moving up the seam then down to circle my entrance, separated only by a scrap of now damp material.

My hips flex, seeking more, and he tsks my greediness. "All in due time, baby. I told you, we have all night. And I intend to take my time with you." Nimble fingers peel my panties aside, and my body clamps around them as they press deep inside. "God, you're so wet."

His fingers move faster, hindered by the tight confines of my jeans, but as he moves, his palm grinds against my pubic bone, applying pressure in all the right places. I rock against him, chasing my orgasm, feeling it build, gaining momentum. At the last minute, his fingers slide out, spreading wetness up my center as he rubs my clit in fast circles. My eyelids flutter and I melt. Becoming one with the mattress as I write beneath him. My thighs clench together, trapping his hand as the orgasm rocks my body.

"Damn, that was beautiful," he whispers before claiming my parted lips. In my weakened state, my arms circle his neck to draw him close, craving the heat of his body against mine.

"I need you inside me," the words fall out. Sounding desperate and needy. I need to feel him. *All* of him. "Please." My hands fumble, unfastening three buttons before he covers my hands to finish the task.

"Is this what you want?" he fists his cock in his hand, giving it a few strokes as I nod, unable to tear my eyes away. His body is perfect, in every sense of the word. Long, muscular legs. Strong arms, one covered in tattoos down to his wrist. Wide shoulders narrow to a lean waist, with defined abdominal muscles and a deep V that points straight to his impressive manhood. "Lie back."

I follow his command, heart hammering in my chest. It's been months since I've been intimate with a man, and I want him more than I've ever wanted anyone. Now that I've sampled what his hands can do, I want it all.

Correction, I *need* it all.

With a deft hand, he unfastens my bra, letting it fall down my shoulders before peeling it from my body. Every nerve is on high alert, and I shiver when his fingers trail down my side. He sucks my nipple between his teeth, biting down then soothing the sting with a sweeping pass of his tongue. He moves to the other and gives it the same attention. Kissing his way down my stomach, he pauses to tug at the denim with his teeth. I suddenly feel as if the material is smothering me. Reaching between us, I tear at the button and zipper in my haste to remove my jeans.

I'm completely naked, vulnerable and laid out before him, but I don't feel the slightest bit shy. The look in his eyes tells me he appreciates what he sees. He settles between my legs, and my head falls back against the pillows while his tongue takes me to places I've never known existed. Justin wasn't a big fan of oral sex, at least not in the role as the giver. Oh, he'd certainly appreciated every blowjob I'd given him, but when it came time to return the favor, he acted as if it were a torturous act. For the longest time, I thought something might be wrong with me. Maybe I'd been plagued with some funky-tasting vagina, or something awful and embarrassing like that. But all that evaporates with the first swipe of Brantley's tongue when he looks up at me with lust in his amber eyes and says I taste sweeter than anything he's ever known. He may be exaggerating, but it only proves my ex had been a selfish asshole.

"Yes. Yes. Oh, god, yes," I cry out as his tongue dips and swipes over the needy little bud. It's clear he's no stranger in the art of pleasuring a woman. The way his tongue brushes over my clit in slow, expert strokes makes me feel as if he's an artist and I'm his greatest masterpiece. Watching him stare up at me from between my legs sends me over the edge.

"I swear I could spend the rest of my life watching you come."

"Careful, or I just may take you up on that offer." When he

kisses me, I tentatively swipe my tongue over his lips, tasting my arousal when I pull it back in. When he moans, it's sexy as hell. Knowing I'm the one responsible for that sound emboldens me to keep going.

My fingers wrap around his thick cock. In slow strokes, I tease my thumb over the crown, spreading his arousal as I trace my way down the length of his shaft. His breath quickens, and I rise to my knees, keeping one hand around him while pushing him back on the bed with the other. His eyes flicker with excitement when I lean forward.

"Cassie, you don't have to do—" he whispers weakly, his words trailing off as I lower my mouth, swirling my tongue as I grip the base of him in my hand. "God, that feels so good. Too good."

I make a few passes with my tongue before he reaches down and pulls me back to his mouth. "I won't be able to last if you keep that up." Flipping me on my back, he stretches a hand to the bedside table and brings back a strip of condoms. Smiling down at me before tearing one off and tossing the remaining packets aside.

"Hurry, I need to feel you," I shamelessly beg, and he obliges by sliding inside, giving me everything I ask for and then some. Inch by glorious inch he fills me until our bodies meet as one. He feels so good, but he's huge, and for a few seconds, it's uncomfortable.

"Are you okay? I'm not hurting you, am I?" he asks tenderly.

"You're a lot for a girl to handle," I reply breathlessly. "Just give me a minute to get used to you." I turn my head away, breathing through my discomfort, but he turns my face back to him and captures my lips in a wet kiss.

"Sweetheart, look at me," he gently commands between kisses. "Focus on me, nothing else. Just look into my eyes and I promise it'll feel good. Better than good." His tongue glides along the swell of my bottom lip, and I meet him with a flick of my own tongue. We begin rocking our hips, slowly at first, then picking up the pace as we learn each other's rhythm.

"Oh. Oh yes. God, that feels so good. So amazing." My eyes flutter closed and I cry out as the orgasm builds with an intensity that's sure to break me apart. I feel him everywhere. My mouth, my neck, deep inside me. He leaves no part of me untouched. Being with him is everything I thought it would be and more, and this is only the first time. He's promised me an entire night of pleasure

It all feels good. Better than good. Just as he promised. His mouth is on mine, one hand in my hair while the other holds my wrists above my head as he rocks into my awaiting body. He draws back again, and I raise my hips to meet him on the downward thrust. His body slams into me, striking the furthest recesses of my body. Again and again, yet I can't seem to get enough. Hard thrusts pin me down against the mattress. He's taking charge, and I'm his captive. But I don't want to be set free. I would gladly remain here forever if he'd only promise this for all of eternity. Crying out in ecstasy, I ride the final wave of pleasure as he gives in to his own release.

BRANTLEY

I'm in big trouble.

That's the thought running through my head right now. Second only to *that felt way better than I'd hoped it would.*

Sound strange? Well, it should. I guess part of me had been wishing we would get it out of our system and pretend like it never happened. Now she's beside me, sleeping in my arms, and all I can think about is waking her up and taking my lips on a journey across her hot as hell body before sinking deep inside her again.

I *love* sex. In fact, I challenge you to find a twenty-one year old guy who doesn't share that sentiment. I lost my virginity at the ripe old age of fifteen and never once looked back with remorse. I've met a lot of nice girls, and some who were merely looking for a good time. For the most part I'm always up for it, and I know without a doubt I've spent my fair share of time trying to hook up, though that's no longer where my head is.

I remember walking on campus for the first time, full of confidence and certain I wasn't going to be one of those losers who fell in love freshmen year. A month later I met Vanessa, and despite being surrounded by thousands of beautiful girls, hers was the only face I saw. On the outside, Vanessa had been a beautiful girl. But appearances can be deceiving, especially to a young punk who's just moved a thousand miles away from home and finally getting it on the regular. After three months of dating, I really thought she was the one.

Cassie stirs, her muscles twitching as she yawns and stretches beside me. She twists around to face me, and when I lean forward to give her a kiss her hand immediately covers her mouth.

"Morning breath," she whispers from behind her hand.

"Don't care," I push her hand away, "I still want to kiss you."

Her lips are soft, her mouth warm as she welcomes my tongue inside to mingle with hers. Concern over hygiene is quickly forgotten as the kiss intensifies and she rolls on top of me, her legs opening wide as she straddles my thighs. Hovering above me, her pert nipples tease against my skin as she reaches between us to roll a condom down my length. My fingers dig into her hips as I tease her clit with the tip of my cock.

"Umm, that feels nice," she purrs against my neck. Her hips roll and her eyes flutter closed when I fill her in one powerful thrust. I raise my knees and she leans back, using them for leverage as she rotates her hips in slow, teasing circles.

"That's it, ride me, baby." Her hands brace against my chest as she rocks her slick pussy over my shaft. "Fuck, I love your tight little pussy." I rise to meet her, holding her body against me until we're face-to-face. My lips lock over the soft flesh of her neck and suck, leaving behind a faint bruise when I pull away. Grabbing hold of her ass, I drive deep with every thrust until the sound of our bodies slapping together is the only sound filling the room.

"Holy shit, you're so deep this way. God, it feels good. So, so good."

I grunt in agreement, unable to speak as I savor the connection we're sharing. I don't want to think about practice. Or classes. Or my parents' marriage. Hell, I don't care about food, water, or any of the other essentials we may need. I just want to stay here in this moment. I don't want to lose this feeling. Everything about her just feels so fucking perfect. We kiss with an intensity I haven't shared with anyone else. Our lips move in perfect unison, like we've been doing this forever, and it feels too good to stop. So I don't. Instead of breaking free, I devour her, claiming her mouth as my own as I grasp her hips and pound into her, over and over until we finally break for air and my name falls on a whisper from her trembling lips.

"Good morning." She gives me a lazy smile as I pull out and dispose of the condom.

"It is now," I growl, kissing the tip of her nose before heading to the bathroom. "Are you hungry?" I call out as I finish brushing my teeth.

"Starving. We should go back to that diner and get more French toast."

I walk back into the room to find her still in bed under the covers, and I get an idea. Smiling, I crawl my way up her body and snatch the blanket away before she has a chance to react. My fingers find the ticklish spots behind her knees and soon she's thrashing beneath me.

"No, no, no, please stop," she begs breathlessly. "Seriously, if you don't stop, I'll pee in your bed." I pull my hands back and take a moment to appreciate the vision lying beneath me. Her blond hair is fanned out around her face, and these insanely blue eyes stare back at me. I look at them and swear they can see right through me. She's naked, and her smooth skin is like a magnet for my mouth and hands. If we hadn't just had sex, or the fact my stomach won't stop growling, I'd bury my face between her legs and leave her with one final memory before we go back to the way we were before.

Damn, do I really want to give all of this up?

"I'll take you for French toast on one condition," I grin up at her mischievously and her brow lifts in question. "You share your sausage with me."

"Get your own sausage." She swats a hand at my head, but I'm too fast and duck away before she makes contact.

"Oh, come on. You don't even eat it, it just sits there all lonely and cold on your plate." I bend and retrieve her jeans before tossing them at her.

"Fine, you can have my sausage, but I'm getting extra whipped cream."

"You can have all the cream you want, any time, baby." I cup my hand over my cock, intending it to be a joke, but cringe as soon as the words leave my mouth and I see the pained look on her face. It's bad enough I gave in and broke every one of Scott's rules more than a few times; now I'm making crass remarks as if she's just another bunny passing through my bed. The fact I even allowed myself to speak to her that way reminds me I need to keep my feelings in check. My heart may be falling for her, but that doesn't mean I won't fight like hell to prevent it from happening. "You about ready?" My demeanor visibly shifts as I turn and grab my keys from the dresser. Before stepping into the hall, I crack the door and check to be sure no one is around to see us sneaking out together.

She doesn't say much on the way to breakfast, and what started out as a great morning seems to keep going downhill once we're seated. We manage to make small talk while eating, but it's clear something has shifted between us. This is exactly what I feared would happen. I'm not looking for a relationship. And I definitely don't know how to act around her now that we've had sex. When she's in my bed, or in my arms, that's when I'm at ease. That's where I don't question my actions. I know how to please a woman. But Vanessa had made it clear I had no fucking clue how to treat a woman. That may have been four years ago, but her words still ring in my head as if they've just been spoken.

When I finally drop her off in front of South Quad, I'm almost relieved to see her go. Maybe this is how it should be. I mean, I was afraid that things would get weird between us after sex, but it was bound to happen. We had a really good thing going, but we'd gotten greedy thinking we could go from one to the other without losing something along the way.

She reaches for the door handle and, being the stubborn ass I am, I'm about to let her walk away. Her parting glance is a mixture of confusion and disappointment. It messes with my already conflicted brain, and I know I can't let things end this way. Truth is, I don't want to give her up. I want it all. The friendship. The laughter. The sex. I know there may be something more buried beneath the surface, but I'm not ready to acknowledge that fact just yet.

I grab hold of her arm and stop her before the door fully opens. "Cassie, please wait. I'm sorry things got weird between us. I was hoping we could avoid all that shit and just fall back into you and me. You know, the way we were before."

She turns in her seat and closes her eyes before speaking in a soft voice. "I thought I could handle it. The sex, I mean. You gave me ample opportunity to walk away. But I just wanted to be with you so badly. It's all I've wanted since the morning we met. So I agreed because I knew if I said I couldn't handle it, you'd never ask me again. I wasn't ready to pass that up. Maybe if we would have stopped after last night, I might have been okay, but then this morning happened, and I don't know, I felt something between us and it scared me. I'm already thinking about the next time, only there isn't going to be a next time." I open my mouth to speak, but she lifts her hand to silence me. "It's okay, B. I knew the rules going in, but I'm tired of rules where you're concerned. I'm tired of pretending I don't want you. I enjoy being with you, and not just physically. You make me laugh, and you make me feel safe. I don't want to lose what we have, but at the same time I think I need time to think this through. Clearly, I don't always make the best decisions where you're concerned."

Hearing her words hurt more than I was expecting. While I'm not looking for a relationship, I'm not ready to lose her either. The thought of not hearing her voice at night before I fall asleep makes my balls feel like they're stuck between two hockey sticks. As sick as it is, I've come to depend on her far more than I ever realized. Maybe even more than she depends on me. I want to tell her we can have it all. But I'm not sure I can give her what she wants. What she deserves from me.

I reach over and twine our fingers like I always do, and when she doesn't pull away, I have a glimmer of hope. "When you say time, how long are we talking? A day or two?" I probably sound pathetic, but right now, I don't care.

"Honestly, I'm not sure. Being with you makes me so happy, but it also makes me weak. I'm blinded by all of these feelings stirring inside me. I want a world with you that has no rules. I want to be able to kiss you whenever I feel like it and not worry about who may catch us. And to be honest, it scares the hell out of me that I'm feeling this way so soon, but you have that effect on me. You look at me and it's like I'm consumed in flames. The extinguisher is within my grasp, but I'm too scared to use it, because if I do, then all the good I'm feeling will disappear."

She stifles a sob and it kills me to see her hurting. My arms immediately reach out and pull her close, our lips pressing together for a fleeting kiss. "Oh, baby, I don't want to lose the good either. Fuck. This is exactly what I was afraid of. What can I do? Tell me anything, and I'll do it."

"I'm afraid I may be falling for you," her voice is barely a whisper, and my heart caves inside my chest, because she's asking for something I can't give. My whole heart. How can I give her my heart when it's already been shattered and all that's left are fragmented pieces that have been taped together?

"Anything but that," I bury my face in her neck, "I'm not capable of more, Cassie."

"Why not? I don't understand. Help me understand," she sobs

When I don't answer, she pulls back, putting distance between us. I want nothing more than to hold her tight and go back to where we were this morning. Back before my stupid fears got in the way. Back to the safety of my bed, where rules and codes and brotherhood cease to exist. Back to where it was just the two of us and all we cared about was making each other happy. But that's not going to happen, because at the end of the day, I'm the same selfish asshole who knew all the risks, yet still dove in headfirst. Right now, I'm caught in that place between my head and my heart, and I'm not sure which one to follow, but I know I need to make a choice or run the risk of choking on my own fears.

"I'm not sure where this leaves us, but I'll call you when I finally figure it out. Goodbye, B." And with that, she lets go of my hand, and I watch helplessly as she walks away. I remain in front of her building, hoping she'll turn around and wave one last time, but she doesn't.

As the large wooden door to South Quad closes, I realize I may have lost her, and right now, that's not something I want to deal with.

CASSIE

"Did you guys hear? Our boy, Maxwell has a secret crush on our resident stripper," Jonah announces as our heads turn to Maxwell for confirmation.

It's Wednesday evening, and several of us have gathered in the common area outside the room Jonah shares with Maxwell and three other guys. We started hanging at the beginning of the semester, but lately I've been a little preoccupied and have missed out on the last three weeks of gossip. Steve's over in the corner, taking pictures and posting them on Snapchat. I'm sharing an oversized beanbag with Roni. Jonah's on the loveseat, and Chloe's sitting on his lap. I had no idea they were an item, so it appears I have a lot to catch up on. And when I look over at Maxwell, he's leaning casually against the wall, but his eyes are shooting daggers in his roommate's direction.

"Get in line, buddy. Her performances are the talk of the frat house," Roni quips, and Maxwell visibly tenses.

"Yeah, he's been spending most of his free time at that club. He's even got a mason jar over his bed stuffed with singles,"

Jonah says teasingly.

"It's not a crush, asshole," Maxwell replies defensively. "I just enjoy checking out her tits. I mean, come on, have you seen them?"

"Can't say that I have," I answer dryly.

"Oh, fuck, she's packing the most gorgeous set of DD's I've ever seen. Her nipples are always standing at attention and I just want to bury my face in there and let my tongue go to town," he says dreamily, and it's obvious he's envisioning her rack now based on the size of the tent in his jeans.

Roni's jaw nearly hits the floor when she notices where my finger is pointing. "Holy shit, Maxwell. Who knew you were packing a gun of that caliber." Maxwell's face goes red, and he cups his hand over his sweatpants. It doesn't matter that she has a built-in booty call, now that she's noticed, it's all she can focus on.

"Speaking of big guns, I wanted to ask Cassie about her new romance. Tell me, are the rumors true?" Chloe waggles her eyebrows, and suddenly all eyes in the room are on me. I chew the inside of my cheek and shake my head.

"Sorry, I wouldn't know."

Jonah coughs into his hand, "Bullshit!"

"It's true. Nothing's happened between us, we just hang out and stuff," I flash my best smile and swallow the golf ball in my throat.

"Yeah, I know. It's the *stuff* I want to hear more about. Stacy Preston tells everyone he was the best lay she's ever had. That's why she's always hanging around the rink. She may wear other jerseys, but that's just to piss him off so he'll want her again,"

Chloe rambles, but I tune her out because I don't want to hear anymore. Despite B's claim that she was selfish in bed, the fact she was ever in bed with him pisses me off. I hated her before; I hate her even more now.

I go quiet as the topic shifts to the celebration party after last week's football victory. I'd been at the same party, but while they discuss who drank the most shots, my mind drifts to Brantley carrying me up to John's room. That's where everything had changed for me. I'd opened my mouth and poured out my soul. His offer hadn't been a relationship. It was an offer of sex, and I'd grabbed onto it without thinking twice. I'd known what I was agreeing to at the time, so why am I second-guessing that decision now? Of course, I'd like more than just sex, but I'm beginning to think Roni's booty call lifestyle may be the ticket to keeping your heart out of the equation.

Saying my goodbyes to the group, I walk back to our room and get ready for bed. As I settle beneath the blankets, I scroll through my social media pages. Ashley's posted numerous selfies on IG. Including one where she and Scott are in his bed. She's on her back with Scott's head between her legs, and it's posted with the hashtag #GLgoaliescoresbig. I know she only posted that to warn off the bunnies, because it's not her style to brag about the sex life she shares with my brother. Davis has several IG posts that show a party taking place at their apartment. I scan each image, trying to see if Brantley's hooked up with someone, namely Stacy, but he's always with a group of guys.

Then I come across Brantley's last post and my heart rate picks up. It's a picture of a bottle of tequila, with two shot glasses and a shaker of salt, and the caption reads *thinking of you tonight* with a lime wedge emoticon.

I know I wanted time apart, but I had no idea it would be this hard. We've been inseparable for the past three months; now the silence between us is deafening. Walking away had been a necessary step, and it's taken every ounce of strength I have not to contact him. I was scared. It's the only logical explanation for what I said in his truck. Scared of falling in love with him. Scared of losing him. Scared of needing him more than he needs me.

Fighting the urge to reply, I close my eyes and allow sleep to take me away.

"Ohmygod would you stop checking your phone? With all of that sighing you sound absolutely pitiful," Roni tosses a crumpled-up piece of paper at my head.

She's had to endure my pitiful breakdowns over the past week, choosing to keep me company over sex with her boyfriend. I feel bad about keeping her from him, but right now, I need her with me. When she's around, it keeps me from caving and calling him. When I said I needed time, I had no idea how slowly it would creep by once all the joy had been taken from my life. I know that sounds melodramatic, but I feel as if I haven't smiled in ages.

I remember this one time when I was six, and my parents took me to Navy Pier in downtown Chicago. There was a vendor holding a giant bouquet of the most colorful balloons I'd ever seen. I'd begged my dad for one, and he'd suggested I wait until after we'd ridden the Ferris wheel. I'd cried until he finally caved and bought me a red one. I'd carried it proudly, holding the string tightly as we walked the pier. When we climbed into the gondola, my dad offered to hold my balloon, but I'd refused. The wheel began to turn and we rose higher and higher, and I'd panicked and let go of the string. I remember watching helplessly as the balloon floated further from reach. With each pass of the wheel I could still see my balloon, but I couldn't get it back. I'd been crushed. I'd had something I treasured, but then I'd gotten scared and let it go when I should have held on tighter.

That's sort of the way I feel now. Brantley was my balloon, and I panicked and let him slip through my grasp. The only difference is, the wind hasn't carried him away. He's still within my reach, but if I go to him, I'm not sure what it is I'd be reaching for. I know he doesn't want a relationship, but why not? Where do you go after crossing the line from friends to lovers? Can lovers go back to being friends? Is that what I want? It feels as if I've tasted the forbidden fruit and now I'm being punished. I've been banished from the Garden of Eden, but it was by my own hand.

I fall back against the pillows and throw an arm over my eyes. I'm such an idiot.

I've been utterly miserable and it's all my fault.

"If you're that sad just call and tell him you've changed your mind and want to jump his bones again."

"You really think it's that's simple? Sex is the answer to everything, right? How am I supposed to pretend it didn't mean anything? I've never been *that* girl before."

"Do you miss hanging out with him?"

"Yes." There's no hesitation in my response. "But the sex was pretty incredible too." At this, she giggles and leaps over to join me on my twin mattress.

"So have both."

"What are you saying?" I ask warily.

"Be his fuck buddy; that way you get the best of everything," she announces casually. "The way I see it, this is your only option. You clearly need this man in your life, and you'd be a fool not to have him in your bed. You practically said so yourself. This way it's a win-win." She waits for me to say something, but all I can think about is how much I miss him. "Let's go. We're busting out of the land of gloom and doom." She tugs harder, and I let out another sigh. "Uh uh, there will be no more moping today. Come on, it's a gorgeous day out there. Let's go soak up some rays."

"Fine, but I can't promise what kind of company I'll be. I'm suffering over here." I push out my lip and show her my best pouting face.

"You'll get no sympathy from me for self-inflicted suffering. You hold the power to turn it around," she retorts as she slips her Ray Bans in place.

"What are you talking about? He's the one who said we should have sex then go back to being friends. I think *he's* the one holding all the power."

"My dear, sweet Cassie. You really have no clue, do you?" she points a manicured nail at my lady bits. "That space between your legs holds a magic box that lover boy has already sampled, and by the look on your face I'm assuming he did a lot of sampling. I can guarantee you he won't say no if you offer him another chance to unleash it's power."

"You're crazy. I don't have a magic vagina," I say, shaking my head at her logic. Call me crazy, but right now my lady bits aren't feeling very magical. If anything, spending the last few days alone has left me feeling lonely and horny.

"Maybe not, but in your heart you know I'm right."

I flash her the first smile I've smiled in days and mentally run through everything I ever learned from Harry Potter.

You know, just in case...

As we approach the grassy area outside the auditorium, Roni begins tugging on my arm, encouraging me to walk faster. There's a game of touch-football being played on the lawn, not an unusual occurrence for this particular part of campus, but when the guys playing happen to be half the men's hockey team a crowd is bound to gather. My heart leaps at the prospect of seeing B again.

We claim a patch of grass and drop down to join the oglefest. Is that even a word? If not, it should be, because the men gathered here this afternoon are definitely worthy of ogling. Less than fifteen feet away, a herd of bunnies have taken up residence, no surprise there, and it's all I can do not to gag every time I hear one of them cheering for B. Thinking back to my first night in Ann Arbor, I remember the comment Scotty had made about multiple girls in Brantley's bed. Now that we've been intimate, it leaves me wondering which of these girls he's taken back to his apartment. Jealousy rises to the surface when I realize that maybe my magic box doesn't possess the kind of special powers Roni was referring to. Maybe mine was just another notch in his belt. I quickly brush that thought away and do my best to focus on the game, but it's hard to look out there and see anyone but him.

I watch the next three plays and study the way he moves. I watch the way the muscles in his back ripple when he raises an arm to throw a pass, and I think about the way they'd contracted during his climax. The rise and fall of his chest after sprinting for a touchdown reminds me of the first time I took him in my mouth and he'd fallen apart beneath me.

Sitting here is pure torture. I should get up and leave. Guard my heart from the pain I'm sure to inflict upon it by staying here. But I can't bring myself to walk away again. Just being in his presence has me feeling lighter than I had been before arriving. At one point our eyes connect and I can tell he's surprised to see me. A small smirk tugs at the corner of his mouth before he gathers his team around him in a huddle. No more than thirty seconds pass before they break and Davis begins calling out numbers and something else I can't quite understand. The play begins and the guys start to scatter. Before I know what's happening, I see Davis lowering his arm to deliver a pass right into B's awaiting hands, and before I know it, he falls to the ground and somehow ends up with his head in my lap.

"Hey, you," a smile forms on my lips when his amber eyes meet mine, "nice play."

"Pretty smooth, huh? I'll let you in on a little secret." His finger beckons me to lean down so he can whisper in my ear. "This little stunt wasn't exactly an accident."

"No, really?" I flutter my lashes and feign surprise. Being this close reminds me how much I've missed him.

"Cross my heart." He makes an X over his chest and a sad smile appears. My hand instinctively cups his cheek, and the warmth of his skin burns straight through me. "God, I've missed you."

I don't know if it's the look in his eyes or the feel of his hand as our fingers twine together then break apart far too soon, but I come to the conclusion that I don't want whatever it is we have to end. I need him, and I'll take whatever it is he's willing to give me.

"Bet I've missed you more," I quip, and my flirty response is rewarded with a wicked grin.

Davis' hand reaches down, interrupting our moment, to lift Brantley back to a standing position. Our little reunion lasts less than a minute.

"Quit screwing around, Cage. We're trying to play a game here," Davis grumbles, shaking his head at his teammate.

"Will you stick around?" His eyes plead with me to say yes, so I nod my head and turn to find Roni wearing a smug grin.

"What are you smiling about?" I ask, working hard to contain a smirk of satisfaction. *He missed me.*

"You're a clever little vixen. I believe I've underestimated you, Cassie Rivers," she clucks her tongue, giving me a sideways glance. "With a mere touch of your hand you had that man begging with puppy dog eyes."

"I have no idea what you're talking about." We're both giggling before I finish getting the words out.

The game finishes with Brantley's team taking the win, and the guys go their separate ways, while the bunnies scamper after them in pairs. A few circle around Brantley, slowing him down on his way back to me, but surprisingly I'm not the least bit affected by it. I can't hear what they're asking him. I only see him shake his head in response before brushing past them to get to me. He comes to a stop and towers over me with his hands on his hips.

Without a word, I tip my head back and flash him a toothy grin.

"I've missed that goofy smile. Get over here, woman," he extends his arms and pulls me to a standing position. Once I'm on my feet, he surprises me by bending his head and placing a soft kiss on my lips.

"B! What are you doing?" I hiss, "Someone might see you."

"Nah, they're not paying attention to us. Feel like taking a walk?"

"I'd love that." He wraps an arm around my waist and I lean into him as we cut across campus. When we reach the path, I guide him in the direction of my dorm.

"Cassie, I'm really sorry about the way we left things. I've been a wreck since you left my truck. God, I wanted so badly to jump out and chase you down."

"It's okay. In a way I'm glad you didn't. I needed that time alone. It was hard, but it was good for me. It gave me time to figure some things out."

"Oh, yeah? What kind of things?" he stops walking and leads me off the path behind a row of shrubbery. He blows out a heavy breath, and when I look up, I can see he's nervous. Taking his hands in mine, I offer a smile to ease his worry.

"I was thinking maybe we're being too hasty by trying to pretend nothing happened. What if there were other options?"

"Go on," he prods.

My hands fidget between us as I search for the right words. "Well, I was thinking that *maybe* we could try the FWB approach."

It's clear my suggestion takes him by surprise when his mouth opens but nothing comes out. For a split second I wish I could take it back. Embarrassment washes over me and I take a step back, squeezing my eyes shut as I imagine a spell that would magically erase the last three minutes.

The sound of his throaty chuckle is what makes me open my eyes, and when I do I find him staring at me with a hunger I've never seen. "Why, Cassandra Rivers, I don't believe I've ever heard sexier words come out of your mouth," he nuzzles his nose over my neck, trailing his tongue in its wake, and I melt in his arms. "Just so we're clear, what kind of benefits are we talking about?" The teasing lilt in his voice is music to my ears.

"You *know*," my voice quivers when his tongue tickles the outer shell of my ear. His lips hover, and the heat of his breath mixes with my cool skin to send shivers down my spine.

"You mean we can keep fucking while acting as if nothing's changed? Is that what my little sex kitten is proposing?" his mouth is on me, firm and unyielding in its attack. I run my hands over his bare skin, skimming the waistband of his shorts before reaching in and settling on his bare ass.

"That's exactly what I'm proposing. Think you can handle that, Superman?" He answers by redirecting my hand to the front of his shorts. He's thick and hot to the touch, and my mouth waters when I think about the last time we were together.

"I can handle it just fine, Dimples. What I need to know is, can *you*?" his eyes search mine, all playfulness gone as he waits for my response. This is it. My chance to walk away and spare my heart the damage it's sure to endure. He's offering me everything he's capable of giving. The question is, do I agree to his terms even though I want more? Walk away now and live with the memories. Or stick around and savor every moment we have together, regardless of the cost.

The choice is easy.

I rock forward on the balls of my feet and bring my lips to his ear. "Bring. It. On." An animalistic growl falls from his parted lips as he lowers his mouth to mine. For the next five minutes we're nothing but hands and teeth as we fight to get closer, both chasing something unseen, something just beyond our reach, yet we're desperate to catch it. He strokes my breast with his thumb, teasing just enough to make me crave more. My soft whimpers encourage him, begging him to do more. I'm lost to his touch, so much so I forget where we are and who might see us.

"Baby, I'm dying to have you in my bed, but are you sure this is what you want? You're not just saying this because you think it's what I want to hear?" I strain forward, craving his lips, but he holds me at arm's length and forces me to look at him. "Cassie?"

My gaze travels his body, firm and still sweaty from the game. From his dark, messy hair to the firm thighs I've straddled on more than one occasion, he's all man. And right now he's offering himself to me if I'm up to playing it his way.

"This *is* what I want. I need this too." As soon as I say the words his hands are back on me, grabbing me by the seat of my pants to pull me to his waist. I lock my ankles around him and feel his arousal line up against my opening. If it weren't for the clothing separating us, he'd bury himself inside me.

I kiss my way up his neck and whisper in his ear. "I've got the dorm to myself tonight."

"Shit," he lowers his forehead to mine. "I have practice in thirty minutes. That's not enough to do everything I want to do to you." I frown against his lips but nod my head in understanding. "I'll be done with practice at nine. Be ready for me." He commands before giving me a kiss that makes my knees weak and leaves my lips burning for more.

Once I'm on my own, a shadow of doubt creeps in and I wonder if I'm capable of handling this new role.

I'm Brantley Cage's sex kitten...

I close my eyes and pray we both come out of this unscathed, but something tells me that's an impossible request.

BRANTLEY

Only two minutes are left in the game with the score tied at 2-2. Vickers circles the net and passes off to Masterson, directing the play away from GL territory. The puck is intercepted by Owens and carried back into our offensive zone, and he fires a shot that goes wide and to the right of the net. It's picked up by a Boston forward, who weaves between our D-men as if they're standing still. He passes it off to Owens, but we've got him surrounded and it goes loose. Davis is on it in a flash and on a breakaway carries the puck across the red line just as I leave the bench and hustle after him to cover the play.

Mitchell comes out of nowhere and body checks me from behind, and I'm slammed against the boards. "Give it up, pretty boy," he grimaces.

"Fuck you," I growl and ram my stick in his gut. The pain in my back is intense from where his shoulder connected, but I'm the first to skate away.

The entire game has played out this way. Mitchell stepped on the ice looking for a fight, and tonight he found one. Normally,

I'm the level-headed player on the ice. I let my skating and stick handling do the talking, not my fists. But today my head isn't in the game, and I've allowed him to get to me. Between the two of us, we've spent more time in the sin bin than anyone else. Any other game it's the last place I want to be, but this guy's an asshole and Coach knows it. Though that doesn't stop him from reaming my ass out every time I'm on the bench.

We're on Boston's ice today, and so far it's been a tight game. We've skated our asses off; we're tired and looking to finish with a much needed win. I look to my left and see Davis skating toward the net. Once again, Mitchell is behind me as we follow every move Nelson makes. Mitchell is bulky, and it slows him down. I'm tall but lean, and I'm fast. Lightning fast. Nelson passes me the puck and I circle behind the net and pass off to Davis, who tips it in through the five hole, scoring us the winning goal.

"Fuck, yeah, that was awesome!" I shout, gathering the back of his helmet in my gloved hands. Nelson skates over, and I flash him a winning smile. "Great setup, Nelson."

Our celebration is cut short by Coach ushering us off the ice. We have to shower and catch a bus back to Ann Arbor, and we're on a tight schedule. I've just finished pulling off my skates when the sound of Coach's voice silences the celebratory chatter in the locker room. I look up just in time to see a clipboard whizzing past my left shoulder. It's a good thing Masterson just headed for the showers, or else he'd have taken a hit to the back of the head.

"That victory is hardly worth celebrating. You may have won, but you were sloppy out there. At this point in the game, I expect more from all of you." He focuses his anger on me as he approaches. "Especially you, Cage. You are the assistant captain; these guys look for you to be an example. What the hell were you doing out there? We almost lost that one because you couldn't keep your temper in check." Coach Bishop is normally a level-headed guy, but he has a low tolerance for penalties taken for fighting.

"Coach, that guy was an asshole. You should have heard the shit he was throwing at me," I argue.

"I've told you boys time and again you need to be the bigger man. You're a damn good player, Brantley. You shouldn't waste your time polishing the pine. You want to fight and spend half the game in the penalty box, that's fine. But save it for when you're on someone else's bench. Until then, your ass belongs to me, and I want you on the ice and doing the job you were recruited to do. Remember that next time some dickhead tries to get under your skin." And with that, he storms off, leaving his clipboard on the floor behind me.

"Hey, man, Mitchell's a giant D-bag. He deserved everything you dished out, and then some," Rivers declares, clapping me on the shoulder on his way to the showers.

When we board the bus I look for a quiet seat near the front so I can be alone and reflect on today's game. Even though we won, my mood is sour. Coach was right. I never should've let him get to me like that. I'd gone in there with my head somewhere else. I blame Cassie and the fact that sex with her has taken over my life. That girl is a total sex maniac. And I'm not complaining, but there have been a few nights this week where I didn't fall asleep until well past three in the morning. That's what happens when you have roommates and one of them just happens to be an overprotective brother you're lying to.

I lose myself on social media, checking for posts about the game. The game was televised, so it's no surprise to find my pages littered with comments about how I kicked ass, or nearly lost it for the team. Some praised my actions while others called me a selfish asshole. I skim through a few posts and feel a jolt of pride when I find Cassie has bitched out one of my attackers. Poor asshole has no clue he just had his ass handed to him by a pixie with the sexiest dimples ever. I pull up her contact and shoot her a quick text.

Me: Thinking about u...
Her: Oh yeah? Sexy thoughts I hope...
Me: R there any other kind?
Her: For u? No way. I saw the game. How r u?
Me: Mad as hell. Wish I were there 2 hold u.
Her: You'll see me tomorrow night.
Me: Sweet dreams, Dimples.

Either the guys know I need some time to myself, or they're too tired to notice, but no one bothers to fill the empty seat next to me. The bus is quiet. Too quiet after a win. Coach's outburst in the locker room seems to have us all thinking about our performance tonight. Sure, we won, but Coach had been right, it was a sloppy win. The two goals that had slipped past Rivers were the same shots he's stopped a thousand times before. We lost Thompson during the second period after a concussion left him unable to continue, and that loss had been hard to recover from. He's one of our best forwards, and coach had to send in one of the rookies to take his spot on the line.

I end up dozing off while scrolling through photos of Cassie.

My favorite is one I took two mornings ago when she was in my bed. The sun was streaming through the window, landing on the pillow beside me where her head rested. She was staring up at me with this smoldering gaze. She looked so beautiful I had to take a photo. Her pink lips are parted to speak, but I've forgotten what she even said, because the look in her eyes said she wanted me, and those had been the words I'd listened to right before burying myself balls deep inside her warmth.

"Wake up, sleepyhead." I crack open one heavy eyelid and find Rivers sitting beside me.

"Hey. What time is it?" I ask through a yawn.

"After eleven. Coach says we should be home around midnight. I don't know about you but I'm looking forward to sleeping in my own bed." I nod my head in agreement as I have every intention of falling into bed and staying there for the next eight hours. "Who's Candy?" he asks, squinting at the phone he's holding.

I love my roommates, but they're nosey as hell, which is precisely why I never changed Candy's name to Cassie once I found out who she really was. I figured this would be safer. Turns out I'd been right. I reach over and snag it from his hand, discreetly closing out the photo as I do, and read the text she sent while I was sleeping. Six words are all it takes to make me hard.

They're sweeter when I'm with u.

"Just a girl I met."

"Judging from what I read I take it you've been *properly* introduced," he gives me a wink and a jab to the ribs and my heart pounds in my chest. This is the first time we've been alone since Cassie and I started fucking around, and I hope like hell I don't look as guilty as I feel. "Where does one meet a girl named Candy anyhow?"

"She's a performer at the um... the Landing Strip." The lie slips easily past my lips. "She was in town and I ran into her. We've hooked up a few times."

"Dude, you're banging a stripper? That's hot as hell. Way to go, man." We bump fists.

"Yeah, pretty hot," I laugh and turn to look out the window, wondering when I became someone who lies to his best friend without blinking an eye. "So, how are things with Ash?"

"Shit, man. I don't know anymore. Most of the time it seems like things are great, but lately I've been getting this weird vibe from her."

"What kind of vibe?" I ask, eager to shift the focus away from my guilt-laden sex life.

"Like I'm not giving her enough," he answers flatly.

"Wow, that's... That's rough dude." I hold it together for all of five seconds before I'm doubled over in laughter.

"No, that's not what I'm implying. Asshole. I've got plenty to offer her in *that* department. I'm talking about marriage. She wants us to get married, have kids and all that shit," he states, giving me a frustrated scowl.

"I take it that's not on *your* radar?"

"Yeah, in five years. Maybe. But I'm heading to the pros next summer. I guess I expected to be going there alone. The way she sees it, we should be looking at apartments together." He drops his head, looking defeated.

I'm the last person to give advice on relationships, but this is my best friend and his future may be in jeopardy. "What'd you expect, Scott? You've been together for two years. For a woman, that's practically a lifetime. I hate to say I told you so, but I did. I warned you this would happen when you started spending every waking moment with her. Give a woman that kind of power over you and the next thing you know they're moving in and picking out china patterns, and you're left wondering where the fuck your life went."

"Christ, that bitch really did a number on you," he says quietly.

"Yeah, I guess she did."

I don't like to think about all the shit that went down between Vanessa and I, but every so often it happens and I'm reminded why I've avoided falling in love. I'd rather stick to random sex. Over the years, there've been a few girls I've gone back to for a repeat hook-up. Cassie is one of those girls. When I'm with her, I forget about all the other shit that fills my head and we just have fun. Today's been a shit-filled day, and I really need to lose myself in someone. Thanksgiving break is this week, which means everyone I know will be heading home, while I sit in an empty apartment, watching football and eating a frozen turkey dinner. This may be our last opportunity to meet up before she boards a train to Chicago. I'm not sure why, but tonight, that bothers me.

Me: U awake?

Her: Umm hmm. And u interrupted me.

This peaks my curiosity a little bit.

Me: What r u doing?

Her: Thinking of u. Touching myself...

Now I'm curious *and* hard.

Me: The bus pulls in around midnight. U alone?

Her: Roni's here, but she's a heavy sleeper.

Me: R u DTF?

Her: My fingers are soaked. Does that answer your question?

Fuck if that's not a sexy image to have stuck in my head. I adjust my junk and look out the window to gage how close we are to campus.

Me: I want to be the one who makes you come.

Her: Then get your ass over here.

"Can you catch a ride with Davis?" I check with Rivers as we're getting off the bus. "I've got someplace I need to be."

"No problem, buddy. Have a good time." He winks and gives me a slap on the back before leaving to find Davis.

I shoot a quick text to let her know I'm at her door, and she answers immediately and pulls me in for a sloppy, wet kiss. She's dressed for bed, and I slip my calloused hands under her shirt just to feel her. I'm dying to get her naked and on the bed, but she's pressed up against me, fucking my mouth with her tongue. My dick is so hard it's already cresting the band of my sweatpants. I walk her to the bed, where she lies back and stretches out an arm to draw me to her. The mattress dips when I rest one knee beside her and lower my face to hers.

"Hi," she greets in a breathy whisper that shoots straight to my crotchal region, "what took you so long?" My arm extends behind my head to remove my shirt while Cassie slides my sweatpants down my thighs. This position puts her at eye level with my dick, and when her tongue sneaks out to moisten her lips, it jerks in response. Forming a circle with her fingers, she lowers her hand down the entire length of my shaft then tightens her grip and reverses the motion. I blow out a shuddery groan as she runs the flat of her thumb in a small circle and coats the tip in precum. Taking pity on my throbbing shaft, she opens her mouth, and I watch through half-lidded eyes as the crown disappears between her soft lips. I cup the back of her head in my hand, loving the sleepy look her eyes get whenever she goes down on me, and it takes every ounce of willpower I have not to take over and jam my dick against the back of her throat. When her warm tongue slices through my slit, I have to clamp my ass cheeks to keep from blowing my load.

"Slow down, baby." She releases me with a pop and stares up with those sleepy eyes. I jerk my head in the direction of her roommate's sleeping form. "You sure she's out cold?"

"Positive," she drawls and lifts her top to reveal two beautiful nipples that beckon my mouth. "Now get down here and fuck me already," she commands, and my ass clenches again.

Climbing under the blankets, I cover her body with mine and capture her mouth in a kiss. "Since when are you so bossy in bed?" I chuckle, sucking her lower lip between my teeth before resuming the kiss.

"Since you interrupted my private party with promises of making me come." She gives my lip a playful nip and whimpers. "I'm dying here."

"Oh, that's right. Why don't you show me where you left off?" I rasp, drawing a nipple into my mouth as she guides my hand to the heated flesh between her legs. Christ, she wasn't kidding. She's soaking wet. I circle her opening with my thumb then trace up her slit, slowly spreading her arousal over the swollen bud. I ease a finger inside and give my hand a few lazy strokes. When she moans, I bring my lips to her ear and whisper, "Is this where you left off?"

She squirms beneath me with parted lips and eyes half-closed. "Almost," she coos, and I add a second finger inside and tease my thumb over her clit. The breathy sound she releases makes me horny as fuck, and I respond by pumping my hand faster. I drag my thumb over her opening to get it nice and wet then work the tiny bud into a frenzy. Her pussy grinds against my hand while I lavish her tits with soft, open-mouthed kisses that leave her a whimpering mess.

"How about now? Is this about where you were?" I murmur around her pebbled nipple.

"So close," she answers breathlessly. When I slip a third finger deep inside, she lifts her hips and frantically bucks against my hand before releasing a shuddery moan. "Yesss."

"Jesus, baby. You're fucking killing me." I throw her leg over my shoulder and bury my face between her legs. With the first swipe of my tongue, her knees come together in an attempt to stop me. But that's only because she's sensitive from the orgasm I've just given her. Flattening my tongue, I start at her opening and lick my way through her lips with slow, repeated strokes before focusing on her clit. When I do this, her legs splay open and her knees press into the mattress as she rocks against my face.

"Does that feel good?" I hum against her swollen flesh. I already know the answer. I just love hearing her response.

"Yes," she rasps and grabs the back of my head, "it feels sooo fucking good. Almost too good."

"You want me to stop?" I chuckle as she rocks her hips, bringing her mound back to my lips.

"Don't. You. Dare." Her words are choppy as she lets go and rewards me with her release.

I love performing oral sex on a woman. The first time we fucked, she told me how her ex was all take and no give. Me? I'm a giver. That's not to say I don't love a great blowjob. I most certainly do. Hell, I challenge you to find any guy over the age of fifteen who'd turn down a BJ. But I digress... Back to her pussy. First of all, she waxes, which is a good thing. A great thing, really. But she's not bare. She's has them leave the thinnest strip of hair, and it's incredibly sexy when I'm inside her and look down to where we're joined and see that little strip. Something about that turns me on, big time. Then, there's her scent. The best way to describe it would be a salty, musky, citrusy combination. I don't know what she does to make it that way, but it's like the sweetest fragrance. I could lick her pussy every damn day and you wouldn't hear a single complaint out of me.

Once she's sated, I crawl up her body, leaving a trail of kisses every few inches. Her arms circle my neck as my cock settles in the cradle of her thighs. I stare down at where she's lying beneath me. She's wearing her satisfied sex face. Her lips are full and her eyelids are droopy. I love that I'm responsible for giving her that look.

"Are you happy?" I kiss her tentatively on the lips.

"Mmmm hmmm. So happy." She kisses me back, swirling her tongue with mine. I'm certain she can taste herself on me, and knowing that is a big turn on. "Now it's time for you to be happy," she smiles seductively and starts to shimmy down the bed, but I reach out and stop her. "Is something wrong?"

I shake my head and bring her back to the pillow. "Nothing's wrong. I've just had a shitty day, and watching you come made it so much better. Now I just want to forget, and the only way I'm gonna do that is by losing myself inside you. Right now, that's all I need. Is that okay?"

"Of course it's okay. Come here." Her mouth parts, and she extends her tongue to meet mine. Our tongues wrestle outside our mouths until we crash together in a sloppy, sexy kiss. The tip of my cock nudges her entrance, and it's so warm and wet, my vision goes white and everything stops. Including me. I hover over her, bracing my weight on my forearms.

"Fuck," I hiss through clenched teeth.

"What is it?" She starts to sit up, and the change in position presses me further inside. When her inner walls tighten around my shaft, my eyes roll all the way back in my head.

"My wallet's in the truck." I reluctantly ease out and kneel between her legs with my head down. I'm ready to haul my ass down three flights of stairs and across two city blocks, naked, just to grab my stash of condoms. I've never had unprotected sex. *Ever.* And there are reasons for that. STDs are an obvious one. But also because Vanessa pulled some shit that scarred me for life.

"It's okay, B. I'm on birth control. I get the shot and everything. I trust you," she angles her head and brushes her lips over my neck.

"I don't know, baby. It's still pretty risky. I've never had sex without a condom." I'm trying to remain strong, but it's hard when her soft tongue teases over my skin. "We need to be careful. I don't need another reason for Scott to—"

Her hand on my cock shuts me up when the pads of her

fingers delicately stroke the underside of my shaft. With every pull of her hand my tip brushes against the hot, pebbled bud, making her purr in my ear.

"I haven't done this before either. But we'll be careful. I need to feel you inside me with nothing between us. Just once. I'll make you feel better." Her lips form a seal over my neck, licking and sucking. Bruising to the point of pleasured pain. "You can finish in my mouth if that makes the decision easier."

I hang my head, torn between what I *need* and what I probably *should* do. Of course, my needs are going to end up winning this one.

They always do.

"Go ahead, baby. Lose yourself in me," she plants her feet firmly on the mattress and spreads her legs for me. I line myself up with her opening and hiss as I watch the head slowly disappear. I continue watching as her tight pussy swallows every last inch until our bodies become one, and tell myself I never want to use a condom with her again.

"Fuck." I fall forward, bracing my weight on my forearms as I fight to get my breathing under control. It's not entirely easy, because being bare inside her feels A-Ma-Zing. "You feel... so good," I can barely choke out the words. I reverse my hips then rock forward, gliding easily within her slick walls.

"I love the way you feel too," she stretches her hand to where we're joined, and when her fingers brush the base of my shaft, I snap my hips and drive deeper. The soft, keening noise she makes tells me she wants more.

Our lips brush together as our rhythm increases. With each rotation of my hips she rises to meet me. At one point, I drop to my elbow, knee digging into the mattress for leverage, as our bodies slap together and I lose myself completely. My balls draw tight against my body, signaling I'm close. Our mouths meet in a sloppy kiss that deepens as she comes and her pussy contracts around my cock. It feels so incredible, I almost forget I'm not wearing a condom. I quickly pull out and damn near growl when Cassie's lips envelop me just in time for hot ribbons of my release to meet the back of her throat.

My bones feel as if they've turned to jelly, and I collapse beside her on the narrow mattress. It's a good thing she's so tiny or else my ass would hang off the edge of her damn bed. I wrap my arms around her and rest my lips on her temple as we both recover. No sexual encounter has even come close to comparing to what we just shared, and I'm already calculating when we'll be able to meet up again. Except for our breathing, the room is completely quiet. Until her roommate rolls over and interrupts the silence.

"So, I guess the rumors are true. Christ, Brantley. If only you'd held out another minute I would've come too. Now, if you two are finished with your fuckfest, some of us would like to get some sleep," she announces before turning to face the wall.

"I thought you said she was a heavy sleeper," I whisper through muffled laughter.

"I may have stretched the truth, just a little," she giggles, and doesn't stop until I shut her up the only way I know how.

With my tongue...

We must have fallen asleep after her roommate's confession, and at some point I rolled over and the pain in my back made it impossible to fall back asleep on her narrow bed. I stagger through the door sometime after four in the morning. The room is dark except for the sliver of moonlight that shines through the blinds. I drop my keys in the glass dish we keep by the door and head to the kitchen for a glass of water.

"Late night," says a gruff voice in the dark.

"Jesus, Davis!" I flip the light switch and find him sitting at the kitchen table. "You scared the crap out of me." I reach for a glass and turn on the tap. "How long have you been sitting there?"

"Not long." He drums his fingers over the polished wood. "How long has it been going on?"

"What are you talking about?" I ask warily.

"Come on, Brantley. You really need me to spell it out?" He gives me a look that tells me he already knows, so there's no sense trying to come up with another lie. I glance nervously over my shoulder and back to him. "He's not here," he says flatly, already knowing my question. I pull out a chair and sit down across from him.

"Who told you?"

"No one. I figured it out for myself. Actually, it wasn't all that hard. I've noticed the change in your behavior. The way you look at her when she's around. You also go out of your way to avoid Rivers. You two were always thick as thieves. I guess it all added up to tell me you're fucking Cassie." He shrugs and leans back in his chair. I'm quiet as I try and gage his level of anger. His voice is calm, and he doesn't appear to be pissed I've gone against my best friend's wishes.

"I never intended for it to happen. And it hasn't been going on long, just since the night of her recital. Either way, I know I fucked up."

"Why do you say that?" His eyes narrow. "Do you like her?"

"Of course I like her."

"Do you care about her?"

"Hell, yes. I'd do anything for her," I answer defensively.

"Then I fail to see where you fucked up. So you went against the code. Big fucking deal. If Rivers finds out, he'll probably kick your ass, but he'll get over it and forgive you. But if you're just screwing around with her and she gets her heart broken, I'll be the one to kick your sorry ass. Cassie's my friend and I care about her. I don't want to see her get hurt," he pushes away from the table and stands.

"I don't want to hurt her either," I admit.

"Then don't," he replies and leaves the room.

"Davis, wait," I call after him, "are you going to say anything to him?"

"No," he says quietly, "I think I'll leave that to you."

CASSIE

The train to Chicago leaves in two hours, but I can't bring myself to leave without saying goodbye to Brantley. We've both been really busy this week, so we've only had time to talk on the phone. I remember him saying his plane leaves at two, which means I have just enough time to surprise him before he heads to the airport.

He answers the door dressed in a pair of sweatpants and nothing else. They hang low on his hips, and for a moment I'm distracted by the view.

"Hey." He smiles stiffly as he grips the top of the door with his right hand. "I figured you'd be at the train station by now."

"I thought you'd be leaving for the airport by now. I wanted to come over and say goodbye," I answer sweetly, then step inside and greet him with a heated kiss.

"Whoa." He licks his lips after we pull apart, "I like the way you say goodbye."

I look around the apartment and quickly assess there's something he isn't telling me. "You want to tell me what's going on?"

He scratches the back of his head and gives his shoulder a partial shrug. "My plans sort of changed."

It's only then I realize he may not be alone, and I take a step back toward the door. It hadn't dawned on me he may be sleeping with other girls. I'd foolishly assumed that while we were in the FWB stage, we would be exclusive. It was an easy assumption on my part. It's not as if I have many guys beating down my door. But he *is* #2 on that stupid conquest list. He has hundreds of girls waiting in line.

I need to get out of here.

"Cassie?" He eyes me suspiciously. "Are you okay?" He reaches out and removes my hand from the doorknob. "Where're you going? You just got here."

"It's just... I thought... I thought maybe you had another girl here," I stammer and chew the side of my cheek.

"Why the hell would you think that?" He gives a snort of derision before pulling me into his arms. "Go check for yourself. There's no one else here. It's only me, the television, and a freezer full of food. Oh, and now there's you." He grips my face in his hands and claims my mouth. His tongue makes lazy circles over mine and with every stroke his fingers weave through my hair to draw us closer. I can feel his arousal pressing against my stomach and I'm not surprised. He's always in the mood.

"Wait," I break our connection, "you're not going to Colorado?" He bites down on my lip before soothing it with his tongue.

"Nope. My parents wanted to get away, so I'm left here to fend for myself." He makes a sad face. "Don't you feel sorry for me?" He takes my hand in his and guides it down the front of his pants. I circle my fingers around him and stroke down to the base. His head rests on my shoulder, so I hear every little moan he makes when I work my hand over his thick shaft. There's an inch gap between the tip of my thumb and middle finger, and my mouth waters when I think of how incredible it feels when he's inside me.

Without warning, he picks me up and walks over to the kitchen table. He turns a chair around before setting me back on my feet. In one quick motion, he drops his sweats to the floor and takes a seat. He draws his bottom lip between his teeth and seduces me with his amber eyes as he lifts my skirt up to my waist. I straddle his legs, and he holds me by the hips as he guides me over his erection. Guess after the other night he's decided not to bother with a condom. I start to remind him but change my mind.

"Wait, I have a proposition." I tease my opening over the engorged head.

"Can it wait until I'm inside you?" He gives his hips a quick thrust and breaches my opening. I counter by pulling mine back.

"I'll have sex with you only if you agree to come to Chicago with me. Spend Thanksgiving with my family." I feather soft kisses down his neck. "I promise," my tongue teases over the flat of his nipple, "to make it," I rub my arousal over the head of his cock, "worth your while."

"You really think that's a good idea?" I nod, slowly rolling my hips as he continues, "And you really want me there?"

"Mmm hmm."

"Then we'd better hurry if we're gonna catch that train." He smiles wickedly before filling me in one fluid motion.

We climb the steps to the front porch of my childhood home, and I'm about to open the door when I feel his fingers tighten their grip around mine.

"Are you *positive* your parents are okay with me crashing their holiday?"

I give his hand a gentle squeeze and sigh. This is the third time he's asked this question since leaving Ann Arbor. Once he'd finished showing me how amazing chair sex can be, he'd stuffed clothes and toiletries into a backpack, while I placed a call to mom and told her I was bringing him along. As expected, she assured me she would love having another mouth to feed. Mom was always the June Cleaver of our neighborhood. Dinner was always on the table by six, and a freshly baked dessert was sure to follow. Friends were considered family and welcome at our table anytime. I know without a doubt that once we walk through the door, mom will go out of her way to make sure he's properly welcomed.

"B, I promise you have nothing to worry about. Besides, *I* want you here, and that's all that matters."

He leans forward and gently cups my face in his hands as his mouth covers mine. The kiss is soft, nothing like the one he'd given me in the train lavatory. Where that one had been frantic, like he couldn't get enough, he takes his time with this one, savoring it as if he were a man eating his last meal.

"I wanted to do that one more time, just in case it's the last chance I get for the next few days." I give him my brightest smile then drop his hand and push open the door.

Turns out I'd been right about mom. We barely make it through the door before she has B wrapped up in her arms. She gushes over him, going on and on about how much he's grown since she last saw him. Then she loops her arm through his and gives him a full tour of the house, making sure to point out every photo she has of me, even the hideous school photos taken during my awkward phase. He's a good sport about it, laughing at all the right times and answering every question she fires at him. While we prepare dinner, dad drags him off to the den for a little male bonding over a beer and hockey on ESPN.

Now, I'm standing at the kitchen counter, one arm wrapped around a large bowl, the other holding a potato masher, while staring into the den with a smile plastered on my face. The very fact he's sitting in the house I grew up in feels better than I'd ever imagined. I know this somehow goes beyond our arrangement, but neither of us have been very good at playing by the rules where this relationship is concerned. Not that I would call what we have a relationship, but it definitely feels as if there's something more between us. I want so badly to ask him why he's against falling in love. He once told me he wasn't capable of it, but I disagree. The way he treats me is proof he's capable of showing love. Maybe the problem is that he can't bring himself to receive it.

"He sure is easy on the eyes, isn't he?" Mom sneaks up behind me and looks over my shoulder in the direction of the den.

"I suppose," I answer, pretending as if I haven't noticed his charming good looks.

Her raised brow tells me she isn't buying it. "Sweetheart, you don't fool me for one second. I know you're sleeping with him." She pulls the bowl and masher from my hands to finish the task.

"What makes you think that?" My voice cracks and I search my brain for anything we may have done when we'd thought no one had been looking.

"Call it a mother's intuition," she winks and continues matchmaking while mashing potatoes. "That, and the fact you haven't stopped staring at each other since the two of you entered this house. Look at how well he gets along with your father. My father hated your dad when he first met him. Trust me, snatch this boy up while he's still available." She opens the oven to give the steaks a final baste of garlic butter before setting the pan on top of the stove.

"I'm curious, how do you know he doesn't already have a girlfriend?"

"I asked him and he told me."

"What the hell, mom? You can't go around asking guys if they're single."

"You can if you're a mother who wants to see grandchildren before she's too old to play with them," she quips tartly. "Listen, honey, I get that you're young and sex is more of a casual thing to your generation. But at some point there'll come a time when you'll want more. I just think he would be a great catch."

"Mom, wait." I grab her by the arm and lower my voice. "You can't say anything about us to dad or Scotty."

"Cassie, I wouldn't do that to you. But your father already knows you've had sex. You do remember the night he caught Justin in your bed?" Her perfectly shaped brow shoots up an inch.

"Please, don't remind me," I shudder. "It's just that Brantley doesn't want Scotty to know about us. He thinks we're merely friends. I guess there's this code between them Brantley promised not to break. I don't want to cause problems."

"Well, that's just nonsense. Your brother has no right to tell anyone who they can or cannot be with. I'm quite certain if your friend out there had a sister Scott took a shine to he wouldn't allow some pact to stop him."

"Please, mom. Just do this for me."

"Fine. I won't say a word. But I still say you should stake claim on him. You two would make the prettiest babies together."

"Mom!" I shake my head and begin to wonder if I should have stayed in Ann Arbor with B where we could have watched TV and eaten our frozen meals in peace.

Later that evening, after my parents say goodnight and head to their room, I slip downstairs and stand outside the room where Brantley is staying. His back is to me as he rifles through his backpack, searching for something. I clear my throat, alerting him to my presence as I step forward and lock the door behind me. I lean against the door and my breath catches in my throat when I see the look in his eyes. I know that look. It says he wants to finish what we started on the train. Heat courses through my veins as I stare at his bare chest, and the memory of what took place between us increases the aching need between my thighs.

"I'll be right back. I have to use the restroom," I whispered.

"Okay," he whispered back, lifting his arms as I untangled my legs from his lap. "Wait, do you have anything to eat? I'm starving."

"I think there's a granola bar in my purse. Help yourself." I offered before making my way to the restroom. The room smelled of deodorizer, and I wrinkled my nose in disgust, eager to do my business and get back to my book and the man waiting for me. I'd been in the middle of a heated scene when nature rudely interrupted the moment, leaving me aroused. As I opened the door to leave I was quickly forced back inside by a very intense looking hockey player.

"What are you doing?" I asked in a hushed voice.

"There's something I need to do." He licked his lips and stared at my mouth as if he intended to devour me.

"Then I'll just step out and leave you to it." A smirk filled my face as I wormed my way to the door. His arm rested on the sink, preventing my escape. "I have no desire to watch, if that's what you're hoping."

"I don't have to use the bathroom." His voice was low and seductive as he reached into his pocket. "I found something in your purse, and I'm dying to try it out."

My insides quaked when I realized what he was about to reveal. I'd bought it on a whim. His money had burnt a whole in my pocket during the entire demonstration. The woman had promised this particular vibrator, when used properly, would take my orgasm to the next level. I had yet to discover its possibilities, having thrown it in my purse the night of the party and forgetting about it, because Brantley provided all the pleasure a girl could ask for.

"What are you doing?" I hissed when he grasped the device in his right hand and lifted the hem of my skirt. With a gleam in his eye, he twisted the handle and an audible hum filled the confined space. My skin tingled as he rolled the latex over my clenched thighs. "B, we can't do this here. Someone might—" My voice faltered when his hand teased the front of my panties. I widened my stance, offering a silent invitation for him to continue, and was soon rewarded with a throaty chuckle in my ear. His fingers tugged at the fabric, pulling it aside, and a whimper fell from my lips when the blissful vibration met my swollen clit.

"That's it, baby, just roll with it. Feels good, right?" He growled the words against my neck before sinking his teeth into the soft skin, delivering a sting of pain that was immediately soothed by his heated tongue.

I mumbled incoherently, incapable of an intelligent response, as the sensation between my legs began its slow burn. His finger dipped, lowering the tip of the vibrator until it breached my opening and slipped inside. My head lolled to the side, and his mouth was there, kissing my neck, whispering the sexiest words I'd ever heard. I rolled my hips, seeking more, and he rewarded me with two quick thrusts of his hand. I reached between my legs, and my fingers came back soaked in my arousal. He bent down, covering my fingers with his mouth, and proceeded to lick both digits clean.

"You are so fucking sexy. Do you have any idea what you do to me?" Unable to respond, I leaned against him for support as his hand worked the toy in and out with quick, pulsating thrusts. Then his mouth was on mine, his hand shoved mine aside to rub the latex over my hardened nub while his fingers pumped hard and fast, filling me with each delicious stroke.

I braced my hands on the counter as the pressure mounted and couldn't hold back any longer. "I'm coming." My moans fell breathlessly into lips that muffled my cries of pleasure.

His arms surrounded me and supported my weight until I was able to stand without wobbling. When we finally made eye contact, a blush turned my face a deep shade of crimson. It wasn't as if he'd never witnessed one of my orgasms, but somehow this one seemed different. More personal. I hid my face in his chest and couldn't help giggling now that it was over. "I think *you may have broken me that time."*

Someone banged on the door and asked if I was okay, and our laughter filled the tiny room.

A room that now smelled of deodorizer and sex.

His chest rumbled with laughter as he lowered his head for a kiss. "Best twenty dollars I ever spent."

"Hey, gorgeous." His husky voice pulls me back to the present. "You lost or something?" His words tease but there's nothing playful about the kiss he gives me. "I've been wanting to do that all night."

I'm still reeling when he grasps my hand and guides me toward the bed. "Scotty will be here tomorrow."

"Guess that means I'll have to be on my best behavior." He lowers his mouth to mine and steals a greedy kiss. "What do you say, Dimples. You feel like being bad with me one last time?"

"I thought you'd never ask." We fall back on the bed, and he spends the next hour loving every inch of my body with expert hands and a wicked mouth. Later, when we're sated and too tired to move, he cradles me in his arms. "Who knew being bad would feel so good?"

"We knew." He lets out a growl while giving my shoulder a playful bite.

"Can I ask you a question?" My fingers trace circles through the patch of hair on his chest.

"Of course." There's no hesitation in his reply.

"It's about Vanessa." His hand stills.

"That's not an easy subject for me."

"I'm sorry. I just was wondering... You know what, it doesn't matter. Forget I mentioned anything. Can we just go back to what we were doing?" I'm rambling, worried my digging will drive a wedge between us when things are going so well. I wouldn't have brought it up, but talking with my mom got me thinking again.

"Cassie, just ask. I'll tell you anything you want to know."

The hand on my back stills as he steels himself for the question he knows I'm seeking the answers to. "What did she do to you?"

A measured sigh falls from his lips before he speaks again. "You want the long or short story?"

"I guess whichever story you feel like sharing." I answer softly.

"We'd been dating for three months when I knew I was in love with her. I'm talking can't eat, can't sleep, can't think about anything else. I couldn't afford to take her out, so we spent most of our time in our rooms, or making out in the library. My life revolved around four things. Hockey. My teammates. Sex. And Vanessa. In that order. Remember what you were saying about your ex, and how he never put you first? Well, I guess that's how Vanessa must have felt. But she was wrong. I did love her. I loved her so much, my heart ached."

He reaches for my hand, threading our fingers together as if touching me gives him strength. I remain still, afraid to move out of fear he may stop talking.

"She used to say I had no idea what love was. That I didn't know how to treat a woman. I don't know. At the time, I guess she was right. She was my first love. But I had no clue what I was doing. Six months into our relationship, I found out she was sleeping with another guy. I loved her, so I'd been too stubborn to believe the rumors, until Scott sent me a photo of her kissing the guy outside the frat house. She probably never thought she'd get caught. But she underestimated my best friend's loyalty."

His hand drops and he begins mindlessly stroking my side boob with the edge of his finger.

"We broke up, and I shut down. Two weeks passed before she came to my dorm, crying her eyes out, begging me to take her back. When I told her to leave, she dropped to her knees and said she was pregnant with my kid. She told me she was sorry for everything and said she still loved me. She said by not putting her first, I'd pushed her into his arms, and the sick thing was, I actually believed her. I spent the next month scared out of my mind, trying to figure out how to raise a kid and stay in school."

"So what happened? Did she keep the baby?"

"That's the kicker. She was never pregnant. She made that shit up so I would pay more attention to her. She played with my heart and it nearly destroyed me."

I lift my head and look into his sad eyes. "That's awful. I'm so sorry you had to go through that, but not every girl is out to break your heart."

"Maybe so, but I don't ever want to go through that pain again. I think our arrangement works. I like you. You like me. We have fun and get along perfectly. And the sex is hot as hell. Why ruin a good thing by throwing the L-word into the mix?" When I don't answer right away, he brings my hand to his mouth for a kiss.

"Thank you for opening up to me. I know it wasn't easy, but it helps me understand where you're coming from."

"I've only shared that with a few people. Truthfully, I'm glad you asked me about it."

The fact he opened up and trusted me with his darkest pain is not lost on me. It makes me want to hold him in my arms and kiss him until the pain of the past becomes a forgotten memory.

"Justin's cheating wasn't the only reason I broke up with him. There were other things. Things I've never told anyone."

"What kind of things?" he asks warily.

"Well, for starters, there were many times when he was verbally abusive. He would guilt me into spending time with him. He never encouraged me to follow my dreams. Don't get me wrong. He wasn't horrible, but it still wasn't right. Justin had this vision of how he wanted me to be. For the longest time we would argue about it. After a while it became easier to just be who he wanted me to be."

"Why'd you put up with that? Did you think you didn't deserve better?"

"I was in love with him. At least I thought I was. I don't know what to think anymore."

"Sounds as if we both have valid reasons for keeping things carefree."

"I'm not so sure it's that easy. It's hard to tell your heart what to do. I don't know about you, but mine seems to have a mind of its own."

He brings a hand to my chin and lifts my face to his. "Cassie, you are having fun, aren't you?"

"Of course I'm having fun. You're my best friend. You make me laugh." His hand slips between us, and I squirm when his thumb brushes against my sex. "And you worship my body on a daily basis." He leaves two wet kisses on my neck before bringing his lips to my ear.

"See. Perfect, just the way it is." Our lips meet briefly before he pulls me into his lap. "You have to promise you'll tell me when this stops being fun. I mean it, Cassie. The minute things change, you need to tell me. I can't risk losing you because I'm too fucked in the head to handle anything more."

"B, you're not going to lose me—"

"Cassie, please." Those two words come out low and tortured, each one piercing my heart. "Promise me."

"Okay, baby, I promise." And then he's there, teasing my skin with wet, open-mouthed kisses that leave me panting his name.

"Does that feel good?" he toys my nipple between his teeth as he rolls me onto my back. I pull him back to my mouth, savoring the warmth of his tongue as it seduces me with each fevered stroke. His eyes close when he fills me, and when my muscles clamp around him, he grunts his approval. What starts out slow quickly accelerates as every thrust he delivers drives him deeper inside. His head falls forward, and my lips seek out the heated flesh on his neck.

"I promise." I tell him once more as the warmth of his release fills me.

BRANTLEY

I'm not a coward. At least I've never believed I was. Heights don't frighten me. I have no trouble being stuck in tight spaces. Hell, I'm not even afraid of failure, because every failure I've suffered through has made me stronger. But right now, there are two things I fear.

Falling in love.

Losing Scott's trust.

I'll be honest, I'm nervous about Scott's reaction to finding me in his parents' living room. Obviously, he'll be surprised, but he may also become suspicious. So far, my friendship with Cassie has worked to his benefit. As long as she's spending time with me, it lessens the guilt he feels for not spending time with her. So far, he seems cool with the idea of us spending so much time together, but that's only because he trusts me to look out for her. That was *before* we slept together. I'm worried he's going to take one look at our faces when we're together and see right through our lies. So I make a decision to avoid her by sitting across from her at the table; that way I won't be tempted. I have to admit, it's hard keeping my hands to myself, especially when I know all the right places to touch.

I hear his voice, long before he enters the room, and do my best to act natural. Cassie catches my eye and gives me a quick wink that says *it'll be okay,* and I thank her with my brightest smile. My smile quickly turns to surprise when I learn he's not alone.

"Hey, everyone, look who I found outside. Mom, hope you don't mind another mouth to feed," his raucous laughter fills the room as he steps aside to reveal his guest. I recognize this guy. He plays for Minnesota. All of a sudden, the pieces start falling into place.

This guy's her ex.

"Justin?" A pained expression fills Cassie's face when he pulls her in for an embrace. "How are you?"

"I'm good. Better now that I'm back home. I've missed you." He holds her in his arms, their reunion unfolding right before my eyes, and when his lips settle over hers, I'm left with feelings I'm not ready to face. It's bad enough knowing they've had sex, but I also know this is the guy she gave her virginity to. She's told me stories about their relationship. Stories of how selfish he was in bed, and how he'd never given her more than one orgasm at a time. Hell, I gave her three just this morning, and that was before we made it to the shower. After what she told me last night, it takes everything I have not to rip this asshole's head off. Seeing his hand on her back makes me want to beat on my chest and announce to everyone she's mine. To hell with loyalty and worry over losing my best friend. Bottled rage seeps into the cracks of my heart, and I envision myself ripping her from his arms and fucking her right in front of him just to show him how it's done.

Scott's brow furrows when his eyes lock on my scowl, and for a moment I'm sure everyone can read my mind. "Cage? What the hell are you doing in my living room? I thought you were Colorado bound?" Relieved, my shoulders shrug as he makes his way across the room.

"Those plans sort of fell through, so Cassie invited me here." I answer casually.

"Well, I needed *someone* to keep me company during that five-hour train ride," she replies, stepping away from Justin to hug her brother. As she pulls away she looks over and gives me an apologetic smile.

"I don't care how you got here. I'm just glad to see you, brother. It's been too damn long." I step forward, and he pulls me in for a hug. "Happy Thanksgiving. Make sure to save room for mom's pecan pie. You deserve it after being stuck with this one for that amount of time." He hooks a thumb Cassie's way, and she slugs him in the arm as payback.

"Kids, no fighting. I swear, sometimes I think you're both still teenagers," she scolds them and then ushers us all to the table.

Fuming over the fact that Justin's kiss is still fresh on her lips, I ditch my plan of avoiding her and, like a caveman, stake my claim by stealing the chair beside her before he sits down. She gives me a puzzled look, as if she has no idea what's gotten into me, and all I can do is smile in return. Mr. Rivers carves the turkey, and there's a flurry of activity as dishes are passed and everyone fills their plate. Before we begin eating, he sets aside the carving knife and asks us all to go around and share one thing we're thankful for this year. I always dread these situations. I never know the right thing to say, or I'm so worried about saying the wrong thing I end up blanking out and say nothing at all. I listen as each one offers something meaningful, and all I can think about is how thankful I am to have a friend with benefits. I can't actually say *that*, now can I? *Wait, can I?* Justin goes next, and he rambles on about the blessing of seeing Cassie again, and she gives him a strained smile, but I find it interesting when it's her turn she doesn't share the same sentiment.

"I'm thankful for family, the new friends I've made, and real life superheroes," she says with a smirk, and I want to reach over and kiss that smirk away. Her answer seems to piss Justin off, and that settles my inner caveman. I discreetly reach over and run my hand up her leg, stopping only when I reach the juncture of her thighs. My fingertips brush her panties, and a rush of adrenaline surges through me when her legs clamp around my hand.

"Superheroes? What the hell kind of answer is that? Women are crazy." Scott declares with a shake of his head. "You're up, Cage, though how you'll follow that one I'll never know."

I should come up with something sappy, like I'm thankful my dad is alive and healthy, or I'm thankful to have a family to share the holiday with. Then her hand covers mine and my dick hardens to the point where I can no longer think straight. My thumb slides under the fabric, and I rake my nail over the little bud. Her eyes close, and she reaches for a glass of water. We're surrounded by her family, and her dickhead ex, yet she doesn't stop me. When her left hand wraps around my unit, I blurt out the first thought that pops in my head. "I'm thankful that twenty dollars is all it takes to have a good time."

"Dude," Scott busts out laughing, "is that all you had to spend on the stripper you hooked up with last week?"

The room goes silent, seconds tick by like minutes, and her fingers squeeze me so tightly I damn near flinch. Luckily, their dad comes to my rescue by telling us all to start eating. I hang my head, feeling like a complete asshole. I'm certain they must be wondering how fast they can kick my ass out the door. Hell, I'm already plotting my escape after I swallow my turkey and sweet potatoes.

Then, her dad speaks again, and some of the tension dissipates. "Twenty bucks. Is that all it costs these days?" Everyone around the table laughs. Everyone except Cassie. She releases her hold and shoves my hand away.

So much for a Thanksgiving hand job.

I try to get her alone so I can explain the stripper comment, but between Scott and an ex-boyfriend who's glued to her fucking hip, it's next to impossible. She won't even look at me, and I've tried everything I can think of to get her attention. When it's time to head over to the neighbors' cocktail party, I have no desire to go. I need to straighten this shit out, but in order to do that, I need to get her away from an ex who's clearly looking to get back together. Scott leaves to spend the rest of the weekend in Ohio with Ashley, meaning all of her attention is now monopolized by the guy whose jaw I'm about to break. I finally see an opening when she excuses herself to go to the bathroom, and I quietly follow her down the darkened hallway.

"What are you doing?" she hisses when I squeeze through the door before she can get it closed.

"Just be quiet and listen to me for two minutes." She glowers but crosses her arms and waits for me to continue. "I never hooked up with a stripper."

"Then why would Scotty say that? He wouldn't just make that up."

"We were on the bus, coming back from our game against Boston, and he saw your response to my text. You know, the one about your dreams being sweeter when you're with me."

"Wait," she catches my forearm in a death grip, "am I still Candy in your contacts? Please say yes." Panic crosses her face at the prospect of Scott finding out.

"Yes." She lets out a huge sigh of relief and relaxes against the counter. "And that's why he started asking about you, and the whole name thing. I panicked and told him you were just some stripper I'd met." Her body visibly softens and when she steps forward and drops her forehead against my chest, I fold my arms around her. "Believe me, if he knew you were Candy, you'd have heard about it by now."

"So I just spent the last hour angry with you for nothing?" She frowns.

"Oh, I wouldn't say it was for nothing." There's a devilish gleam in my eye as I lower my mouth and steal a kiss. "Now we get to enjoy the best part of being friends who fuck and fight."

"Oh, really? What's that?" She runs her nails down my back.

"Make-up sex," I smile and brush my lips over hers in a soft kiss. I'm thinking we'll head back to her parents' house. But when Cassie pops the buttons on my fly and wraps her lips around my dick, I discover she has other plans.

After our bathroom hook-up, she leads me into the hall. We

only make it three feet before she pulls me against the wall and guides my hand under her shirt. I sneak a quick glance over my shoulder, because we're in the middle of her neighbors' fucking house and I'm feeling her up against a wall. I don't want us to get caught, but the thought of someone watching is a bit of a turn-on.

"I've heard that turkey makes some people sleepy. I'm starting to think it makes you horny," I give her nipple a playful tweak.

"Then maybe you should feed me turkey every day," she answers huskily.

"Maybe I will." I give her a wink and look over my shoulder one more time. Off in the distance I see her ex watching us. I know I probably shouldn't, but I pin her against the wall and give her a kiss that leaves her breathless. Full of tongue and groping, and I believe there was even a little grinding going on. When I look back, he's gone, but there's no doubt he received my message loud and clear. The message being, *She's mine, so back the fuck off.*

She stares up at me. Lips parted. Skin flushed. Eyes full of adoration.

My chest tightens, and I realize there's one fear I haven't acknowledged.

I'm scared to death of losing her.

The fact I'm even thinking this way tells me my feelings for her go way beyond the lie we've been hiding behind. That crap I'd been spouting last night about keeping things carefree now burns like acid on my tongue. Right now, holding her in my arms, I know the very promise I asked her to make is one I have no intention of keeping.

As crazy as it sounds, I'm starting to think it would be wise to put some distance between us, before one of us winds up getting hurt.

CASSIE

You know the old saying if it seems too good to be true then it probably is...

Well, things *were* great. Really, *really* great.

Our time in Chicago had a profound effect on me. It changed me. Changed the way I look at us. I know that I'm in love with him. And I'm almost certain he loves me too.

From the moment we met I've had a crush on him. Over time that crush turned to longing. We've spent so much time together. I never questioned when the feelings I'd been harboring began to take root. I knew early on he felt something for me, and I suspected it was something much deeper than he was willing to admit. In a way, we've constructed our own twisted puzzle, pieced together with so many truths and lies neither of us seem to notice those pieces, however jagged their edges, fit together perfectly.

Life got pretty busy for both of us after returning to Ann Arbor. I'm busy studying for finals. I've memorized most of the chapters covered in my psych lecture, and thanks to my private tutor, I'm fairly certain I'll pass calculus with a solid B-. Just last week, I started working on a new song with Mitch, the guy from my composition class, so we've been spending a lot of time in a rehearsal room.

Hockey and school have always kept Brantley busy, but two weeks ago, he picked up a part-time job bussing tables at a restaurant downtown to earn extra money for Christmas. That means if I want to see him on the days we can't hang out, I have to jump on a bus and finish my homework while the team practices. After Thanksgiving, Roni severed all ties with Josh, claiming a certain hockey player had caught her eye, so she often joins me. We huddle under a blanket and try our best to focus on our assignments, but once the guys take the ice, it's pretty hard to focus on anything else.

Last weekend he had a night off, so we went out and bought a Christmas tree. Then, we took it back to his place and decorated it with supplies we'd picked up at Target. Jordan and Davis wanted to help, so I gave them the task of stringing the lights after Brantley spent thirty minutes making sure the tree was perfectly straight. We each took turns hanging ornaments, making sure to fill every available branch, and when we were finished we turned off the lights and sat on the floor to enjoy its beauty. Scotty came home with a pizza, and the five of us talked for hours, sharing our favorite childhood memories of Christmas mornings.

Tonight I'm alone as I approach the arena. My Chucks scuff quickly over the concrete in my haste to escape the cold outdoors, only to immediately subject myself to the frigid temperature inside the rink. I tried telling myself I should stay home tonight, but we've barely spoken this week, and I can't shake the feeling he's hiding something from me.

The guys are on the ice, and practice appears to be in full swing. I scan the jerseys, searching for #27, and when I find him, my heart swells. I love watching him skate. Love the way he looks in his practice jersey. He glides gracefully over the ice. His fluid movements transport him from one end of the ice to the other in no time at all. That same sexy confidence I see in the bedroom carries over to his performance as a player. I stand behind a wall of wood and Plexiglas, transfixed by the man before me. He's covered in gear, but I know every inch of the gorgeous body hidden beneath it by heart. I've memorized every line, every muscle, every vein. I know what makes him shudder, and I know how to make him moan. He could just as easily make the same statement about me. He knows me better than I even know myself. That's why the physical distance is tearing me apart. But it's not just sex that I miss. I miss they way we used to be. The way we were before sex.

I miss us.

Practice is about to wrap up, and at this point, the guys are running simple skate-and-shoot drills against the freshmen players, which are ridiculously unbalanced. It's hardly fair to put a freshmen player up against someone of Davis' or Brantley's caliber; those two dominate when they're on the ice. He looks over to where I'm standing and acknowledges me with a tip of his chin and a wink. When it's his turn, he kicks off with his skate and weaves side to side, maneuvering the puck with ease, and when he reaches the end, he draws his arm back and sends the puck flying into the net. When he skates past a group of bunnies,

I notice the way he acknowledges them, but when he reaches the section where I'm standing, he lifts his glove and blows me a kiss on his way to the locker room. My heart leaps with joy at the simple gesture, because it tells me he still cares.

Once practice is over, I hang around until the guys have had their showers, and hide in a darkened corner to watch as everyone exits the locker room. Everyone except Brantley. Once I know the coast is clear, I tentatively enter the room and search for him. There's a long hall with two rooms on the left. One is a meeting area where they watch footage of their games, and study their opponents. The other is an office I assume belongs to Coach Bishop. On the right, the hall opens to a large area lined with lockers and benches for the players. This area leads to the shower room. I don't find him in the locker room, so I can only assume he's still in the shower, or maybe he's already left and I just missed seeing him.

As I approach I hear running water and a voice. His voice. I stop and toe my shoes off before entering the steamy room. From where I stand, I can see him. His back is to me, and his hands are braced against the tile. Water runs over his back and he's speaking softly, either to himself or someone else. At this point, I'm not sure. I brace myself for the worst and bridge the distance between us. Sensing he's no longer alone, he turns his head and looks surprised to see me.

"Cassie, what are you doing back here?" He frowns.

His question offends me, and when he doesn't make a move toward me I step into the stall with him.

"Why do you think I'm here? I was worried about you. About us. We hardly see each other anymore."

"I'm fine. I told you, I've been really busy." He scrubs a hand over his face before pinching the bridge of his nose between two fingers.

"You've been in here a really long time. And when I came in, you were talking to yourself. Is there something going on you're not telling me?" My fists clench at my sides in frustration, because I don't know if I should be angry or confused. The shaky feeling in my legs tells me it's something worse.

I'm terrified.

"I've got a few things on my mind I need to mull over, and I wanted to do it *alone*," he snaps, and I tense at the harshness in his voice.

Okay. This conversation is going nowhere fast. Guess I'll have to be more direct. I pull myself up to my full height, though he still towers over me, and step under the water with him. Fully clothed.

"Are you crazy?" he yells, just as I blurt out, "Are you dumping me?"

He stops and stares as rivulets of water stream down my face. He moves me back a half-step, so I'm no longer drowning, and rests his hands on my elbows. His face registers confusion, and I don't really blame him. We aren't dating. We're not a couple. Hell, we're not even in a relationship. And we sure as hell haven't said the unspoken L-word. Bottom line— I'm not sure what we are anymore.

"Baby, no." He folds me in his arms as he rocks me back and forth under the spray. "I'm not dumping you. How can you even think that? From the moment we met, you've consumed me." His voice softens as he cups my face in his strong hands.

"Because I miss you, B. Because I need you." My voice breaks as the words get stuck in my throat. "And I thought..." I look down and see my hands are shaking. I'm in a steamy room, with hot water beating down on me, yet I can't stop shivering.

"Believe me when I tell you, there's no one else on this earth worth thinking about. I'm just dealing with shit only I can fix." He lowers his face to mine before continuing. "I told you, I'm messed up. There are things happening between us, and I just wasn't prepared for it. I'm trying to figure out what it all means." His thumb traces the curve of my lip as he studies my expression. "Now, what else were you going to say?"

"What do you mean?" I blink up at him in confusion.

"You said you *thought* something. What was it?" his lips brush mine in a tender kiss as he waits for my answer.

"I was going to say that I thought you needed me too." It's a good thing he's close, because I've whispered the words so softly even I barely hear them.

His body sags against mine. "That's the problem, Dimples. I'm scared I may need you too much."

No other words are spoken. Instead, we close our eyes and kiss until we forget about everything else. We kiss the way we did the first time we met.

Before rules and promises were broken.

Before lies were told.

Back when things were simple.

Back when we were *just* friends.

Back when we were still *us*.

And it was perfect. Except for one small problem.

When I open my eyes, I'm still in love with him.

BRANTLEY

"There's no denying their lines are strong this year," Jordan announces as the waitress places our drinks on the table. "I've watched the footage of their last four games, and McFarland scored three goals in one game alone, not to mention the goals and assists he racked up in the other three games."

I look around the table and realize how much I've missed these guys. It's been a long time since the four of us stopped for a beer after practice. After talking about Scott's love life and teasing Jordan over his lack of one, the topic has naturally switched to hockey. More specifically, the game scheduled against Minnesota after we return from Christmas break.

"Yeah, we're going to have to tighten up that second line if we want any chance of taking away a win. Let's talk with Coach about getting in some extra ice time before we take off this week. Cage, why don't you see if Taylor's willing to push the D-men harder in practice?" Rivers tosses out sarcastically. There's no denying our last two losses were because we've been weak in the defensive zone. I'm not solely responsible for our poor performance on the ice, but when you tack on the fact I'm sleeping with his sister, it only adds to the guilt I'm already carrying.

"Let's not forget their goalie is a strong contender for the Richter Award. His stats are pretty stellar, so if we want any hope of scoring, we'll have to attack hard," Davis reminds us.

"Spiker may be good, but Rivers has been solid in the crease this season. He's averaged twenty-eight saves per game, and he's also a contender. If you ask me, I think he'll be the one to take it." I tip my beer in Scott's direction. He offers a nod of thanks, but doesn't let the praise go to his head. Like the rest of us, he's played the game long enough to know anything can happen, and if you're not careful, the direction your career was taking can suddenly veer off path and it would all end in the blink of an eye.

"Hey, what time are you guys heading out tomorrow?" I ask casually. Jordan scored tickets for the Kid Rock concert tomorrow night in Cincinnati. Ashley is also going, which comes as no surprise, but it works in their favor because her family lives in Cincinnati and they plan on getting hammered and spending the night at their house.

"Charger's pulling out at three, and there's room for your sexy ass if you've changed your mind," Rivers replies, making sure to toss in a cheeky wink at the end.

While a part of me would love to go along for the ride, I'd already told them I couldn't because I had to work at the restaurant. But that's a lie. I don't have to work. Cassie's coming over to watch a movie and celebrate Christmas before we both head back home for break.

When we left Chicago, I'd known things between us had shifted. It spooked me, because I'm not sure either of us is ready to admit our true feelings. Cassie's not ready for Scott to find out about us. And honestly, neither am I. The guilt I've been carrying is a heavy burden, but it doesn't change the way I feel about her. I'm not going to lie, the last few weeks have been rough, but we're both trying to work through it. Cassie says she wants to get through Christmas and then come clean about our relationship.

Cause that's what this is...

A relationship.

I'm still not sure how it happened. Me letting her in. I've been running from love for so long, I figured if I kept wasting time with girls who were forgettable, it would never catch up with me. So, I've spent the last four years using casual sex as a shield, secretly believing it would protect my heart from further damage.

And then I met her...

Cassie isn't like all the other girls. And there's nothing forgettable about her.

She came into my life like a sudden downpour. Showering me with love and hope when I'd least expected it. But exactly when I'd needed her the most.

Tonight, she's hanging out with her roommate and some guy named Mitch from her music class. They've been working on a project together these last few weeks, and claimed they needed a break from the monotony of the rehearsal room.

"Thanks, but I have to work at four. I'll be there till closing. But have a good time and try to stay out of trouble." I'm looking at Davis when I say this, because he always seems to get himself in a bind whenever we're out. I blame it on his charming good looks, but Rivers says it's because he runs his mouth too much.

"Hey, you can't have fun without finding a little trouble. The two go hand-in-hand. Ain't that right, Cage?" Davis retorts. I look over and scowl and that fucker has the nerve to wink at me!

Cocky son of a bitch.

"God, would somebody please kill me so I don't have to endure another Kelly Clarkson wannabe," Rivers beats his forehead on the table. We all look toward the stage, where a blond is doing her best to keep up with the lyrics on the screen, but she still sounds like a dying hyena. "How the hell did we forget it was karaoke night?"

"Aw, come on, it's not so bad. That chick who sang Katy Perry was smokin' hot," Davis smiles wickedly. "She even gave me her phone number."

"Why am I not surprised?" I say, rolling my eyes.

"Yeah, what can I say? Chicks just seem to throw themselves at me," he deadpans. We're all laughing at his remark when he leans over and smacks me with the back of his hand as he points in the direction of the stage. "Hey, Scott, isn't that Cassie?"

Rivers turns around and when he sees her he does a double take. "Huh, I guess it is. I didn't know she hung out here." He gives his shoulder a quick shrug. "But I'm not surprised she's up on that stage."

"Why's that?" Jordan asks.

"Because she has an amazing voice," I answer quietly. Scott scowls as if he may be about to say something, but he lets it go. My gaze shifts to the stage, where she's holding a microphone and waiting for her opening note. The music starts up, and it's a techno-synthesizer beat I've become very familiar with over the past few months, because she's made me listen to it on more than one occasion.

She begins the song standing in place, but once she reaches the chorus, she starts strutting across the stage, singing about love being insanity and clarity all at the same time. Gone is the shy girl I walked home after finding her crying in a bathroom. In her place is a woman who dropped to her knees and owned me in her neighbors' bathroom. The same woman who'd moaned shamelessly while I brought her to climax with my fingers and a cheap latex toy.

The woman on stage exudes raw sexuality, and my dick has definitely taken notice.

But that's not the only part of me that notices.

I know everything about her. Every freckle on her nose. The sparkle that gleams in her left eye just before she comes. Every sigh of contentment. And the dimple that pops just after we've kissed. I could go on and on.

The crowd loves her. They love it when she raises her fist to punctuate certain words. And they scream like crazy every time she hits an unbelievably high note. She steps into the crowd, weaving her way through tables while continuing the song. A few guys at a table near the front reach out and snack her on the ass, and I push myself out of my chair.

"Easy, Casanova," Davis holds me back with a strong grip on my forearm. I sit back down and rub my hand over the back of my neck in frustration.

"Holy shit, Rivers. Your sister is fucking awesome!" Jordan stares up at the stage with his mouth hanging open.

"She is pretty amazing, isn't she?" he says in wonder.

When the song is over, the crowd goes bat-shit crazy and demands an encore. My heart swells with pride, because I've been telling her all along she's going to be a star. It doesn't take long for the next song to start, and it's a slow one. I also know this song. It's "Holding Out for a Hero" by Elise Lieberth. She had me listen to it on the train ride home, and after it was through playing, she said the song reminded her of me.

Even though I've heard her sing many times, I'm still mesmerized by her performance. The whole place goes quiet as she sings, and when she asks if there's a Superman to sweep her off her feet, I could swear our eyes lock.

Davis places a hand on my shoulder and leans forward, speaking in a low tone. "I realize you're having a moment right now, but I advise you to wipe that look off your face before he figures out you're in love with her." My eyes dart to his, and he merely raises his brow in response. "Just thought you should know."

Love?

Me?

BRANTLEY

"Are you *sure* you want to wait until after dinner to exchange gifts?" She calls to me from the living room.

I come down the stairs and find her on her knees under the tree, trying to find the perfect spot for my present. When she turns her head, I'm right behind her, and her eyes travel the length of my frame before meeting my gaze. I can't resist chuckling at her persistence before crouching down beside her. I skim my finger along her cheek before tapping the end of her button nose.

"Positive." I slide my hand around the back of her head and give a gentle tug until our lips are millimeters apart. "I think someone needs to learn some patience." Our lips meet for three quick kisses before I stand and take her by the hand. "Come on, time for that movie."

The movie is half over and we've spent most of it making out. So far, we've stuck to kissing and fondling with our clothes on. It's actually really nice, and I can't remember the last time I've had this much fun with my clothes on. Every time her hands go to unbutton my jeans, I just lift her arm and place it back around my neck. I look at it as building the anticipation, but it's driving Cassie out of her ever-loving mind.

"You're no fun." She sticks out her bottom lip and pouts.

I stop kissing her neck and narrow my eyes. "Did you just call me boring?"

She doesn't say anything, just looks at me and nods once. In one fluid motion, I stand and throw her over my shoulder. As I march toward the front door, she's giggling and slapping at my ass. The cold air hits immediately, and when she realizes where I'm going, her giggles turn into pleading.

"Brantley, no! Don't you dare." I keep walking until we reach the pile of snow to the right of the sidewalk and carefully toss her in the slushy mound. "Are you crazy? I'm not dressed for this!" She rises to a sitting position and places her hands on her hips. I'm laughing so hard I fail to see her hands reaching up to yank me down beside her. Now we're both cold and wet, so I do the only logical thing that comes to mind. I make a sloppy snow angel. A moment later, she makes one too and when I turn to her, still laughing, I find her staring at me with something more than laughter in her eyes.

"B, I lo—" I lean over and cover her mouth with mine, effectively cutting her off.

I know what she was about to say, and I'm not sure I'm ready to hear it. Right now, we're living in the fantasy world we've created, and everything feels so good here. I'm afraid if we say the words, we're opening ourselves up to a reality that's sure to destroy us.

I kiss her deeply, hoping my lips are able to convey what I'm feeling inside.

"Brantley," she says through chattering teeth, "I'm turning into a popsicle. Can we maybe take this back inside?"

"Oh, shit, baby, I'm sorry," I scoop her up and dash back inside where it's nice and warm. We're both a soaking wet mess, so I take her upstairs to my room. "Why don't you take a shower to warm up while I go downstairs and start dinner. Is breakfast okay?"

"It's perfect, just like you," she whispers, lifting up on her tiptoes to kiss me again. "There's only one teeny problem. I don't have anything dry to put on." She lifts her wet shirt over her head and tosses it on the bathroom floor, and I'm momentarily distracted by how great her tits look in the lacy, red bra she's wearing.

"No worries, just grab anything of mine." I give her nipple a tease with my thumb before turning to start dinner. "See you in a few minutes."

"Tease." She throws me a wink before adding her bra to the pile. "Make me extra sausage."

"You never eat your sausage," I remind her.

"I know, but *you* do." I can't stop smiling as I make my way down the stairs.

My back is turned when she enters the room. The pancake batter is ready to go, and I have sausage and bacon finishing up on the stove.

"There's orange juice on the counter, and I've already popped the cork on the champagne if you'd like a mimosa," I call over my shoulder as I take the meat out of the pan. "I thought we could pretend like it's Christmas morning and—" I turn around and forget everything I was about to say.

She's standing in my kitchen, dressed in nothing but my old practice jersey and a pair of blue-stripped tube socks. She's so small it hangs past her knees, and the collar falls off one shoulder. Her blond hair hangs down in loose curls and her face has been scrubbed clean.

In all my life, I've never seen a more beautiful sight.

"Is everything okay? I hope you don't mind me wearing this," she looks down and tugs nervously at the jersey as I fight to swallow the lump in my throat. "I just figured it's so long it takes away the need for pants. If it bothers—" She stops talking when I cut her off for the second time tonight.

My left hand threads through her hair as our lips crash together. Her mouth is warm, just like her skin, and when my tongue slides inside, she whimpers. My fingers trail down her leg to find the hem of my shirt, and when I reach the apex of her thighs, I'm met with her bare pussy.

"No panties?" I smile devilishly.

"I figured it was redundant." Her shoulder lifts an inch. "You'd probably end up tearing them off."

"I like the way you think."

Keeping my hand between her legs, I lift her up and place her on the kitchen table. Stepping into the empty space between her legs, I tease my tongue over her lips before trailing it down the hollow of her throat.

Her soft whimpers encourage me as I lower one side of the jersey's collar to expose her naked breast. My lips cover the taut peak, and I swirl my tongue in slow circles until she squirms beneath me. Moving to the other nipple, I repeat the seduction while she rubs herself over my knuckle until her soft purrs turn into moans.

I release her nipple with a loud pop and lower myself into the chair positioned directly in front of her. Lifting her by the hips, my hands slide the jersey up to her waist. I could take it off, but seeing her in it has my dick harder than the fucking Hope diamond. My hands go to her knees, easing them apart ever so slowly until I'm rewarded with the sight of her glistening folds.

"Mmmm," I say, leaning my head in for a taste.

"Uh, Brantley," she wiggles her hips and braces herself on her elbows, "what are you doing?"

I stop what I'm doing and tip my head back to meet her smirk with one of my own, "Eating, of course."

Taking her by the ankles, I drag her back to my mouth and dine until her soft cries tell me she's had enough.

"That mouth of yours should be registered as a lethal weapon." A contented smile fills her face as she reaches out for me to help her up.

"I take it you enjoyed that," I say with confidence, wiping my mouth with the back of my hand.

"Duh." She offers a throaty laugh and palms the aching bulge in my pants. "But what about you? Do you enjoy doing that?"

"Are you kidding?" I smile and drop my pants to the floor. "Best meal I've ever eaten."

"Yeah? Well, you haven't had dessert yet," she counters, curling her leg around mine to urge me closer. Lust fills her gorgeous, blue eyes, and all I can think about is covering her in sticky, sweet caramel and feasting until I fall into a sugar coma.

Her arms circle my waist, drawing me in so the tip of my

arousal brushes against the tiny bundle of nerves. Her lips part and her eyes flutter closed as she eagerly tilts her pelvis to take me. With one hand in her hair and the other splayed across her lower back, I roll my hips and slowly guide the blunt head inside. Her inner muscles contract and pull, guiding me in at a luxuriously slow pace.

I love the way her body reacts to the intrusion. The shuddery gasp when I crest her opening. The hiss she sucks in as her muscles stretch to accommodate me. Followed by the long, contented sigh we both release when I'm all the way in.

"Sweet Jesus," I growl in her ear, "being inside you tops everything I've ever done."

My lips find the spot on her neck that drives her crazy, and her head rolls lazily to one side as I lavish her with wet kisses.

"Better than kicking Kazmierski's ass?" she teases with a snap of her pelvis I feel clear down to my toes.

I bite her tender flesh then soothe the sharp sting with soft strokes of my tongue. "Sooo much better."

She writhes on the table, lowering her chin to her chest and moaning ever so softly. I don't like the change, because it means I can't see her eyes. I fist my hand in her hair and give a gentle yank.

Her pupils dilate, telling me she likes it when I get a little rough. "Better than winning the Frozen Four?"

"I told you," I growl, slamming my cock so deep she whimpers and claws at my shoulders. "Nothing compares. Nuh-thing."

Her fingers grip the back of my scalp, smashing our mouths together in a hungry kiss. I angle my head to the left, savoring the push and pull of her lips as her tongue twists and turns with mine in a slow dance of seduction.

As I roll my hips, she arches her back to meet me. Her legs tighten their grip around my waist, increasing the friction between us. With every stroke the base of my shaft grinds against her engorged clit and she responds by sucking my tongue deeper into her mouth. I pull back, leaving only the crown safely nestled inside, then hammer back into her in one powerful stroke. Her head falls forward to rest on my shoulder, and I continue thrusting, giving it everything I've got, until I damn near pass out from the intense pleasure coursing through me.

"I love you," she whispers quietly.

My body stills at her words, but my brain doesn't slow down. It kicks into overdrive.

She loves me?

Gripping my face in her hands, she presses one tender kiss to my lips, and this time looks me straight in the eye when she repeats it. "I love you, Brantley."

She loves me...

My head is spinning.

I've spent the last four years believing that hearing the words *I love you* would only bring me pain.

All it had taken to prove me wrong had been hearing the right woman say them.

She loves me!

Sliding my hands under her ass, I pick her up and take her against the pantry door. Her arms cling tightly around my neck as I pound relentlessly into her tiny body. Canned goods knock together every time her ass slams against the door, and when her orgasm reaches a crescendo she bites down hard on my shoulder as I fill her with my release.

By now, we're both a panting, sweaty mess. My pants are around my ankles, and her legs are draped over my forearms. I slowly lower her to the floor and pull up my pants, not bothering to button them before I cup my hands over her face and place a soft kiss on her swollen lips.

Unable to tear my gaze away, I rest my forehead on hers and take a deep breath to steady my nerves for what I need to say.

"Cassie, I—" I'm unable to get the words out before an angry voice bellows behind me and we both freeze.

"You lying motherfucker!" I'm torn away from her and thrown onto the kitchen table. "The whole time? You were fucking her the whole time!"

"Scott, it wasn't like th—" my words are cut off when his fist connects with my jaw. It hurts like hell, but this time I remain standing.

At this point, Cassie's screaming, and when Scott turns his anger on her, I use my hand to move her safely behind me.

"Just friends, huh? I can't believe you went behind my back." His face reflects nothing but disgust when he points his finger at me. "Why him? He's not good enough for you."

"Hey!" I interject, taking offense to the insult he's just hurtled at my expense.

"Cassie, he'll sleep with anything that walks. Hell, he's slept with half the chicks on campus, and now you've let him fuck you too. Don't you know he'll only break your heart?" His hands pull violently at the ends of his hair as he angrily paces the kitchen floor. "Christ, you're no better than his faithful puck bunnies."

I charge at him, lowering my shoulder as I connect, and we both slam against the wall. We're an equal match in strength and throw one another around the kitchen with great force, denting the fridge and breaking the table as we both land on it. As we wrestle, he pins me down and starts pounding my face with his fist. Blood gushes from my nose, and by the crunching sound it made when he hit me, I'm pretty sure it's broken.

Cassie jumps on her brother's back and starts pummeling him with her small fists, screaming at the top of her lungs.

"Stop it! You're going to kill him!" her high-pitched screams echo in my ears. "Scotty, please, I love him," she cries out, distracting him enough for me to deliver a two-handed blow to the chest. He staggers back, knocking Cassie to the ground with a loud thud and she scrambles to the corner.

I take advantage of the opening and pounce on him. After he landed first blow, I'd been willing to let it go, seeing as how I had deceived him. But after the cruel things he said to Cassie and seeing the pain on her face, I can't hold back any longer.

I have him pinned against the counter, nailing him with my fist, knee, elbow.

Whatever.

With every swing that connects, the guilt I've been carrying piles onto my shoulders like lead weights until, ultimately, it consumes me and I'm left staring at the mess I've made.

Two people.

Two people I love more than anything else in this world.

Two people whose lives have just been ruined by my selfish choices.

The best friend who trusted me...

The girl who thinks of me as her hero...

Fuck that. I'm no hero. I'm nothing more than a broken mess. Inside *and* out.

Hell, I don't deserve either of them.

Rivers stands, wiping the blood from his nose on his sleeve before delivering the final blow. "I can't believe you both went behind my back. I trusted you, Cage. I fucking trusted you would look out for her, but instead you took advantage of that trust and you took advantage of my sister. You son of a bitch. I can't even look at you anymore. "

Tears pour down Cassie's cheeks as she's faced with the consequences of our actions. I'd already known something like this would happen. I tried telling her from the very start, but she wouldn't listen.

Neither of us had truly listened.

Until now, it had all been a game. But in every game, no matter how well you both play, there's always going to be someone who loses.

Her eyes fall to mine, and even through her tears I can tell she expects me to rescue her. But I can't. How can I save her when I can't even save myself?

She reaches out for me to take her hand, and just like that the walls that used to guard my heart are once again resurrected. "Come on, B. Let's get out of here."

"You need to go home. Now." I meet her gaze with eyes that feel empty and a heart heavy as stone.

"Pack your shit and get out of my house," he says, putting an arm around his sister's waist.

"Scotty, you need to let us explain. We love—"

"Love?" His laughter mocks her. "You're wasting your time, Cassie. Cage doesn't fall in love." She shoves him away and takes a step in my direction.

"That's not true! He does love me!" She turns and her eyes plead with me. "B, tell him."

I open my mouth. Wanting desperately to tell her what she needs to hear. And what I need to say.

But I don't...

"Go home, Cassie!" She sucks in a breath, her blue eyes filling with tears, and another piece of my heart shatters. The last thing I see is her running out the door before Rivers' fist connects with my eye.

CASSIE

"Go home!"

Those two words ring loudly in my ears as my socked feet pound the wet pavement. It's snowing out. I guess it must have started sometime after we'd made our snow angels.

I look over and there they are. Side by side and somewhat disfigured thanks to the awkward angle in which we'd fallen. Fresh snow now covers the ground, but if you look closely, you can still see the handprint he'd left when he'd rolled over to kiss me.

He'd known what I was about to say. That's why he'd kissed me. To shut me up.

He hadn't been ready then, so what had changed in the last hour? I'd told him not once, but twice in the kitchen. The look in his eyes clearly indicated he liked hearing it. And the way he responded told me he felt the same way.

He'd been about to say it too. I'm sure of it. Then Scott stormed in and destroyed everything.

Including Brantley.

Why was he always trying to come between us?

Tears sting my eyes, making it impossible to see where I'm going, which is why I collide with Davis at the end of the driveway.

"Whoa, Cassie, slow down. Where are you going?" he casts a nervous glance toward the house before frowning at my appearance. "Sweetie, you're going to freeze to death dressed like that." He slips off his jacket and wraps it around my shoulders. "What's happening in there?"

I collapse against him and begin sobbing uncontrollably as he guides me over to Scott's car.

"What the fuck is going on?" Jordan demands, repeating the question, and they both look to me for answers.

"Brantley," I manage to choke out, "he's hurt. Scotty came home. They fought. There's so much blood."

"What the fuck?" Davis mutters under his breath. "Jordan, go inside and make sure they haven't killed each other. I'm going to take Cassie home," he orders. Jordan doesn't hesitate. He bounds up the stairs and throws open the front door to check on his friends.

I'm having trouble believing what just happened. I've never seen my brother so angry. So full of raw emotion. Could he really hate Brantley all because of some stupid code?

We're both quiet for the first few minutes of the ride, but the drumming of his thumbs on the steering wheel tells me he's waiting for me to tell him what happened.

"We were going to tell him after Christmas. Brantley wanted to tell him sooner, but I begged him to wait," our eyes meet briefly before I have to look away because of the guilt I'm feeling.

"I just needed a little more time."

"Time to do what?" he places his hand over mine to offer a comforting squeeze.

"Make him fall in love with me," I lean my head against the cool glass and picture the look on his face when he'd yelled at me.

Brantley never yelled at me. In fact, he's never even raised his voice before today. He's always so caring. So protective. Even when Scott had turned his anger on me, it had been Brantley's natural reaction to shield me. Scott's words were harsh, but the accusations he made against Brantley were completely false and uncalled for.

B has never once treated me like a puck bunny. Even when we were just fooling around he'd shown me tremendous respect. And I know he's hurting right now. He values my brother's friendship, and because of me that bond has been destroyed. He never wanted a relationship, but that never stopped me from pushing his limits until it was too late to turn back.

"You've got nothing to worry about there. Dude's been in love since the moment he met you," Davis chuckles and downshifts as we turn the corner.

"Yeah, right," I scoff, "he went out of his way to avoid me. I'd hardly call that love at first sight."

"Oh, he was in love. He just didn't know it yet." He deadpans, throwing the car in park when we reach our destination.

My fingers fidget nervously in my lap before I'm able to meet his concerned gaze. We've grown close this semester. I reflect on all the Wednesday lunch dates we've shared. Like Brantley, he's kind-hearted and fiercely loyal. I find myself wondering how my brother could turn his back on someone he once considered a brother. It just doesn't make sense.

None of this does.

"And what about now? You think he's figured it out by now?" I ask quietly, taking a deep breath I don't realize I'm holding until he answers and I finally let it out.

"It's not really my place to tell you that," he begins, then he releases a heavy sigh before adding, "but yeah, I truly believe he's head over heels in love with you. But it's not going to be easy for him. Scott's friendship meant the world to him, and you saw how pissed your brother was."

"If you knew he was that angry then why didn't you and Jordan stop him? You had to know what was going to happen when he got inside the house."

"Scott asked us to wait outside to give him time to talk to both of you. I know it sounds crazy, but this has been coming for a long time. Those two haven't seen eye to eye for the last year. Ashley drove a pretty good wedge between them," he crosses his arms over the steering wheel and looks up at the stars, appearing to be deep in thought. "He broke up with her tonight, at the concert. That's why we were headed home early. He was already pissed and driving fast. Then he got a call from your ex saying you've been screwing Cage. Well, as you can imagine, he drove like a bat out of hell the rest of the way home, muttering under his breath and cursing up a storm."

Justin? How the hell would he have found out about us?

"He said some really awful things about Brantley. If they're truly best friends, why would he do that?"

"Cage was a mess when that shit went down with Vanessa.

292

Scott really helped him through all that. Those two were already close, but that seemed to make their bond stronger. Soon, they were inseparable, and then Scott met Ashley. At first, he was able to divide his time between hockey, Ashley, and everything else. But a year ago, Ashley decided Scott needed to be up her ass twenty-four-seven. Cage gave him shit about it. Personally, I think it was because he was secretly jealous Scott had found something he'd lost. He's tried for years to play it off like he didn't want a relationship, but then he met you and everything else took second place. I think that says a lot. Don't you?"

"I'm scared, Davis. He yelled at me tonight. He's never done that," I worry my bottom lip between my teeth, wishing desperately life was a giant remote and I could just press the rewind button and change the last two hours. "I realize things got pretty intense in there, but you weren't there. You didn't see the cold look in his eyes," I swallow hard and angrily brush the tears from my face. "We were so close to figuring it all out. Now I'm terrified he'll throw it all away."

He leans across the console and pulls me in for a hug. The angle is awkward, but I rest my head on his broad shoulder and find comfort in the stroke of his hand on my back. "Give him some time, Cassie. Cage is a smart guy. He'll figure it out. You both will."

"I hope so," I whisper and close my eyes. "God, I hope so."

CASSIE

Time...

Why does it seem to fly when you're doing something you love, but drags ass when you're miserable?

I manage to survive three days without contacting him. Instead of dwelling on what happened, I try my best to focus on what Davis told me. Surely he knew what he'd been talking about when he said Brantley loved me. Being he'd never actually said the words, and with every day of silence that's passed, it's hard to ignore the doubt clinging to the edges of my already fragile heart.

I remember what it felt like when I'd fallen in love with Justin. He was the first boy I ever kissed, and my heart used to race when he'd score a goal and point to me so I'd know he'd done it just for me. Everything with Justin had been over the top. He always made a grand show of letting everyone know I was his girl. It was his way of staking claim. At the time, I thought nothing of it. Later, I came to realize I no longer wanted to be someone's property, especially when he didn't even respect me.

Unlike Justin, Brantley never treated me as a possession. He treated me as if I were a prize. Often I would find him staring, and he'd give me a look that said he wasn't completely sure if he deserved me. But nothing could have been further from the truth. When we met I'd been an emotional wreck, but he'd gone out of his way to care for me.

Loving B had been easy. He made me feel safe. He made me feel wanted. He's never shown me anything but respect. He took all of my insecurities and gave me a confidence I never knew I possessed. In some ways we were complete opposites, but other times, we were one and the same.

I was a storm and he was my sun. And when we came together we formed one hell of a rainbow.

Some say we never should have been together. But I say we make perfect sense.

"You have another delivery," Roni announces, entering the room with another vase of brightly-colored flowers. She walks over to my desk, places them on the only empty space available, then tosses me the attached card.

That makes four bouquets and countless phone calls from Scott. Not to mention the lengthy voicemail Justin left last night after I refused to answer his calls. He gave me some sob story of how concerned he'd been for my safety, claiming a guy like Brantley would only break my heart. So naturally, he had to share his concern with Scott.

Please. Like he gave two fucks about the condition of my heart.

I deleted that one and chose to ignore the accompanying texts that continued to pop up throughout the night. By this morning I'd had enough and blocked his number entirely. Something I should have done a long time ago.

I'd heard too much from everyone I *didn't* want to talk to, and not one word from the *only* one who mattered.

"Are you going to class today?" She takes a seat on the edge of the bed and runs a hand up and down my arm. "Break starts tomorrow. You should go and at least pick up your final papers."

"Pass," I pull the pillow over my face.

"Cassie." She yanks the pillow away and forces me to look at her. "This is no way to act. Look, you're hurt I get that. But are you just going to let him go back to Colorado without talking to him? I think you're letting him off too easily."

"Oh yeah? So what would you suggest? Maybe I should try offering to be his fuck buddy again," I say sarcastically. "Wait, I already did that."

"Hey, don't knock that suggestion. Look where it got you."

"Hiding in my bed with more questions than answers? Yeah, thanks for that." I roll my eyes and pull the covers over my head like a child.

"Hey, don't blame me. It's not my fault you're afraid to call Scott out on his bullshit," she accuses.

I throw the covers back and abruptly sit up to argue.

"What the hell does that mean?"

"I'm just saying, you transferred to GL to get away from a controlling asshole and re-connect with your brother. But he never made time for you and was totally on board with Brantley being your friend. It's not your fault you developed feelings for one another; it was inevitable. Two attractive people in their sexual prime. Hell, your brother's a fucking idiot for not seeing this coming. And who is he to dictate who you, or anyone else for that matter, can date? All this time you've been hiding behind a label when you both should have had the balls to confront his ass and tell him to either accept it or fuck off."

Her words strike a chord deep within me. I've spent my entire life avoiding conflict. As a child I was always the one to conform. I can't count how many times I allowed girls in high school to walk all over me. Looking back, that's probably why Justin had been drawn to me. He knew he could suggest something and I'd go right along with it, even when I may have disagreed.

I'd been the same way with Scott. He was my big brother. I looked up to him. No matter what it was, if he was doing it, I wanted to do it too. If he didn't like something, it usually meant I wouldn't like it either. But not because I'd formulated my own opinion. His approval meant everything to me. Then he moved away to college, and I was left to stand on my own two feet. For the first time in my life I was free to make my own choices, and that was a scary feeling. Justin swooped in and took over my voice, and for a while I willingly handed it over to him. Until I found the strength to take it back. But when it comes to Scott, it seems I'm not there yet.

Pursuing Brantley had been my first real act of defiance against Scott. Maybe it had something to do with my breakup with Justin. But I think the real reason had simply been Brantley's reaction when he'd learned who I was. The look on his face when he spoke about that fucking bro code Scott hung over their heads has been stamped on my brain. His stupid rules make me feel as if he's still trying to make decisions for me, as if I'm a silly teenager who can't possibly know what's good for her.

But I *do* know.

I know Brantley Cage is the best thing that's ever happened

to me. Our friendship had been born out of need, yet somehow it still felt organic. We make each other laugh, and we wipe each other's tears. We talk about our fears, and encourage one another to chase our dreams.

Sleeping with him had been a choice.

And one I'll never regret.

But falling in love...

Falling in love had been inevitable.

By seven o'clock, I've grown tired of the silent treatment. Veronica was right. I can't let him fly back to Colorado without giving him a piece of my mind. Due to Christmas break, the buses aren't running, so I have to take an Uber. Earlier, I'd thought about all the places he could possibly be and only one made sense. He has to be at the arena. It's one of his favorite places to go, especially when he has something on his mind.

The building is closed for break, but I had the foresight to ask Davis if he had a key. Just so happens he did, and now I'm using it to let myself in. Davis said Brantley has been staying at the frat house with John, and I know he hates it there. He also informed me when Brantley has a lot on his mind, he tends to hide out in the weight room. So that's where I'm heading now.

The building is dark, and I have to use the flashlight on my phone to read the plaques on the doors. Halfway down the main corridor there's a small hallway on the right. I round the corner and come face-to-face with the door to the weight room. The door is one that only opens on this side of the building with one of those card access readers. Lucky for me, I'd already counted on that and came prepared. I swipe my student ID and open the door.

The room is huge, filled with every piece of equipment imaginable. A bank of treadmills line the entire outer wall, while hundreds of free weights take up space on the opposite interior wall. Large, padded squares dot various sections of the floor, while floor-to-ceiling mirrors decorate the wall behind the free weights. I assume this is so they can make sure they have proper form and don't injure themselves. Like the hallway, the room is mostly dark, with only half the room illuminated.

He's sitting on a bench by the free weights. His back is to me, and he's facing an empty wall. For a moment I think he's just sitting there, but as I inch closer, I spot the large dumbbell in his hand and see he's doing arm curls. He's wearing ear buds, so he doesn't hear me approach, and with every rep of the weight I see the pop in his veins and the bulge of his bicep. He's shirtless, and a sheen of perspiration glistens over the expanse of his muscular back.

Being this close makes my heart race. I know it's only been three days, but suddenly it seems as though it's been a lifetime. Taking a deep breath for strength, I step out of the shadows and finally come into view. He senses movement, which makes him turn his head, and when our eyes meet in the mirror, I choke back a sob.

His face is a complete mess. Both eyes have dark bruises beneath them as a result of the broken nose. The left side of his bottom lip is split, and dried blood fills the large crack that's there. And there's a bruise lining his left jaw. That was from the first blow.

My eyes never leave his as I make my way over to where he's sitting. I circle the bench, and when he doesn't stop me, I kneel in front of him, filling the space between his legs. His breathing is heavy, and it's the only sound I hear as I lift my hand to cup his cheek. The knuckles of his right hand are cracked and dotted with dried blood. With the opposite hand, I gently bring his fingers to my lips. Covering each digit with soft kisses before reaching his thumb. Never taking my eyes off his, I circle the tip of his thumb with my tongue before drawing it all the way into my warm mouth. An audible sigh escapes his damaged lips as the weight he's holding drops to the mat with a thud. Using his free hand, he threads his fingers around the nape of my neck and pulls me up to meet his waiting lips.

I don't care that the last words he spoke were a dismissal.

I don't care that it's been days since he last touched me.

I only focus on the relief coursing through me when his damaged mouth covers mine in the sweetest kiss I've ever experienced.

Reaching between us, I close my fingers around the thin cord and pop the buds from his ears. Though my mind swirls with questions, I don't voice them. Instead, I speak with my hands as they skim over the hard plains of his abdominal muscles, taking care to avoid the bruise on his ribs as I work my way up his chest. I boldly press my lips to his chest and my tongue sweeps over the heated flesh in long, languid strokes, stopping only when I've reached his earlobe.

His hands fist the back of my shirt, and all I can think about is getting naked with him in this room. I press myself further into him, feeling the length of his arousal as it grinds against the flat of my belly.

"I've missed you, so much."

His hands tighten their grip, and he releases a sigh of his own. "Cassie, you shouldn't be here. Anyone could come in and—"

"I don't care about someone seeing us. I don't care about any of that anymore. The only thing I care about is you and what's happening between us. Don't you see? We don't have to hide anymore. We can be together and no longer be saddled by guilt." Though my words are muffled by his flesh I know he hears because his shoulders sag as if he's carrying the weight of the world on them.

"Baby, I wish it were that easy. Jesus, I wish I could be everything you need me to be." He cups a hand under my chin and gently lifts my head to meet his gaze. "I'm so sorry for yelling at you, but I needed you to get out of there. It was the only way I could protect you."

"B, don't you know by now that I only feel safe when I'm with you? Without you, I'm empty and weak. I need *you* more than anything else."

I don't give him a chance to argue, I just kiss him. Gently at first, but then I'm no longer able to hold back. He opens, granting me access to explore and tease his tongue with mine. Soon, he's giving as much as he takes, cupping my ass in his hands and lifting me until I straddle his waist. My lips begin to travel as I slowly rock my pelvis back and forth, leaving open-mouthed kisses down his neck, nipping and suckling from one side to the other.

"Cassie, stop. I can't do this." He pulls back to meet my hurt gaze.

"I know why you're doing this." I draw a breath, letting it out on a long exhale. "You don't trust me with your heart. You're afraid if you give it to me there's a chance it could be broken again."

"It's been shattered once. I'm afraid next time it won't get broken. It'll be obliterated," he says quietly.

I press a single kiss to his lips. "You're my Superman. You're not supposed to be afraid of anything."

"Even Superman had weaknesses."

I flatten my hands against his chest and push back, needing to see his face.

There's pain masked beneath the blood and bruises. By looking in his eyes I know what's happening.

I'm losing him.

My greatest fear is happening right before my eyes, and there's not a damn thing I can do to stop it.

"You coward," I accuse through trembling lips. When he doesn't defend himself, I can't help shaking my head. "You're running away instead of fighting for us."

Letting out a frustrated huff, he stands and paces the floor, then turns and points to his face.

"I *did* fight for us! I'm wearing the fucking scars to prove it. Christ, what more do you want from me?" his chest heaves as he looks down at me with pain in his eyes and anguish on his battered face.

"I want you to tell me it wasn't a mistake, and that I'm not the only one in this room who fell in love." I plead with him.

He brings a hand to his mouth, and his eyes meet mine for the briefest of moments before closing.

"It wasn't a mistake."

I wait for him to keep going. To hear him say he loves me and needs me more than his next breath. But the words never come. It's almost as if the last months never occurred. That everything between us was just a beautiful dream that turned into one horrific nightmare. My heart cracks, standing still as if it's stopped beating.

"Fuck you, Brantley Cage. Fuck you and your goddamn fears," I cry out in despair, beating my fists against his chest. "Fuck you for being so sexy. For coming to my rescue, and for—"

Out of nowhere, he grabs my face, smashing his mouth over mine, forcing his wicked tongue deep inside. Goosebumps prick my flesh. But I'm far from being cold. I meld into him. Tongues spiraling round and round like a wild tornado. Kissing me like he owns me. Kissing me until I'm dizzy and we're both gasping for air.

"Fuck you, Cassie. Fuck you for making me fall in love with you," he growls. Then he storms out of the room and leaves me to process what just happened.

Did he just say what I think he said?

BRANTLEY

This just hasn't been my night.

I came to the arena with the hope of being alone. Being at the frat house means I've had zero privacy for three fucking days. I suppose I could go back to the house, but I really don't feel like going another round with Rivers. Dude's got a mean right hook, and I've got the busted nose and bruises to prove it. I'm fairly certain he doesn't look much better, but I haven't laid eyes on him since I stormed off that night.

I talked to Davis after I left, and he told me he'd given Cassie a ride home. He said she was a mess, and he asked what the hell I'd been thinking kicking her out when she hadn't been wearing clothes. Honestly, once the fists started flying, I'd forgotten everything else. But after speaking with him, it all came crashing back on me.

Making snow angels in the yard.

Cassie standing behind me in my jersey.

Screwing against the pantry door.

I swear to god she looked so fucking beautiful, I half expected animated wildlife to start circling her and singing. Like something out of a Disney movie or some crazy shit like that.

I felt so many things when I looked at her. I wanted to have my way with her on the kitchen table, then take her up to my room and beg her to never leave me. I wanted to tell her to keep my jersey and wear it every goddamn day. I wanted to tell her that no matter how hard I'd tried to fight it, I'd fallen deeply in love with her.

I should have known the fantasy we'd created was too good to be true. We'd been playing house for so long, I'd forgotten our walls were made of glass. Sooner or later, reality was bound to come crashing in.

Hearing Rivers say that shit to Cassie left a deep gash in my heart. Not only because it hurt to hear him saying those things about me. But also because in a way he'd been right. I *have* been with my fair share of women over the last four years. And I've made it abundantly clear to everyone with ears I'm not looking for a relationship. When Cassie came along, I'd been quick to tell her the same thing. She seemed content to simply be my friend, so spending time with her had been easy. Natural even. But every day, a little piece of her had wormed its way into my every thought. My every desire. My heart.

I want to believe what Cassie and I share is the real thing. But Vanessa had claimed to love me, and look how that turned out. After that heartbreak, it's been hard for me to freely hand over my heart to someone else. It's not because I don't believe Cassie will take care of it. I've been guarding it so long, I'm afraid I may not trust myself to give her my *whole* heart. Hell, after the way it was obliterated, I'm not even sure how much of it's left to give away. And she deserves nothing less than all of it.

So that's the question I've been asking myself since that night in my kitchen. Can I give it away and risk being hurt again? I'll keep searching until I find the answer. But I don't think it's fair to ask her to wait around while I try to figure it out.

I hadn't been prepared to see her tonight. I've skipped classes all week just to avoid running into her. I didn't want her seeing my face all messed up. I knew it would only make her feel guilty for not talking to Scott ourselves instead of letting him find out on his own. Davis told me how he found out, and the next time I see that prick, Justin, I'll be sure to kick his punk ass. Davis kindly pointed out I'll get my chance when we go against Minnesota after break. I'll gladly spend the night in the sin bin if it means I get to pound his face into the ice.

I make it back to the locker room and see the light on in Coach's office. *Christ, I cannot catch a break tonight.* There's no way I'm getting past his office without him seeing me, so I might as well say hello.

"Knock, knock," I lean in the doorway and wait for him to call me in. I know I could walk right in and take a seat across from him, but I'm not sure if he had the same idea as me and was counting on having the space to himself.

"Brantley, I'm surprised to see you here this late. Sit down and keep me company." He tosses his glasses on the desk and rubs a hand over his tired eyes.

"Well, I don't want to bother you. I just wanted to say hi, and wish you a Merry Christmas."

"Nonsense, get in here. I wanted to talk with you about something anyway." He points to an empty seat and then lowers his index finger. I take that to mean *park your ass in that chair*, which I've heard him tell me on more than one occasion, so I do as his finger says.

"I've waited three days for you or Rivers to have the balls to tell me what the hell went down between you two," his brow arches as he waits for me to respond. When I don't, he adds, "I'm still waiting."

"It was just a simple misunderstanding." I give my shoulder a shrug as if it's no big deal.

"Bullshit!" he barks, and the force of his voice knocks me back in my chair. "Two of my best players come in looking as if they've gone a few rounds with Mike Tyson, and you're going to sit there and tell me it was a simple misunderstanding?"

"He didn't like that I've been messing around with his sister," I concede.

"Yeah, I've noticed Cassie's been attending a lot of practices." He leans forward and scratches a hand over his chin. "So, what happened, he pull the big brother card on you?"

"Basically, but it goes deeper than that," I go quiet, and he takes that time to study my face. "He said I'm not good enough for her. You think maybe that's true?"

"First of all, I hate you even have to ask me that question. It tells me you actually believe that shit. Let me tell you something, Cage. You're a great kid. There's not a doubt in my mind you're more than good enough for this young woman. But it doesn't really matter what I think. What matters is what *you* think."

I draw a deep breath and let out a loud whoosh of air. "I want to be worthy of her love."

He nods his head and scratches his chin again. "I see. Are you in love with her?"

"Yes," I answer right away.

A smug smile fills his face as he sits back with his hands behind his head and stares.

"Why are you looking at me like that?" I ask defensively.

"Nothing. I just like the way you didn't even hesitate when I asked that question. So what's next?"

"Not sure. Guess I need some time to think it through."

"Sounds like you're afraid of getting hurt again. I get that. What you went through was rough for a kid your age. But, in all the years I've known you I've never seen you back down when something you wanted was within reach."

He gets up and walks around to where I'm sitting, then leans against the edge of the desk, arms crossed over his chest.

"Allow me to make an analogy. It's the final game of the Frozen Four. Score is tied with fifteen seconds left on the clock and it's your puck. Spiker's in the net and he's all over the crease, leaving only the thinnest chance of scoring. Do you take the shot anyway?"

It's a no-brainer.

"Hell, yeah, I do. I have to take it. I wouldn't waste an opportunity to knock the chip off Spiker's shoulder, not to mention I wouldn't want to let my team down." He just looks at me and does that head bob thing again.

"Interesting. Allow me to draw another scenario. It's the Stanley Cup Finals. You're playing D for the Chicago—"

"But I'm not going to Chicago. I'm going to Detroit," I interject.

"Please, allow me to finish. You're with Chicago and it's down to the final seconds of game seven. It's all on you, and Rivers has been on top of his game all night. Stopping every shot on goal. The puck races down the ice, and at the last minute it's handed off to you, because you have an opening. Now, do you hesitate to take the shot because Rivers is your friend, and by scoring you'll strip him of the opportunity to win the cup? Or, do you take the shot?"

"Fuck, no. I'd still take the shot," I say with certainty. There's no doubt in my mind. Not because of what went down between us, but because of our love of the game. It's what we'd both expect of each other.

"Why, Brantley? Why would you still take that shot?"

"Because, I'd be a fucktard for passing up that opportunity. And because he'd expect nothing less of me."

"Good answer." He gives me a pat me on the shoulder and goes back to his chair. He doesn't say anything else, so I assume the analogy lesson is over and I passed. I get up and head for the door when his voice stops me. "Cage?"

"Yeah?" I turn my head and look at him over my shoulder.

"You *do* realize that in both of those analogies Cassie was the goal. Right?"

I think about it for a minute then scrub my hand down my face. "I do now."

"Right. I just have one more question. Why aren't you taking the shot?"

Good question.

I don't answer. Mainly because I can't right now. But he did give me something to think about.

CASSIE

"I'm making cookies," mom announces, pulling the mixer and her favorite bowl from the cabinet. "Wanna help?"

"Sure," I shrug and continue to bounce my heel off the cabinet door.

"Okay, first things first, grab a carton of eggs and two sticks of butter from the fridge."

"I think by *help* you mean be your gopher," I tease, then jump down from my perch atop the counter and retrieve the items. While I'm there, I snag a slice of cold pizza leftover from last night's dinner.

"Which cookies are you making this year?" I lean on the counter beside her and take a giant bite.

"White chocolate with macadamias, of course," she answers over the whirl of the mixer.

I smile, appreciating her efforts to try and cheer me up.

"I know what my baby girl likes." Her right eye closes in what's supposed to be a wink but ends up looking more like a nervous twitch.

With a mouth full of pizza, I reach over and pat her on the arm, "Pfhank ewe."

Her eyes roll to the ceiling. "Sweetie, it's not ladylike to talk with your mouth full."

"It's also not ladylike to say fuck, but you say it all the time," I remind her.

"That's just splitting hairs," she argues as I pop the last bite in my mouth, "and it's not even a fair comparison. There will *always* be a time where fuck is the only word that fits. Talking with your mouth full of pizza is just—"

"Gross," Scott finishes, coming up behind her and placing a kiss on her cheek. "Morning," he says to both of us. Mom smiles and returns the greeting. I, however, do neither.

"Scott, we were just making cookies. Would you like to help us? It'll be just like old times." She gives him a smile that reads *you're making cookies whether you like it or not* and hands him the mixer.

"What the hell. Sounds like fun. Cass, remember that time we—"

"You know what? I've suddenly lost my appetite for cookies. If you'll excuse me," I brush past them, not missing the defeated look on my mother's face as I grab my coat and walk out the back door.

I grew up on a dead-end street, which was great when we were kids. We would ride bikes and rollerblade for hours on end. During the summer months, dad would set up two nets, and before you knew it, there would be a crowd of neighborhood kids playing an impromptu game of roller hockey that would last long past the streetlights coming on. I liked the idea of having friends around if I wanted to go out, but oftentimes I just wanted quiet. Our house was always loud, full of people and a hockey game on television. I used to sneak down to the pond at the end of the street and sit for hours, reading or writing music. It was always so peaceful. Over time, it became my sanctuary.

I guess that's why my feet brought me here now. I'd left the house just to avoid Scott. We've been home for three days, and I have yet to have a conversation with him, but that hasn't stopped him from trying to corner me. Mom told us we need to sit down and air our grievances, while dad told her to let it be and leave our grievances to work themselves out. To be honest, I don't know how I feel about it.

It's easy for me to place all the blame on Scott, but it probably isn't fair. It hadn't been his fault I'd run from heartbreak in Minnesota and ended up at Great Lakes just to be closer to him. How could I really fault him for not realizing that sometimes a girl just needs her big brother? I mean, I'd never actually told him, so how could he have known?

But Brantley knew. That day in the diner, he'd listened as I poured my heart out, and he'd remembered. To be honest, that's probably why he'd been so protective of me early on. He knew I needed someone to look out for me, and he knew Scott had been too preoccupied to notice.

There was something about what Scott said that hadn't sat well with me. Actually, none of it had, but one thing in particular kept niggling away at my brain.

Brantley is a really great guy. He's smart, thoughtful, supportive. He's kind and gentle with me. Unlike Justin, not once has he ever laid a hand on me in anger. But above all else, he was a loyal friend. If you take all of those qualities and match them with what Scott said, things just didn't add up. Why wouldn't Brantley be good enough for me?

I was so lost in my own head I failed to hear the footsteps behind me. I guess that's why I react the way I do when he speaks.

"I thought I'd find you here." Every muscle in my body stiffens at the sound of Justin's voice. "Why have you been avoiding me?"

I spin around so fast he doesn't have time to react to my open hand until it connects with his cheek, and the resulting smack echoes around us.

"What the fuck is wrong with you?" he screams, clutching his face as if I've drawn blood.

If only.

"Me? You've got some nerve showing up here as if I owe you something. I owe you jack shit!" My nostrils flare as I stand toe-to-toe with the man I once trusted with my heart.

What a fool I'd been. But no more.

"Oh, I get what this is. It's about him, right? Cage is a fucking loser. I know his type. He'll talk sweet. Say anything to get you in bed. He'll fuck you a while before he grows tired of you and decides to stick it somewhere else." He's seething with rage. Spittle gathers on either side of his mouth and it's started to foam. The effect it has reminds me of a rabid dog.

"Sounds to me like you've just described yourself. Or have you forgotten you were once the sweet talker who fucked me over." My eyes narrow, daring him to deny it.

"You fucking bitch!" He grabs me by the arm, jerking so hard it feels as if it's been pulled out of its socket. "You think you can replace me with him? I've got news for you, sweetheart. You'll never find someone who'll treat you as well as I did."

I choke out a laugh, suddenly feeling fearless in his presence. "God, I hope not. You were the worst kind of asshole. Brantley is two hundred times the man you'll ever be."

"Be careful, Cassie. You don't want to say anything you may regret later. You know, I could fuck you right here and no one would ever know." His mouth is so close his breath heats my skin. "How do you think pretty boy would feel about that?"

"Just try and fuck me, and you're going to find out. He'll fucking kill you," I spit in his face.

Spit slides down his cheek as he throws his head back in laughter. "Oh, yeah, well Cage isn't here now, is he?"

"No, but I am. Take your fucking hands off her, Fairfax," Scott's booming voice thunders clear across the pond, and the next thing I know, Justin is lifted off the ground and thrown a good ten feet. Justin, being the stubborn ass he is, tries to pull himself up, but the heel of Scott's Timberland pushes him back to the ground. "If you know what's good for you, you'll stay down."

"Cassie," he turns to me, "was this the first time he's laid a hand on you?" My eyes dart to Justin's, and his go wide with fear, pleading with me to cover his sorry ass. I look back to my brother, all two hundred and ten pounds of him, and shake my head no.

Normally, I'm not a violent person, being non-confrontational and all. But there are times when I'm willing to make an exception. For two years, I allowed Justin to control me, mentally and physically. Though most of the beatings I took were of a verbal nature, there were several occasions when Justin's temper would get the better of him and he would yank me by the arm, like today. There were even times when he would get mad and initiate sex just so he could hit me and later claim it was because he'd been caught up in the moment. But I knew better, and the bruises on my ass and legs would take weeks to fade.

So, when Scotty responds to my admission of Justin's little secret by beating the shit out of him, I don't so much as flinch. Bastard had it coming. Every punch he absorbs is a silent victory for not only me, but also for Brantley. He too had been an unsuspecting victim of Justin's twisted jealousy. And when Justin rolls over and cries like a baby, his sobs are sweet music to my ears.

My fingers skim the smooth finish of the baby grand that sits proudly in the center of the room, making it the focal point of the music studio dad built for me as a surprise for my sixteenth birthday. My thumb settles on middle C, and I finger out a scale. One key at a time. The last time I was in this room, Brantley had been with me. It was Thanksgiving evening, after we'd left the Mendoza's party. I'd brought him back here and we made love on this very piano bench.

My hand runs over the hot pink material. My mother's contribution to the room. She's all too familiar with my obsession of all things pink. Now, this cushion holds a lot more sentimental value.

That night when we kissed, things had felt different between us. I can't explain it except to say nothing felt rushed. Gone was the urgency to tear each other's clothes off and get busy. We kissed slowly. We explored each other with our hands. And when he finally claimed me he did it at a painstakingly slow pace that left every part of my body doing its own victory dance.

Through no direction of my own, my fingers find their place on the keys, and soon I'm playing the first song I ever played for him. The one I sang on his bedroom floor when he'd almost kissed me. I don't even realize I'm singing until I'm on the second chorus and tears are streaming down my face.

Come back to me, I'm begging you darlin'
Come back to me, I'll believe in you this time.
The bed's too big without you, don't leave me alone tonight.
Come back to me, I'll make everything alright.
Come back to me, I'll make everything alright.

"You have a beautiful voice," Scott says quietly, trying not to startle me. "Have I ever told you that?"

He makes his way into the room, stops at the end of the piano, and watches me with a wary eye.

Even though he came to my rescue today, we still haven't addressed the elephant in the room. But I have a feeling we're about to.

"No. You never have."

His eyes soften, and it looks as though he may start crying. My first thought is I can't recall a time I've ever seen him cry.

Then, I remember the day years ago when I'd broken my arm. Scott and his buddies had been rollerblading at the school, daring each other to perform stunts while not wearing any protective gear. As usual, I'd followed him and wanted to join in. Scott tried to make me go back home, but I'd stubbornly refused. I wanted to impress him. The first few stunts I was challenged with had been simple, and when I'd successfully completed each one, his face would light up. All was going well, until Travis Burke dared me to jump two flights of stairs then ride the railing on the last set. *Watch and learn*, I'd told him. As I skated my warm-up, Scotty had pulled me aside and told me I didn't need to go through with the stunt. I just gave him a wink and jokingly told him to have a stretcher ready, just in case. I cleared the first set of steps with ease, landing and tucking my knees back up for the second set. I'd executed the second landing perfectly, but when my wheels hit the railing, I hadn't accounted for the two-inch thick wad of gum that had been stuck to the metal. When the side of my wheels met the hardened obstacle, it caused me to flip two times in the air before I landed on the railing and rolled lifelessly to the ground.

Scotty had picked me up and run two miles, barefoot, holding me close and crying the entire way. He'd blamed himself for that break and spent the next six weeks hovering over me. He'd even put his artistic abilities to good use on my cast look to make it look as if I had a sleeve tattoo. I was only fourteen at the time. I guess in his own way he's been looking out for me ever since.

"I've been a shitty big brother." He heaves a sigh and motions to the other half of the bench. He doesn't sit until I nod my okay.

"I wouldn't say shitty. You've had your moments." I nudge him with my shoulder, and he gives me a gentle nudge back.

"Why didn't you tell me Justin was hurting you?"

"I don't know. You were already in Michigan and we'd sorta lost touch. I'd always looked up to you. It was hard for me to admit the first adult decision I'd made had been a poor one."

"God, when the hell did I turn into such a prick?" He drags one finger across the piano keys.

"You really want me to answer that?" I give him a look.

"No," he says quietly. "That song you were just playing, does it have anything to do with Cage?"

"If I say yes, will you start yelling at me again? Tell me what a horrible person he is and how he's not good enough?"

Regret fills his face when our eyes meet, but I'm not quite finished.

"Do you remember the morning when you introduced me to Brantley?" The sounds of C, D, and E ring quietly in the background as my fingers fidget over the keys. "That day you told me Brantley was the best friend you ever had. You called him loyal and said that no matter what, you knew he'd always have your back. You even said you trusted him."

"You're right. I did say those things."

"What I'm having trouble understanding is how you can say all of those wonderful things about him one minute, then turn around and spew horrible things about him the next. You stood in front of both of us and told me he wasn't good enough for me." I twist on the seat to face him, "Why would you say that?"

"It's complicated, Cass," his fingers run through his hair, leaving it sticking up in all directions.

"So, un-complicate it for me, Scotty." I fold my arms across my chest and wait.

"Well, first off, there was a bro code that he not only broke, he fucking obliterated it."

I open my mouth to reply, but all that comes out is a frustrated scream. With both my hands I give him a hard shove to the chest, knocking him back a ways on the bench.

"I'm so fucking sick of hearing about that goddamn code! It's just a stupid set of rules used to try and dictate people's actions. How dare you think you have the right to tell Brantley, or me, who we can or cannot fuck."

"Cassie, come on. Don't use that word."

"Seriously? What did you think we were doing when we spent all that time together? Frankly, I don't give a rat's ass if it makes you uncomfortable. I fucked Brantley Cage. Yeah, I said it. I fucked him and I liked it. Hell, I liked it so much I went and fell in love with him. And he fell in love with me. And everything was great until you swooped in on your proverbial high horse and fucked us both. Well, Scotty, all I can say is, no, thank you very fucking much!"

I push myself off the bench and start to leave, but I'm stopped in my tracks by a giant arm circling my waist.

"Everything spiraled out of control that night. First Ashley, then that call. I lost my head. I don't know what else to say. There were times when I suspected maybe something was going on. That night we went to the movies and he just showed up out of the blue. That day he chased you out of the house when you caught him in bed with Natasha. Then you brought him home for Thanksgiving. By the way, did mom and dad have any clue you two were dating then?"

"Maybe a small clue," I smile sheepishly. "If it makes you feel any better, we didn't sleep together until the weekend of my recital. In Brantley's defense, he tried really hard to respect your wishes."

"Oh, I'll bet he did," he scoffs.

"No, really. That first night I stayed at your apartment, I woke up to find him in bed with me. He had no idea who I was when I threw myself at him, but once he found out, he couldn't get away fast enough. He kept going on about how you were going to kill him if you found out. After that first kiss, he really didn't stand a chance. I'd already set my sights on him and was determined to make him notice me. Once we started spending time together, we both knew we'd found something special."

He reaches up to take hold of my hand and pulls me back down on the bench. I gently stroke the bruise on his jaw.

"I'm sorry I lied to you. But you once said that you trusted him more than anyone else. If you truly love me, then shouldn't he be the man you trust to take care of me? He *is* what's best for me. And you're just going to have to accept we're in love."

"I know that. But it's not easy. To me, you'll always be the little girl who looked up to me and wanted to do everything I was doing."

"I'll always look up to you. You're my big brother and I love you. And right now, I need my big brother's support." He gives my hand a small squeeze. "Scotty, I *really* love him."

"Cassie, I know deep down that Cage will never hurt you. He'll be faithful, and I know without a doubt he'd risk his life to protect you. That's the Brantley I know and love."

"Thank you for saying that. It means a lot. But I know someone who needs to hear that more than I do. Promise me you'll talk to him."

"It's a promise."

"So, just like that, you and Ashley are over? Is that really what you wanted?" Now that our grievances have been aired, I feel it's time I start showing my support. After all, it feels as if our relationship just rounded the corner into adulthood. I'm hoping this is a promise of things to come between us.

"I didn't set out that night planning to break up with her. But it was the right thing to do. We were headed in different directions. Ashley wanted to settle down and have kids within a couple of years. I'm nowhere near that stage of life. For the past two years we've practically been joined at the hip. If that's what marriage is like, I'm not ready for it. I love her, but I'm man enough to admit she deserves more."

"I'm sorry. I know how that must hurt. Two years is a huge chunk of your life. But I understand where you're coming from. You're about to embark on a whole new adventure. You don't want to be held back by someone who's forcing you to be someone you're not."

"Was that how things were with Justin? Was he a control freak as well?" He chuckles at this, but we both give a nod of understanding.

"I'm glad you're finally doing something for yourself. Hey, if you ever get lonely you know the way to South Quad. My door is always open for you."

Without warning, I'm pulled in for one of Scotty's bear hugs. The last time he gave me one was the day he left to attend Great

Lakes. That fact is not lost on me, and soon I find myself crying. But not because I'm sad. These tears are falling, because for the first time in four years, I feel like I have my big brother again.

Later that night, I pull out my phone and type out a message, wishing I could be there to deliver it in person.

Merry Christmas, B. I miss you. Love, Dimples

BRANTLEY

"Are you sure you can't stay? It feels as if you've just gotten here," mom busies herself with straightening the bed, while I'm busy stuffing dirty clothes in my suitcase.

"Mom, it's been two weeks already. I really need to get back and take care of my shit." I turn and give her a kiss on the cheek.

Coming home had turned out better than I'd expected. It was nice to spend time with Chris again. For the first time in years, my status as a hockey player took a backseat and we were just two brothers hanging out and catching up.

After a long talk with my dad, I have a better understanding as to what he'd been going through before his heart attack. Business had taken a nosedive and they'd been struggling to make ends meet. He'd been worried about letting mom down. Worried he wouldn't be able to provide. He was afraid she would wake up one day and see him for the failure he saw himself to be. He assured me nothing happened with the other woman. He said he just needed to confess his fears to someone other than mom because he didn't want her to think of him as weak. She'd listened thoughtfully and without judgement. She then told him a man will look at his failures and consider himself weak. While a woman is able to see not only the failures, but the strength it takes to overcome them.

Mom continues to fuss. Rearranging items I've just packed. I head to the bathroom to collect my toothbrush and razor, and when I return I find she's dumped everything on the bed and is now in the process of refolding every item.

"What are you doing? Everything was fine the way it was." I step in front of her and gently shoo her away.

"Fine," her hands go up, "but don't blame me if you get home and all of your clothes are wrinkled." She reaches out and grabs one last shirt, unable to resist the urge to fold it properly. "What's this?"

She holds up a thin rectangular box up for me to inspect. It's wrapped in black paper and adorned in blue ribbon that's been smashed beyond repair by the contents of my suitcase. Seeing as how I wasn't the one to pack it, I can only assume it's something Davis hid when I wasn't looking. He'd been the only one home when I'd stopped by to pick up my clothes.

"No clue," I huff out a laugh, "probably something from one of the guys." My fingers work quickly, tearing at the paper with new curiosity. Tossing aside the lid, I fold back the tissue paper and reveal a comic book.

"A comic book?" Mom's nose wrinkles.

"It's not just a comic book. It's a Superman 1939 First Series collectible. This must have cost a fortune." Lifting it carefully, my eyes dart back to the box for any sign of a card.

"Well, someone put some thought into that gift. I'm willing

to bet something like that wasn't easy to find," her hand reaches down and lifts the tissue. "There's something else in here."

"What is it?" I reluctantly set down the comic and stare at the T-shirt she's holding up. It's black, with a blue and silver design. The same colors as my GL uniform. The design on the front is a play on Superman's logo, but custom designed just for me. Only one person could have done this.

Mom studies the design closer before turning to me. "Are those supposed to be skate blades?" she asks, tracing her finger over the diamond-shaped design surrounding the giant letter B.

"Yep," I take the shirt and examine it closer. There's small tag stitched to the lower left side, and when I read what is written I start laughing.

Designed by Dimples

I feel a hand on my shoulder and turn to find mom smiling. "It looks good on you."

"What looks good?" my eyes shift between the shirt I'm wearing and the one I'm holding.

Her head cocks to the side as the smile broadens across her face. "Love."

"Thank you for flying United Airlines flight 831 non-stop to Detroit. At this time, we are boarding all passengers seated in first class."

I remain in my seat, knowing it will be a good twenty minutes before they call my zone. A text from Davis confirms he'll meet me in Detroit. Now I just need to figure out what I'm going to say to Cassie. I'm hoping she'll speak to me. The last time I heard from her had been a text to say Merry Christmas. My reply had been just as concise.

There is *one* thing being apart taught me. I learned I'm much happier when she's by my side.

They finally call my zone, and when it comes time for the attendant to scan my ticket, the damn machine starts beeping.

"Uh oh. Mr. Cage, there seems to be a problem with the seat you've booked."

"What sort of problem are we talking about?" I ask calmly. Though calm is not what I'm feeling at the moment. I need to get home.

"It appears the seat was somehow broken during the last flight, and it was missed on the final walkthrough. Thanks to a last minute cancellation, we were able to bump you up to first class. I'm terribly sorry for the inconvenience."

"No problem at all."

I'm escorted to my new seat and stow my suitcase in the overhead bin. Nodding to the couple beside me, I buckle up and settle in for the three-hour flight.

Every few minutes, I sneak a glance at the guy seated next to me. He looks familiar, though for the life of me I can't place him. A couple of times he's caught me checking him out. This time when our eyes meet, he reaches for the woman's hand. After that, I vow to keep my eyes trained forward for the rest of the flight.

Well, maybe just one more glance.

His hair is jet-black and wild on top. It looks pretty cool. His arms are covered in tattoos that extend past his knuckles. The ink is intricately beautiful. The last thing I notice is the flash of silver on either side of his bottom lip, and I find myself wondering if it hurt when he had them done.

I take off my jacket and tuck it under the seat. Deciding music will be a good distraction, I pop in the ear buds and scroll through my app. Sam Hunt. James Bay. Paradox. It takes me a few seconds to realize this is the playlist of Cassie's favorites. My finger hovers over the song by Paradox before I scroll to a different playlist.

"I've heard some of those Paradox tunes are pretty good. You a fan?" tattooed guy asks. His voice is deep. Much deeper than I'd expected.

I stop scrolling and slide back to the previous screen. "I've only recently been introduced to their music. My girl—" Shit. What do I even call her? I've ignored her for two fucking weeks. She may not want me to call her anything at all. "Um... this girl I know. She's like their biggest fan. You should see her face when she talks about the lead singer," I notice that the blond beside him looks as if she's about to crack up, but I just keep babbling. "She goes on and on about his tattoos and lip ri—"

I look right at him and shake my head. Surely, I must be red in the face. I feel like an idiot. I *knew* this guy looked familiar. I just never thought I'd be seated next to him on a domestic flight bound for Detroit.

"Sebastian Miles," he extends a hand and I take it.

"Brantley Cage. It's an honor to meet you."

"Sorry about that. Sometimes I just can't help myself." He smiles and now I totally get it. I'm comfortable enough with my own masculinity to admit this guy is pretty damn good-looking.

"Don't let him fool you, Brantley. He just needs his daily ego boost," says the beautiful woman next to him. He presses a kiss to her lips and then introduces her.

"Brantley, I'd like you to meet my beautiful wife, Brooke." We shake hands, and I catch Sebastian checking out my arm.

"Nice ink. You get that done in Denver?"

"Ann Arbor. Name Brand Tattoos."

"Yeah? I've been there. Jeff did this for me last year when I was in town." He lifts his sleeve to show me the chef's knife on his bicep. It looks as if it's coming out of his arm. He hooks his head toward his wife. "She's a chef." I look at it more closely and see her name is scripted on the handle of the knife.

"I hope this isn't the part where you tell me she actually stabbed you one time and that's your memento," I joke, and thankfully they both laugh.

"Nah, nothing like that. But she did pierce me. Right here," his fingers tap over his heart, "first time I met her. When she looked at me, I swear I felt it right in my heart. After that, I was hooked."

"Aww, sweetie," she gives him a chaste kiss, "you're such a romantic."

Watching the two of them makes me miss home even more. I wonder if Cassie and I ever looked like that together? Davis once said we were obvious.

"So, Brantley. Tell me more about this girl." Sebastian turns to me.

"Which girl?" I stall.

"The one who may or may not be your girlfriend."

"Ah, that one." I fidget with the leather bracelet Chris gave me for Christmas. "Her name is Cassie, and we were really good friends who turned into something more."

"Why do I get the feeling there's more to this sad story?"

This is strange for me, because I've never been in a position to open up to a complete stranger. Yet, I find myself wanting to tell him more. I take solace in the fact that Cassie likes his music, so in a way it feels as if there's a connection of some sort.

"Probably because there is," I huff out a nervous laugh. "She's my best friend's kid sister." They both give a knowing nod. "And I fell in love with her."

"Ouch." Sebastian's brow raises and he claps me on the shoulder while laughing. "How bad of a beating did you take?"

"Dude, you have no idea." I join him in laughing at my own expense. Then, I find myself sharing our sordid tale, finishing with the discovery I made this morning.

"Oh, Brantley. My heart aches for you. I can see how much you love her. Trust me, I know what it's like to love someone again after heartbreak. I had the same worries about Sebastian. I wasn't sure I had enough of my heart left to offer. I used to think the shattered pieces wouldn't be enough for him. Once I trusted myself to give as much love as I'd been given, the broken pieces were finally made whole," Brooke exclaims through teary eyes.

"Baby, don't cry. It all worked out." His arm goes around her in a show of love and support. "Brantley, you said you fell in love with her, but what have you done to prove it? If you can't answer that just yet, then here's what you need to do. Go home and get reacquainted with your romantic side. Go back to the beginning, to whatever it was that brought you together in the first place. Text her. Shower her with gifts. Do something for her and expect nothing in return. You get my point? She needs to know you'd risk anything to have her. She needs to know no matter what, you'll always be there for her."

I lean forward and lock eyes with Brooke. "Is that how he was with you in the beginning?"

"Yes, except with Sebastian, it was the beginning, middle, and everything in between. He's the most romantic soul I've ever known."

Later, as we exit the plane, he shakes my hand and tells me to keep in touch. It isn't until I watch them leave that I realize I never got a picture to show Cassie.

Back to the beginning, huh?

I can do that.

Me: Hey, Candy. Was hoping u might have time 2 discuss guitar lessons.

I pocket my phone. Not expecting a response, but still hopeful.

To my surprise, one comes right away.

Her: Depends. Who's Candy?

Me: Oh, she's this sexy blond I met.

Her: Then ur out of luck. I have red hair and look like a cartoon character.

Me: No prob. I think cartoons are sexy.

Her: Weirdo... So, if I'm Candy, who ru?

Me: How 'bout you just call me Superman?

Her: Gee, I don't know.

Me: Uh oh... Sounds as if u doubt Superman's existence.

Her: I don't know. Seems kinda silly. Don't u think?

Me: What if I told u Superman IS real and he's very much in love with u?

Her: If that's true then I guess I would tell him to prove it.

BRANTLEY

Operation Dimples was already in motion.

She asked me to prove my love, and that's what I intend to do.

For starters, this morning I had her favorite breakfast delivered to her dorm. French toast with powdered sugar, the syrup heated, and extra sausage.

After lunch, I had two dozen pink roses sent to the lecture hall where her music theory class meets. I paid the delivery guy twenty extra bucks to personally walk them up to her seat.

And thanks to my connections on campus, I arranged to have the campus radio channel play only music by Paradox all day. They were even able to pipe it into every hallway and outside the buildings.

I also send short text messages to her throughout the day.

My lips miss you

Heard the train today and got aroused. Is that weird?

$3f''(x) + 5xf(x) = 11$

I throw the last one in just to make her laugh. I don't want her thinking I've only missed her body. But that doesn't mean I haven't. Because I've missed *all* of her so fucking much. Being apart is killing me.

I head into practice early to try and connect with Coach before he heads into a meeting. I need to thank him for the heart-to-heart he shared with me before Christmas. Not only do I have a great deal of respect for the guy, but what he said really hit home.

Traffic on State is bumper to bumper, and by the time I park and head inside the arena his meeting has already started. I've got another forty-five minutes to kill before I have to suit up. I don't feel like getting caught up in the traffic jam outside, so I figure I'll just head to the weight room and knock out a few hundred sit-ups. As I round the corner, I see Cassie coming down the hall.

My god. Why does she have to be so beautiful? It's really not fair to think I can resist her. Telling myself I'll just ask for one kiss, I duck back behind the wall and wait for her. When she rounds the corner and finds me there, she lets out a startled gasp.

"Goddammit, Brantley, you scared the crap out of me." She raises a delicate hand to her throat.

"Sorry, I just... I had to see you." I reach out and tentatively brush the back of my hand down her cheek. "You okay?"

A contented sigh passes her lips as she leans into my touch.

"I've had an interesting day." Her eyes lift, and she peers up at me through long lashes. "The roses were beautiful."

Has it always been this easy between us?

"Not nearly as beautiful as you." I hook my pinky with hers and a ghost of a smile lifts the corners of her mouth.

One kiss. That's all I need.

"Thank you." Her smile widens, until the little divots appear. And I'm done for.

"Do you have any idea how I feel about you?" Her head shakes gently from side to side, but a twitch of her lip tells me she has a small idea. "I am so deeply in love with you." I allow myself to get lost in her a little longer, our pinkies swinging gently to and fro. "Would it be alright if I kissed you?"

"I was kinda hoping you would," she answers breathlessly.

My lips brush over hers. Hesitantly at first. Sampling her as if it's the first kiss we've shared. She tastes of strawberries and cream. Just as I remember. My tongue passes over her bottom lip, but doesn't seek entry. I kiss every inch of her lips. From top to bottom and side to side. Over and over I kiss her lips until we pull apart and we both let out a whoosh of air.

"Wow," she fans a hand over her face, "that was..."

"Yeah." My thumb traces the gentle curve of her kiss-swollen lip. "It was."

BRANTLEY

Packing your shit to leave the home you've shared with your best buddies is not an easy thing to do. Screw that. It's fucking hard. It's a wonder someone doesn't write a country song about it. Hell, it has all parts that make up a tale of woe. Memories made. Memories forgotten. Leaving behind those you've come to call your family. Heartbreak. It's all here, and currently being thrown into the boxes laid out on my bed.

John's older brother has an apartment just outside of town, and he said I could crash with him for a few months until graduation. It's not where I want to be, but it's better than staying at the frat. I'm not sure I can handle too many more nights of sleeping on a futon. It's seriously starting to mess with my performance on the ice.

I'm in the bathroom, sorting through my junk drawer, when I hear the knock. I don't bother getting up, I just call out for them to come in. It's probably Masterson; he's the only in the house who still thinks of knocking before entering.

"Hey."

I lift my eyes from the drawer to find Scott standing in the doorway. He looks dejected and uncomfortable. For some reason, this doesn't make me feel happy. It makes me sad that this is what we've become.

"Hey." I stand, just in case things turn ugly again. "Sorry, I thought I'd have the place to myself while I packed. I'll get out of here as fast as I can," I tuck the box under my arm and brush past him.

"How was your Christmas?" he asks, hands in his pockets as if to announce he's only here to talk.

"It was okay," I answer warily. "I got to spend a few days with Chris, so that was cool. Yours?"

"It was good once Cassie finally started speaking to me," he laughs. "We were in the same house for three whole days before she said anything other than fuck off."

I'm unable to suppress my grin. I can totally picture her tiny ass telling him that.

That's my girl.

"Have you talked to her since you got back?" He's no longer in the doorway. Now he's over by the dresser, pretending to look at stuff.

"Saw her yesterday for a few minutes." I stuff a few more things into a box while keeping a watchful eye on his hands. If he's going to charge at me, this time I want to be prepared. My jaw still hurts like a bitch.

"Are you really moving out?" This time when he moves, he sits on the edge of the bed. My body finally relaxes.

"Rivers, what are you doing here? You told me to get out, and I gave it a lot of thought over break and decided that's probably for the best." I lean back against the desk with my arms resting at my sides.

He doesn't say anything. Just covers his face with his hands and blows out a puff of air. Me? I watch and wait.

"I said and did some things that night I'm not proud of. I was out of line. Hitting you like that. And I was wrong to say those things. Christ, Brantley. Deep down you have to know I didn't mean what I said. It was just hard for me to think of you two together. Then, I come home and find you that way. I mean, it was obvious what you'd been up to, and I guess that just fueled the fire."

"You know, I'm man enough to admit it was shitty of me to look you in the eye and lie to you about my feelings for Cassie. But I never intended for any of it to happen. It just did. And I don't regret a minute of it. That's how I know my love for her is real. 'Cause at the end of the day, I'd risk everything to keep it. Even if it means losing you as a friend. I love her more than anything, bro'. I need you to believe that."

There's a long pause. A lot of emotions pass over his face. Finally ending in a small smile.

"I'm trusting you to take care of her." His eyes actually tear up when our eyes meet.

"You *know* I will," I answer confidently.

"Yeah, I know. Listen, I'm really sorry for saying those things. For not being the kind of friend you needed. For being an overall prick for the past nine months." We both laugh at this truth.

"I don't want you to leave. And Davis and Masterson are ready to kick my ass if I let you get out of here. I have to be honest, I don't think I can take another ass whipping. Going around with your crazy ass damn near killed me. Have you been watching that MMA shit again?" He rubs at his side and grimaces.

God, I've missed this asshole.

"So, you're okay with me dating your sister?"

"Not only am I okay with it, I insist. She threatened me as well. I'm warning you, man, she may be little, but she's a pistol."

"Yeah, she recently introduced me to that side of her." Now it's my turn to grimace.

"You know, she gave her ex a verbal smackdown. Even slapped the shit out of him. I heard that slap all the way down the street."

"He better not have fucking touched her," I growl.

"Unfortunately for him, he did. And it wasn't the first time either." I start for the door, but he stops me. "Easy, killer. I took care of it."

"By taking care of it you better mean you knocked his head off."

"Among other things, yes. Suffice it to say, it may be a while before he can easily chew solid foods. And I may have cracked a few of his ribs when I kicked him. Should I go on?"

"Please do. This story is music to my ears."

He continues regaling me with the beating of Justin while helping me unpack. And when Davis and Masterson come home, we all head over to Skeeps. I bring them up to speed on Operation Dimples, and we're all in agreement that while Cassie may be in love with me, my silence has hurt her. I need to show her I'm here for her and will never run out on her again. Proverbially speaking, it's time to hang up my skates.

I don't know how long we were there. Playing darts. Drinking beer. Plotting my next romantic gesture. May have been hours, or it could have been days. The point is, none of us cared. It was just like old times. Us. Beer. And a whole lot of laughter.

All in all, it had been a great day.

⊲♦⊳

After talking it over with the guys, I decided I needed to come up with a gesture to show Cassie just how much I love her. The only problem is that it has to be grand. And it has to be soon. That kiss we shared only made me want her more, and I vowed to put her heart before my physical needs.

Temporarily, at least.

Tonight is our game against Minnesota. The tension in the locker room this week has been thick. But as a team, we've never looked better. After two months of play, the lines are finally cohesive, thanks to a few of Coach's well-timed pep talks. Basically, he sat us all down and told us to start working together or get the fuck off the ice. He didn't actually put it *that* way, but it was implied. Bottom line, we all got the point.

I've just finished tossing my apron in the laundry bin when my phone buzzes in my pocket. Normally, I'm not scheduled to work on days when I have games, but Anthony had called in sick and they needed someone to cover his lunch shift. I've worked at this restaurant off and on for the past two years. The owner, Donnie, is great. He lets me work whenever it fits *my* schedule, and not the other way around, which is unusual for high-end restaurants.

"Yo, what's up?" I answer as I'm leaving the break room.

"What time do you get out of there?" Rivers yells into the phone. It sounds as if he's inside a washing machine.

"Just leaving now. What the hell is that noise?" I throw a parting wave to a couple of waiters gathered by the POS station.

"I'm at the car wash. Have you given any more thought to what you're going to do?"

"Are you kidding? It's all I've been thinking about. I'm over here wracking my brain and coming up empty. Short of hiring the Goodyear Blimp to do a flyover, I've got nothing."

He gives a snort of laughter. "You'll think of something. Just make sure it's big. This *is* my baby sister you're trying to romance."

"Yeah, yeah. Sometimes I think I liked it better when you were left in the dark." I laugh loudly, attracting the attention of a few customers. I mouth *sorry* as I pass, then lock eyes with a familiar face.

Rivers is saying something, but I don't hear him. The gears in my head start churning, and all of a sudden it hits me.

"Rivers," I cut him off, "about that gesture. I think I have an idea..."

CASSIE

Him: Can I ask u something?

   Me: I'm all thumbs.

   Him: If we could go back and do it over, would u change anything?

   Me: No. I think we got it right the first time. Would u?

   Him: I wouldn't have left u the way I did.

   Me: You're back now. That's all that matters.

   Him: Will u come 2 my game tonight? I need 2 see u.

   Me: I'll be there.

"What the hell are you smiling about over there?" Roni grumbles. "Wait, don't tell me. Another romantic gesture from Mr. Stamina?"

"Ha ha. You're just jealous and you know it." I toss a throw pillow at her head.

"Pfft. What's to be jealous of? It's not as if he's some guy who looks like sex on skates who goes out of his way to make you feel special." She bats her lashes playfully. "I mean, seriously, who could *possibly* fit that description?"

"B does." I flash an exaggerated grin.

"Yeah, rub it in, why don't ya." She flops on the bed next to me. "What's Mr. Romance up to now?"

"He asked if I'd go watch him play."

"So, what are you thinking, do you want to go?"

"Yeah. I really do. Will you go with me?"

"It'll be a hardship, but if it means that much to you, I'll take one for the team." She gives a dramatic sigh.

"Just so long as you're not taken *by* the team. Lord knows we don't need another bunny in training."

"Sweetie, you and I both know there's no training required. Matter of fact, just call me Head Bunny from now on." Her tongue pokes the side of her cheek while one hand bobs in front of her mouth.

"Ohmygod, you are in need of serious help." She falls back with her head in my lap, and we laugh until our sides hurt.

The arena is relatively packed this evening. I know the rivalry between these two teams is fierce, but I wasn't counting on having a hard time finding seats.

"I told you we should have left earlier," I grumble. "Now I'll have to watch him from the nosebleed section."

"Don't go getting your Victoria's in a wad." She waves me off. "He'll be just as sexy from up there as he would if we were in the front row."

"I wouldn't know about that. I've never made it to the front row," I huff and begin the long trudge to the top.

"Excuse me," comes a male voice from behind us. "Cassie Rivers?"

"Yeah." I turn and find two security guards there. "Can I help you with something?"

"If you'll follow us down front, we have two seats waiting for you and Miss Parker."

I raise a brow at Roni, but she simply offers a one-shoulder shrug and follows them back down the stairs, all the way to the section behind the bench.

Right away, I sense that something is weird. The large panel of plexiglass separating the fans from the bench is completely missing. One of the nets has been pushed to the side, and a section of red carpet covers center ice. As if all of this weren't already strange enough, a grand piano has been rolled out and left sitting in the center of the carpet.

I'm so busy trying to figure out what's going on, I don't even notice that someone's walked out on the ice and has taken a seat at the piano. I also don't question why my normally chatty roommate has suddenly gone quiet. I assume she's just as baffled as I am.

"Do they usually have musical guests for rivalry games?" I snap my head in Roni's direction, but she's too busy texting to notice I'm talking to her.

"I'm sorry, did you say something?" she asks innocently.

A familiar voice comes over the sound system, grabbing my attention before I can respond.

"Good evening, everyone. Before you all start checking your tickets, I want to assure you that you *are* in the right place."

"Why is Sebastian Miles at a GL game?" I look around, speaking to no one in particular. This night could *not* get any crazier.

"I realize this may be a little unorthodox, but a friend of mine contacted me today and told me he needed help showing his girl how much he loves her. Being a romantic myself, I had to say yes," Sebastian's sexy voice drawls into the microphone.

The players take the ice, followed by their coaches, and skate over to their benches. Scotty and Davis are directly in front of me. But there's no sign of #27.

"You need to come with me, sis," Scotty takes hold of one hand, while Davis takes the other. They lift me over the bench and position me so my ass balances on the wall and my legs dangle into the rink.

"Scotty, what's going on?" I look nervously between him and Davis.

"You told the man to prove it. Now sit back, and let him prove it."

"Cassie," Sebastian's smooth voice calls to me, "this song is for you. It's not an original, but seeing as how Charlie is a friend, I don't think he'll mind. I hope I'll do it justice."

My stomach leaps, because I know what he's about to play. Charlie Puth's "One Call Away" is my anthem for B.

He opens with the first note, and I'm immediately giddy because he's singing to ME! Then a lone figure skates out on the ice. Dressed in blue jeans and a white button-down. I've never seen him out of uniform on the ice. He looks so incredibly sexy it's downright sinful. No man should have the right to look that good and be this amazing.

Sebastian is singing, as Brantley skates around the rink. Showing everyone watching all of his moves. Trust me. The man has serious moves. Who knew he was capable of dancing on skates. But the graceful sway of his hips mesmerizes me. When the chorus hits and Brantley rips open his shirt, revealing the T-shirt I had made for him, I don't know whether to laugh or cry. So I do both. And when he skates over to me, I lose it. I push off the wall and wrap my arms and legs around him. Without missing a beat, he skates backwards around the rink with me in his arms. Kissing me silly while Sebastian 'freaking' Miles serenades us.

"Told you Superman was real." He presses his forehead to mine.

"Does this mean you'll keep running to my rescue?" I gently tease.

"I'll always come running for you, doll." He skates backwards, our song playing in the background, and he's staring, his amber eyes filled with love. "God, I've missed you. Walking away was the biggest mistake I've ever made. I miss holding you in my arms. The feel of your lips on mine. I miss our movie nights and listening to you play your guitar. And your touch... I miss that so much. The way you used to run your fingers through my hair at night until I fell asleep. I miss all of it. But most of all I miss the sound of your laughter, because every time I heard it, I knew I was making you happy. It made me feel as if I was finally doing something right. I'm sorry for hurting you. For not trusting that what we've found is everything that's been missing from my life."

"I've missed you so much. I don't ever want to be apart again. I don't think my heart can take it."

"Baby, I'm not going anywhere. Ever again. I learned something while I was away. I learned that by believing in me and loving me, you healed my shattered heart. You took all the jagged pieces and made me whole again. So, in a way, you've rescued me too."

"I've never doubted you. I believe it was our brokenness that brought us together. But if rescuing was what you needed, I can promise I'll go to the ends of the earth for you. As long as we're together, we can survive anything." I nuzzle my cheek into his, oblivious to the eyes watching our every move. "Guess this kinda makes me your sidekick, huh?"

"Nah, you're better than a sidekick." I can feel the pull of his smile against my skin. "You're my Jersey Girl."

I pull back to meet his eyes. "Brantley Cage, are you asking me to wear your jersey?"

"You bet your sweet ass I am." He nips playfully at my lip. "And later, if I'm lucky, that's all you'll be wearing."

"Oh, I think that can be arranged." A wide grin fills my face and he affectionately kisses each divot.

As the song begins to wind down and the faces of the crowd blur around me, he meets my gaze, and all the love he holds for me is reflected behind those amber eyes. With my heart full of love and a happiness I've never known, I lean in and press my lips tenderly to his.

"I love you, B."

"I love you too, Dimples."

ACKNOWLEDGEMENTS

There are so many amazing people I need to thank for supporting me on this project. It truly was a labor of love.

First and foremost, my family. Dan, you are the best husband a girl could ever hope for. Thank you for your patience and your undying love. It was easy to write about a male lead with a Superman complex. You've been my Superman since the first night we met and you came to my rescue. You've been saving me ever since, and for that, I love you! My kids, Taylor and David. I'm sorry for all of the missed moments. The forgotten dinners. I hope it goes without saying that I love you to the moon and back!

My daughter, Taylor - Thank you for designing such a beautiful cover for this book! This one is my personal fave. Thank you for the beautiful book teasers, new banners, and for putting up with me. I know I drive you crazy, and I'm hard to work with, but I wouldn't want to do this without you.

Melissa Mendoza - I thank God every single day for bringing you into my life. In a short span of time you have become a trusted friend. A shoulder to cry on. Someone to laugh with. And someone to bitch with! Knowing you are in my corner makes even the darkest of days brighter. I say this all the time, but I sincerely mean it. I could not do this without you. I mean, I probably could, but why the fuck would I want to? Sharing this with you makes it so much more fun! Thank you for putting up with my brand of crazy. For all the last minute changes I put you through. For reading every line I write. Even the ones that don't get published. You are my rock and my soul sister. I can't wait for Norfolk!!

Christine Tovey - This book is an extension of my love for you! I love how we connected over Tucker and Gracie. I love all of the inspirational images you send me. And I love knowing you are in my corner. Supporting me. Championing me. Pushing me to write this story, and the next! You truly are a bright light in my life. You're not only an amazing blogger. You're my maple dealer. A shoulder to lean on. And a friend. I love you!! Watch out! Davis is coming next!!!

Sarah Piechuta - Sharing this journey with you has been such an amazing ride. You fell in love with B right from the start. You helped me shape him into the character he came to be. Knowing you loved these characters as much as I did made me work that much harder to put out something we both could be proud of. I sincerely hope you stick around for the rest of this series. I can't wait for you to see what the rest of these guys have to offer the book-loving world!

Jess Hodges - My quiet cheerleader. We don't talk often, but when we do, it's as if time has stood still. I love sharing my stories with you. You always make me feel like I wrote them just for you, which is exactly how an author wants the reader to feel. Always know that a little piece of you goes into every story I write. Love you, lady!

Helena Hunting - What do you say to the author who created your greatest BBF crush? The same one who took the time to read this story (in its absolute rawest form) and gave me feedback and tips to make this story better? Thank you just doesn't seem like enough. But seriously, THANK YOU! I'm honored you were a part of this process. I want you to know I listened to everything you said and took copious notes! You're amazing and a true example of what being an Indie author is all about.

To my editor, Julia Goda, and formatter, CP Smith - I'm so glad I met you both! I had a lot of fun sharing this project with each of you. Thank you so much for everything you did to help make this my best book to date!

Melanie Harlow - Thank you for answering this fellow Michigan girl's plea for help. Without hesitation, you offered to promote my cover reveal and kicked off my release party. Having you share this moment with me was a dream come true.

To Terra Kelly, Christine Tovey, and Claudia Burgoa - You three make me laugh on a daily basis. What would I do without Christine's wake up post? The Gospel According to Skye? Or the support I get from each of you? I don't know. But I definitely know I DON'T want to find out! Love you girls so much!!

To all of my amazing ladies in the VIP Room - You ROCK! Thank you for all of the pimping and support you show me and my books!

Sandy Young - My beautiful sister and confidant. I can't thank you enough for listening to me ramble about my characters. Just knowing you are always there for me makes me very happy. I love you very much!

John Grover - Thank you so much for taking the time to answer all of my questions about college hockey. You're an amazing player and it was a pleasure to work with you.

My YpsiChicks: Shawn Miracle, Theresa Likert, Tracy Bashaw, Lisa Helton, Cathy Griggs, and Jana Creps. Girls, what would I do without you! I think it's time we meet up again!

A special note of thanks needs to be given to the following individuals who have each taken time out of their day to support and encourage me along the way: Jamie Reinhardt, Kathleen Rivest, Jaime Burns, Anne Mercier, Anita Ingram, everyone at Alpha Book Club, Karen Monasterio, Autumn Hardin, Jennifer

Marie, Jacks Williams, Audra Innis, Jo Overfield, and Stacy Aube.

To all of the amazing authors who came out to support me during my release party - Melanie Harlow, Celia Aaron, Carrie Aarons, Lissette Kristensen, Lisa B. Kamps, Melody Hack Gatto, Ariel Marie, Nikki Belaire, GM Scherbert, Sarah Greyson, and Claudia Burgoa. Thank you all SO much!

To ALL of the bloggers and readers who took the time to read Brantley and Cassie's story, thank you for supporting me in this journey. Without all of you, this wouldn't be possible. So thank you, from the bottom of my heart. Visit my Facebook page Rhonda James, Author, my website, or follow me on Twitter to stay up to date on my upcoming projects.

Finally, if you've read this book, or anything else written by me, please take a moment and consider leaving a review. Indie authors thrive on feedback, and we are all encouraged by the positive and negative reviews we receive. We can only grow and improve by listening to the feelings invoked by our stories. Thank you for your consideration.

ABOUT THE AUTHOR

Rhonda James is a romance author who loves a good HEA, believes nice guys don't finish last, and strives to create a book boyfriend for all her readers.

Rhonda is married and lives in Michigan with her family. In her spare time you can find her talking to readers, cooking new creations in her kitchen, or just spending time with her family.

Some of her guilty pleasures are mastering such things as diving into a good book, wasting time on Facebook, and indulging in dark chocolate, though she may do one more than the other.

If you'd like to keep up with the latest news, releases, help promote Rhonda's books and upcoming contests, be sure to find her on her social networks.

Facebook AuthorRLJames

Twitter @AuthorRljames

Website rhondajames.org

JERSEY GIRL PLAYLIST on SPOTIFY

https://play.spotify.com/user/rhondajames/playlist/5eIzNb2kxffL0cA /RquxG0

Made in the USA
San Bernardino, CA
04 June 2016